Collector's Library

FATHER BROWN

Selected Stories

FATHER BROWN

Selected Stories

G. K. Chesterton

with an Afterword by

DAVID PINCHING

Collector's Library

The first Father Brown story
was published in 1911
This edition published in 2003 by
Collector's Library
an imprint of CRW Publishing Limited
69 Gloucester Crescent, London NW1 7EG

ISBN 1 904633 05 6

4 6 8 10 9 7 5

Typeset in Great Britain by Antony Gray
Printed and bound in China by Imago

Contents

THE SCANDAL OF FATHER BROWN

FATHER BROWN

Selected Stories

The Blue Cross

Between the silver ribbon of morning and the green glittering ribbon of sea, the boat touched Harwich and let loose a swarm of folk like flies, among whom the man we must follow was by no means conspicuous – nor wished to be. There was nothing notable about him, except a slight contrast between the holiday gaiety of his clothes and the official gravity of his face. His clothes included a slight, pale grey jacket, a white waistcoat, and a silver straw hat with a grey-blue ribbon. His lean face was dark by contrast, and ended in a curt black beard that looked Spanish and suggested an Elizabethan ruff. He was smoking a cigarette with the seriousness of an idler. There was nothing about him to indicate the fact that the grey jacket covered a loaded revolver, that the white waistcoat covered a police card, or that the straw hat covered one of the most powerful intellects in Europe. For this was Valentin himself, the head of the Paris police and the most famous investigator of the world; and he was coming from Brussels to London to make the greatest arrest of the century.

Flambeau was in England. The police of three countries had tracked the great criminal at last from Ghent to Brussels, from Brussels to the Hook of Holland; and it was conjectured that he would take some advantage of the unfamiliarity and confusion of the Eucharistic Congress, then taking place in London. Probably he would travel as some minor clerk or secretary connected with it; but, of course,

Valentin could not be certain; nobody could be certain about Flambeau.

It is many years now since this colossus of crime suddenly ceased keeping the world in a turmoil; and when he ceased, as they said after the death of Roland, there was a great quiet upon the earth. But in his best days (I mean, of course, his worst) Flambeau was a figure as statuesque and international as the Kaiser. Almost every morning the daily paper announced that he had escaped the consequences of one extraordinary crime by committing another. He was a Gascon of gigantic stature and bodily daring; and the wildest tales were told of his outbursts of athletic humour; how he turned the *juge d'instruction* upside down and stood him on his head, 'to clear his mind'; how he ran down the Rue de Rivoli with a policeman under each arm. It is due to him to say that his fantastic physical strength was generally employed in such bloodless though undignified scenes; his real crimes were chiefly those of ingenious and wholesale robbery. But each of his thefts was almost a new sin, and would make a story by itself. It was he who ran the great Tyrolean Dairy Company in London, with no dairies, no cows, no carts, no milk, but with some thousand subscribers. These he served by the simple operation of moving the little milk-cans outside people's doors to the doors of his own customers. It was he who had kept up an unaccountable and close correspondence with a young lady whose whole letter-bag was intercepted, by the extraordinary trick of photographing his messages infinitesimally small upon the slides of a microscope. A sweeping simplicity, however, marked many of his experiments. It is said he once repainted all the numbers in a street in the dead of night merely to divert one traveller into a trap. It is quite certain that he invented a portable pillar-box, which he put up at corners in quiet suburbs on the chance of strangers dropping postal orders into it. Lastly he was known to be a startling acrobat; despite his huge figure, he could leap like a grasshopper and melt into the treetops like a monkey. Hence the great Valentin, when he set out to find Flambeau, was perfectly well aware that his adventures would not end when he had found him.

But how was he to find him? On this the great Valentin's ideas were still in process of settlement.

There was one thing which Flambeau, with all his dexterity of disguise, could not cover, and that was his singular height. If Valentin's quick eye had caught a tall apple-woman, a tall grenadier, or even a tolerably tall duchess, he might have arrested them on the spot. But all along his train there was nobody that could be a disguised Flambeau, any more than a cat could be a disguised giraffe. About the people on the boat he had already satisfied himself; and the people picked up at Harwich or on the journey limited themselves with certainty to six. There was a short railway official travelling up to the terminus, three fairly short market-gardeners picked up two stations afterwards, one very short widow lady going up from a small Essex town, and a very short Roman Catholic priest going up from a small Essex village. When it came to the last case, Valentin gave it up and almost laughed. The little priest was so much the essence of those Eastern flats: he had a face as round and dull as a Norfolk dumpling; he had eyes as empty as the North Sea; he had several brown-paper parcels which he was quite incapable of collecting. The Eucharistic Congress had doubtless sucked out of their local stagnation many such creatures, blind and helpless, like moles disinterred. Valentin was a sceptic in the severe style of France, and could have no love for priests. But he could have pity for them, and this one might have provoked pity in anybody. He had a large, shabby umbrella, which constantly fell on the floor. He did not seem to know which was the right end of his return ticket. He explained with a moon-calf simplicity to everybody in the carriage that he had to be careful, because he had something made of real silver 'with blue stones' in one of his brown-paper parcels. His quaint blending of Essex flatness with saintly simplicity continuously amused the Frenchman till the priest arrived (somehow) at Stratford with all his parcels, and came back for his umbrella. When he did the last, Valentin even had the good nature to warn him not to take care of the silver by telling everybody about it. But to whomever he talked, Valentin kept his eye open for someone else; he looked out steadily for anyone, rich or poor, male or female, who was well up to six feet; for Flambeau was four inches above it.

He alighted at Liverpool Street, however, quite conscientiously secure that he had not missed the criminal so far. He then went to Scotland Yard to regularise his position and arrange for help in case of need; he then lit another cigarette and went for a long stroll in the streets of London. As he was walking in the streets and squares beyond Victoria, he paused suddenly and stood. It was a quaint, quiet square, very typical of London, full of an accidental stillness. The tall, flat houses round looked at once prosperous and uninhabited; the square of shrubbery in the centre looked as deserted as a green Pacific islet. One of the four sides was much higher than the rest, like a dais;

and the line of this side was broken by one of London's admirable accidents – a restaurant that looked as if it had strayed from Soho. It was an unreasonably attractive object, with dwarf plants in pots and long, striped blinds of lemon yellow and white. It stood specially high above the street, and in the usual patchwork way of London, a flight of steps from the street ran up to meet the front door almost as a fire-escape might run up to a first-floor window. Valentin stood and smoked in front of the yellow-white blinds and considered them long.

The most incredible thing about miracles is that they happen. A few clouds in heaven do come together into the staring shape of one human eye. A tree does stand up in the landscape of a doubtful journey in the exact and elaborate shape of a note of interrogation. I have seen both these things myself within the last few days. Nelson does die in the instant of victory; and a man named Williams does quite accidentally murder a man named Williamson; it sounds like a sort of infanticide. In short, there is in life an element of elfin coincidence which people reckoning on the prosaic may perpetually miss. As it has been well expressed in the paradox of Poe, wisdom should reckon on the unforeseen.

Aristide Valentin was unfathomably French; and the French intelligence is intelligence specially and solely. He was not 'a thinking machine'; for that is a brainless phrase of modern fatalism and materialism. A machine only *is* a machine because it cannot think. But he was a thinking man, and a plain man at the same time. All his wonderful successes, that looked like conjuring, had been gained by plodding logic, by clear and commonplace French thought. The French electrify the world not by starting any paradox, they electrify it by carrying out a truism. They carry a truism so far – as in the French Revolution. But exactly because Valentin understood reason, he understood the limits of reason. Only a man who knows nothing of motors talks of motoring without petrol; only a man who knows nothing of reason talks of reasoning without strong, undisputed first principles. Here he had no strong first principles. Flambeau had been missed at Harwich; and if he was in London at all, he might be anything from a tall tramp on Wimbledon Common to a tall toastmaster at the Hôtel Métropole. In such a naked state of nescience, Valentin had a view and a method of his own.

In such cases he reckoned on the unforeseen. In such cases, when he could not follow the train of the reasonable, he coldly and carefully followed the train of the unreasonable. Instead of going to the right places – banks, police stations, rendezvous – he systematically went to the wrong places; knocked at every empty house, turned down every *cul de sac*, went up every lane blocked with rubbish, went round every crescent that led him uselessly out of the way. He defended this crazy course quite logically. He said that if one had a clue this was the worst way; but if one had no clue at all it was the best, because there was just the chance that any oddity that caught the eye of the pursuer might be the same that had caught the eye of the pursued. Somewhere a man must begin, and it had better be just where another man might stop. Something about that flight of steps up to the shop, something about the quietude and quaintness of the restaurant, roused all the detective's rare romantic fancy and made him resolve to strike at random. He went up the steps, and sitting down by the window, asked for a cup of black coffee.

It was halfway through the morning, and he had not breakfasted; the slight litter of other breakfasts stood about on the table to remind him of his hunger; and adding a poached egg to his order, he proceeded musingly to shake some white sugar into his coffee, thinking all the time about Flambeau. He remembered how Flambeau had escaped, once by a pair of nail scissors, and once by a house on fire; once by having to pay for an unstamped letter, and once by getting people to look through a telescope at a comet that might destroy the world. He thought his detective brain as good as the criminal's, which was true. But he fully realised the disadvantage. 'The criminal is the creative artist; the detective only the critic,' he said with a sour smile, and lifted his coffee cup to his lips slowly, and put it down very quickly. He had put salt in it.

He looked at the vessel from which the silvery powder had come; it was certainly a sugar-basin; as unmistakably meant for sugar as a champagne-bottle for champagne. He wondered why they should keep salt in it. He looked to see if there were any more orthodox vessels. Yes, there were two salt-cellars quite full. Perhaps there was some speciality in the condiment in the salt-cellar. He tasted it; it was sugar. Then he looked round at the restaurant with a refreshed air of interest, to see if there were any other traces of that singular artistic taste which puts the sugar in the salt-cellar and the salt in the sugar-basin. Except for an odd splash of some dark fluid on one of the white-papered walls, the whole place appeared neat, cheerful and ordinary. He rang the bell for the waiter.

When that official hurried up, fuzzy-haired and

somewhat blear-eyed at that early hour, the detective (who was not without an appreciation of the simpler forms of humour) asked him to taste the sugar and see if it was up to the high reputation of the hotel. The result was that the waiter yawned suddenly and woke up.

'Do you play this delicate joke on your customers every morning?' enquired Valentin. 'Does changing the salt and sugar never pall on you as a jest?'

The waiter, when this irony grew clearer, stammeringly assured him that the establishment had certainly no such intention; it must be a most curious mistake. He picked up the sugar-basin and looked at it; he picked up the salt-cellar and looked at that, his face growing more and more bewildered. At last he abruptly excused himself, and hurrying away, returned in a few seconds with the proprietor. The proprietor also examined the sugar-basin and then the salt-cellar; the proprietor also looked bewildered.

Suddenly the waiter seemed to grow inarticulate with a rush of words.

'I zink,' he stuttered eagerly, 'I zink it is those two clergymen.'

'What two clergymen?'

'The two clergymen,' said the waiter, 'that threw soup at the wall.'

'Threw soup at the wall?' repeated Valentin, feeling sure this must be some Italian metaphor.

'Yes, yes,' said the attendant excitedly, and pointing at the dark splash on the white paper; 'threw it over there on the wall.'

Valentin looked his query at the proprietor, who came to his rescue with fuller reports.

'Yes, sir,' he said, 'it's quite true, though I don't

suppose it has anything to do with the sugar and salt. Two clergymen came in and drank soup here very early, as soon as the shutters were taken down. They were both very quiet, respectable people; one of them paid the bill and went out; the other, who seemed a slower coach altogether, was some minutes longer getting his things together. But he went at last. Only, the instant before he stepped into the street he deliberately picked up his cup, which he had only half emptied, and threw the soup slap on the wall. I was in the back room myself, and so was the waiter; so I could only rush out in time to find the wall splashed and the shop empty. It didn't do any particular damage, but it was confounded cheek; and I tried to catch the men in the street. They were too far off though; I only noticed they went round the corner into Carstairs Street.'

The detective was on his feet, hat settled and stick in hand. He had already decided that in the universal darkness of his mind he could only follow the first odd finger that pointed; and this finger was odd enough. Paying his bill and clashing the glass doors behind him, he was soon swinging round into the other street.

It was fortunate that even in such fevered moments his eye was cool and quick. Something in a shop-front went by him like a mere flash; yet he went back to look at it. The shop was a popular greengrocer and fruiterer's, an array of goods set out in the open air and plainly ticketed with their names and prices. In the two most prominent compartments were two heaps, of oranges and of nuts respectively. On the heap of nuts lay a scrap of cardboard, on which was written in bold, blue chalk, 'Best tangerine oranges, /o a penny'. On the oranges was the equally clear and exact description, 'Finest Brazil nuts, 4*d.* a lb.'. M. Valentin looked at these two placards and fancied he had met this highly subtle form of humour before, and that somewhat recently. He drew the attention of the red-faced fruiterer, who was looking rather sullenly up and down the street, to this inaccuracy in his advertisements. The fruiterer said nothing, but sharply put each card into its proper place. The detective, leaning elegantly on his walking-cane, continued to scrutinise the shop. At last he said: 'Pray excuse my apparent irrelevance, my good sir, but I should like to ask you a question in experimental psychology and the association of ideas.'

The red-faced shopman regarded him with an eye of menace; but he continued gaily, swinging his cane. 'Why,' he pursued, 'why are two tickets wrongly placed in a greengrocer's shop like a shovel hat that has come to London for a holiday? Or, in case I do not make myself clear, what is the mystical association which connects the idea of nuts marked as oranges with the idea of two clergymen, one tall and the other short?'

The eyes of the tradesman stood out of his head like a snail's; he really seemed for an instant likely to fling himself upon the stranger. At last he stammered angrily: 'I don't know what you 'ave to do with it, but if you're one of their friends, you can tell 'em from me that I'll knock their silly 'eads off, parsons or no parsons, if they upset my apples again.'

'Indeed?' asked the detective, with great sympathy. 'Did they upset your apples?'

'One of 'em did,' said the heated shopman; 'rolled 'em all over the street. I'd 'ave caught the fool but for havin' to pick 'em up.'

'Which way did these parsons go?' asked Valentin.

'Up that second road on the left-hand side, and then across the square,' said the other promptly.

'Thanks,' said Valentin, and vanished like a fairy. On the other side of the second square he found a policeman, and said: 'This is urgent, constable; have you seen two clergymen in shovel hats?'

The policeman began to chuckle heavily. 'I 'ave, sir; and if you arst me, one of 'em was drunk. He stood in the middle of the road that bewildered that – '

'Which way did they go?' snapped Valentin.

'They took one of them yellow buses over there,' answered the man; 'them that go to Hampstead.'

Valentin produced his official card and said very rapidly: 'Call up two of your men to come with me in pursuit,' and crossed the road with such contagious energy that the ponderous policeman was moved to almost agile obedience. In a minute and a half the French detective was joined on the opposite pavement by an inspector and a man in plain clothes.

'Well, sir,' began the former, with smiling importance, 'and what may – ?'

Valentin pointed suddenly with his cane. 'I'll tell you on the top of that omnibus,' he said, and was darting and dodging across the tangle of the traffic. When all three sank panting on the top seats of the yellow vehicle, the inspector said: 'We could go four times as quick in a taxi.'

'Quite true,' replied their leader placidly, 'if we only had an idea of where we were going.'

'Well, where *are* you going?' asked the other, staring.

Valentin smoked frowningly for a few seconds; then, removing his cigarette, he said: 'If you *know* what a man's doing, get in front of him; but if you want to guess what he's doing, keep behind him. Stray when he strays; stop when he stops; travel as slowly as he. Then you may see what he saw and may act as he acted. All we can do is to keep our eyes skinned for a queer thing.'

'What sort of a queer thing do you mean?' asked the inspector.

'Any sort of queer thing,' answered Valentin, and relapsed into obstinate silence.

The yellow omnibus crawled up the northern roads for what seemed like hours on end; the great detective would not explain further, and perhaps his assistants felt a silent and growing doubt of his errand. Perhaps, also, they felt a silent and growing desire for lunch, for the hours crept long past the normal luncheon hour, and the long roads of the North London suburbs seemed to shoot out into length after length like an infernal telescope. It was one of those journeys on which a man perpetually feels that now at last he must have come to the end of the universe, and then finds he has only come to the beginning of Tufnell Park. London died away in draggled taverns and dreary scrubs, and then was unaccountably born again in blazing high streets and blatant hotels. It was like passing through thirteen separate vulgar cities all just touching each other. But though the winter twilight was already threatening the road ahead of them, the Parisian detective still sat silent and watchful, eyeing the frontage of the streets that slid by on either side. By the time they had left Camden Town behind, the policemen were nearly asleep; at least, they gave something like a jump as Valentin leapt erect, struck a hand on each man's shoulder, and shouted to the driver to stop.

They tumbled down the steps into the road without realising why they had been dislodged; when they looked round for enlightenment they found Valentin triumphantly pointing his finger towards a window on the left side of the road. It was a large window, forming part of the long façade of a gilt and palatial public house; it was the part reserved for respectable dining, and labelled 'Restaurant'. This window, like all the rest along the frontage of the hotel, was of frosted and figured glass, but in the middle of it was a big, black smash, like a star in the ice.

'Our cue at last,' cried Valentin, waving his stick; 'the place with the broken window.'

'What window? What cue?' asked his principal assistant. 'Why, what proof is there that this has anything to do with them?'

Valentin almost broke his bamboo stick with rage.

'Proof!' he cried. 'Good God! The man is looking for proof! Why, of course, the chances are twenty to one that it has *nothing* to do with them. But what else can we do? Don't you see we must either follow one wild possibility or else go home to bed?' He banged his way into the restaurant, followed by his companions, and they were soon seated at a late luncheon at a little table, and looking at the star of smashed glass from the inside. Not that it was very informative to them even then.

'Got your window broken, I see,' said Valentin to the waiter, as he paid his bill.

'Yes, sir,' answered the attendant, bending busily over the change, to which Valentin silently added an enormous tip. The waiter straightened himself with mild but unmistakable animation.

'Ah, yes, sir,' he said. 'Very odd thing, that, sir.'

'Indeed? Tell us about it,' said the detective with careless curiosity.

'Well, two gents in black came in,' said the waiter; 'two of those foreign parsons that are running about. They had a cheap and quiet little lunch, and one of them paid for it and went out. The other was just going out to join him when I looked at my change again and found he'd paid me more than three times too much. "Here," I says to the chap who was nearly out of the door, "you've paid too much." "Oh," he says, very cool, "have we?" "Yes," I says, and picks up the bill to show him. Well, that was a knockout.'

'What do you mean?' asked his interlocutor.

'Well, I'd have sworn on seven Bibles that I'd put 4*s.* on that bill. But now I saw I'd put 14*s.*, as plain as paint.'

'Well?' cried Valentin, moving slowly, but with burning eyes, 'and then?'

'The parson at the door he says, all serene, "Sorry to confuse your accounts, but it'll pay for the window." "What window?" I says. "The one I'm going to break," he says, and smashed that blessed pane with his umbrella.'

All the enquirers made an exclamation; and the inspector said under his breath: 'Are we after escaped lunatics?' The waiter went on with some relish for the ridiculous story: 'I was so knocked silly for a second, I couldn't do anything. The man marched out of the place and joined his friend just round the corner. Then they went so quick up Bullock Street that I couldn't catch them, though I ran round the bars to do it.'

'Bullock Street,' said the detective, and shot up that thoroughfare as quickly as the strange couple he pursued.

Their journey now took them through bare brick ways like tunnels; streets with few lights and even with few windows; streets that seemed built out of the blank backs of everything and everywhere. Dusk was deepening, and it was not easy even for the London policemen to guess in what exact direction they were treading. The inspector, however, was pretty certain that they would eventually strike some part of Hampstead Heath. Abruptly one bulging and gas-lit window broke the blue twilight like a bull's-eye lantern; and Valentin stopped an instant before a little garish sweet-stuff shop. After an instant's hesitation he went in; he stood amid the gaudy colours of the confectionery with entire gravity and bought thirteen chocolate cigars with a certain care. He was clearly preparing an opening; but he did not need one.

An angular, elderly young woman in the shop had regarded his elegant appearance with a merely automatic enquiry; but when she saw the door behind him blocked with the blue uniform of the inspector, her eyes seemed to wake up.

'Oh,' she said, 'if you've come about that parcel, I've sent it off already.'

'Parcel!' repeated Valentin; and it was his turn to look enquiring.

'I mean the parcel the gentleman left – the clergyman gentleman.'

'For goodness' sake,' said Valentin, leaning forward with his first real confession of eagerness, 'for Heaven's sake tell us what happened exactly.'

'Well,' said the woman, a little doubtfully, 'the clergymen came in about half an hour ago and bought some peppermints and talked a bit, and then went off towards the Heath. But a second after, one of them runs back into the shop and says, "Have I left a parcel?" Well, I looked everywhere and couldn't see one; so he says, "Never mind; but if it should turn up, please post it to this address," and he left me the address and a shilling for my trouble. And sure enough, though I thought I'd looked everywhere, I found he'd left a brown-paper parcel, so I posted it to the place he said. I can't remember the address now; it was somewhere in Westminster. But as the thing seemed so important, I thought perhaps the police had come about it.'

'So they have,' said Valentin shortly. 'Is Hampstead Heath near here?'

'Straight on for fifteen minutes,' said the woman, 'and you'll come right out on the open.' Valentin sprang out of the shop and began to run. The other detectives followed him at a reluctant trot.

The street they threaded was so narrow and shut in by shadows that when they came out unexpectedly into the void common and vast sky they were startled to find the evening still so light and clear. A perfect dome of peacock-green sank into gold amid the blackening trees and the dark violet distances. The glowing green tint was just deep enough to pick out in points of crystal one or two stars. All that was left of the daylight lay in a golden glitter across the edge of Hampstead and that popular hollow which is called the Vale of Health. The holiday makers who roam this region had not wholly dispersed: a few couples sat shapelessly on benches; and here and there a distant girl still shrieked in one of the swings. The glory of heaven deepened and darkened around the sublime vulgarity of man; and standing on the slope and looking across the valley, Valentin beheld the thing which he sought.

Among the black and breaking groups in that distance was one especially black which did not break – a group of two figures clerically clad. Though they seemed as small as insects, Valentin could see that one of them was much smaller than the other. Though the other had a student's stoop and an inconspicuous manner, he could see that the man was well over six feet high. He shut his teeth and went forward, whirling his stick impatiently. By the time he had substantially diminished the distance and magnified the two black figures as in a vast microscope, he had perceived something else; something which startled him, and yet which he had somehow expected. Whoever was the tall priest, there could be no doubt about the identity of the short one. It was his friend of the Harwich train, the stumpy little *curé* of Essex whom he had warned about his brown-paper parcels.

Now, so far as this went everything fitted in finally and rationally enough. Valentin had learned by his enquiries that morning that a Father Brown from Essex was bringing up a silver cross with sapphires, a relic of considerable value, to show some of the foreign priests at the congress. This undoubtedly was the 'silver with blue stones'; and Father Brown undoubtedly was the little greenhorn in the train. Now there was nothing wonderful about the fact that what Valentin had found out Flambeau had also found out; Flambeau found out everything. Also there was nothing wonderful in the fact that when Flambeau heard of a sapphire cross he should try to steal it; that was the most natural thing in all natural history. And most certainly there was nothing wonderful about the fact that Flambeau should have it all his own way with such a silly sheep as the man with the umbrella and the parcels. He was the sort of man whom anybody could lead on a string to the North Pole; it was not surprising that an actor like Flambeau, dressed as another priest, could lead him to Hampstead Heath. So far the crime seemed clear enough; and while the detective pitied the priest for his helplessness, he almost despised Flambeau for condescending to so gullible a victim. But when Valentin thought of all that had happened in between, of all that had led him to his triumph, he racked his brains for the smallest rhyme or reason in it. What had the stealing of a blue-and-silver cross from a priest from Essex to do with chucking soup at wallpaper? What had it to do with calling nuts oranges, or with paying for windows first and breaking them afterwards? He had come to the end of his chase; yet somehow he had missed the middle of it. When he failed (which was seldom), he had usually grasped the clue, but nevertheless missed the criminal. Here he had grasped the criminal, but still he could not grasp the clue.

The two figures that they followed were crawling like black flies across the huge green contour of a hill. They were evidently sunk in conversation, and perhaps did not notice where they were going; but they were certainly going to the wilder and more silent heights of the Heath. As their pursuers gained on them, the latter had to use the undignified attitudes of the deerstalker, to crouch behind clumps of trees and even to crawl prostrate in deep grass. By these ungainly ingenuities the hunters even came close enough to the quarry to hear the murmur of the discussion, but no word could be distinguished except the word 'reason' recurring frequently in a high and almost childish voice. Once, over an abrupt dip of land and a dense tangle of thickets, the detectives actually lost the two figures they were following. They did not find the trail again for an agonising ten minutes, and then it led round the brow of a great dome of hill overlooking an amphitheatre of rich and desolate sunset scenery. Under a tree in this commanding yet neglected spot was an old ramshackle wooden seat. On this seat sat the two priests still in serious speech together. The gorgeous green and gold still clung to the darkening horizon; but the dome above was turning slowly from peacock-green to peacock-blue, and the stars detached themselves more and more like solid jewels. Mutely motioning to his followers, Valentin contrived to creep up behind the big branching tree, and, standing there in deathly silence, heard the words of the strange priests for the first time.

After he had listened for a minute and a half, he was gripped by a devilish doubt. Perhaps he had dragged the two English policemen to the wastes of a nocturnal heath on an errand no saner than seeking figs on thistles. For the two priests were talking exactly like priests, piously, with learning and leisure, about the most aerial enigmas of theology. The little Essex priest spoke the more simply, with his round face turned to the strengthening stars; the other talked with his head bowed, as if he were not even worthy to look at them. But no more innocently clerical conversation could have been heard in any white Italian cloister or black Spanish cathedral.

The first he heard was the tail of one of Father Brown's sentences, which ended: '. . . what they really meant in the Middle Ages by the heavens being incorruptible.'

The taller priest nodded his bowed head and said: 'Ah, yes, these modern infidels appeal to their reason; but who can look at those millions of worlds and not feel that there may well be wonderful universes above us where reason is utterly unreasonable?'

'No.' said the other priest; 'reason is always reasonable, even in the last limbo, in the lost borderland of things. I know that people charge the Church with lowering reason, but it is just the other way. Alone on earth, the Church makes reason really supreme. Alone on earth, the Church affirms that God Himself is bound by reason.'

The other priest raised his austere face to the spangled sky and said: 'Yet who knows if in that infinite universe – ?'

'Only infinite physically,' said the little priest, turning sharply in his seat, 'not infinite in the sense of escaping from the laws of truth.'

Valentin behind his tree was tearing his fingernails with silent fury. He seemed almost to hear the sniggers of the English detectives whom he had brought so far on a fantastic guess only to listen to the metaphysical gossip of two mild old parsons. In his impatience he lost the equally elaborate answer of the tall cleric, and when he listened again it was again Father Brown who was speaking: 'Reason and justice grip the remotest and the loneliest star. Look at those stars. Don't they look as if they were single diamonds and sapphires? Well, you can imagine any mad botany or geology you please. Think of forests of adamant with leaves of brilliants. Think the moon is a blue moon, a single elephantine sapphire. But don't fancy that all that frantic astronomy would make the smallest difference to the reason and justice of conduct. On plains of opal, under cliffs cut out of pearl, you would still find a notice-board, "Thou shalt not steal." '

Valentin was just in the act of rising from his rigid and crouching attitude and creeping away as softly as might be, felled by the one great folly of his life. But something in the very silence of the tall priest made him stop until the latter spoke.

When at last he did speak, he said simply, his head bowed and his hands on his knees: 'Well, I still think that other worlds may perhaps rise higher than our reason. The mystery of heaven is unfathomable, and I for one can only bow my head.'

Then, with brow yet bent and without changing by the faintest shade his attitude or voice, he added: 'Just hand over that sapphire cross of yours, will you? We're all alone here, and I could pull you to pieces like a straw doll.'

The utterly unaltered voice and attitude added a strange violence to that shocking change of speech. But the guarder of the relic only seemed to turn his head by the smallest section of the compass. He seemed still to have a somewhat foolish face turned to the stars. Perhaps he had not understood. Or, perhaps, he had understood and sat rigid with terror.

'Yes,' said the tall priest, in the same low voice and in the same still posture, 'yes, I am Flambeau.' Then, after a pause, he said: 'Come, will you give me that cross?'

'No,' said the other, and the monosyllable had an odd sound.

Flambeau suddenly flung off all his pontifical pretensions. The great robber leaned back in his seat and laughed low but long.

'No,' he cried; 'you won't give it me, you proud

prelate. You won't give it me, you little celibate simpleton. Shall I tell you why you won't give it me? Because I've got it already in my own breast-pocket.'

The small man from Essex turned what seemed to be a dazed face in the dusk, and said, with the timid eagerness of the 'private secretary': 'Are – are you sure?'

Flambeau yelled with delight.

'Really, you're as good as a three-act farce,' he cried. 'Yes, you turnip, I am quite sure. I had the sense to make a duplicate of the right parcel, and now, my friend, you've got the duplicate, and I've got the jewels. An old dodge, Father Brown – a very old dodge.'

'Yes,' said Father Brown, and passed his hand through his hair with the same strange vagueness of manner. 'Yes, I've heard of it before.'

The colossus of crime leaned over to the little rustic priest with a sort of sudden interest.

'*You* have heard of it?' he asked. 'Where have *you* heard of it?'

'Well, I mustn't tell you his name, of course,' said the little man simply. 'He was a penitent, you know. He had lived prosperously for about twenty years entirely on duplicate brown-paper parcels. And so, you see, when I began to suspect you, I thought of this poor chap's way of doing it at once.'

'Began to suspect me?' repeated the outlaw with increased intensity. 'Did you really have the gumption to suspect me just because I brought you up to this bare part of the heath?'

'No, no,' said Brown with an air of apology. 'You see, I suspected you when we first met. It's that little bulge up the sleeve where you people have the spiked bracelet.'

'How in Tartarus,' cried Flambeau, 'did you ever hear of the spiked bracelet?'

'Oh, one's little flock, you know!' said Father Brown, arching his eyebrows rather blankly. 'When I was a curate in Hartlepool, there were three of them with spiked bracelets. So, as I suspected you from the first, don't you see, I made sure that the cross should go safe, anyhow. I'm afraid I watched you, you know. So at last I saw you change the parcels. Then, don't you see, I changed them back again. And then I left the right one behind.'

'Left it behind?' repeated Flambeau, and for the first time there was another note in his voice beside his triumph.

'Well, it was like this,' said the little priest, speaking in the same unaffected way. 'I went back to that sweet-shop and asked if I'd left a parcel, and gave them a particular address if it turned up. Well, I knew I hadn't; but when I went away again I did. So, instead of running after me with that valuable parcel, they have sent it flying to a friend of mine in Westminster.' Then he added rather sadly: 'I learnt that, too, from a poor fellow in Hartlepool. He used to do it with handbags he stole at railway stations, but he's in a monastery now. Oh, one gets to know, you know,' he added, rubbing his head again with the same sort of desperate apology. 'We can't help being priests. People come and tell us these things.'

Flambeau tore a brown-paper parcel out of his inner pocket and rent it in pieces. There was nothing but paper and sticks of lead inside it. He sprang to his feet with a gigantic gesture, and cried: 'I don't believe you. I don't believe a bumpkin like you could manage all that. I believe you've still got the stuff on you, and if you don't give it up – why, we're all alone, and I'll take it by force!'

'No,' said Father Brown simply, and stood up also; 'you won't take it by force. First, because I really haven't still got it. And, second, because we are not alone.'

Flambeau stopped in his stride forward.

'Behind that tree,' said Father Brown, pointing, 'are two strong policemen and the greatest detective alive. How did they come here, do you ask? Why, I brought them, of course! How did I do it? Why, I'll tell you if you like! Lord bless you, we have to know twenty such things when we work among the criminal classes! Well, I wasn't sure you were a thief, and it would never do to make a scandal against one of our own clergy. So I just tested you to see if anything would make you show yourself. A man generally makes a small scene if he finds salt in his coffee; if he doesn't, he has some reason for keeping quiet. I changed the salt and sugar, and *you* kept quiet. A man generally objects if his bill is three times too big. If he pays it, he has some motive for passing unnoticed. I altered your bill, and *you* paid it.'

The world seemed waiting for Flambeau to leap like a tiger. But he was held back as by a spell; he was stunned with the utmost curiosity.

'Well,' went on Father Brown, with lumbering lucidity, 'as you wouldn't leave any tracks for the police, of course somebody had to. At every place we went to, I took care to do something that would get us talked about for the rest of the day. I didn't do much harm – a splashed wall, spilt apples, a broken window; but I saved the cross, as the cross will always be saved. It is at Westminster by now. I rather wonder you didn't stop it with the Donkey's Whistle.'

'With the what?' asked Flambeau.

'I'm glad you've never heard of it,' said the priest, making a face. 'It's a foul thing. I'm sure you're too good a man for a Whistler. I couldn't have countered it even with the Spots myself; I'm not strong enough in the legs.'

'What on earth are you talking about?' asked the other.

'Well, I did think you'd know the Spots,' said Father Brown, agreeably surprised. 'Oh, you can't have gone so very wrong yet!'

'How in blazes do you know all these horrors?' cried Flambeau.

The shadow of a smile crossed the round, simple face of his clerical opponent.

'Oh, by being a celibate simpleton, I suppose,' he said. 'Has it never struck you that a man who does next to nothing but hear men's real sins is not likely to be wholly unaware of human evil? But, as a matter of fact, another part of my trade, too, made me sure you weren't a priest.'

'What?' asked the thief, almost gaping.

'You attacked reason,' said Father Brown. 'It's bad theology.'

And even as he turned away to collect his property, the three policemen came out from under the twilight trees. Flambeau was an artist and a sportsman. He stepped back and swept Valentin a great bow.

'Do not bow to me, *mon ami*,' said Valentin, with silver clearness. 'Let us both bow to our master.'

And they both stood an instant uncovered, while the little Essex priest blinked about for his umbrella.

The Secret Garden

Aristide Valentin, Chief of the Paris Police, was late for his dinner, and some of his guests began to arrive before him. These were, however, reassured by his confidential servant, Ivan, the old man with a scar and a face almost as grey as his moustaches, who always sat at a table in the entrance hall – a hall hung with weapons. Valentin's house was perhaps as peculiar and celebrated as its master. It was an old house, with high walls and tall poplars almost overhanging the Seine; but the oddity – and perhaps the police value – of its architecture was this: that there was no ultimate exit at all except through this front door, which was guarded by Ivan and the armoury. The garden was large and elaborate, and there were many exits from the house into the garden. But there was no exit from the garden into the world outside; all round it ran a tall, smooth unscalable wall with special spikes at the top; no bad garden, perhaps, for a man to reflect in whom some hundred criminals had sworn to kill.

As Ivan explained to the guests, their host had telephoned that he was detained for ten minutes. He was, in truth, making some last arrangements about executions and such ugly things; and though these duties were rootedly repulsive to him, he always performed them with precision. Ruthless in the pursuit of criminals, he was very mild about their punishment. Since he had been supreme over French – and largely over European – police methods, his great influence had been honourably used for the mitigation of sentences and the purification of prisons. He was one of the great humanitarian French freethinkers; and the only thing wrong with them is that they make mercy even colder than justice.

When Valentin arrived he was already dressed in black clothes and the red rosette – an elegant figure, his dark beard already streaked with grey. He went straight through his house to his study, which opened on the grounds behind. The garden door of it was open, and after he had carefully locked his box in its official place, he stood for a few seconds at the open door looking out upon the garden. A sharp moon was fighting with the flying rags and tatters of a storm, and Valentin regarded it with a wistfulness unusual in such scientific natures as his. Perhaps such scientific natures have some psychic prevision of the most tremendous problem of their lives. From any such occult mood, at least, he quickly recovered, for he knew he was late and that his guests had already begun to arrive. A glance at his drawing-room when he entered it was enough to make certain that his principal guest was not there, at any rate. He saw all the other pillars of the little party: he saw Lord Galloway, the English Ambassador – a choleric old man with a russet face like an apple, wearing the blue ribbon of the Garter. He saw Lady Galloway, slim and thread-like, with silver hair and a face sensitive and superior. He saw her daughter, Lady Margaret Graham, a pale and pretty girl with an elfish face and copper-coloured hair. He saw the Duchess of Mont St Michel, black-eyed and opulent, and with her two daughters, black-eyed and opulent also. He saw Dr Simon, a typical French scientist, with glasses, a pointed brown beard, and a forehead barred with those parallel wrinkles which are the penalty of superciliousness, since they come through constantly elevating the eyebrows. He saw Father Brown of Cobhole, in Essex, whom he had recently met in England. He saw – perhaps with more interest than any of those – a tall man in uniform, who had bowed to the Galloways without receiving any very hearty acknowledgment, and who now advanced alone to pay his respects to his host. This was Commandant O'Brien, of the French Foreign Legion. He was a slim yet somewhat swaggering figure, clean-shaven, dark-haired, and blue-eyed, and as seemed natural in an officer of that famous regiment of victorious failures and successful suicides, he had an air at once dashing and melancholy. He was by birth an Irish gentleman, and in boyhood had known the Galloways – especially Margaret Graham. He had left his country after some crash of debts, and now expressed his complete freedom from British etiquette by swinging about in uniform, sabre and spurs. When he bowed to the Ambassador's family, Lord and Lady Galloway bent stiffly, and Lady Margaret looked away.

But for whatever old causes such people might be interested in each other, their distinguished host was not specially interested in them. No one of them at least was in his eyes the guest of the evening. Valentin was expecting, for special reasons, a man of world-wide fame, whose friendship he had secured during some of his great detective tours and triumphs in the United States. He was expecting Julius K. Brayne, that multimillionaire whose colossal and even crushing endowments of small religions have occasioned so much easy sport and easier solemnity for the American and English papers. Nobody could quite make out whether Mr Brayne was an atheist or a Mormon, or a Christian Scientist; but he was ready to pour money into any intellectual vessel, so long as it was an untried vessel. One of his hobbies was to wait for the American Shakespeare – a hobby more patient than angling. He admired Walt Whitman, but thought that Luke P. Tanner, of Paris, Pa., was more 'progressive' than Whitman any day. He liked anything that he thought 'progressive'. He thought Valentin 'progressive', thereby doing him a grave injustice.

The solid appearance of Julius K. Brayne in the room was as decisive as a dinner bell. He had this great quality, which very few of us can claim, that his presence was as big as his absence. He was a huge fellow, as fat as he was tall, clad in complete evening black, without so much relief as a watch-chain or a ring. His hair was white and well brushed back like a German's; his face was red, fierce and cherubic, with one dark tuft under the lower lip that threw up that otherwise infantile visage with an effect theatrical and even Mephistophelean. Not long, however, did that *salon* merely stare at the celebrated American; his lateness had already become a domestic problem, and he was sent with all speed into the dining-room with Lady Galloway upon his arm.

Except on one point the Galloways were genial and casual enough. So long as Lady Margaret did not take the arm of that adventurer O'Brien her father was quite satisfied; and she had not done so; she had decorously gone in with Dr Simon. Nevertheless, old Lord Galloway was restless and almost rude. He was diplomatic enough during dinner, but when, over the cigars, three of the younger men – Simon the doctor,

Brown the priest, and the detrimental O'Brien, the exile in a foreign uniform – all melted away to mix with the ladies or smoke in the conservatory, then the English diplomatist grew very undiplomatic indeed. He was stung every sixty seconds with the thought that the scamp O'Brien might be signalling to Margaret somehow; he did not attempt to imagine how. He was left over the coffee with Brayne, the hoary Yankee who believed in all religions, and Valentin, the grizzled Frenchman who believed in none. They could argue with each other, but neither could appeal to him. After a time this 'progressive' logomachy had reached a crisis of tedium; Lord Galloway got up also and sought the drawing-room. He lost his way in long passages for some six or eight minutes: till he heard the high-pitched, didactic voice of the doctor, and then the dull voice of the priest, followed by general laughter. They also, he thought with a curse, were probably arguing about 'science and religion'. But the instant he opened the *salon* door he saw only one thing – he saw what was not there. He saw that Commandant O'Brien was absent, and that Lady Margaret was absent, too.

Rising impatiently from the drawing-room, as he had from the dining-room, he stamped along the passage once more. His notion of protecting his daughter from the Irish-Algerian ne'er-do-well had become something central and even mad in his mind. As he went towards the back of the house, where was Valentin's study, he was surprised to meet his daughter, who swept past with a white, scornful face, which was a second enigma. If she had been with O'Brien, where was O'Brien? If she had not been with O'Brien, where had she been? With a sort of senile and passionate suspicion he groped his way to the dark back parts of the mansion, and eventually found a servants' entrance that opened on to the garden. The moon with her scimitar had now ripped up and rolled away all the storm-wrack. The argent light lit up all four corners of the garden. A tall figure in blue was striding across the lawn towards the study door; a glint of moonlit silver on his facings picked him out as Commandant O'Brien.

He vanished through the French windows into the house, leaving Lord Galloway in an indescribable temper, at once virulent and vague. The blue-and-silver garden, like a scene in a theatre, seemed to taunt him with all that tyrannic tenderness against which his worldly authority was at war. The length and grace of the Irishman's stride enraged him as if he were a rival instead of a father; the moonlight maddened him. He was trapped as if by magic into a garden of troubadours, a Watteau fairyland; and, willing to shake off such amorous imbecilities by speech, he stepped briskly after his enemy. As he did so he tripped over some tree or stone in the grass; looked down at it first with irritation and then a second time with curiosity. The next instant the moon and the tall poplars looked at an unusual sight – an elderly English diplomatist running hard and crying or bellowing as he ran.

His hoarse shouts brought a pale face to the study door, the beaming glasses and worried brow of Dr Simon, who heard the nobleman's first clear words. Lord Galloway was crying: 'A corpse in the grass – a bloodstained corpse'. O'Brien at least had gone utterly from his mind.

'We must tell Valentin at once,' said the doctor,

when the other had brokenly described all that he had dared to examine. 'It is fortunate that he is here'; and even as he spoke the great detective entered the study, attracted by the cry. It was almost amusing to note his typical transformation; he had come with the common concern of a host and a gentleman, fearing that some guest or servant was ill. When he was told the gory fact, he turned with all his gravity instantly bright and businesslike; for this, however abrupt and awful, was his business.

'Strange, gentlemen,' he said, as they hurried out into the garden, 'that I should have hunted mysteries all over the earth, and now one comes and settles in my own backyard. But where is the place?' They crossed the lawn less easily, as a slight mist had begun to rise from the river; but under the guidance of the shaken Galloway they found the body sunken in deep grass – the body of a very tall and broad-shouldered man. He lay face downwards, so they could only see that his big shoulders were clad in black cloth, and that his big head was bald, except for a wisp or two of brown hair that clung to his skull like wet seaweed. A scarlet serpent of blood crawled from under his fallen face.

'At least,' said Simon, with a deep and singular intonation, 'he is none of our party.'

'Examine him, doctor,' cried Valentin rather sharply. 'He may not be dead.'

The doctor bent down. 'He is not quite cold, but I am afraid he is dead enough,' he answered. 'Just help me to lift him up.'

They lifted him carefully an inch from the ground, and all doubts as to his being really dead were settled at once and frightfully. The head fell away. It had been entirely sundered from the body; whoever had cut his throat had managed to sever the neck as well. Even Valentin was slightly shocked. 'He must have been as strong as a gorilla,' he muttered.

Not without a shiver, though he was used to anatomical abortions, Dr Simon lifted the head. It was slightly slashed about the neck and jaw, but the face was substantially unhurt. It was a ponderous, yellow face, at once sunken and swollen, with a hawk-like nose and heavy lids – the face of a wicked Roman emperor, with, perhaps, a distant touch of a Chinese emperor. All present seemed to look at it with the coldest eye of ignorance. Nothing else could be noted about the man except that, as they had lifted his body, they had seen underneath it the white gleam of a shirt front defaced with a red gleam of blood. As Dr Simon said, the man had never been of their party. But he might very well have been trying to join it, for he had come dressed for such an occasion.

Valentin went down on his hands and knees and examined with his closest professional attention the grass and ground for some twenty yards round the body, in which he was assisted less skilfully by the doctor, and quite vaguely by the English lord. Nothing rewarded their grovellings except a few twigs, snapped or chopped into very small lengths, which Valentin lifted for an instant's examination, and then tossed away.

'Twigs,' he said gravely; 'twigs, and a total stranger with his head cut off; that is all there is on this lawn.'

There was an almost creepy stillness, and then the unnerved Galloway called out sharply: 'Who's that? Who's that over there by the garden wall?'

A small figure with a foolishly large head drew

waveringly near them in the moonlit haze; looked for an instant like a goblin, but turned out to be the harmless little priest whom they had left in the drawing-room.

'I say,' he said meekly, 'there are no gates to this garden, do you know.'

Valentin's black brows had come together somewhat crossly, as they did on principle at the sight of the cassock. But he was far too just a man to deny the relevance of the remark. 'You are right,' he said. 'Before we find out how he came to be killed, we may have to find out how he came to be here. Now listen to me, gentlemen. If it can be done without prejudice to my position and duty, we shall all agree that certain distinguished names might well be kept out of this. There are ladies, gentlemen, and there is a foreign ambassador. If we must mark it down as a crime, then it must be followed up as a crime. But till then I can use my own discretion. I am the head of the police; I am so public that I can afford to be private. Please Heaven, I will clear every one of my own guests before I call in my men to look for anybody else. Gentlemen, upon your honour, you will none of you leave the house till tomorrow at noon; there are bedrooms for all. Simon, I think you know where to find my man, Ivan, in the front hall; he is a confidential man. Tell him to leave another servant on guard and come to me at once Lord Galloway, you are certainly the best person to tell the ladies what has happened, and prevent a panic. They also must stay. Father Brown and I will remain with the body.'

When this spirit of the captain spoke in Valentin he was obeyed like a bugle. Dr Simon went through to the armoury and routed out Ivan, the public detective's private detective. Galloway went to the drawing-room and told the terrible news tactfully enough, so that by the time the company assembled there the ladies were already startled and already soothed. Meanwhile the good priest and the good atheist stood at the head and foot of the dead man motionless in the moonlight, like symbolic statues of their two philosophies of death.

Ivan, the confidential man with the scar and the moustaches, came out of the house like a cannon ball, and came racing across the lawn to Valentin like a dog to his master. His livid face was quite lively with the glow of this domestic detective story, and it was with almost unpleasant eagerness that he asked his master's permission to examine the remains.

'Yes; look, if you like, Ivan,' said Valentin, 'but don't be long. We must go in and thrash this out in the house.'

Ivan lifted his head, and then almost let it drop.

'Why,' he gasped, 'it's – no, it isn't; it can't be. Do you know this man, sir?'

'No,' said Valentin indifferently; 'we had better go inside.'

Between them they carried the corpse to a sofa in the study, and then all made their way to the drawing-room.

The detective sat down at a desk quietly, and even with hesitation; but his eye was the iron eye of a judge at assize. He made a few rapid notes upon paper in front of him, and then said shortly: 'Is everybody here?'

'Not Mr Brayne,' said the Duchess of Mont St Michel, looking round.

'No,' said Lord Galloway, in a hoarse, harsh voice.

'And not Mr Neil O'Brien I fancy. I saw that gentleman walking in the garden when the corpse was still warm.'

'Ivan,' said the detective, 'go and fetch Commandant O'Brien and Mr Brayne. Mr Brayne, I know, is finishing a cigar in the dining-room; Commandant O'Brien, I think, is walking up and down the conservatory. I am not sure.'

The faithful attendant flashed from the room, and before anyone could stir or speak Valentin went on with the same soldierly swiftness of exposition.

'Everyone here knows that a dead man has been found in the garden, his head cut clean from his body. Dr Simon, you have examined it. Do you think that to cut a man's throat like that would need great force? Or, perhaps, only a very sharp knife?'

'I should say that it could not be done with a knife at all,' said the pale doctor.

'Have you any thought,' resumed Valentin, 'of a tool with which it could be done?'

'Speaking within modern probabilities, I really haven't,' said the doctor, arching his painful brows. 'It's not easy to hack a neck through even clumsily, and this was a very clean cut. It could be done with a battle-axe or an old headsman's axe, or an old two-handed sword.'

'But, good heavens!' cried the Duchess, almost in hysterics; 'there aren't any two-handed swords and battle-axes round here.'

Valentin was still busy with the paper in front of him. 'Tell me,' he said, still writing rapidly, 'could it have been done with a long French cavalry sabre?'

A low knocking came at the door, which for some unreasonable reason, curdled everyone's blood like the knocking in *Macbeth*. Amid that frozen silence Dr

Simon managed to say: 'A sabre – yes, I suppose it could.'

'Thank you,' said Valentin, 'Come in, Ivan.'

The confidential Ivan opened the door and ushered in Commandant Neil O'Brien, whom he had found at last pacing the garden again.

The Irish officer stood disordered and defiant on the threshold. 'What do you want with me?' he cried.

'Please sit down,' said Valentin in pleasant, level tones. 'Why, you aren't wearing your sword! Where is it?'

'I left it on the library table,' said O'Brien, his brogue deepening in his disturbed mood. 'It was a nuisance, it was getting –'

'Ivan,' said Valentin: 'please go and get the Commandant's sword from the library.' Then, as the servant vanished: 'Lord Galloway says he saw you leaving the garden just before he found the corpse. What were you doing in the garden?'

The Commandant flung himself recklessly into a chair. 'Oh,' he cried in pure Irish; 'admirin' the moon. Communing with Nature, me boy.'

A heavy silence sank and endured, and at the end of it came again that trivial and terrible knocking. Ivan reappeared, carrying an empty steel scabbard. 'This is all I can find,' he said.

'Put it on the table,' said Valentin, without looking up.

There was an inhuman silence in the room, like that sea of inhuman silence round the dock of the condemned murderer. The Duchess's weak exclamations had long ago died away. Lord Galloway's swollen hatred was satisfied and even sobered. The voice that came was quite unexpected.

'I think I can tell you,' cried Lady Margaret, in that clear, quivering voice with which a courageous woman speaks publicly. 'I can tell you what Mr O'Brien was doing in the garden, since he is bound to silence. He was asking me to marry him. I refused; I said in my family circumstances I could give him nothing but my respect. He was a little angry at that; he did not seem to think much of my respect. I wonder,' she added, with rather a wan smile, 'if he will care at all for it now. For I offer it him now. I will swear anywhere that he never did a thing like this.'

Lord Galloway had edged up to his daughter, and was intimidating her in what he imagined to be an undertone. 'Hold your tongue, Maggie,' he said in a thunderous whisper. 'Why should you shield the fellow? Where's his sword? Where's his confounded cavalry – '

He stopped because of the singular stare with which his daughter was regarding him, a look that was indeed a lurid magnet for the whole group.

'You old fool!' she said, in a low voice without pretence of piety; 'what do you suppose you are trying to prove? I tell you this man was innocent while with me. But if he wasn't innocent, he was still with me. If he murdered a man in the garden, who was it who must have seen – who must at least have known? Do you hate Neil so much as to put your own daughter – '

Lady Galloway screamed. Everyone else sat tingling at the touch of those satanic tragedies that have been between lovers before now. They saw the proud, white face of the Scotch aristocrat and her lover, the Irish adventurer, like old portraits in a dark house. The long silence was full of formless historical memories of murdered husbands and poisonous paramours.

In the centre of this morbid silence an innocent voice said: 'Was it a very long cigar?'

The change of thought was so sharp that they had to look round to see who had spoken.

'I mean,' said little Father Brown, from the corner of the room. 'I mean that cigar Mr Brayne is finishing. It seems nearly as long as a walking stick.'

Despite the irrelevance there was assent as well as irritation in Valentin's face as he lifted his head.

'Quite right,' he remarked sharply. 'Ivan, go and see about Mr Brayne again, and bring him here at once.'

The instant the factotum had closed the door, Valentin addressed the girl with an entirely new earnestness.

'Lady Margaret,' he said, 'we all feel, I am sure, both gratitude and admiration for your act in rising above your lower dignity and explaining the Commandant's conduct. But there is a hiatus still. Lord Galloway, I understand, met you passing from the study to the drawing-room, and it was only some minutes afterwards that he found the garden and the Commandant still walking there.'

'You have to remember,' replied Margaret, with a faint irony in her voice, 'that I had just refused him, so we should scarcely have come back arm in arm. He is a gentleman, anyhow; and he loitered behind – and so got charged with murder.'

'In those few moments,' said Valentin gravely, 'he might really – '

The knock came again, and Ivan put in his scarred face.

'Beg pardon, sir,' he said, 'but Mr Brayne has left the house.'

'Left!' cried Valentin, and rose for the first time to his feet.

'Gone. Scooted. Evaporated,' replied Ivan, in humorous French. 'His hat and coat are gone, too; and I'll tell you something to cap it all. I ran outside the house to find any traces of him, and I found one, and a big trace, too.'

'What do you mean?' asked Valentin.

'I'll show you,' said his servant, and reappeared with a flashing naked cavalry sabre, streaked with blood about the point and edge. Everyone in the room eyed it as if it were a thunderbolt; but the experienced Ivan went on quite quietly: 'I found this,' he said, 'flung among the bushes fifty yards up the road to Paris. In other words, I found it just where your respectable Mr Brayne threw it when he ran away.'

There was again a silence, but of a new sort. Valentin took the sabre, examined it, reflected with unaffected concentration of thought, and then turned a respectful face to O'Brien. 'Commandant,' he said, 'we trust you will always produce this weapon if it is wanted for police examination. Meanwhile,' he added, slapping the steel back in the ringing scabbard, 'let me return you your sword.'

At the military symbolism of the action the audience could hardly refrain from applause.

For Neil O'Brien, indeed, that gesture was the turning-point of existence. By the time he was wandering in the mysterious garden again in the colours of the morning the tragic futility of his ordinary mien had fallen from him; he was a man with many reasons for happiness. Lord Galloway was a gentleman, and had offered him an apology. Lady Margaret was something better than a lady, a woman at least, and had perhaps given him something better than an apology, as they drifted among the old flower-beds before breakfast. The whole company was more light-hearted and humane, for though the riddle of the death remained, the load of suspicion was lifted off them all, and sent flying off to Paris with the strange millionaire – a man they hardly knew. The devil was cast out of the house – he had cast himself out.

Still, the riddle remained; and when O'Brien threw himself on a garden seat beside Dr Simon, that keenly scientific person at once resumed it. He did not get much talk out of O'Brien, whose thoughts were on pleasanter things.

'I can't say it interests me much,' said the Irishman frankly, 'especially as it seems pretty plain now. Apparently Brayne hated this stranger for some reason; lured him into the garden, and killed him with my sword. Then he fled to the city, tossing the sword away as he went. By the way, Ivan tells me the dead man had a Yankee dollar in his pocket. So he was a countryman of Brayne's, and that seems to clinch it. I don't see any difficulties about the business.'

'There are five colossal difficulties,' said the doctor quietly; 'like high walls within walls. Don't mistake me. I don't doubt that Brayne did it; his flight, I fancy, proves that. But as to how he did it. First difficulty: why should a man kill another man with a great hulking sabre, when he can almost kill him with a pocket knife and put it back in his pocket? Second difficulty: why was there no noise or outcry? Does a man commonly see another come up waving a scimitar and offer no remarks? Third difficulty: a servant watched the front door all the evening; and a rat cannot get into Valentin's garden anywhere. How did the dead man get into the garden? Fourth difficulty: given the same conditions, how did Brayne get out of the garden?'

'And the fifth,' said Neil, with eyes fixed on the English priest, who was coming slowly up the path.

'Is a trifle, I suppose,' said the doctor, 'but I think an odd one. When I first saw how the head had been slashed, I supposed the assassin had struck more than once. But on examination I found many cuts across the truncated section; in other words, they were struck *after* the head was off. Did Brayne hate his foe so fiendishly that he stood sabring his body in the moonlight?'

'Horrible!' said O'Brien, and shuddered.

The little priest, Brown, had arrived while they were talking, and had waited, with characteristic shyness, till they had finished. Then he said awkwardly: 'I say, I'm sorry to interrupt. But I was sent to tell you the news!'

'News?' repeated Simon, and stared at him rather painfully through his glasses.

'Yes, I'm sorry,' said Father Brown mildly. 'There's been another murder, you know.'

Both men on the seat sprang up, leaving it rocking.

'And, what's stranger still,' continued the priest, with his dull eyes on the rhododendrons, 'it's the same disgusting sort; it's another beheading. They found the second head actually bleeding in the river, a few yards along Brayne's road to Paris; so they suppose that he – '

'Great Heaven!' cried O'Brien. 'Is Brayne a monomaniac?'

'There are American vendettas,' said the priest impassively. Then he added: 'They want you to come to the library and see it.'

Commandant O'Brien followed the others towards the inquest, feeling decidedly sick. As a soldier, he loathed all this secretive carnage; where were these extravagant amputations going to stop? First one head was hacked off, and then another; in this case (he told himself bitterly) it was not true that two heads were better than one. As he crossed the study he almost staggered at a shocking coincidence. Upon Valentin's table lay the coloured picture of yet a third bleeding head; and it was the head of Valentin himself. A second glance showed him it was only a Nationalist paper, called *The Guillotine*, which every week showed one of its political opponents with rolling eyes and writhing features just after execution; for Valentin was an anti-clerical of some note. But O'Brien was an Irishman, with a kind of chastity even in his sins; and his gorge rose against that great brutality of the intellect which belongs only to France. He felt Paris as a whole, from the grotesques on the Gothic churches to the gross caricatures in the newspapers. He remembered the gigantic jests of the Revolution. He saw the whole city as one ugly energy, from the sanguinary sketch lying on Valentin's table up to where, above a mountain and forest of gargoyles, the great devil grins on Notre Dame.

The library was long, low, and dark; what light entered it shot from under low blinds and had still some of the ruddy tinge of morning. Valentin and his servant Ivan were waiting for them at the upper end of a long, slightly-sloping desk, on which lay the mortal remains, looking enormous in the twilight. The big black figure and yellow face of the man found in the garden confronted them essentially unchanged. The second head, which had been fished from among the river reeds that morning, lay streaming and dripping beside it; Valentin's men were still seeking to recover the rest of this second corpse, which was supposed to be afloat. Father Brown, who did not seem to share O'Brien's sensibilities in the least, went up to the second head and examined it with his blinking care. It was little more than a mop of wet, white hair, fringed with silver fire in the red and level morning light; the face, which seemed of an ugly, empurpled and perhaps criminal type, had been much battered against trees or stones as it tossed in the water.

'Good-morning, Commandant O'Brien,' said Valentin, with quiet cordiality. 'You have heard of Brayne's last experiment in butchery, I suppose?'

Father Brown was still bending over the head with white hair, and he said, without looking up: 'I suppose it is quite certain that Brayne cut off this head, too.'

'Well, it seems common sense,' said Valentin, with his hands in his pockets. 'Killed in the same way as the other. Found within a few yards of the other. And sliced by the same weapon which we know he carried away.'

'Yes, yes; I know,' replied Father Brown, submissively. 'Yet, you know, I doubt whether Brayne could have cut off this head.'

'Why not?' enquired Dr Simon, with a rational stare.

'Well, doctor,' said the priest, looking up blinking, 'can a man cut off his own head? I don't know.'

O'Brien felt an insane universe crashing about his ears; but the doctor sprang forward with impetuous practicality and pushed back the wet, white hair.

'Oh, there's no doubt it's Brayne,' said the priest quietly. 'He had exactly that chip in the left ear.'

The detective, who had been regarding the priest with steady and glittering eyes, opened his clenched mouth and said sharply: 'You seem to know a lot about him, Father Brown.'

'I do,' said the little man simply. 'I've been about with him for some weeks. He was thinking of joining our church.'

The star of the fanatic sprang into Valentin's eyes; he strode towards the priest with clenched hands. 'And, perhaps,' he cried, with a blasting sneer: 'perhaps he was also thinking of leaving all his money to your church.'

'Perhaps he was,' said Brown stolidly; 'it is possible.'

'In that case,' cried Valentin, with a dreadful smile: 'you may indeed know a great deal about him. About his life and about his – '

Commandant O'Brien laid a hand on Valentin's arm. 'Drop that slanderous rubbish, Valentin,' he said: 'or there may be more swords yet.'

But Valentin (under the steady, humble gaze of the priest) had already recovered himself. 'Well,' he said shortly: 'people's private opinions can wait. You gentlemen are still bound by your promise to stay; you must enforce it on yourselves – and on each other. Ivan here will tell you anything more you want to know; I must get to business and write to the authorities. We can't keep this quiet any longer. I shall be writing in my study if there is any more news.'

'Is there any more news, Ivan?' asked Dr Simon, as the chief of police strode out of the room.

'Only one more thing, I think, sir,' said Ivan, wrinkling up his grey old face; 'but that's important, too, in its way. There's that old buffer you found on the lawn,' and he pointed without pretence of reverence at the big black body with the yellow head. 'We've found out who he is, anyhow.'

'Indeed!' cried the astonished doctor; 'and who is he?'

'His name was Arnold Becker,' said the under-detective, 'though he went by many aliases. He was a wandering sort of scamp, and is known to have been in America; so that was where Brayne got his knife into him. We didn't have much to do with him ourselves, for he worked mostly in Germany. We've communicated, of course, with the German police. But, oddly enough, there was a twin brother of his, named Louis Becker, whom we had a great deal to do with. In fact, we found it necessary to guillotine him only yesterday. Well, it's a rum thing, gentlemen, but when I saw that fellow flat on the lawn I had the greatest jump of my life. If I hadn't seen Louis Becker guillotined with my own eyes, I'd have sworn it was Louis Becker lying there in the grass. Then, of course, I remembered his twin brother in Germany, and following up the clue – '

The explanatory Ivan stopped, for the excellent reason that nobody was listening to him. The Commandant and the doctor were both staring at Father Brown, who had sprung stiffly to his feet, and was holding his temples tight like a man in sudden and violent pain.

'Stop, stop, stop!' he cried; 'stop talking a minute, for I see half. Will God give me strength? Will my brain make the one jump and see all? Heaven help me! I used to be fairly good at thinking. I could paraphrase any page in Aquinas once. Will my head split – or will it see? I see half – I only see half.'

He buried his head in his hands, and stood in a sort of rigid torture of thought or prayer, while the other three could only go on staring at this last prodigy of their wild twelve hours.

When Father Brown's hands fell they showed a face quite fresh and serious, like a child's. He heaved a huge sigh, and said: 'Let us get this said and done with as quickly as possible. Look here, this will be the quickest way to convince you all of the truth.' He turned to the doctor. 'Dr Simon,' he said, 'you have a strong headpiece, and I heard you this morning asking the five hardest questions about this business. Well, if you will now ask them again, I will answer them.'

Simon's pince-nez dropped from his nose in his doubt and wonder, but he answered at once. 'Well, the first question, you know, is why a man should kill another with a clumsy sabre at all when a man can kill with a bodkin?'

'A man cannot behead with a bodkin,' said Brown, calmly, 'and for *this* murder beheading was absolutely necessary.'

'Why?' asked O'Brien, with interest.

'And the next question?' asked Father Brown.

'Well, why didn't the man cry out or anything?' asked the doctor; 'sabres in gardens are certainly unusual.'

'Twigs,' said the priest gloomily, and turned to the window which looked on the scene of death. 'No one saw the point of the twigs. Why should they lie on that lawn (look at it) so far from any tree? They were not snapped off; they were chopped off. The murderer occupied his enemy with some tricks with the sabre, showing how he could cut a branch in mid-air, or what not. Then, while his enemy bent down to see the result, a silent slash, and the head fell.'

'Well,' said the doctor slowly, 'that seems plausible

enough. But my next two questions will stump anyone.'

The priest still stood looking critically out of the window and waited.

'You know how all the garden was sealed up like an airtight chamber,' went on the doctor. 'Well, how did the strange man get into the garden?'

Without turning round, the little priest answered: 'There never was any strange man in the garden.'

There was a silence, and then a sudden cackle of almost childish laughter relieved the strain. The absurdity of Brown's remark moved Ivan to open taunts.

'Oh!' he cried; 'then we didn't lug a great fat corpse on to a sofa last night? He hadn't got into the garden, I suppose?'

'Got into the garden?' repeated Brown reflectively. 'No, not entirely.'

'Hang it all,' cried Simon, 'a man gets into a garden, or he doesn't.'

'Not necessarily,' said the priest, with a faint smile. 'What is the next question, doctor?'

'I fancy you're ill,' exclaimed Dr Simon sharply; 'but I'll ask the next question if you like. How did Brayne get out of the garden?'

'He didn't get out of the garden,' said the priest, still looking out of the window.

'Didn't get out of the garden?' exploded Simon.

'Not completely,' said Father Brown.

Simon shook his fists in a frenzy of French logic. 'A man gets out of a garden, or he doesn't,' he cried.

'Not always,' said Father Brown.

Dr Simon sprang to his feet impatiently. 'I have no time to spare on such senseless talk,' he cried angrily.

'If you can't understand a man being on one side of the wall or the other, I won't trouble you further.'

'Doctor,' said the cleric very gently 'we have always got on very pleasantly together. If only for the sake of old friendship, stop and tell me your fifth question.'

The impatient Simon sank into a chair by the door and said briefly: 'The head and shoulders were cut about in a queer way. It seemed to be done after death.'

'Yes,' said the motionless priest, 'it was done so as to make you assume exactly the one simple falsehood that you did assume. It was done to make you take for granted that the head belonged to the body.'

The borderland of the brain, where all the monsters are made, moved horribly in the Gaelic O'Brien. He felt the chaotic presence of all the horsemen and fish-women that man's unnatural fancy has begotten. A voice older than his first fathers seemed saying in his ear: 'Keep out of the monstrous garden where grows the tree with double fruit. Avoid the evil garden where died the man with two heads.' Yet, while these shameful symbolic shapes passed across the ancient mirror of his Irish soul, his Frenchified intellect was quite alert, and was watching the odd priest as closely and incredulously as all the rest.

Father Brown had turned round at last, and stood against the window with his face in dense shadow; but even in that shadow they could see it was pale as ashes. Nevertheless, he spoke quite sensibly, as if there were no Gaelic souls on earth.

'Gentlemen,' he said; 'you did not find the strange body of Becker in the garden. You did not find any strange body in the garden. In face of Dr Simon's rationalism, I still affirm that Becker was only partly present. Look here!' (pointing to the black bulk of the mysterious corpse); 'you never saw that man in your lives. Did you ever see this man?'

He rapidly rolled away the bald-yellow head of the unknown, and put in its place the white-maned head beside it. And there, complete, unified, unmistakable, lay Julius K. Brayne.

'The murderer,' went on Brown quietly, 'hacked off his enemy's head and flung the sword far over the wall. But he was too clever to fling the sword only. He flung the *head* over the wall also. Then he had only to clap on another head to the corpse, and (as he insisted on a private inquest) you all imagined a totally new man.'

'Clap on another head!' said O'Brien, staring. 'What other head? Heads don't grow on garden bushes, do they?'

'No,' said Father Brown huskily, and looking at his boots; 'there is only one place where they grow. They grow in the basket of the guillotine, beside which the Chief of Police, Aristide Valentin, was standing not an hour before the murder. Oh, my friends, hear me a minute more before you tear me in pieces. Valentin is an honest man, if being mad for an arguable cause is honesty. But did you ever see in that cold, grey eye of his that he is mad? He would do anything, *anything*, to break what he calls the superstition of the Cross. He has fought for it and starved for it, and now he has murdered for it. Brayne's crazy millions had hitherto been scattered among so many sects that they did little to alter the balance of things. But Valentin heard a whisper that Brayne, like so many scatterbrained sceptics, was drifting to us; and that was quite a different thing. Brayne would pour supplies into the impoverished and pugnacious Church of France; he would support six Nationalist newspapers like *The Guillotine*. The battle was already balanced on a point, and the fanatic took flame at the risk. He resolved to destroy the millionaire, and he did it as one would expect the greatest of detectives to commit his only crime. He abstracted the severed head of Becker on some criminological excuse, and took it home in his official box. He had that last argument with Brayne, that Lord Galloway did not hear the end of; that failing, he led him out into the sealed garden, talked about swordsmanship, used twigs and a sabre for illustration, and – '

Ivan of the Scar sprang up. 'You lunatic,' he yelled; 'you'll go to my master now, if I take you by – '

'Why, I was going there,' said Brown heavily; 'I must ask him to confess, and all that.'

Driving the unhappy Brown before them like a hostage or sacrifice, they rushed together into the sudden stillness of Valentin's study.

The great detective sat at his desk apparently too occupied to hear their turbulent entrance. They paused a moment, and then something in the look of that upright and elegant back made the doctor run forward suddenly. A touch and a glance showed him that there was a small box of pills at Valentin's elbow, and that Valentin was dead in his chair; and on the blind face of the suicide was more than the pride of Cato.

The Queer Feet

If you meet a member of that select club, 'The Twelve True Fishermen', entering the Vernon Hotel for the annual club dinner, you will observe, as he takes off his overcoat, that his evening coat is green and not black. If (supposing that you have the star-defying audacity to address such a being) you ask him why, he will probably answer that he does it to avoid being mistaken for a waiter. You will then retire crushed. But you will leave behind you a mystery as yet unsolved and a tale worth telling.

If (to pursue the same vein of improbable conjecture) you were to meet a mild, hard-working little priest, named Father Brown, and were to ask him what he thought was the most singular luck of his life, he would probably reply that upon the whole his best stroke was at the Vernon Hotel, where he had averted a crime and, perhaps, saved a soul, merely by listening to a few footsteps in a passage. He is perhaps a little proud of this wild and wonderful guess of his, and it is possible that he might refer to it. But since it is immeasurably unlikely that you will ever rise high enough in the social world to find 'The Twelve True Fishermen', or that you will ever sink low enough among slums and criminals to find Father Brown, I fear you will never hear the story at all unless you hear it from me.

The Vernon Hotel, at which The Twelve True Fishermen held their annual dinners, was an institution such as can only exist in an oligarchical society which has almost gone mad on good manners. It was that topsy-turvy product – an 'exclusive' commercial enterprise. That is, it was a thing which paid, not by attracting people, but actually by turning people away. In the heart of a plutocracy tradesmen become cunning enough to be more fastidious than their customers. They positively create difficulties so that their wealthy and weary clients may spend money and diplomacy in overcoming them. If there were a fashionable hotel in London which no man could enter who was under six foot, society would meekly make up parties of six-foot men to dine in it. If there were an expensive restaurant which by a mere caprice of its proprietor was only open on Thursday afternoon, it would be crowded on Thursday afternoon. The Vernon Hotel stood, as if by accident, in the corner of a square in Belgravia. It was a small hotel; and a very inconvenient one. But its very inconveniences were considered as walls protecting a particular class. One inconvenience, in particular, was held to be of vital importance: the fact that practically only twenty-four people could dine in the place at once. The only big dinner table was the celebrated terrace table, which stood open to the air on a sort of veranda overlooking one of the most exquisite old gardens in London. Thus it happened that even the twenty-four seats at this table could only be enjoyed in warm weather; and this making the enjoyment yet more difficult made it yet more desired. The existing owner of the hotel was a Jew named Lever; and he made nearly a million out of it, by making it difficult to get into. Of course he combined with this limitation in the scope of his enterprise the most careful polish in its performance. The wines and cooking were really as good as any in Europe, and the demeanour of the attendants exactly mirrored the fixed mood of the English upper class. The proprietor knew all his waiters like the fingers on his hand; there were only fifteen of them all told. It was much easier to become a Member of Parliament than to become a waiter in that hotel. Each waiter was trained in terrible silence and smoothness, as if he were a gentleman's servant. And, indeed, there was generally at least one waiter to every gentleman who dined.

The club of The Twelve True Fishermen would not have consented to dine anywhere but in such a place, for it insisted on a luxurious privacy; and would have been quite upset by the mere thought that any other club was even dining in the same building. On the occasion of their annual dinner the Fishermen were in the habit of exposing all their treasures, as if they were in a private house, especially the celebrated set of fish knives and forks which were, as it were, the insignia of the society, each being exquisitely wrought in silver in the form of a fish, and each loaded at the hilt with one large pearl. These were always laid out for the fish course, and the fish course was always the most magnificent in that magnificent repast. The society had a vast number of ceremonies and observances, but it had no history and no object; that was where it was so very aristocratic. You did not have to be anything in order to be one of the Twelve Fishers; unless you were already a certain sort of person, you never even heard of them. It had been in existence twelve years. Its president was Mr Audley. Its vice-president was the Duke of Chester.

If I have in any degree conveyed the atmosphere of this appalling hotel, the reader may feel a natural wonder as to how I came to know anything about it, and may even speculate as to how so ordinary a person as my friend Father Brown came to find himself in that golden gallery. As far as that is concerned, my story is simple, or even vulgar. There is in the world a very aged rioter and demagogue who breaks into the most refined retreats with the dreadful information that all men are brothers, and wherever this leveller went on his pale horse it was Father Brown's trade to follow. One of the waiters, an Italian, had been struck down with a paralytic stroke that afternoon; and his Jewish employer, marvelling mildly at such superstitions, had consented to send for the nearest Popish priest. With what the waiter confessed to Father Brown we are not concerned, for the excellent reason that the cleric kept it to himself; but apparently it involved him in writing out a note or statement for the conveying of some message or the righting of some wrong. Father Brown, therefore, with a meek impudence which he would have shown equally in Buckingham Palace, asked to be provided with a room and writing materials. Mr Lever was torn in two. He was a kind man, and had also that bad imitation of kindness, the dislike of any difficulty or scene. At the same time the presence of one unusual stranger in his hotel that evening was like a speck of dirt on something just cleaned. There was never any borderland or ante-room in the Vernon Hotel, no people waiting in the hall, no customers coming in on chance. There were fifteen waiters. There were twelve guests. It would be as startling to find a new guest in the hotel that night as to find a new brother taking breakfast or tea in one's own family. Moreover, the priest's appearance was second-rate and his clothes muddy; a mere glimpse of him afar off might precipitate a crisis in the club. Mr Lever at last hit on a plan to cover, since he might not obliterate, the disgrace. When you enter (as you never will) the Vernon Hotel, you pass down a short passage decorated with a few dingy but important pictures, and come to the main vestibule and lounge which opens on your right into passages leading to the public rooms, and on your left to a similar passage pointing to the kitchens and offices of the hotel. Immediately on your left hand is the corner of a glass office, which abuts upon the lounge – a house within a house, so to speak, like the old hotel bar which probably once occupied its place.

In this office sat the representative of the proprietor (nobody in this place ever appeared in person if he could help it), and just beyond the office, on the way to the servants' quarters, was the gentlemen's cloakroom, the last boundary of the gentlemen's domain. But between the office and the cloakroom was a small private room without other outlet, sometimes used by the proprietor for delicate and important matters, such as lending a duke a thousand pounds or declining to lend him sixpence. It is a mark of the magnificent tolerance of Mr Lever that he permitted this holy place to be for about half an hour profaned by a mere priest, scribbling away on a piece of paper. The story which Father Brown was writing down was very likely a much better story than this one, only it will never be known. I can merely state that it was very nearly as long, and that the last two or three paragraphs of it were the least exciting and absorbing.

For it was by the time he had reached these that the priest began a little to allow his thoughts to wander and his animal senses, which were commonly keen, to awaken. The time of darkness and dinner was drawing on; his own forgotten little room was without a light, and perhaps the gathering gloom, as occasionally happens, sharpened the sense of sound. As Father Brown wrote the last and least essential part of his document, he caught himself writing to the rhythm of a recurrent noise outside, just as one sometimes thinks to the tune of a railway train. When he became conscious of the thing he found what it was: only the ordinary patter of feet passing the door, which in an hotel was no very unlikely matter. Nevertheless, he stared at the darkened ceiling, and listened to the sound. After he had listened for a few seconds dreamily, he got to his feet and listened intently, with his head a little on one side. Then he sat down again and buried his brow in his hands, now not merely listening, but listening and thinking also.

The footsteps outside at any given moment were such as one might hear in any hotel; and yet, taken as a whole, there was something very strange about them. There were no other footsteps. It was always a very silent house, for the few familiar guests went at once to their own apartments, and the well-trained waiters were told to be almost invisible until they were wanted. One could not conceive any place where there was less reason to apprehend anything irregular. But these footsteps were so odd that one could not decide to call them regular or irregular. Father Brown followed them with his finger on the edge of the table, like a man trying to learn a tune on the piano.

First, there came a long rush of rapid little steps, such as a light man might make in winning a walking race. At a certain point they stopped and changed to a sort of slow-swinging stamp, numbering not a quarter of the steps, but occupying about the same time. The moment the last echoing stamp had died away would come again the run or ripple of light, hurrying feet, and then again the thud of the heavier walking. It was certainly the same pair of boots, partly because (as has been said) there were no other boots about, and partly because they had a small but unmistakable creak in them. Father Brown had the kind of head that cannot help asking questions; and on this apparently trivial question his head almost split. He had seen men run in order to jump. He had seen men run in order to slide. But why on earth should a man run in order to walk? Or, again, why should he walk in order to run? Yet no other description would cover the antics of this invisible pair of legs. The man was either walking very fast down one-half of the corridor in order to walk very slow down the other half; or he was walking very slow at one end to have the rapture of walking fast at the other. Neither suggestion seemed to make much sense. His brain was growing darker and darker, like his room.

Yet, as he began to think steadily, the very blackness of his cell seemed to make his thoughts more vivid; he began to see as in a kind of vision the fantastic feet capering along the corridor in unnatural or symbolic attitudes. Was it a heathen religious dance? Or some entirely new kind of scientific exercise? Father Brown began to ask himself with more exactness what the steps suggested. Taking the slow step first; it certainly was not the step of the proprietor. Men of his type walk with a rapid waddle, or they sit still. It could not be any servant or messenger waiting for directions. It did not sound like it. The poorer orders (in an oligarchy) sometimes lurch about when they are slightly drunk, but generally, and especially in such gorgeous scenes, they stand or sit in constrained attitudes. No; that heavy yet springy step, with a kind of careless emphasis, not specially noisy, yet not caring what noise it made, belonged to only one of the animals of this earth. It was a gentleman of western Europe, and probably one who had never worked for his living.

Just as he came to this solid certainty, the step changed to the quicker one, and ran past the door as feverishly as a rat. The listener remarked that though this step was much swifter it was also much more noiseless, almost as if the man were walking on tiptoe. Yet it was not associated in his mind with secrecy, but with something else – something that he could not remember. He was maddened by one of those half-memories that make a man feel half-witted. Surely he had heard that strange, swift walking somewhere. Suddenly he sprang to his feet with a new idea in his head, and walked to the door. His room had no direct outlet on the passage, but let on one side into the glass office, and on the other into the cloakroom beyond. He tried the door into the office, and found it locked. Then he looked at the window, now a square pane full of purple cloud cleft by livid sunset, and for an instant he smelt evil as a dog smells rats.

The rational part of him (whether the wiser or not) regained its supremacy. He remembered that the proprietor had told him that he should lock the door, and would come later to release him. He told himself that twenty things he had not thought of might explain the eccentric sounds outside; he reminded himself that there was just enough light left to finish his own proper work. Bringing his paper to the window so as to catch the last stormy evening light, he resolutely plunged once more into the almost completed record. He had written for about twenty minutes, bending closer and closer to his paper in the lessening light; then suddenly he sat upright. He had heard the strange feet once more.

This time they had a third oddity. Previously the unknown man had walked, with levity indeed and lightning quickness, but he had walked. This time he ran. One could hear the swift, soft, bounding steps coming along the corridor, like the pads of a fleeing and leaping panther Whoever was coming was a very strong, active man, in still yet tearing excitement. Yet, when the sound had swept up to the office like a sort of whispering whirlwind, it suddenly changed again to the old slow, swaggering stamp.

Father Brown flung down his paper, and, knowing the office door to be locked, went at once into the cloakroom on the other side. The attendant of this place was temporarily absent, probably because the only guests were at dinner, and his office was a sinecure. After groping through a grey forest of overcoats, he found that the dim cloakroom opened on the lighted corridor in the form of a sort of counter or half-door, like most of the counters across which we have all handed umbrellas and received tickets. There was a light immediately above the semicircular arch of this opening. It threw little illumination on Father Brown himself, who seemed a mere dark outline against the dim sunset window behind him. But it threw an almost theatrical light on the man who stood outside the cloakroom in the corridor.

He was an elegant man in very plain evening-dress; tall, but with an air of not taking up much room; one felt that he could have slid along like a shadow where many smaller men would have been obvious and obstructive. His face, now flung back in the lamplight, was swarthy and vivacious, the face of a foreigner. His figure was good, his manners good-humoured and confident; a critic could only say that his black coat was a shade below his figure and manners, and even bulged and bagged in an odd way. The moment he caught sight of Brown's black silhouette against the sunset, he tossed down a scrap of paper with a number and called out with amiable authority: 'I want my hat and coat, please; I find I have to go away at once.'

Father Brown took the paper without a word, and obediently went to look for the coat; it was not the first menial work he had done in his life. He brought it and laid it on the counter; meanwhile, the strange gentleman who had been feeling in his waistcoat pocket, said, laughing: 'I haven't got any silver; you can keep this.' And he threw down half a sovereign, and caught up his coat.

Father Brown's figure remained quite dark and still; but in that instant he had lost his head. His head was always most valuable when he had lost it. In such moments he put two and two together and made four million. Often the Catholic Church (which is wedded to common sense) did not approve of it. Often he did not approve of it himself. But it was a real inspiration – important at rare crises – when whosoever shall lose his head the same shall save it.

'I think, sir,' he said civilly, 'that you have some silver in your pocket.'

The tall gentleman stared. 'Hang it,' he cried. 'If I give you gold, why should you complain?'

'Because silver is sometimes more valuable than

gold,' said the priest mildly; 'that is, in large quantities.'

The stranger looked at him curiously. Then he looked still more curiously up the passage towards the main entrance. Then he looked back at Brown again, and then he looked very carefully at the window beyond Brown's head, still coloured with the after-glow of the storm. Then he seemed to make up his mind. He put one hand on the counter, vaulted over as easily as an acrobat and towered above the priest, putting one tremendous hand upon his collar.

'Stand still,' he said, in a hacking whisper. 'I don't want to threaten you, but – '

'I do want to threaten you,' said Father Brown, in a voice like a rolling drum. 'I want to threaten you with the worm that dieth not, and the fire that is not quenched.'

'You're a rum sort of cloakroom clerk,' said the other.

'I am a priest, Monsieur Flambeau,' said Brown, 'and I am ready to hear your confession.'

The other stood gasping for a few moments, and then staggered back into a chair.

The first two courses of the dinner of The Twelve True Fishermen had proceeded with placid success. I do not possess a copy of the menu; and if I did it would not convey anything to anybody. It was written in a sort of super-French employed by cooks, but quite unintelligible to Frenchmen. There was a tradition in the club that the hors-d'oeuvres should be various and manifold to the point of madness. They were taken seriously because they were avowedly useless extras, like the whole dinner and the whole club. There was also a tradition that the soup course should be light and unpretending – a sort of simple and austere vigil for the feast of fish that was to come. The talk was that strange, slight talk which governs the British Empire, which governs it in secret, and yet would scarcely enlighten an ordinary Englishman even if he could overhear it. Cabinet Ministers on both sides were alluded to by their Christian names with a sort of bored benignity. The Radical Chancellor of the Exchequer, whom the whole Tory party was supposed to be cursing for his extortions, was praised for his minor poetry, or his saddle in the hunting-field. The Tory leader, whom all Liberals were supposed to hate as a tyrant, was discussed and, on the whole, praised – as a Liberal. It seemed somehow that politicians were very important. And yet, anything seemed important about them except their politics. Mr Audley, the chairman, was an amiable, elderly man who still wore Gladstone collars; he was a kind of symbol of all that phantasmal and yet fixed society. He had never done anything – not even anything wrong. He was not fast; he was not even particularly rich. He was simply in the thing; and there was an end of it. No party could ignore him, and if he had wished to be in the Cabinet he certainly would have been put there. The Duke of Chester, the vice-president, was a young and rising politician. That is to say, he was a pleasant youth, with flat, fair hair and a freckled face, with moderate intelligence and enormous estates. In public his appearances were always successful and his principle was simple enough. When he thought of a joke he made it, and was called brilliant. When he could not think of a joke he said that this was no time for trifling, and was called able. In private, in a club of his own class, he was simply quite pleasantly frank and silly, like a schoolboy. Mr Audley, never having been in politics, treated them a little more seriously. Sometimes he even embarrassed the company by phrases suggesting that there was some difference between a Liberal and a Conservative. He, himself, was a Conservative, even in private life. He had a roll of grey hair over the back of his collar like certain old-fashioned statesmen, and seen from behind he looked like the man the empire wants. Seen from the front he looked like a mild, self-indulgent bachelor, with rooms in the Albany – which he was.

As has been remarked, there were twenty-four seats at the terrace table, and only twelve members of the club. Thus they could occupy the terrace in the most luxurious style of all, being ranged along the inner side of the table, with no one opposite, commanding an uninterrupted view of the garden, the colours of which were still vivid, though evening was closing in somewhat luridly for the time of year. The chairman sat in the centre of the line, and the vice-president at the right-hand end of it. When the twelve guests first trooped into their seats it was the custom (for some unknown reason) for all the fifteen waiters to stand lining the wall like troops presenting arms to the king, while the fat proprietor stood and bowed to the club with radiant surprise, as if he had never heard of them before. But before the first chink of knife and fork this army of retainers had vanished, only the one or two required to collect and distribute the plates darting about in deathly silence. Mr Lever, the proprietor, of course had disappeared in convulsions of courtesy long before. It would be exaggerative, indeed irreverent, to say that he ever positively appeared again. But when the important course, the fish course, was being brought on, there was – how shall I put it? – a vivid shadow, a projection of his personality, which told that he was hovering near. The sacred fish course consisted (to the eyes of the vulgar) in a sort of monstrous pudding, about the size and shape of a wedding cake, in which some considerable number of interesting fishes had finally lost the shapes which God had given to them. The Twelve True Fishermen took up their celebrated fish knives and fish forks, and approached it as gravely as if every inch of the pudding cost as much as the silver fork it was eaten with. So it did, for all I know. This course was dealt with in eager and devouring silence; and it was only when his plate was nearly empty that the young duke made the ritual remark: 'They can't do this anywhere but here.'

'Nowhere,' said Mr Audley, in a deep bass voice, turning to the speaker and nodding his venerable head a number of times. 'Nowhere, assuredly, except here. It was represented to me that at the Café Anglais – '

Here he was interrupted and even agitated for a moment by the removal of his plate, but he recaptured the valuable thread of his thoughts. 'It was represented to me that the same could be done at the Café Anglais. Nothing like it, sir,' he said, shaking his head ruthlessly, like a hanging judge. 'Nothing like it.'

'Overrated place,' said a certain Colonel Pound, speaking (by the look of him) for the first time for some months.

'Oh, I don't know,' said the Duke of Chester, who was an optimist, 'it's jolly good for some things. You can't beat it at – '

A waiter came swiftly along the room, and then stopped dead. His stoppage was as silent as his tread;

but all those vague and kindly gentlemen were so used to the utter smoothness of the unseen machinery which surrounded and supported their lives, that a waiter doing anything unexpected was a start and a jar. They felt as you and I would feel if the inanimate world disobeyed – if a chair ran away from us.

The waiter stood staring a few seconds, while there deepened on every face at table a strange shame which is wholly the product of our time. It is the combination of modern humanitarianism with the horrible modern abyss between the souls of the rich and poor. A genuine historic aristocrat would have thrown things at the waiter, beginning with empty bottles, and very probably ending with money. A genuine democrat would have asked him, with a comrade-like clearness of speech, what the devil he was doing. But these modern plutocrats could not bear a poor man near to them, either as a slave or as a friend. That something had gone wrong with the servants was merely a dull, hot embarrassment. They did not want to be brutal, and they dreaded the need to be benevolent. They wanted the thing, whatever it was, to be over. It was over. The waiter, after standing for some seconds rigid, like a cataleptic, turned round and ran madly out of the room.

When he reappeared in the room, or rather in the doorway, it was in company with another waiter, with whom he whispered and gesticulated with southern fierceness. Then the first waiter went away, leaving the second waiter, and reappeared with a third waiter. By the time a fourth waiter had joined this hurried synod, Mr Audley felt it necessary to break the silence in the interests of tact. He used a very loud cough, instead of the presidential hammer, and said: 'Splendid work young Moocher's doing in Burma. Now, no other nation in the world could have – '

A fifth waiter had sped towards him like an arrow, and was whispering in his ear: 'So sorry. Important! Might the proprietor speak to you?'

The chairman turned in disorder, and with a dazed stare saw Mr Lever coming towards them with his lumbering quickness. The gait of the good proprietor was indeed his usual gait, but his face was by no means usual. Generally it was a genial copper-brown; now it was a sickly yellow.

'You will pardon me, Mr Audley,' he said, with asthmatic breathlessness. 'I have great apprehensions. Your fish plates, they are cleared away with the knife and fork on them!'

'Well, I hope so,' said the chairman, with some warmth.

'You see him?' panted the excited hotel keeper; 'you see the waiter who took them away? You know him?'

'Know the waiter?' answered Mr Audley indignantly. 'Certainly not!'

Mr Lever opened his hands with a gesture of agony. 'I never send him,' he said. 'I know not when or why he come. I send my waiter to take away the plates, and he find them already away.'

Mr Audley still looked rather too bewildered to be really the man the empire wants; none of the company could say anything except the man of wood – Colonel Pound – who seemed galvanised into an unnatural life. He rose rigidly from his chair, leaving all the rest sitting, screwed his eyeglass into his eye, and spoke in a raucous undertone as if he had half-forgotten how to speak. 'Do you mean,' he said, 'that somebody has stolen our silver fish service?'

The proprietor repeated the open-handed gesture with even greater helplessness; and in a flash all the men at the table were on their feet.

'Are all your waiters here?' demanded the colonel, in his low, harsh accent.

'Yes; they're all here. I noticed it myself,' cried the young duke, pushing his boyish face into the inmost ring. 'Always count 'em as I come in; they look so queer standing up against the wall.'

'But surely one cannot exactly remember,' began Mr Audley, with heavy hesitation.

'I remember exactly, I tell you,' cried the duke excitedly. 'There never have been more than fifteen waiters at this place, and there were no more than fifteen tonight, I'll swear: no more and no less.'

The proprietor turned upon him, quaking in a kind of palsy of surprise. 'You say – you say,' he stammered, 'that you see all my fifteen waiters?'

'As usual,' assented the duke. 'What is the matter with that?'

'Nothing,' said Lever, with a deepening accent, 'only you did not. For one of zem is dead upstairs.'

'There was a shocking stillness for an instant in that room. It may be (so supernatural is the word death) that each of those idle men looked for a second at his soul, and saw it as a small dried pea. One of them – the duke, I think – even said with the idiotic kindness of wealth: 'Is there anything we can do?'

'He has had a priest,' said the Jew, not untouched.

'Then, as to the clang of doom, they awoke to their own position. For a few weird seconds they had really felt as if the fifteenth waiter might be the ghost of the dead man upstairs. They had been dumb under that oppression, for ghosts were to them an embarrassment, like beggars. But the remembrance of the silver broke the spell of the miraculous; broke it abruptly and with a brutal reaction. The colonel flung over his chair and strode to the door. 'If there was a fifteenth man here, friends,' he said, 'that fifteenth fellow was a thief. Down at once to the front and back doors and secure everything; then we'll talk. The twenty-four pearls are worth recovering.'

'Mr Audley seemed at first to hesitate about whether it was gentlemanly to be in such a hurry about anything; but, seeing the duke dash down the stairs with youthful energy, he followed with a more mature motion.

At the same instant a sixth waiter ran into the room, and declared that he had found the pile of fish plates on a sideboard, with no trace of the silver.

The crowd of diners and attendants that tumbled helter-skelter down the passages divided into two groups. Most of the Fishermen followed the proprietor to the front room to demand news of any exit. Colonel Pound, with the Chairman, the vice-president, and one or two others, darted down the corridor leading to the servants' quarters, as the more likely line of escape. As they did so they passed the dim alcove or cavern of the cloakroom, and saw a short, black-coated figure, presumably an attendant, standing a little way back in the shadow of it.

'Hallo there!' called out the duke. 'Have you seen anyone pass?'

The short figure did not answer the question directly, but merely said: 'Perhaps I have got what you are looking for, gentlemen.'

They paused, wavering and wondering, while he quietly went to the back of the cloakroom, and came back with both hands full of shining silver, which he laid out on the counter as calmly as a salesman. It took the form of a dozen quaintly shaped forks and knives.

'You – you – ' began the colonel, quite thrown off his balance at last. Then he peered into the dim little room and saw two things: first, that the short, black-clad man was dressed like a clergyman; and, second, that the window of the room behind him was burst, as if someone had passed violently through.

'Valuable things to deposit in a cloakroom, aren't they?' remarked the clergyman, with cheerful composure.

'Did – did you steal those things?' stammered Mr Audley, with staring eyes.

'If I did,' said the cleric pleasantly, 'at least I am bringing them back again.'

'But you didn't,' said Colonel Pound, still staring at the broken window.

'To make a clean breast of it, I didn't,' said the other, with some humour. And he seated himself quite gravely on a stool.

'But you know who did,' said the colonel.

'I don't know his real name,' said the priest placidly; 'but I know something of his fighting weight, and a great deal about his spiritual difficulties. I formed the physical estimate when he was trying to throttle me, and the moral estimate when he repented.'

'Oh, I say – repented!' cried young Chester, with a sort of crow of laughter.

Father Brown got to his feet, putting his hands behind him. 'Odd, isn't it,' he said, 'that a thief and a vagabond should repent, when so many who are rich and secure remain hard and frivolous, and without fruit for God or man? But there, if you will excuse me, you trespass a little upon my province. If you doubt the penitence as a practical fact, there are your knives and forks. You are The Twelve True Fishers, and there are all your silver fish. But He has made me a fisher of men.'

'Did you catch this man?' asked the colonel, frowning.

Father Brown looked him full in his frowning face. 'Yes,' he said, 'I caught him, with an unseen hook and an invisible line which is long enough to let him wander to the ends of the world, and still to bring him back with a twitch upon the thread.'

There was a long silence. All the other men present drifted away to carry the recovered silver to their comrades, or to consult the proprietor about the queer condition of affairs. But the grim-faced colonel still sat sideways on the counter, swinging his long, lank legs and biting his dark moustache.

At last he said quietly to the priest: 'He must have been a clever fellow, but I think I know a cleverer.'

'He was a clever fellow,' answered the other, 'but I am not quite sure of what other you mean.'

'I mean you,' said the colonel, with a short laugh. 'I don't want to get the fellow jailed; make yourself easy about that. But I'd give a good many silver forks to know exactly how you fell into this affair, and how you got the stuff out of him. I reckon you're the most up-to-date devil of the present company.'

Father Brown seemed rather to like the saturnine candour of the soldier. 'Well,' he said, smiling, 'I mustn't tell you anything of the man's identity, or his own story, of course; but there's no particular reason why I shouldn't tell you of the mere outside facts which I found out for myself.'

He hopped over the barrier with unexpected activity, and sat beside Colonel Pound, kicking his short legs like a little boy on a gate. He began to tell the story as easily as if he were telling it to an old friend by a Christmas fire.

'You see, colonel,' he said, 'I was shut up in that small room there doing some writing, when I heard a pair of feet in this passage doing a dance that was as queer as the dance of death. First came quick, funny little steps, like a man walking on tiptoe for a wager; then came slow, careless, creaking steps, as of a big man walking about with a cigar. But they were both made by the same feet, I swear, and they came in rotation; first the run and then the walk, and then the run again. I wondered at first idly, and then wildly why a man should act these two parts at once. One walk I knew; it was just like yours, colonel. It was the walk of a well-fed gentleman waiting for something, who strolls about rather because he is physically alert than because he is mentally impatient. I knew that I knew the other walk, too, but I could not remember what it was. What wild creature had I met on my travels that tore along on tiptoe in that extraordinary style? Then I heard a clink of plates somewhere; and the answer stood up as plain as St Peter's. It was the walk of a waiter – that walk with the body slanted forward, the eyes looking down, the ball of the toe spurning away the ground, the coat tails and napkin flying. Then I thought for a minute and a half more. And I believe I saw the manner of the crime, as clearly as if I were going to commit it.'

Colonel Pound looked at him keenly, but the speaker's mild grey eyes were fixed upon the ceiling with almost empty wistfulness.

'A crime,' he said slowly, 'is like any other work of art. Don't look surprised; crimes are by no means the only works of art that come from an infernal workshop. But every work of art, divine or diabolic, has one indispensable mark – I mean, that the centre of it is simple, however much the fulfilment may be complicated. Thus, in *Hamlet,* let us say, the grotesqueness of the grave-digger, the flowers of the mad girl, the fantastic finery of Osric, the pallor of the ghost and the grin of the skull are all oddities in a sort of tangled wreath round one plain tragic figure of a man in black. Well, this also,' he said, getting slowly down from his seat with a smile, 'this also is the plain tragedy of a man in black. Yes,' he went on, seeing the colonel look up in some wonder, 'the whole of this tale turns on a black coat. In this, as in *Hamlet*, there are the rococo excrescences – yourselves, let us say. There is the dead waiter, who was there when he could not be there. There is the invisible hand that swept your table clear of silver and melted into air. But every clever crime is founded ultimately on some one quite simple fact – some fact that is not itself mysterious. The mystification comes in covering it up, in leading men's thoughts away from it. This large and subtle and (in the ordinary course) most profitable crime, was built on the plain fact that a gentleman's evening dress is the same as a waiter's. All the rest was acting, and thundering good acting, too.'

'Still,' said the colonel, getting up and frowning at his boots. 'I am not sure that I understand.'

'Colonel,' said Father Brown, 'I tell you that this archangel of impudence who stole your forks walked up and down this passage twenty times in the blaze of all the lamps, in the glare of all the eyes. He did not go and hide in dim corners where suspicion might have searched for him. He kept constantly on the move in the lighted corridors, and everywhere that he went he seemed to be there by right. Don't ask me what he was like; you have seen him yourself six or seven times tonight. You were waiting with all the other grand people in the reception room at the end of the passage there, with the terrace just beyond. Whenever he came among you gentlemen, he came in the lightning style of a waiter, with bent head, flapping napkin and flying feet. He shot out on to the terrace, did something to the tablecloth, and shot back again towards the office and the waiters' quarters. By the time he had come under the eye of the office clerk and the waiters he had become another man in every inch of his body, in every instinctive gesture. He strolled among the servants with the absent-minded insolence which they have all seen in their patrons. It was no new thing to them that a swell from the dinner party should pace all parts of the house like an animal at the zoo; they know that nothing marks the Smart Set more than a habit of walking where one chooses. When he was magnificently weary of walking down that particular passage he would wheel round and pace back past the office; in the shadow of the arch just beyond he was altered as by a blast of magic, and went hurrying forward again among the Twelve Fishermen, an obsequious attendant. Why should the gentlemen look at a chance waiter? Why should the waiters suspect a first-rate walking gentleman? Once or twice he played the coolest tricks. In the proprietor's private quarters he called out breezily for a syphon of soda water, saying he was thirsty. He said genially that he would carry it himself, and he did; he carried it quickly and correctly through the thick of you, a waiter with an obvious errand. Of course, it could not have been kept up long, but it only had to be kept up till the end of the fish course.

'His worst moment was when the waiters stood in a row; but even then he contrived to lean against the wall just around the corner in such a way that for that important instant the waiters thought him a gentleman, while the gentlemen thought him a waiter. The rest went like winking. If any waiter caught him away from the table, that waiter caught a languid aristocrat. He had only to time himself two minutes before the fish was cleared, become a swift servant, and clear it himself. He put the plates down on a sideboard, stuffed the silver in his breast pocket, giving it a bulgy look, and ran like a hare (I heard him coming) till he came to the cloakroom. There he had only to be a plutocrat again – a plutocrat called away suddenly on business. He had only to give his ticket to the cloakroom attendant, and go out again elegantly as he had come in. Only – only I happened to be the cloakroom attendant.'

'What did you do to him?' cried the colonel, with unusual intensity. 'What did he tell you?'

'I beg your pardon,' said the priest immovably, 'that is where the story ends.'

'And the interesting story begins,' muttered Pound. 'I think I understand his professional trick. But I don't seem to have got hold of yours.'

'I must be going,' said Father Brown.

They walked together along the passage to the entrance hall, where they saw the fresh, freckled face of the Duke of Chester, who was bounding buoyantly along towards them.

'Come along, Pound,' he cried breathlessly. 'I've been looking for you everywhere. The dinner's going again in spanking style, and old Audley has got to make a speech in honour of the forks being saved. We want to start some new ceremony, don't you know, to commemorate the occasion. I say, you really got the goods back, what do you suggest?'

'Why,' said the colonel, eyeing him with a certain sardonic approval. 'I should suggest that henceforward we wear green coats instead of black. One never knows what mistakes may arise when one looks so like a waiter.'

'Oh, hang it all!' said the young man, 'a gentleman never looks like a waiter.'

'Nor a waiter like a gentleman, I suppose,' said Colonel Pound, with the same lowering laughter on his face. 'Reverend sir, your friend must have been very smart to act the gentleman.'

Father Brown buttoned up his commonplace overcoat to the neck, for the night was stormy, and took his commonplace umbrella from the stand.

'Yes,' he said; 'it must be very hard work to be a gentleman; but, do you know, I have sometimes thought that it may be almost as laborious to be a waiter.'

And saying 'Good-evening,' he pushed open the heavy doors of that palace of pleasures. The golden gates closed behind him, and he went at a brisk walk through the damp, dark streets in search of a penny omnibus.

The Invisible Man

In the cool blue twilight of two steep streets in Camden Town, the shop at the corner, a confectioner's, glowed like the butt of a cigar. One should rather say, perhaps, like the butt of a firework, for the light was of many colours and some complexity, broken up by many mirrors and dancing on many gilt and gaily-coloured cakes and sweetmeats. Against this one fiery glass were glued the noses of many guttersnipes, for the chocolates were all wrapped in those red and gold and green metallic colours which are almost better than chocolate itself; and the huge white wedding cake in the window was somehow at once remote and satisfying, just as if the whole North Pole were good to eat. Such rainbow provocations could naturally collect the youth of the neighbourhood up to the ages of ten or twelve. But this corner was also attractive to youth at a later stage; and a young man, not less than twenty-four, was staring into the same shop window. To him, also, the shop was of fiery charm, but this attraction was not wholly to be explained by chocolates; which, however, he was far from despising.

He was a tall, burly, red-haired young man, with a resolute face but a listless manner. He carried under his arm a flat, grey portfolio of black-and-white sketches which he had sold with more or less success to publishers ever since his uncle (who was an admiral) had disinherited him for Socialism, because of a lecture which he had delivered against that economic theory. His name was John Turnbull Angus.

Entering at last, he walked through the confectioner's shop into the back room, which was a sort of pastry-cook restaurant, merely raising his hat to the young lady who was serving there. She was a dark, elegant, alert girl in black, with a high colour and very quick, dark eyes; and after the ordinary interval she followed him into the inner room to take his order.

His order was evidently a usual one. 'I want, please,' he said with precision, 'one halfpenny bun and a small cup of black coffee.' An instant before the girl could turn away he added, 'Also, I want you to marry me.'

The young lady of the shop stiffened suddenly, and said: 'Those are jokes I don't allow.'

The red-haired young man lifted grey eyes of an unexpected gravity.

'Really and truly,' he said, 'it's as serious – as serious as the halfpenny bun. It is expensive, like the bun; one pays for it. It is indigestible, like the bun. It hurts.'

The dark young lady had never taken her dark eyes off him, but seemed to be studying him with almost tragic exactitude. At the end of her scrutiny she had something like the shadow of a smile, and she sat down in a chair.

'Don't you think,' observed Angus, absently, 'that it's rather cruel to eat these halfpenny buns? They might grow up into penny buns. I shall give up these brutal sports when we are married.'

The dark young lady rose from her chair and walked to the window, evidently in a state of strong but not unsympathetic cogitation. When at last she swung round again with an air of resolution, she was bewildered to observe that the young man was carefully laying out on the table various objects from the shop-window. They included a pyramid of highly coloured sweets, several plates of sandwiches, and the two decanters containing that mysterious port and sherry which are peculiar to pastry-cooks. In the middle of this neat arrangement he had carefully let down the enormous load of white sugared cake which had been the huge ornament of the window.

'What on earth are you doing?' she asked.

'Duty, my dear Laura,' he began.

'Oh, for the Lord's sake, stop a minute,' she cried, 'and don't talk to me in that way. I mean what is all that?'

'A ceremonial meal, Miss Hope.'

'And what is *that*?' she asked impatiently, pointing to the mountain of sugar.

'The wedding-cake, Mrs Angus,' he said.

The girl marched to that article, removed it with some clatter, and put it back in the shop-window; she then returned, and, putting her elegant elbows on the table, regarded the young man not unfavourably, but with considerable exasperation.

'You don't give me any time to think,' she said.

'I'm not such a fool,' he answered; 'that's my Christian humility.'

She was still looking at him; but she had grown considerably graver behind the smile.

'Mr Angus,' she said steadily, 'before there is a minute more of this nonsense I must tell you something about myself as shortly as I can.'

'Delighted,' replied Angus gravely. 'You might tell me something about myself, too, while you are about it.'

'Oh, do hold your tongue and listen,' she said. 'It's nothing that I'm ashamed of, and it isn't even anything that I'm specially sorry about. But what would you say if there were something that is no business of mine and yet is my nightmare?'

'In that case,' said the man seriously, 'I should suggest that you bring back the cake.'

'Well, you must listen to the story first,' said Laura persistently. 'To begin with, I must tell you that my father owned the inn called the "Red Fish" at Ludbury, and I used to serve people in the bar.'

'I have often wondered,' he said, 'why there was a kind of a Christian air about this one confectioner's shop.'

'Ludbury is a sleepy, grassy little hole in the Eastern Counties, and the only kind of people who ever came to the "Red Fish" were occasional commercial travellers, and for the rest, the most awful people you can see, only you've never seen them. I mean little, loungy men, who had just enough to live on, and had nothing to do but lean about in bar-rooms and bet on horses, in bad clothes that were just too good for them. Even these wretched young rotters were not very common at our house; but there were two of them that were a lot too common – common in every sort of way. They both lived on money of their own, and were wearisomely idle and overdressed. But yet I was a bit sorry for them, because I half believe they slunk into our little empty bar because each of them had a slight deformity; the sort of thing that some yokels laugh at. It wasn't exactly a deformity either; it was more an oddity. One of them was a surprisingly small man, something like a dwarf, or at least like a jockey. He was not at all jockeyish to look at, though, he had a round black head and a well-trimmed black beard, bright eyes like a bird's; he jingled money in his pockets; he jangled a great gold watch chain; and he never turned up except dressed just too much like a gentleman to be one. He was no fool, though, though a futile idler; he was curiously clever at all kinds of things that couldn't be the slightest use; a sort of impromptu conjuring; making fifteen matches set fire to each other like a regular firework; or cutting a banana or some such thing into a dancing doll. His name was Isidore Smythe; and I can see him still, with his little dark face, just coming up to the counter, making a jumping kangaroo out of five cigars.

'The other fellow was more silent and more ordinary; but somehow he alarmed me much more than poor little Smythe. He was very tall and slight, and light-haired; his nose had a high bridge, and he might almost have been handsome in a spectral sort of way; but he had one of the most appalling squints I have ever seen or heard of. When he looked straight at you, you didn't know where you were yourself, let alone what he was looking at. I fancy this sort of disfigurement embittered the poor chap a little; for while Smythe was ready to show off his monkey tricks anywhere, James Welkin (that was the squinting man's name) never did anything except soak in our bar parlour, and go for great walks by himself in the flat, grey country all round. All the same, I think Smythe, too, was a little sensitive about being so small, though he carried it off more smartly. And so it was that I was really puzzled, as well as startled, and very sorry, when they both offered to marry me in the same week.

'Well, I did what I've since thought was perhaps a silly thing. But, after all, these freaks were my friends in a way; and I had a horror of their thinking I refused them for the real reason, which was that they were so impossibly ugly. So I made up some gas of another sort, about never meaning to marry anyone who hadn't carved his way in the world. I said it was a point of principle with me not to live on money that was just inherited like theirs. Two days after I had talked in this well-meaning sort of way, the whole trouble began. The first thing I heard was that both of them had gone off to seek their fortunes, as if they were in some silly fairy tale.

'Well, I've never seen either of them from that day to this. But I've had two letters from the little man called Smythe, and really they were rather exciting.'

'Ever heard of the other man?' asked Angus.

'No, he never wrote,' said the girl, after an instant's hesitation. 'Smythe's first letter was simply to say that he had started out walking with Welkin to London; but Welkin was such a good walker that the little man dropped out of it, and took a rest by the roadside. He happened to be picked up by some travelling show, and, partly because he was nearly a dwarf, and partly because he was really a clever little wretch, he got on quite well in the show business, and was soon sent up to the Aquarium, to do some tricks that I forgot. That was his first letter. His second was much more of a startler, and I only got it last week.'

The man called Angus emptied his coffee-cup and regarded her with mild and patient eyes. Her own mouth took a slight twist of laughter as she resumed: 'I suppose you've seen on the hoardings all about this "Smythe's Silent Service"? Or you must be the only person that hasn't. Oh, I don't know much about it, it's some clockwork invention for doing all the housework by machinery. You know the sort of thing: 'Press a button – a butler who never drinks". "Turn a handle – ten housemaids who never flirt". You must have seen the advertisements. Well, whatever these machines are, they are making pots of money; and they are making it all for that little imp whom I knew down in Ludbury. I can't help feeling pleased the poor little chap has fallen on his feet; but the plain fact is, I'm in terror of his turning up any minute and telling me he's carved his way in the world – as he certainly has.'

'And the other man?' repeated Angus with a sort of obstinate quietude.

Laura Hope got to her feet suddenly. 'My friend,' she said: 'I think you are a witch. Yes, you are quite right. I have not seen a line of the other man's writing; and I have no more notion than the dead of what or where he is. But it is of him that I am frightened. It is he who is all about my path. It is he who has half driven me mad. Indeed, I think he has driven me mad; for I have felt him where he could not have been, and I have heard his voice when he could not have spoken.'

'Well, my dear,' said the young man, cheerfully, 'if he were Satan himself, he is done for now you have told somebody. One goes mad all alone, old girl. But when was it you fancied you felt and heard our squinting friend?'

'I heard James Welkin laugh as plainly as I hear you speak,' said the girl, steadily. 'There was nobody there, for I stood just outside the shop at the corner, and could see down both streets at once. I had forgotten how he laughed, though his laugh was as odd as his squint. I had not thought of him for nearly a year. But it's a solemn truth that a few seconds later the first letter came from his rival.'

'Did you ever make the spectre speak or squeak, or anything?' asked Angus, with some interest.

Laura suddenly shuddered, and then said with an unshaken voice: 'Yes. Just when I had finished reading the second letter from Isidore Smythe announcing his success, just then, I heard Welkin say: "He shan't have you, though." It was quite plain, as if he were in the room. It is awful; I think I must be mad.'

'If you really were mad,' said the young man, 'you would think you must be sane. But certainly there seems to me to be something a little rum about this unseen gentleman. Two heads are better than one – I spare you allusions to any other organs – and really, if you would allow me, as a sturdy, practical man, to bring back the wedding-cake out of the window – '

Even as he spoke, there was a sort of steely shriek in the street outside, and a small motor, driven at devilish speed, shot up to the door of the shop and stuck there. In the same flash of time a small man in a shiny top hat stood stamping in the outer room.

Angus, who had hitherto maintained hilarious ease from motives of mental hygiene, revealed the strain of his soul by striding abruptly out of the inner room and confronting the newcomer. A glance at him was quite sufficient to confirm the savage guesswork of a man in love. This very dapper but dwarfish figure, with the spike of black beard carried insolently forward, the clever unrestful eyes, the neat but very nervous fingers, could be none other than the man just described to him: Isidore Smythe, who made dolls out of banana skins and matchboxes: Isidore Smythe, who made millions out of undrinking butlers and unflirting housemaids of metal. For a moment the two men, instinctively understanding each other's air of possession, looked at each other with that curious cold generosity which is the soul of rivalry.

Mr Smythe, however, made no allusion to the ultimate ground of their antagonism, but said simply and explosively: 'Has Miss Hope seen that thing on the window?'

'On the window?' repeated the staring Angus.

'There's no time to explain other things,' said the small millionaire shortly. 'There's some tomfoolery going on here that has to be investigated.'

He pointed his polished walking-stick at the window, recently depleted by the bridal preparations of Mr Angus; and that gentleman was astonished to see along the front of the glass a long strip of paper pasted, which had certainly not been on the window when he had looked through it some time before. Following the energetic Smythe outside into the street, he found that some yard and a half of stamp paper had been carefully gummed along the glass outside, and on this was written in straggly characters: 'If you marry Smythe, he will die.'

'Laura,' said Angus, putting his big red head into the shop, 'you're not mad.'

'It's the writing of that fellow Welkin,' said Smythe gruffly. 'I haven't seen him for years, but he's always bothering me. Five times in the last fortnight he's had threatening letters left at my flat, and I can't even find out who leaves them, let alone if it is Welkin himself. The porter of the flats swears that no suspicious characters have been seen, and here he has pasted up a sort of dado on a public shop window, while the people in the shop – '

'Quite so,' said Angus modestly, 'while the people in the shop were having tea. Well, sir, I can assure you I appreciate your common sense in dealing so directly with the matter. We can talk about other things afterwards. The fellow cannot be very far off yet, for I swear there was no paper there when I went last to the window, ten or fifteen minutes ago. On the other hand, he's too far off to be chased, as we don't even know the direction. If you'll take my advice, Mr Smythe, you'll put this at once in the hands of some energetic enquiry man, private rather than public. I know an extremely clever fellow, who has set up in business five minutes from here in your car. His name's Flambeau, and though his youth was a bit stormy, he's a strictly honest man now, and his brains are worth money. He lives in Lucknow Mansions, Hampstead.'

'That is odd,' said the little man, arching his black eyebrows. 'I live myself in Himalaya Mansions round the corner. Perhaps you might care to come with me; I can go to my rooms and sort out these queer Welkin documents, while you run round and get your friend the detective.'

'You are very good,' said Angus politely. 'Well, the sooner we act the better.'

Both men, with a queer kind of impromptu fairness, took the same sort of formal farewell of the lady, and both jumped into the brisk little car. As Smythe took the wheel and they turned the great corner of the street, Angus was amused to see a gigantesque poster of 'Smythe's Silent Service', with a picture of a huge headless iron doll, carrying a saucepan with the legend, 'A cook who is never cross'.

'I use them in my own flat,' said the little black-bearded man, laughing, 'partly for advertisement, and partly for real convenience. Honestly, and all above board, those big clockwork dolls of mine do bring you coals or claret or a timetable quicker than any live servants I've ever known, if you know which knob to press. But I'll never deny, between ourselves, that such servants have their disadvantages, too.'

'Indeed' said Angus; 'is there something they can't do?'

'Yes,' replied Smythe coolly; 'they can't tell me who left those threatening letters at my flat.'

The man's motor was small and swift like himself; in fact, like his domestic service, it was of his own invention. If he was an advertising quack, he was one who believed in his own wares. The sense of something tiny and flying was accentuated as they swept up long white curves of road in the dead but open daylight of evening. Soon the white curves came sharper and dizzier; they were upon ascending spirals, as they say in the modern religions. For, indeed, they were cresting a corner of London which is almost as precipitous as Edinburgh, if not quite so picturesque. Terrace rose above terrace, and the special tower of flats they sought, rose above them all to almost Egyptian height, gilt by the level sunset. The change, as they turned the corner and entered the crescent known as Himalaya Mansions, was as abrupt as the opening of a window; for they found that pile of flats sitting above London as above a green sea of slate. Opposite to the mansions, on the other side of the gravel crescent, was a bushy enclosure more like a steep hedge or dyke than a garden, and some way below that ran a strip of artificial water, a sort of canal, like the moat of that embowered fortress. As the car swept round the crescent it passed, at one corner, the stray stall of a man selling chestnuts; and right away at the other end of the curve, Angus could see a dim blue policeman walking slowly. These were the only human shapes in that high suburban solitude; but he had an irrational sense that they expressed the speechless poetry of London. He felt as if they were figures in a story.

The little car shot up to the right house like a bullet, and shot out its owner like a bomb shell. He was immediately enquiring of a tall commissionaire in shining braid, and a short porter in shirt sleeves, whether anybody or anything had been seeking his apartments. He was assured that nobody and nothing had passed these officials since his last enquiries; whereupon he and the slightly bewildered Angus were shot up in the lift like a rocket, till they reached the top floor.

'Just come in for a minute,' said the breathless Smythe. 'I want to show you those Welkin letters. Then you might run round the corner and fetch your friend.' He pressed a button concealed in the wall, and the door opened of itself.

It opened on a long, commodious anteroom, of which the only arresting features, ordinarily speaking, were the rows of tall half-human mechanical figures that stood up on both sides like tailors' dummies. Like tailors' dummies they were headless; and like tailors' dummies they had a handsome unnecessary humpiness in the shoulders, and a pigeon-breasted protuberance of chest; but barring this, they were not much more like a human figure than any automatic machine at a station that is about the human height. They had two great hooks like arms, for carrying trays; and they were painted pea-green, or vermilion, or black for convenience of distinction; in every other way they were only automatic machines and nobody would have looked twice at them. On this occasion, at least, nobody did. For between the two rows of these domestic dummies lay something more interesting than most of the mechanics of the world. It was a white, tattered scrap of paper scrawled with red ink; and the agile inventor had snatched it up almost as soon as the door flew open. He handed it to Angus without a word. The red ink on it actually was not dry, and the message ran: 'If you have been to see her today, I shall kill you.'

There was a short silence, and then Isidore Smythe said quietly: 'Would you like a little whisky? I rather feel as if I should.'

'Thank you; I should like a little Flambeau,' said Angus, gloomily. 'This business seems to me to be getting rather grave. I'm going round at once to fetch him.'

'Right you are,' said the other, with admirable cheerfulness. 'Bring him round here as quick as you can.'

But as Angus closed the front door behind him he saw Smythe push back a button, and one of the clockwork images glided from its place and slid along a groove in the floor carrying a tray with syphon and decanter. There did seem something a trifle weird about leaving the little man alone among those dead servants, who were coming to life as the door closed.

Six steps down from Smythe's landing the man in shirt sleeves was doing something with a pail. Angus stopped to extract a promise, fortified with a prospective bribe, that he would remain in that place until the return with the detective, and would keep count of any kind of stranger coming up those stairs. Dashing down to the front hall he then laid similar charges of vigilance on the commissionaire at the front door, from whom he learned the simplifying circumstance that there was no back door. Not content with this, he captured the floating policeman and induced him to stand opposite the entrance and watch it; and finally paused an instant for a penny-worth of chestnuts, and an enquiry as to the probable length of the merchant's stay in the neighbourhood.

The chestnut seller, turning up the collar of his coat, told him he should probably be moving shortly, as he thought it was going to snow. Indeed, the evening was growing grey and bitter, but Angus, with all his eloquence, proceeded to nail the chestnut man to his post.

'Keep yourself warm on your own chestnuts,' he said earnestly. 'Eat up your whole stock; I'll make it worth your while. I'll give you a sovereign if you'll wait here till I come back, and then tell me whether any man, woman, or child has gone into that house where the commissionaire is standing.'

He then walked away smartly, with a last look at the besieged tower.

'I've made a ring round that room, anyhow,' he said. 'They can't all four of them be Mr Welkin's accomplices.'

Lucknow Mansions were, so to speak, on a lower platform of that hill of houses, of which Himalaya Mansions might be called the peak. Mr Flambeau's semi-official flat was on the ground floor, and presented in every way a marked contrast to the American machinery and cold hotel-like luxury of the flat of the silent service. Flambeau, who was a friend of Angus, received him in a rococo artistic den behind his office, of which the ornaments were sabres, harquebuses, Eastern curiosities, flasks of Italian wine, savage cooking-pots, a plumy Persian cat, and a small dusty-looking Roman Catholic priest, who looked particularly out of place.

'This is my friend, Father Brown,' said Flambeau. 'I've often wanted you to meet him. Splendid weather, this; a little cold for Southerners like me.'

'Yes, I think it will keep clear,' said Angus, sitting down on a violet-striped Eastern ottoman.

'No,' said the priest quietly; 'it has begun to snow.'

And indeed, as he spoke, the first few flakes, foreseen by the man of chestnuts, began to drift across the darkening windowpane.

'Well,' said Angus heavily. 'I'm afraid I've come on business, and rather jumpy business at that. The fact is, Flambeau, within a stone's throw of your house is a fellow who badly wants your help; he's perpetually being haunted and threatened by an invisible enemy – a scoundrel whom nobody has even seen.' As Angus proceeded to tell the whole tale of Smythe and Welkin beginning with Laura's story, and going on with his own, the supernatural laugh at the corner of two empty streets, the strange distinct words spoken in an empty room, Flambeau grew more and more vividly concerned, and the little priest seemed to be left out of it, like a piece of furniture. When it came to the scribbled stamp-paper pasted on the window, Flambeau rose, seeming to fill the room with his huge shoulders.

'If you don't mind,' he said, 'I think you had better tell me the rest on the nearest road to this man's house. It strikes me, somehow, that there is no time to be lost.'

'Delighted,' said Angus, rising also, 'though he's safe enough for the present, for I've set four men to watch the only hole to his burrow.'

They turned out into the street, the small priest trundling after them with the docility of a small dog. He merely said, in a cheerful way, like one making conversation: 'How quick the snow gets thick on the ground.'

As they threaded the steep side streets already powdered with silver, Angus finished his story; and by the time they reached the crescent with the towering flats, he had leisure to turn his attention to the four sentinels. The chestnut seller, both before and after receiving a sovereign, swore stubbornly that he had watched the door and seen no visitor enter. The policeman was even more emphatic. He said he had had experience of crooks of all kinds, in top hats and in rags; he wasn't so green as to expect suspicious characters to look suspicious; he looked out for anybody, and, so help him, there had been nobody. And when all three men gathered round the gilded commissionaire, who still stood smiling astride of the porch, the verdict was more final still.

'I've got a right to ask any man, duke or dustman, what he wants in these flats,' said the genial and gold-laced giant, 'and I'll swear there's been nobody to ask since this gentleman went away.'

The unimportant Father Brown, who stood back, looking modestly at the pavement, here ventured to say meekly: 'Has nobody been up and down stairs, then, since the snow began to fall? It began while we were all round at Flambeau's.'

'Nobody's been in here, sir, you can take it from me,' said the official, with beaming authority.

'Then I wonder what that is?' said the priest, and stared at the ground blankly like a fish.

The others all looked down also; and Flambeau

used a fierce exclamation and a French gesture. For it was unquestionably true that down the middle of the entrance guarded by the man in gold lace, actually between the arrogant, stretched legs of that colossus, ran a stringy pattern of grey footprints stamped upon the white snow.

'God!' cried Angus involuntarily; 'the Invisible Man!'

Without another word he turned and dashed up the stairs, with Flambeau following; but Father Brown still stood looking about him in the snow-clad street as if he had lost interest in his query.

Flambeau was plainly in a mood to break down the door with his big shoulder; but the Scotsman, with more reason, if less intuition, fumbled about on the frame of the door till he found the invisible button; and the door swung slowly open.

It showed substantially the same serried interior; the hall had grown darker, though it was still struck here and there with the last crimson shafts of sunset, and one or two of the headless machines had been moved from their places for this or that purpose, and stood here and there about the twilit place. The green and red of their coats were all darkened in the dusk, and their likeness to human shapes slightly increased by their very shapelessness. But in the middle of them all, exactly where the paper with the red ink had lain, there lay something that looked very like red ink spilled out of its bottle. But it was not red ink.

With a French combination of reason and violence Flambeau simply said 'Murder!' and, plunging into the flat, had explored every corner and cupboard of it in five minutes. But if he expected to find a corpse he found none. Isidore Smythe simply was not in the place, either dead or alive. After the most tearing search the two men met each other in the outer hall with streaming faces and staring eyes. 'My friend,' said Flambeau, talking French in his excitement, 'not only is your murderer invisible, but he makes invisible also the murdered man.'

Angus looked round at the dim room full of dummies, and in some Celtic corner of his Scotch soul a shudder started. One of the life-size dolls stood immediately overshadowing the blood stain, summoned, perhaps, by the slain man an instant before he fell. One of the high-shouldered hooks that served the thing for arms, was a little lifted and Angus had suddenly the horrid fancy that poor Smythe's own iron child had struck him down. Matter had rebelled, and these machines had killed their master. But even so, what had they done with him?

'Eaten him?' said the nightmare at his ear; and he sickened for an instant at the idea of rent, human remains absorbed and crushed into all the acephalous clockwork.

He recovered his mental health by an emphatic effort, and said to Flambeau: 'Well, there it is. The poor fellow has evaporated like a cloud and left a red streak on the floor. The tale does not belong to this world.'

'There is only one thing to be done,' said Flambeau, 'whether it belongs to this world or the other, I must go down and talk to my friend.'

They descended, passing the man with the pail, who again asseverated that he had let no intruder pass, down to the commissionaire and the hovering chestnut man, who rightly reasserted their own watchfulness. But when Angus looked round for his fourth confirmation he could not see it, and called out with some nervousness: 'Where is the policeman?'

'I beg your pardon,' said Father Brown; 'that is my fault. I just sent him down the road to investigate something – that I just thought worth investigating.'

'Well, we want him back pretty soon,' said Angus abruptly, 'for the wretched man upstairs has not only been murdered, but wiped out.'

'How?' asked the priest.

'Father,' said Flambeau, after a pause, 'upon my soul I believe it is more in your department than mine. No friend or foe has entered the house, but Smythe is gone, as if stolen by the fairies. If that is not supernatural, I –'

As he spoke they were all checked by an unusual sight; the big blue policeman came round the corner of the crescent running. He came straight up to Brown.

'You're right, sir,' he panted, 'they've just found poor Mr Smythe's body in the canal down below.'

Angus put his hand wildly to his head. 'Did he run down and drown himself?' he asked.

'He never came down, I'll swear,' said the constable, 'and he wasn't drowned either, for he died of a great stab over the heart.'

'And yet you saw no one enter?' said Flambeau in a grave voice.

'Let us walk down the road a little,' said the priest.

As they reached the other end of the crescent he observed abruptly: 'Stupid of me! I forgot to ask the policeman something. I wonder if they found a light brown sack.'

'Why a light brown sack?' asked Angus, astonished.

'Because if it was any other coloured sack, the case must begin over again,' said Father Brown; 'but if it was a light brown sack, why, the case is finished.'

'I am pleased to hear it,' said Angus with hearty irony. 'It hasn't begun, so far as I am concerned.'

'You must tell us all about it,' said Flambeau, with a strange heavy simplicity, like a child.

Unconsciously they were walking with quickening steps down the long sweep of road on the other side of the high crescent, Father Brown leading briskly, though in silence. At last he said with an almost touching vagueness: 'Well, I'm afraid you'll think it so prosy. We always begin at the abstract end of things, and you can't begin this story anywhere else.

'Have you ever noticed this – that people never answer what you say? They answer what you mean – or what they think you mean. Suppose one lady says to another in a country house, "Is anybody staying with you?" the lady doesn't answer "Yes; the butler, the three footmen, the parlour-maid, and so on," though the parlour-maid may be in the room, or the butler behind her chair. She says: "There is *nobody* staying with us," meaning nobody of the sort you mean. But suppose a doctor enquiring into an epidemic asks, "Who is staying in the house?" then the lady will remember the butler, the parlour-maid, and the rest. All language is used like that; you never get a question answered literally, even when you get it answered truly. When those four quite honest men said that no man had gone into the Mansions, they did not really mean that *no man* had gone into them. They meant no man whom they could suspect of being your man. A man did go into the house, and did come out of it, but they never noticed him.'

'An invisible man?' enquired Angus, raising his red eyebrows.

'A mentally invisible man,' said Father Brown.

A minute or two after he resumed in the same unassuming voice, like a man thinking his way. 'Of course, you can't think of such a man, until you do think of him. That's where his cleverness comes in. But I came to think of him through two or three little things in the tale Mr Angus told us. First, there was the fact that this Welkin went for long walks. And then there was the vast lot of stamp paper on the window. And then, most of all, there were the two things the young lady said – things that couldn't be true. Don't get annoyed,' he added hastily, noting a sudden movement of the Scotsman's head; 'she thought they were true all right, but they couldn't be true. A person *can't* be quite alone in a street a second before she receives a letter. She can't be quite alone in a street when she starts reading a letter just received. There must be somebody pretty near her; he must be mentally invisible.'

'Why must there be somebody near her?' asked Angus.

'Because,' said Father Brown: 'barring carrier-pigeons, somebody must have brought her the letter.'

'Do you really mean to say,' asked Flambeau, with energy, 'that Welkin carried his rival's letters to his lady?'

'Yes,' said the priest. 'Welkin carried his rival's letters to his lady. You see, he had to.'

'Oh, I can't stand much more of this,' exploded Flambeau. 'Who is this fellow? What does he look like. What is the usual get-up of a mentally invisible man?'

'He is dressed rather handsomely in red, blue and gold,' replied the priest promptly with decision, 'and in this striking, and even showy costume he entered

Himalaya Mansions under eight human eyes; he killed Smythe in cold blood, and came down into the street again carrying the dead body in his arms – '

'Reverend sir,' cried Angus, standing still, 'are you raving mad, or am I?'

'You are not mad,' said Brown, 'only a little unobservant. You have not noticed such a man as this, for example.'

He took three quick strides forward, and put his hand on the shoulder of an ordinary passing postman who had bustled by them unnoticed under the shade of the trees.

'Nobody ever notices postmen, somehow,' he said thoughtfully; 'yet they have passions like other men and even carry large bags where a small corpse can be stowed quite easily.'

The postman, instead of turning naturally, had ducked and tumbled against the garden fence. He was a lean fair-bearded man of very ordinary appearance, but as he turned an alarmed face over his shoulder, all three men were fixed with an almost fiendish squint.

Flambeau went back to his sabres, purple rugs and Persian cat, having many things to attend to. John Turnbull Angus went back to the lady at the shop, with whom that imprudent young man contrives to be extremely comfortable. But Father Brown walked those snow-covered hills under the stars for many hours with a murderer, and what they said to each other will never be known.

The Honour of Israel Gow

A stormy evening of olive and silver was closing in, as Father Brown, wrapped in a grey Scotch plaid, came to the end of a grey Scotch valley and beheld the strange castle of Glengyle. It stopped one end of the glen or hollow like a blind alley; and it looked like the end of the world. Rising in steep roofs and spires of sea-green slate in the manner of the old French-Scottish châteaux, it reminded an Englishman of the sinister steeple-hats of witches in fairy tales; and the pine woods that rocked round the green turrets looked, by comparison, as black as numberless flocks of ravens. This note of a dreamy, almost a sleepy devilry, was no mere fancy from the landscape. For there did rest on the place one of those clouds of pride and madness and mysterious sorrow which lie more heavily on the noble houses of Scotland than on any other of the children of men. For Scotland has a double dose of the poison called heredity; the sense of blood in the aristocrat, and the sense of doom in the Calvinist.

The priest had snatched a day from his business at Glasgow to meet his friend Flambeau, the amateur detective, who was at Glengyle Castle with another more formal officer investigating the life and death of the late Earl of Glengyle. That mysterious person was the last representative of a race whose valour, insanity, and violent cunning had made them terrible even among the sinister nobility of their nation in the sixteenth century. None were deeper in that labyrinthine ambition, in chamber within chamber of that palace of lies that was built up around Mary Queen of Scots.

The rhyme in the countryside attested the motive and the result of their machinations candidly:

> As green sap to the simmer trees
> Is red gold to the Ogilvies.

For many centuries there had never been a decent lord in Glengyle Castle; and with the Victorian era one would have thought that all eccentricities were exhausted. The last Glengyle, however, satisfied his tribal tradition by doing the only thing that was left for him to do; he disappeared. I do not mean that he went abroad; by all accounts he was still in the castle, if he was anywhere. But though his name was in the church register and the big red Peerage, nobody ever saw him under the sun.

If anyone saw him it was a solitary manservant, something between a groom and a gardener. He was so deaf that the more businesslike assumed him to be dumb; while the more penetrating declared him to be half-witted. A gaunt, red-haired labourer, with a dogged jaw and chin, but quite black blue eyes, he went by the name of Israel Gow, and was the one silent servant on that deserted estate. But the energy with which he dug potatoes, and the regularity with which he disappeared into the kitchen gave people an impression that he was providing for the meals of a superior, and that the strange earl was still concealed in the castle. If society needed any further proof that he was there, the servant persistently asserted that he was not at home. One morning the provost and the minister (for the Glengyles were Presbyterian) were summoned to the castle. There they found that the gardener, groom and cook had added to his many professions that of an undertaker, and had nailed up his noble master in a coffin. With how much or how little further enquiry this odd fact was passed, did not as yet very plainly appear; for the thing had never been legally investigated till Flambeau had gone north two or three days before. By then the body of Lord Glengyle (if it was the body) had lain for some time in the little churchyard on the hill.

As Father Brown passed through the dim garden and came under the shadow of the château, the clouds were thick and the whole air damp and thundery. Against the last stripe of the green-gold sunset he saw a black human silhouette; a man in a chimney-pot hat, with a big spade over his shoulder. The combination was queerly suggestive of a sexton; but when Brown remembered the deaf servant who dug potatoes, he thought it natural enough. He knew something of the Scotch peasant; he knew the respectability which might well feel it necessary to wear 'blacks' for an official inquiry; he knew also the economy that would not lose an hour's digging for that. Even the man's start and suspicious stare as the priest went by were consonant enough with the vigilance and jealousy of such a type.

The great door was opened by Flambeau himself, who had with him a lean man with iron-grey hair and papers in his hand: Inspector Craven from Scotland Yard. The entrance hall was mostly stripped and empty; but the pale, sneering faces of one or two of the wicked Ogilvies looked down out of the black periwigs and blackening canvas.

Following them into an inner room, Father Brown

found that the allies had been seated at a long oak table, of which their end was covered with scribbled papers, flanked with whisky and cigars. Through the whole of its remaining length it was occupied by detached objects arranged at intervals; objects about as inexplicable as any objects could be. One looked like a small heap of glittering broken glass. Another looked like a high heap of brown dust. A third appeared to be a plain stick of wood.

'You seem to have a sort of geological museum here,' he said, as he sat down, jerking his head briefly in the direction of the brown dust and the crystalline fragments.

'Not a geological museum,' replied Flambeau; 'say a psychological museum.'

'Oh, for the Lord's sake,' cried the police detective, laughing, 'don't let's begin with such long words.'

'Don't you know what psychology means?' asked Flambeau with friendly surprise. 'Psychology means being off your chump.'

'Still I hardly follow,' replied the official.

'Well,' said Flambeau, with decision; 'I mean that we've only found out one thing about Lord Glengyle. He was a maniac.'

The black silhouette of Gow with his top hat and spade passed the window, dimly outlined against the darkening sky. Father Brown stared passively at it and answered: 'I can understand there must have been something odd about the man, or he wouldn't have buried himself alive – nor been in such a hurry to bury himself dead. But what makes you think it was lunacy?'

'Well,' said Flambeau; 'you just listen to the list of things Mr Craven has found in the house.'

'We must get a candle,' said Craven, suddenly. 'A storm is getting up, and it's too dark to read.'

'Have you found any candles,' asked Brown smiling, 'among your oddities?'

Flambeau raised a grave face, and fixed his dark eyes on his friend.

'That is curious, too,' he said. 'Twenty-five candles, and not a trace of a candlestick.'

In the rapidly darkening room and rapidly rising wind, Brown went along the table to where a bundle of wax candles lay among the other scrappy exhibits. As he did so he bent accidentally over the heap of red-brown dust; and a sharp sneeze cracked the silence.

'Hullo!' he said; 'snuff!'

He took one of the candles, lit it carefully, came back and stuck it in the neck of the whisky bottle. The unrestful night air, blowing through the crazy window, waved the long flame like a banner. And on every side of the castle they could hear the miles and miles of black pine wood seething like a black sea around a rock.

'I will read the inventory,' began Craven gravely, picking up one of the papers, 'the inventory of what we found loose and unexplained in the castle. You are to understand that the place generally was dismantled and neglected; but one or two rooms had plainly been inhabited in a simple but not squalid style by somebody; somebody who was not the servant Gow. The list is as follows:

> 'First item. A very considerable hoard of precious stones, nearly all diamonds, and all of them loose, without any setting whatever. Of course, it is natural that the Ogilvies should have family jewels; but

those are exactly the jewels that are almost always set in particular articles of ornament. The Ogilvies would seem to have kept theirs loose in their pockets, like coppers.

'Second item. Heaps and heaps of loose snuff, not kept in a horn, or even a pouch, but lying in heaps on the mantelpieces, on the sideboard, on the piano, anywhere. It looks as if the old gentleman would not take the trouble to look in a pocket or lift a lid.

'Third item. Here and there about the house curious little heaps of minute pieces of metal, some like steel springs and some in the form of microscopic wheels. As if they had gutted some mechanical toy.

'Fourth item. The wax candles, which have to be stuck in bottle necks because there is nothing else to stick them in. Now I wish you to note how very much queerer all this is than anything we anticipated. For the central riddle we are prepared; we have all seen at a glance that there was something wrong about the last earl. We have come here to find out whether he really lived here, whether he really died here, whether that red-haired scarecrow who did his burying had anything to do with his dying. But suppose the worst in all this, the most lurid or melodramatic solution you like. Suppose the servant really killed the master, or suppose the master isn't really dead, or suppose the master is dressed up as the servant, or suppose the servant is buried for the master; invent what Wilkie Collins's tragedy you like, and you still have not explained a candle without a candlestick, or why an elderly gentleman of good family should habitually spill snuff on the piano. The core of the tale we could imagine; it is the fringes that are mysterious. By no stretch of fancy can the human mind connect together snuff and diamonds and wax and loose clockwork.'

'I think I see the connection,' said the priest. 'This Glengyle was mad against the French Revolution. He was an enthusiast for the *ancien régime*, and was trying to re-enact literally the family life of the last Bourbons. He had snuff because it was the eighteenth century luxury; wax candles, because they were the eighteenth century lighting; the mechanical bits of iron represent the locksmith hobby of Louis XVI; the diamonds are for the diamond necklace of Marie Antoinette.'

Both the other men were staring at him with round eyes. 'What a perfectly extraordinary notion!' cried Flambeau. 'Do you really think that is the truth?'

'I am perfectly sure it isn't,' answered Father Brown, 'only you said that nobody could connect snuff and diamonds and clockwork and candles. I give you that connection offhand. The real truth, I am very sure, lies deeper.'

He paused a moment and listened to the wailing of the wind in the turrets. Then he said: 'The late Earl of Glengyle was a thief. He lived a second and darker life as a desperate housebreaker. He did not have any candlesticks because he only used these candles cut short in the lantern he carried. The snuff he employed as the fiercest French criminals have used pepper: to fling it suddenly in dense masses in the face of a captor or pursuer. But the final proof is in the curious coincidence of the diamonds and the small steel wheels. Surely that makes everything plain to you?

Diamonds and small steel wheels are the only two instruments with which you can cut out a pane of glass.'

The bough of a broken pine tree lashed heavily in the blast against the windowpane behind them, as if in parody of a burglar, but they did not turn round. Their eyes were fastened on Father Brown.

'Diamonds and small wheels,' repeated Craven ruminating. 'Is that all that makes you think it the true explanation?'

'I don't think it the true explanation,' replied the priest placidly; 'but you said that nobody could connect the four things. The true tale, of course, is something much more humdrum. Glengyle had found, or thought he had found, precious stones on his estate. Somebody had bamboozled him with those loose brilliants, saying they were found in the castle caverns. The little wheels are some diamond-cutting affair. He had to do the thing very roughly and in a small way, with the help of a few shepherds or rude fellows on these hills. Snuff is the one great luxury of such Scotch shepherds; it's the one thing with which you can bribe them. They didn't have candlesticks because they didn't want them; they held the candles in their hands when they explored the caves.'

'Is that all?' asked Flambeau after a long pause. 'Have we got to the dull truth at last?'

'Oh, no,' said Father Brown.

As the wind died in the most distant pine woods with a long hoot as of mockery, Father Brown, with an utterly impassive face, went on: 'I only suggested that because you said one could not plausibly connect snuff with clockwork or candles with bright stones. Ten false philosophies will fit the universe; ten false theories will fit Glengyle Castle. But we want the real explanation of the castle and the universe. But are there no other exhibits?'

Craven laughed, and Flambeau rose smiling to his feet and strolled down the long table.

'Items five, six, seven, etc.,' he said, 'are certainly more varied than instructive. A curious collection, not of lead pencils, but of the lead out of lead pencils. A senseless stick of bamboo, with the top rather splintered. It might be the instrument of the crime. Only, there isn't any crime. The only other things are a few old missals and little Catholic pictures, which the Ogilvies kept, I suppose, from the Middle Ages – their family pride being stronger than their Puritanism. We only put them in the museum because they seem curiously cut about and defaced.'

The heady tempest without drove a dreadful wrack of clouds across Glengyle and threw the long room into darkness as Father Brown picked up the little illuminated pages to examine them. He spoke before the drift of darkness had passed; but it was the voice of an utterly new man.

'Mr Craven,' said he, talking like a man ten years younger: 'you have got a legal warrant, haven't you, to go up and examine that grave? The sooner we do it the better, and get to the bottom of this horrible affair. If I were you I should start now.'

'Now,' repeated the astonished detective, 'and why now?'

'Because this is serious,' answered Brown; 'this is not spilt snuff or loose pebbles, that might be there for a hundred reasons. There is only one reason I know of for *this* being done; and the reason goes down to the roots of the world. These religious pictures are not just dirtied or torn or scrawled over, which might be done in idleness or bigotry, by children or by Protestants. These have been treated very carefully – and very queerly. In every place where the great ornamented name of God comes in the old illuminations it has been elaborately taken out. The only other thing that has been removed is the halo round the head of the Child Jesus. Therefore, I say, let us get our warrant and our spade and our hatchet, and go up and break open that coffin.'

'What *do* you mean?' demanded the London officer.

'I mean,' answered the little priest, and his voice seemed to rise slightly in the roar of the gale. 'I mean that the great devil of the universe may be sitting on the top tower of this castle at this moment, as big as a hundred elephants, and roaring like the Apocalypse. There is black magic somewhere at the bottom of this.'

'Black magic,' repeated Flambeau in a low voice, for he was too enlightened a man not to know of such things; 'but what can these other things mean?'

'Oh, something damnable, I suppose,' replied Brown impatiently. 'How should I know? How can I guess all their mazes down below? Perhaps you can make a torture out of snuff and bamboo. Perhaps lunatics lust after wax and steel filings. Perhaps there is a maddening drug made of lead pencils! Our shortest cut to the mystery is up the hill to the grave.'

His comrades hardly knew that they had obeyed and followed him till a blast of the night wind nearly flung them on their faces in the garden. Nevertheless they had obeyed him like automata; for Craven found a hatchet in his hand, and the warrant in his pocket;

Flambeau was carrying the heavy spade of the strange gardener; Father Brown was carrying the little gilt book from which had been torn the name of God.

The path up the hill to the churchyard was crooked but short; only under the stress of wind it seemed laborious and long. Far as the eye could see, farther and farther as they mounted the slope, were seas beyond seas of pines, now all aslope one way under the wind. And that universal gesture seemed as vain as it was vast, as vain as if that wind were whistling about some unpeopled and purposeless planet. Through all that infinite growth of grey-blue forests sang, shrill and high, that ancient sorrow that is in the heart of all heathen things. One could fancy that the voices from the underworld of unfathomable foliage were cries of the lost and wandering pagan gods: gods who had gone roaming in that irrational forest, and who will never find their way back to heaven.

'You see,' said Father Brown in low but easy tone, 'Scotch people before Scotland existed were a curious lot. In fact, they're a curious lot still. But in the prehistoric times I fancy they really worshipped demons. That,' he added genially, 'is why they jumped at the Puritan theology.'

'My friend,' said Flambeau, turning in a kind of fury, 'what does all that snuff mean?'

'My friend,' replied Brown, with equal seriousness, 'there is one mark of all genuine religions: materialism. Now, devil-worship is a perfectly genuine religion.'

They had come up on the grassy scalp of the hill, one of the few bald spots that stood clear of the crashing and roaring pine forest. A mean enclosure, partly timber and partly wire, rattled in the tempest to tell them the border of the graveyard. But by the time

Inspector Craven had come to the corner of the grave, and Flambeau had planted his spade point downwards and leaned on it, they were both almost as shaken as the shaky wood and wire. At the foot of the grave grew great tall thistles, grey and silver in their decay. Once or twice, when a ball of thistledown broke under the breeze and flew past him, Craven jumped slightly as if it had been an arrow.

Flambeau drove the blade of his spade through the whistling grass into the wet clay below. Then he seemed to stop and lean on it as on a staff.

'Go on,' said the priest very gently. 'We are only trying to find the truth. What are you afraid of?'

'I am afraid of finding it,' said Flambeau.

The London detective spoke suddenly in a high crowing voice that was meant to be conversational and cheery. 'I wonder why he really did hide himself like that. Something nasty, I suppose; was he a leper?'

'Something worse than that,' said Flambeau.

'And what do you imagine,' asked the other, 'would be worse than a leper?'

'I don't imagine it,' said Flambeau.

He dug for some dreadful minutes in silence, and then said in a choked voice: 'I'm afraid of his not being the right shape.'

'Nor was that piece of paper, you know,' said Father Brown quietly, 'and we survived even that piece of paper.'

Flambeau dug on with a blind energy. But the tempest had shouldered away the choking grey clouds that clung to the hills like smoke and revealed grey fields of faint starlight before he cleared the shape of a rude timber coffin, and somehow tipped it up upon the turf. Craven stepped forward with his axe; a thistle-top touched him, and he flinched. Then he took a firmer stride, and hacked and wrenched with an energy like Flambeau's till the lid was torn off, and all that was there lay glimmering in the grey starlight.

'Bones,' said Craven; and then he added, 'but it is a man,' as if that were something unexpected.

'Is he,' asked Flambeau in a voice that went oddly up and down, 'is he all right?'

'Seems so,' said the officer huskily, bending over the obscure and decaying skeleton in the box. 'Wait a minute.'

A vast heave went over Flambeau's huge figure. 'And now I come to think of it,' he cried, 'why in the name of madness shouldn't he be all right? What is it gets hold of a man on these cursed cold mountains? I think it's the black, brainless repetition; all these forests, and over all an ancient horror of unconsciouness. It's like the dream of an atheist. Pine trees and more pine trees and millions more pine trees – '

'God!' cried the man by the coffin; 'but he hasn't got a head.'

While the others stood rigid the priest, for the first time, showed a leap of startled concern.

'No head!' he repeated, '*No head?*' as if he had almost expected some other deficiency.

Half-witted visions of a headless baby born to Glengyle, of a headless youth hiding himself in the castle, of a headless man pacing those ancient halls or that gorgeous garden, passed in panorama through their minds. But even in that stiffened instant the tale took no root in them and seemed to have no reason in it. They stood listening to the loud woods and the shrieking sky quite foolishly, like exhausted animals.

Thought seemed to be something enormous that had suddenly slipped out of their grasp.

'There are three headless men,' said Father Brown: 'standing round this open grave.'

The pale detective from London opened his mouth to speak, and left it open like a yokel, while a long scream of wind tore the sky; then he looked at the axe in his hands as if it did not belong to him, and dropped it.

'Father,' said Flambeau in that infantile and heavy voice he used very seldom, 'what are we to do?'

His friend's reply came with the pent promptitude of a gun going off.

'Sleep!' cried Father Brown. 'Sleep. We have come to the end of the ways. Do you know what sleep is? Do you know that every man who sleeps believes in God? It is a sacrament; for it is an act of faith and it is a food. And we need a sacrament, if only a natural one. Something has fallen on us that falls very seldom on men; perhaps the worst thing that can fall on them.'

Craven's parted lips came together to say: 'What do you mean?'

The priest turned his face to the castle as he answered: 'We have found the truth; and the truth makes no sense.'

He went down the path in front of them with a plunging and reckless step very rare with him, and when they reached the castle again he threw himself upon sleep with the simplicity of a dog.

Despite his mystic praise of slumber, Father Brown was up earlier than anyone else except the silent gardener; and was found smoking a big pipe and watching that expert at his speechless labours in the kitchen garden. Towards daybreak the rocking storm had ended in roaring rains, and the day came with a curious freshness. The gardener seemed even to have been conversing, but at sight of the detectives he planted his spade sullenly in a bed and, saying something about his breakfast, shifted along the lines of cabbages and shut himself in the kitchen. 'He's a valuable man, that,' said Father Brown. 'He does the potatoes amazingly. Still,' he added, with a dispassionate charity, 'he has his faults; which of us hasn't? He doesn't dig this bank quite regularly. There, for instance,' and he stamped suddenly on one spot. 'I'm really very doubtful about that potato.'

'And why?' asked Craven, amused with the little man's new hobby.

'I'm doubtful about it,' said the other, 'because old Gow was doubtful about it himself. He put his spade in methodically in every place but just this. There must be a mighty fine potato just there.'

Flambeau pulled up the spade and impetuously drove it into the place. He turned up, under a load of soil, something that did not look like a potato, but rather like a monstrous, over-domed mushroom. But it struck the spade with a cold click; it rolled over like a ball, and grinned up at them.

'The Earl of Glengyle,' said Brown sadly, and looked down heavily at the skull.

Then, after a momentary meditation, he plucked the spade from Flambeau, and, saying: 'We must hide it again,' clamped the skull down in the earth. Then he leaned his little body and huge head on the great handle of the spade, that stood up stiffly in the earth, and his eyes were empty and his forehead full of wrinkles. 'If one could only conceive,' he muttered, 'the meaning of this last monstrosity.' And leaning on the large spade handle, he buried his brows in his hands, as men do in church.

All the corners of the sky were brightening into blue and silver; the birds were chattering in the tiny garden trees; so loud it seemed as if the trees themselves were talking. But the three men were silent enough.

'Well, I give it all up,' said Flambeau at last boisterously. 'My brain and this world don't fit each other; and there's an end of it. Snuff, spoilt prayer-books, and the insides of musical boxes – what – '

Brown threw up his bothered brow and rapped on the spade handle with an intolerance quite unusual with him. 'Oh, tut, tut, tut, tut!' he cried. 'All that is as plain as a pikestaff. I understood the snuff and clockwork, and so on, when I first opened my eyes this morning. And since then I've had it out with old Gow, the gardener, who is neither so deaf nor so stupid as he pretends. There's something amiss about the loose items. I was wrong about the torn mass-book, too; there's no harm in that. But it's this last business. Desecrating graves and stealing dead men's heads – surely there's harm in that? Surely there's black magic still in that? That doesn't fit in to the quite simple story of the snuff and the candles.' And, striding about again, he smoked moodily.

'My friend,' said Flambeau, with a grim humour, 'you must be careful with me and remember I was once a criminal. The great advantage of that estate was that I always made up the story myself, and acted it as quick as I chose. This detective business of waiting about is too much for my French impatience. All my life, for good or evil, I have done things at the instant; I always fought duels the next morning; I always paid bills on the nail; I never even put off a visit to the dentist – '

Father Brown's pipe fell out of his mouth and broke into three pieces on the gravel path. He stood rolling his eyes, the exact picture of an idiot. 'Lord, what a turnip I am!' he kept saying. 'Lord, what a turnip!' Then, in a somewhat groggy kind of way, he began to laugh.

'The dentist!' he repeated. 'Six hours in the spiritual abyss, and all because I never thought of the dentist! Such a simple, such a beautiful and peaceful thought! Friends, we have passed a night in hell; but now the sun is risen, the birds are singing, and the radiant form of the dentist consoles the world.'

'I will get some sense out of this,' cried Flambeau, striding forward, 'if I use the tortures of the Inquisition.'

Father Brown repressed what appeared to be a momentary disposition to dance on the now sunlit lawn and cried quite piteously, like a child: 'Oh, let me be silly a little. You don't know how unhappy I have been. And now I know that there has been no deep sin in this business at all. Only a little lunacy, perhaps – and who minds that?'

He spun round once, then faced them with gravity.

'This is not a story of crime,' he said; 'rather it is the story of a strange and crooked honesty. We are dealing with the one man on earth, perhaps, who has taken no more than his due. It is a study in the savage living logic that has been the religion of this race.

'That old local rhyme about the house of Glengyle –

> As green sap to the simmer trees
> Is red gold to the Ogilvies –

was literal as well as metaphorical. It did not merely mean that the Glengyles sought for wealth; it was also true that they literally gathered gold; they had a huge collection of ornaments and utensils in that metal. They were, in fact, misers whose mania took that turn. In the light of that fact, run through all the things we found in the castle. Diamonds without their gold rings; candles without their gold candlesticks; snuff without the gold snuffboxes; pencil-leads without the gold pencil-cases; a walking-stick without its gold top; clockwork without the gold clocks – or rather watches. And, mad as it sounds, because the halos and the name of God in the old missals were of real gold, these also were taken away.'

The garden seemed to brighten, the grass to grow gayer in the strengthening sun, as the crazy truth was told. Flambeau lit a cigarette as his friend went on.

'Were taken away,' continued Father Brown; 'were taken away – but not stolen. Thieves would never have left this mystery. Thieves would have taken the gold snuffboxes, snuff and all; the gold pencil-cases, lead and all. We have to deal with a man with a peculiar conscience, but certainly a conscience. I found that mad moralist this morning in the kitchen garden yonder, and I heard the whole story.

'The late Archbishop Ogilvie was the nearest approach to a good man ever born at Glengyle. But his bitter virtue took the turn of the misanthrope; he moped over the dishonesty of his ancestors, from which, somehow, he generalised a dishonesty of all men. More especially he distrusted philanthropy or free-giving; and he swore if he could find one man who took his exact rights he should have all the gold of Glengyle. Having delivered this defiance to humanity he shut himself up, without the smallest expectation of its being answered. One day, however, a deaf and seemingly senseless lad from a distant village brought him a belated telegram; and Glengyle, in his acrid pleasantry, gave him a new farthing. At least he thought he had done so, but when he turned over his change he found the new farthing still there and a sovereign gone. The accident offered him vistas of sneering speculation. Either way, the boy would show the greasy greed of the species. Either he would vanish, a thief stealing a coin; or he would sneak back with it virtuously, a snob seeking a reward. In the middle of the night Lord Glengyle was knocked up out of his bed – for he lived alone – and forced to open the door to the deaf idiot. The idiot brought with him, not the sovereign, but exactly nineteen shillings and eleven-pence three-farthings in change.

'Then the wild exactitude of this action took hold on the mad lord's brain like fire. He swore he was Diogenes, that had long sought an honest man, and at last had found one. He made a new will, which I have seen. He took the literal youth into his huge, neglected house, and trained him up as his solitary servant and – after an odd manner – his heir. And whatever that queer creature understands, he understood absolutely his lord's two fixed ideas: first, that the letter of right is everything; and second, that he himself was to have the gold of Glengyle. So far, that is all; and that is simple. He has stripped the house of gold, and taken not a grain that was not gold; not so much as a grain of snuff. He lifted the gold leaf off an old illumination, fully satisfied that he left the rest unspoilt. All that I understood; but I could not understand this skull business. I was really uneasy about that human head buried among the potatoes. It distressed me – till Flambeau said the word.

'It will be all right. He will put the skull back in the grave, when he has taken the gold out of the tooth.'

And, indeed, when Flambeau crossed the hill that morning, he saw that strange being, the just miser, digging at the desecrated grave, the plaid round his throat thrashing out in the mountain wind; the sober top hat on his head.

The Hammer of God

The little village of Bohun Beacon was perched on a hill so steep that the tall spire of its church seemed only like the peak of a small mountain. At the foot of the church stood a smithy, generally red with fires and always littered with hammers and scraps of iron; opposite to this, over a rude cross of cobbled paths, was the Blue Boar, the only inn of the place. It was upon this crossway, in the lifting of a leaden and silver daybreak, that two brothers met in the street and spoke; though one was beginning the day and the other finishing it. The Revd and Hon. Wilfred Bohun was very devout, and was making his way to some austere exercises of prayer or contemplation at dawn. Colonel the Hon. Norman Bohun, his elder brother, was by no means devout, and was sitting in evening-dress on the bench outside 'The Blue Boar', drinking what the philosophic observer was free to regard either as his last glass on Tuesday or his first on Wednesday. The colonel was not particular.

The Bohuns were one of the very few aristocratic families really dating from the Middle Ages, and their pennon had actually seen Palestine. But it is a great mistake to suppose that such houses stand high in chivalric traditions. Few except the poor preserve traditions. Aristocrats live not in traditions but in fashions. The Bohuns had been Mohocks under Queen Anne and Mashers under Queen Victoria. But, like more than one of the really ancient houses, they had rotted in the last two centuries into mere drunkards and dandy degenerates, till there had even come a whisper of insanity. Certainly there was something hardly human about the colonel's wolfish pursuit of pleasure, and his chronic resolution not to go home till morning had a touch of the hideous charity of insomnia. He was a tall, fine animal, elderly, but with hair startlingly yellow. He would have looked merely blond and leonine, but his blue eyes were sunk so deep in his face that they looked black. They were a little too close together. He had very long yellow moustaches: on each side of them a fold or furrow from nostril to jaw, so that a sneer seemed to cut into his face. Over his evening clothes he wore a curiously pale yellow coat that looked more like a very light dressing gown than an overcoat, and on the back of his head was stuck an extraordinary broad-brimmed hat of a bright green colour, evidently some oriental curiosity caught up at random. He was proud of appearing in such incongruous attires – proud of the fact that he always made them look congruous.

His brother the curate had also the yellow hair and the elegance, but he was buttoned up to the chin in black, and his face was clean-shaven, cultivated and a little nervous. He seemed to live for nothing but his religion; but there were some who said (notably the blacksmith, who was a Presbyterian) that it was a love of Gothic architecture rather than of God, and that his haunting of the church like a ghost was only another and purer turn of the almost morbid thirst for beauty which sent his brother raging after women and wine. This charge was doubtful, while the man's practical piety was indubitable. Indeed, the charge was mostly an ignorant misunderstanding of the love of solitude and secret prayer, and was founded on his being often found kneeling, not before the altar, but in peculiar places, in the crypts or gallery, or even in the belfry. He was at the moment about to enter the church through the yard of the smithy, but stopped and frowned a little as he saw his brother's cavernous eyes staring in the same direction. On the hypothesis that the colonel was interested in the church he did not waste any speculations. There only remained the blacksmith's shop, and though the blacksmith was a Puritan and none of his people, Wilfred Bohun had heard some scandals about a beautiful and rather celebrated wife. He flung a suspicious look across the shed, and the colonel stood up laughing to speak to him.

'Good-morning, Wilfred,' he said. 'Like a good landlord I am watching sleeplessly over my people. I am going to call on the blacksmith.'

Wilfred looked at the ground and said: 'The blacksmith is out. He is over at Greenford.'

'I know,' answered the other with silent laughter; 'that is why I am calling on him.'

'Norman,' said the cleric, with his eye on a pebble in the road, 'are you ever afraid of thunderbolts?'

'What do you mean?' asked the colonel. 'Is your hobby meteorology?'

'I mean,' said Wilfred, without looking up, 'do you ever think that God might strike you in the street?'

'I beg your pardon,' said the colonel; 'I see your hobby is folklore.'

'I know your hobby is blasphemy,' retorted the religious man, stung in the one live place of his nature. 'But if you do not fear God, you have good reason to fear man.'

The elder raised his eyebrows politely. 'Fear man?' he said.

'Barnes the blacksmith is the biggest and strongest man for forty miles round,' said the clergyman sternly. 'I know you are no coward or weakling, but he could throw you over the wall.'

This struck home, being true, and the lowering line by mouth and nostril darkened and deepened. For a moment he stood with the heavy sneer on his face. But in an instant Colonel Bohun had recovered his own cruel good humour and laughed, showing two doglike front teeth under his yellow moustache. 'In that case, my dear Wilfred,' he said quite carelessly, 'it was wise for the last of the Bohuns to come out partially in armour.'

And he took off the queer round hat covered with green, showing that it was lined within with steel. Wilfred recognised it indeed as a light Japanese or Chinese helmet torn down from a trophy that hung in the old family hall.

'It was the first to hand,' explained his brother airily; 'always the nearest hat – and the nearest woman.'

'The blacksmith is away at Greenford,' said Wilfred quietly; 'the time of his return is unsettled.'

And with that he turned and went into the church with bowed head, crossing himself like one who wishes to be quit of an unclean spirit. He was anxious to forget such grossness in the cool twilight of his tall Gothic cloisters; but on that morning it was fated that his still round of religious exercises should be everywhere arrested by small shocks. As he entered the church, hitherto always empty at that hour, a kneeling figure rose hastily to its feet and came towards the full daylight of the doorway. When the curate saw it he stood still with surprise. For the early worshipper was none other than the village idiot, a nephew of the blacksmith, one who neither would nor could care for the church or for anything else. He was always called 'Mad Joe', and seemed to have no other name; he was a dark, strong, slouching lad, with a heavy white face, dark straight hair, and a mouth always open. As he passed the priest, his moon-calf countenance gave no hint of what he had been doing or thinking of. He had never been known to pray before. What sort of prayers was he saying now? Extraordinary prayers surely.

Wilfred Bohun stood rooted to the spot long enough to see the idiot go out into the sunshine, and even to see his dissolute brother hail him with a sort of avuncular jocularity. The last thing he saw was the colonel throwing pennies at the open mouth of Joe, with the serious appearance of trying to hit it.

This ugly sunlight picture of the stupidity and cruelty of the earth sent the ascetic finally to his prayers for purification and new thoughts. He went up to a pew in the gallery, which brought him under a coloured window which he loved and which always quieted his spirit; a blue window with an angel carrying lilies. There he began to think less about the half-wit, with his livid face and mouth like a fish. He began to think less of his evil brother, pacing like a lean lion in his horrible hunger. He sank deeper and deeper into those cold and sweet colours of silver blossoms and sapphire sky.

In this place half an hour afterwards he was found by Gibbs, the village cobbler, who had been sent for him in some haste. He got to his feet with promptitude, for he knew that no small matter would have brought Gibbs into such a place at all. The cobbler was, as in many villages, an atheist, and his appearance in church was a shade more extraordinary than Mad Joe's. It was a morning of theological enigmas.

'What is it?' asked Wilfred Bohun rather stiffly, but putting out a trembling hand for his hat.

The atheist spoke in a tone that, coming from him, was quite startlingly respectful, and even, as it were, huskily sympathetic.

'You must excuse me, sir,' he said in a hoarse whisper, 'but we didn't think it right not to let you know at once. I'm afraid a rather dreadful thing has happened, sir. I'm afraid your brother – '

Wilfred clenched his frail hands. 'What devilry has he done now?' he cried in involuntary passion.

'Why, sir,' said the cobbler, coughing, 'I'm afraid he's done nothing, and won't do anything. I'm afraid he's done for. You had really better come down, sir.'

The curate followed the cobbler down a short winding stair which brought them out at an entrance rather higher than the street. Bohun saw the tragedy in one glance, flat underneath him like a plan. In the yard of the smithy were standing five or six men, mostly in black, one in an inspector's uniform. They included the doctor, the Presbyterian minister, and the priest from the Roman Catholic chapel to which the blacksmith's wife belonged. The latter was speaking to her, indeed, very rapidly, in an undertone, as she, a magnificent woman with red-gold hair, was sobbing blindly on a bench. Between these two groups, and just clear of the main heap of hammers, lay a man in evening dress, spread-eagled and flat on his face. From the height above Wilfred could have sworn to every item of his costume and appearance, down to the Bohun rings upon his fingers; but the skull was only a hideous splash, like a star of blackness and blood.

Wilfred Bohun gave but one glance, and ran down the steps into the yard. The doctor, who was the family physician, saluted him, but he scarcely took any notice. He could only stammer out: 'My brother is dead. What does it mean? What is this horrible mystery?' There was an unhappy silence; and then the cobbler, the most outspoken man present, answered: 'Plenty of horror, sir,' he said, 'but not much mystery.'

'What do you mean?' asked Wilfred, with a white face.

'It's plain enough,' answered Gibbs. 'There is only one man for forty miles round that could have struck such a blow as that, and he's the man that had most reason to.'

'We must not prejudge anything,' put in the doctor, a tall, black-bearded man, rather nervously; 'but it is competent for me to corroborate what Mr Gibbs says about the nature of the blow, sir; it is an incredible blow. Mr Gibbs says that only one man in this district could have done it. I should have said myself that nobody could have done it.'

A shudder of superstition went through the slight figure of the curate. 'I can hardly understand,' he said.

'Mr Bohun,' said the doctor in a low voice, 'metaphors literally fail me. It is inadequate to say that the skull was smashed to bits like an eggshell. Fragments of bone were driven into the body and the ground like bullets into a mud wall. It was the hand of a giant.'

He was silent a moment, looking grimly through his glasses; then he added: 'The thing has one advantage – that it clears most people of suspicion at one stroke. If you or I or any normally made man in the country were accused of this crime, we should be acquitted as an infant would be acquitted of stealing the Nelson Column.'

'That's what I say,' repeated the cobbler obstinately, 'there's only one man that could have done it, and he's the man that would have done it. Where's Simeon Barnes, the blacksmith?'

'He's over at Greenford,' faltered the curate.

'More likely over in France,' muttered the cobbler.

'No; he is in neither of those places,' said a small and colourless voice, which came from the little Roman priest who had joined the group. 'As a matter of fact, he is coming up the road at this moment.'

The little priest was not an interesting man to look at, having stubbly brown hair and a round and stolid face. But if he had been as splendid as Apollo no one would have looked at him at that moment. Everyone turned round and peered at the pathway which wound across the plain below, along which was indeed walking, at his own huge stride and with a hammer on his shoulder, Simeon the smith. He was a bony and gigantic man, with deep, dark, sinister eyes and a dark chin beard. He was walking and talking quietly with two other men; and though he was never specially cheerful, he seemed quite at his ease.

'My God!' cried the atheistic cobbler; 'and there's the hammer he did it with.'

'No,' said the inspector, a sensible-looking man with a sandy moustache, speaking for the first time. 'There's the hammer he did it with, over there by the church wall. We have left it and the body exactly as they are.'

All glanced round, and the short priest went across and looked down in silence at the tool where it lay.

It was one of the smallest and the lightest of the hammers, and would not have caught the eye among the rest; but on the iron edge of it were blood and yellow hair.

After a silence the short priest spoke without looking up, and there was a new note in his dull voice. 'Mr Gibbs was hardly right,' he said, 'in saying that there is no mystery. There is at least the mystery of why so big a man should attempt so big a blow with so little a hammer.'

'Oh, never mind that,' cried Gibbs, in a fever. 'What are we to do with Simeon Barnes?'

'Leave him alone,' said the priest quietly. 'He is coming here of himself. I know these two men with him. They are very good fellows from Greenford, and they have come over about the Presbyterian chapel.'

Even as he spoke the tall smith swung round the corner of the church and strode into his own yard. Then he stood there quite still, and the hammer fell from his hand. The inspector, who had preserved impenetrable propriety, immediately went up to him.

'I won't ask you, Mr Barnes,' he said, 'whether you know anything about what has happened here. You are not bound to say. I hope you don't know, and that you will be able to prove it. But I must go through the form of arresting you in the King's name for the murder of Colonel Norman Bohun.'

'You are not bound to say anything,' said the cobbler in officious excitement. 'They've got to prove everything. They haven't proved yet that it is Colonel Bohun with the head all smashed up like that.'

'That won't wash,' said the doctor aside to the priest. 'That's out of detective stories. I was the colonel's medical man, and I knew his body better than he did. He had very fine hands, but quite peculiar ones. The second and third fingers were the same in length. Oh, that's the colonel right enough.'

As he glanced at the brained corpse upon the ground the iron eyes of the motionless blacksmith followed them and rested there also.

'Is Colonel Bohun dead?' said the smith quite calmly. 'Then he's damned.'

'Don't say anything! Oh, don't say anything,' cried the atheist cobbler, dancing about in an ecstasy of admiration of the English legal system. For no man is such a legalist as the good Secularist.

The blacksmith turned on him over his shoulder the august face of a fanatic.

'It is well for you infidels to dodge like foxes because the world's law favours you,' he said; 'but God guards His own in His pocket, as you shall see this day.'

Then he pointed to the colonel and said: 'When did this dog die in his sins?'

'Moderate your language,' said the doctor.

'Moderate the Bible's language, and I'll moderate mine. When did he die?'

'I saw him alive at six o'clock this morning,' stammered Wilfred Bohun.

'God is good,' said the smith. 'Mr Inspector, I have not the slightest objection to being arrested. It is you who may object to arresting me. I don't mind leaving the court without a stain on my character. You do mind, perhaps, leaving the court with a bad setback in your career.'

The solid inspector for the first time looked at the blacksmith with a lively eye – as did everybody else, except the short, strange priest, who was still looking down at the little hammer that had dealt the dreadful blow.

'There are two men standing outside this shop,' went on the blacksmith with ponderous lucidity, 'good tradesmen in Greenford whom you all know, who will swear that they saw me from before midnight till daybreak and long after in the committee room of our Revival Mission, which sits all night, we save souls so fast. In Greenford itself twenty people could swear to me for all that time. If I were a heathen, Mr Inspector, I would let you walk on to your downfall; but, as a Christian man, I feel bound to give you your chance and ask you whether you will hear my alibi now or in court.'

The inspector seemed for the first time disturbed and said. 'Of course I should be glad to clear you altogether now.'

The smith walked out of his yard with the same long and easy stride, and returned to his two friends from Greenford, who were indeed friends of nearly everyone present. Each of them said a few words which no one ever thought of disbelieving. When they had spoken the innocence of Simeon stood up as solid as the great church above them.

One of those silences struck the group which are more strange and insufferable than any speech. Madly, in order to make conversation, the curate said to the Catholic priest: 'You seem very much interested in that hammer, Father Brown.'

'Yes, I am,' said Father Brown; 'why is it such a small hammer?'

The doctor swung round on him.

'By George, that's true,' he cried; 'who would use a little hammer with ten larger hammers lying about?'

Then he lowered his voice in the curate's ear and said: 'Only the kind of person that can't lift a large hammer. It is not a question of force or courage between the sexes. It's a question of lifting power in the shoulders. A bold woman could commit ten murders with a light hammer and never turn a hair. She could not kill a beetle with a heavy one.'

Wilfred Bohun was staring at him with a sort of hypnotised horror, while Father Brown listened with his head a little on one side, really interested and attentive.

The doctor went on with more hissing emphasis: 'Why do those idiots always assume that the only person who hates the wife's lover is the wife's husband? Nine times out of ten the person who most hates the wife's lover is the wife. Who knows what insolence or treachery he had shown her – look there?'

He made a momentary gesture towards the red-haired woman on the bench. She had lifted her head at last and the tears were drying on her splendid face. But the eyes were fixed on the corpse with an electric glare that had in it something of idiocy.

The Revd William Bohun made a limp gesture as if waving away all desire to know; but Father Brown, dusting off his sleeve some ashes blown from the furnace, spoke in his indifferent way.

'You are like so many doctors,' he said; 'your mental science is really suggestive. It is your physical science that is utterly impossible. I agree that the woman wants to kill the co-respondent much more than the petitioner does. And I agree that a woman will always pick up a small hammer instead of a big one. But the difficulty is one of physical impossibility. No woman ever born could have smashed a man's skull out flat like that.' Then he added reflectively, after a pause: 'These people haven't grasped the whole of it. The man was actually wearing an iron helmet, and the blow scattered it like broken glass. Look at that woman. Look at her arms.'

Silence held them all up again, and then the doctor said rather sulkily: 'Well, I may be wrong; there are objections to everything. But I stick to the main point. No man but an idiot would pick up that little hammer if he could use a big hammer.'

With that the lean and quivering hands of Wilfred Bohun went up to his head and seemed to clutch his scanty yellow hair. After an instant they dropped, and he cried: 'That was the word I wanted; you have said the word.'

Then he continued, mastering his discomposure: 'The words you said were, "No man but an idiot would pick up the small hammer." '

'Yes,' said the doctor, 'Well?'

'Well,' said the curate, 'no man but an idiot did.' The rest stared at him with eyes arrested and riveted, and he went on in a febrile and feminine agitation.

'I am a priest,' he cried unsteadily, 'and a priest should be no shedder of blood. I – I mean that he should bring no one to the gallows. And I thank God that I see the criminal clearly now – because he is a criminal who cannot be brought to the gallows.'

'You will not denounce him?' enquired the doctor.

'He would not be hanged if I did denounce him,' answered Wilfred, with a wild but curiously happy smile. 'When I went into the church this morning I found a madman praying there – that poor Joe, who has been wrong all his life. God knows what he prayed;

but with such strange folk it is not incredible to suppose that their prayers are all upside down. Very likely a lunatic would pray before killing a man. When I last saw poor Joe he was with my brother. My brother was mocking him.'

'By Jove!' cried the doctor, 'this is talking at last. But how do you explain – '

The Revd Wilfred was almost trembling with the excitement of his own glimpse of the truth. 'Don't you see; don't you see,' he cried feverishly, 'that is the only theory that covers both the queer things, that answers both the riddles. The two riddles are the little hammer and the big blow. The smith might have struck the big blow, but he would not have chosen the little hammer. His wife would have chosen the little hammer, but she could not have struck the big blow. But the madman might have done both. As for the little hammer – why, he was mad and might have picked up anything. And for the big blow, have you never heard, doctor, that a maniac in his paroxysm may have the strength of ten men?'

The doctor drew a deep breath and then said: 'By golly, I believe you've got it.'

Father Brown had fixed his eyes on the speaker so long and steadily as to prove that his large grey, ox-like eyes were not quite so insignificant as the rest of his face. When silence had fallen he said with marked respect: 'Mr Bohun, yours is the only theory yet propounded which holds water every way and is essentially unassailable. I think, therefore, that you deserve to be told, on my positive knowledge, that it is not the true one.' And with that the odd little man walked away and stared again at the hammer.

'That fellow seems to know more than he ought to,'

whispered the doctor peevishly to Wilfred. 'Those popish priests are deucedly sly.'

'No, no,' said Bohun, with a sort of wild fatigue. 'It was the lunatic. It was the lunatic.'

The group of the two clerics and the doctor had fallen away from the more official group containing the inspector and the man he had arrested. Now, however, that their own party had broken up, they heard voices from the others.

The priest looked up quietly and then looked down again as he heard the blacksmith say in a loud voice: 'I hope I've convinced you, Mr Inspector. I'm a strong man, as you say, but I couldn't have flung my hammer bang here from Greenford. My hammer hasn't any wings that it should come flying half a mile over hedges and fields.'

The inspector laughed amicably and said: 'No; I think you can be considered out of it, though it's one of the rummiest coincidences I ever saw. I can only ask you to give us all the assistance you can in finding a man as big and strong as yourself. By George! you might be useful, if only to hold him! I suppose you yourself have no guess at the man?'

'I may have a guess,' said the pale smith, 'but it is not at a man.' Then, seeing the sacred eyes turn towards his wife on the bench, he put his huge hand on her shoulder and said: 'Nor a woman either.'

'What do you mean?' asked the inspector jocularly. 'You don't think cows use hammers, do you?'

'I think no thing of flesh held that hammer,' said the blacksmith in a stifled voice; 'mortally speaking, I think the man died alone.'

Wilfred made a sudden forward movement and peered at him with burning eyes.

'Do you mean to say, Barnes,' came the sharp voice of the cobbler, 'that the hammer jumped up of itself and knocked the man down?'

'Oh, you gentlemen may stare and snigger,' cried Simeon; 'you clergymen who tell us on Sunday in what a stillness the Lord smote Sennacherib. I believe that One who walks invisible in every house defended the honour of mine, and laid the defiler dead before the door of it. I believe the force in that blow was just the force there is in earthquakes, and no force less.'

Wilfred said, with a voice utterly indescribable: 'I told Norman myself to beware of the thunderbolt.'

'That agent is outside my jurisdiction,' said the inspector with a slight smile.

'You are not outside His,' answered the smith; 'see you to it.' And, turning his broad back, he went into the house.

The shaken Wilfred was led away by Father Brown, who had an easy and friendly way with him. 'Let us get out of this horrid place, Mr Bohun,' he said. 'May I look inside your church? I hear it's one of the oldest in England. We take some interest, you know,' he added with a comical grimace, 'in old English churches.'

Wilfred Bohun did not smile, for humour was never his strong point. But he nodded rather eagerly, being only too ready to explain the Gothic splendours to someone more likely to be sympathetic than the Presbyterian blacksmith or the atheist cobbler.

'By all means,' he said; 'let us go in at this side.' And he led the way into the high side entrance at the top of the flight of steps. Father Brown was mounting the first step to follow him when he felt a hand on his shoulder, and turned to behold the dark, thin figure of the doctor, his face darker yet with suspicion.

'Sir,' said the physician harshly, 'you appear to know some secrets in this black business. May I ask if you are going to keep them to yourself?'

'Why, doctor,' answered the priest, smiling quite pleasantly, 'there is one very good reason why a man of my trade would keep things to himself when he is not sure of them, and that is that it is so constantly his duty to keep them to himself when he is sure of them. But if you think I have been discourteously reticent with you or anyone, I will go to the extreme limit of my custom. I will give you two very large hints.'

'Well, sir?' said the doctor gloomily.

'First,' said Father Brown quietly, 'the thing is quite in your own province. It is a matter of physical science. The blacksmith is mistaken, not perhaps in saying that the blow was divine, but certainly in saying that it came by a miracle. It was no miracle, doctor, except in so far as man is himself a miracle, with his strange and wicked and yet half-heroic heart. The force that smashed that skull was a force well known to scientists – one of the most frequently debated of the laws of nature.'

The doctor, who was looking at him with frowning intentness, only said: 'And the other hint?'

'The other hint is this,' said the priest: 'Do you remember the blacksmith, though he believes in miracles, talking scornfully of the impossible fairytale that his hammer had wings and flew half a mile across country?'

'Yes,' said the doctor, 'I remember that.'

'Well,' added Father Brown, with a broad smile, 'that fairy tale was the nearest thing to the real truth that has been said today.' And with that he turned his back and stumped up the steps after the curate.

The Reverend Wilfred, who had been waiting for him, pale and impatient, as if this little delay were the last straw for his nerves, led him immediately to his favourite corner of the church, that part of the gallery closest to the carved roof and lit by the wonderful window with the angel. The little Latin priest explored and admired everything exhaustively, talking cheerfully but in a low voice all the time. When in the course of his investigation he found the side exit and the winding stair down which Wilfred had rushed to find his brother dead, Father Brown ran not down but up, with the agility of a monkey, and his clear voice came from an outer platform above.

'Come up here, Mr Bohun,' he called. 'The air will do you good.'

Bohun followed him, and came out on a kind of stone gallery or balcony outside the building, from which one could see the illimitable plain in which their small hill stood, wooded away to the purple horizon and dotted with villages and farms. Clear and square, but quite small beneath them, was the blacksmith's yard, where the inspector still stood taking notes and the corpse still lay like a smashed fly.

'Might be the map of the world, mightn't it?' said Father Brown.

'Yes,' said Bohun very gravely, and nodded his head.

Immediately beneath and about them the lines of the Gothic building plunged outwards into the void with a sickening swiftness akin to suicide. There is that element of Titan energy in the architecture of the Middle Ages that, from whatever aspect it be seen, it always seems to be rushing away, like the strong back of some maddened horse. This church was hewn out of ancient and silent stone, bearded with old fungoids and stained with the nests of birds. And yet, when they saw it from below, it sprang like a fountain at the stars; and when they saw it, as now, from above, it poured like a cataract into a voiceless pit. For these two men on the tower were left alone with the most terrible aspect of the Gothic: the monstrous foreshortening and disproportion, the dizzy perspectives, the glimpses of great things small and small things great; a topsy-turvydom of stone in the midair. Details of stone, enormous by their proximity, were relieved against a pattern of fields and farms, pygmy in their distance. A carved bird or beast at a corner seemed like some vast walking or flying dragon wasting the pastures and villages below. The whole atmosphere was dizzy and dangerous, as if men were upheld in air amid the gyrating wings of colossal genii; and the whole of that old church, as tall and rich as a cathedral, seemed to sit upon the sunlit country like a cloudburst.

'I think there is something rather dangerous about standing on these high places even to pray,' said Father Brown. 'Heights were made to be looked at, not to be looked from.'

'Do you mean that one may fall over,' asked Wilfred.

'I mean that one's soul may fall if one's body doesn't,' said the other priest.

'I scarcely understand you,' remarked Bohun indistinctly.

'Look at that blacksmith, for instance,' went on Father Brown calmly; 'a good man, but not a Christian – hard, imperious, unforgiving. Well, his Scotch religion was made up by men who prayed on hills and high crags, and learnt to look down on the world more than to look up at heaven. Humility is the mother of giants. One sees great things from the valley; only small things from the peak.'

'But he – he didn't do it,' said Bohun tremulously.

'No,' said the other in an odd voice; 'we know he didn't do it.'

After a moment he resumed, looking tranquilly out over the plain with his pale grey eyes. 'I knew a man,' he said, 'who began by worshipping with others before the altar, but who grew fond of high and lonely places to pray from, corners or niches in the belfry or the spire. And once in one of those dizzy places, where the whole world seemed to turn under him like a wheel, his brain turned also, and he fancied he was God. So that though he was a good man, he committed a great crime.'

Wilfred's face was turned away, but his bony hands turned blue and white as they tightened on the parapet of stone.

'He thought it was given to *him* to judge the world and strike down the sinner. He would never have had such a thought if he had been kneeling with other men upon a floor. But he saw all men walking about like insects. He saw one especially strutting just below him, insolent and evident by a bright green hat – a poisonous insect.'

Rooks cawed round the corners of the belfry; but there was no other sound till Father Brown went on.

'This also tempted him, that he had in his hand one of the most awful engines of nature; I mean gravitation, that mad and quickening rush by which all earth's creatures fly back to her heart when released. See, the inspector is strutting just below us in the smithy. If I were to toss a pebble over this parapet it would be something like a bullet by the time it struck him. If I were to drop a hammer – even a small hammer – '

Wilfred Bohun threw one leg over the parapet, and Father Brown had him in a minute by the collar.

'Not by that door,' he said quite gently; 'that door leads to hell.'

Bohun staggered back against the wall, and stared at him with frightful eyes.

'How do you know all this?' he cried. 'Are you a devil?'

'I am a man,' answered Father Brown gravely; 'and therefore have all devils in my heart. Listen to me,' he said after a short pause. 'I know what you did – at least, I can guess the great part of it. When you left your brother you were racked with no unrighteous rage to the extent even that you snatched up the small hammer, half inclined to kill him with his foulness on his mouth. Recoiling, you thrust it under your buttoned coat instead, and rushed into the church. You pray wildly in many places, under the angel window, upon the platform above, and on a higher platform still, from which you could see the colonel's Eastern hat like the back of a green beetle crawling about. Then something snapped in your soul, and you let God's thunderbolt fall.'

Wilfred put a weak hand to his head, and asked in a low voice: 'How did you know that his hat looked like a green beetle?'

'Oh, that,' said the other with the shadow of a smile, 'that was common sense. But hear me further. I say I know all this; but no one else shall know it. The next step is for you; I shall take no more steps; I will seal this with the seal of confession. If you ask me why, there are many reasons, and only one that concerns you. I leave things to you because you have not yet gone very far wrong, as assassins go. You did not help to fix the crime on the smith when it was easy; or on his wife, when that was easy. You tried to fix it on the imbecile, because you knew that he could not suffer. That was one of the gleams that it is my business to find in assassins. And now come down into the village, and go your own way as free as the wind; for I have said my last word.'

They went down the winding stairs in utter silence, and came out into the sunlight by the smithy. Wilfred Bohun carefully unlatched the wooden gate of the yard, and going up to the inspector, said: 'I wish to give myself up; I have killed my brother.'

The Sign of the Broken Sword

The thousand arms of the forest were grey, and its million fingers silver. In a sky of dark green-blue-like slate the stars were bleak and brilliant like splintered ice. All that thickly wooded and sparsely tenanted countryside was stiff with a bitter and brittle frost. The black hollows between the trunks of the trees looked like bottomless, black caverns of that heartless Scandinavian hell, a hell of incalculable cold. Even the square stone tower of the church looked northern to the point of heathenry, as if it were some barbaric tower among the sea rocks of Iceland. It was a queer night for anyone to explore a churchyard. But, on the other hand, perhaps it was worth exploring.

It rose abruptly out of the ashen wastes of forest in a sort of hump or shoulder of green turf that looked grey in the starlight. Most of the graves were on a slant, and the path leading up to the church was as steep as a staircase. On the top of the hill, in the one flat and prominent place, was the monument for which the place was famous. It contrasted strangely with the featureless graves all round, for it was the work of one of the greatest sculptors of modern Europe; and yet his fame was at once forgotten in the fame of the man whose image he had made. It showed, by touches of the small silver pencil of starlight, the massive metal figure of a soldier recumbent, the strong hands sealed in an everlasting worship, the great head pillowed upon a gun. The venerable face was bearded, or rather whiskered, in the old, heavy Colonel Newcome fashion. The uniform, though suggested with the few strokes of simplicity, was that of modern war. By his right side lay a sword, of which the tip was broken off; on the left side lay a Bible. On glowing summer afternoons wagonettes came full of Americans and cultured suburbans to see the sepulchre; but even then they felt the vast forest land with its one dumpy dome of churchyard and church as a place oddly dumb and neglected. In this freezing darkness of midwinter one would think he might be left alone with the stars. Nevertheless, in the stillness of those stiff woods a wooden gate creaked, and two dim figures dressed in black climbed up the little path to the tomb.

So faint was that frigid starlight that nothing could have been traced about them except that while they both wore black, one man was enormously big, and the other (perhaps by contrast) almost startlingly small. They went up to the great graven tomb of the historic warrior, and stood for a few minutes staring at it. There was no human, perhaps no living, thing for a wide circle; and a morbid fancy might well have wondered if they were human themselves. In any case, the beginning of their conversation might have seemed strange. After the first silence the small man said to the other: 'Where does a wise man hide a pebble?'

And the tall man answered in a low voice: 'On the beach.'

The small man nodded, and after a short silence said: 'Where does a wise man hide a leaf?'

And the other answered: 'In the forest.'

There was another stillness, and then the tall man resumed: 'Do you mean that when a wise man has to hide a real diamond he has been known to hide it among sham ones?'

'No, no,' said the little man with a laugh, 'we will let bygones be bygones.'

He stamped his cold feet for a second or two and then said: 'I'm not thinking of that at all, but of something else; something rather peculiar. Just strike a match, will you?'

The big man fumbled in his pocket, and soon a scratch and a flare painted gold the whole flat side of the monument. On it was cut in black letters the well-known words which so many Americans had reverently read: 'Sacred to the Memory of General Sir Arthur St Clare – Hero and Martyr – who always vanquished his enemies and always spared them, and was treacherously slain by them at last. May God in whom he trusted both reward and revenge him'.

The match burnt the big man's fingers, blackened, and dropped. He was about to strike another, but his small companion stopped him. 'That's all right, Flambeau, old man; I saw what I wanted. Or, rather, I didn't see what I didn't want. And now we must walk a mile and a half along the road to the next inn, and I will try to tell you all about it. For Heaven knows a man should have fire and ale when he dares tell such a story.'

They descended the precipitous path, they relatched the rusty gate, and set off at a stamping, ringing walk down the frozen forest road. They had gone a full quarter of a mile before the smaller man spoke again. He said: 'Yes; the wise man hides a pebble on the beach. But what does he do if there is no beach? Do you know anything of the great St Clare trouble?'

'I know nothing about English generals, Father Brown,' answered the large man, laughing, 'though a little about English policemen. I only know that you have dragged me a precious long dance to all the shrines of this fellow, whoever he is. One would think he got buried in six different places. I've seen a memorial to General St Clare in Westminster Abbey; I've seen a ramping equestrian statue of General St Clare on the Embankment; I've seen a medallion of General St Clare in the street he was born in; and another in the street he lived in; and now you drag me after dark to his coffin in the village churchyard. I am beginning to be a bit tired of his magnificent personality, especially as I don't in the least know who he was. What are you hunting for in all these crypts and effigies?'

'I am only looking for one word,' said Father Brown. 'A word that isn't there.'

'Well,' asked Flambeau, 'are you going to tell me anything about it?'

'I must divide it into two parts,' remarked the priest. 'First there is what everybody knows; and then there is what I know. Now, what everybody knows is short and plain enough. It is also entirely wrong.'

'Right you are,' said the big man called Flambeau cheerfully. 'Let's begin at the wrong end. Let's begin with what everybody knows, which isn't true.'

'If not wholly untrue, it is at least very inadequate,' continued Brown; 'for in point of fact, all that the public knows amounts precisely to this: the public knows that Arthur St Clare was a great and successful English general. It knows that after splendid yet careful campaigns both in India and Africa he was in command against Brazil when the great Brazilian patriot Olivier issued his ultimatum. It knows that on that occasion St Clare with a very small force attacked Olivier with a very large one, and was captured after heroic resistance. And it knows that after his capture, and to the abhorrence of the civilised world, St Clare was hanged on the nearest tree. He was found swinging there after the Brazilians had retired, with his broken sword hung round his neck.'

'And that popular story is untrue?' suggested Flambeau.

'No,' said his friend quietly; 'that story is quite true, so far as it goes.'

'Well, I think it goes far enough!' said Flambeau, 'but if the popular story is true, what is the mystery?'

They had passed many hundreds of grey and ghostly trees before the little priest answered. Then he bit his finger reflectively and said: 'Why, the mystery is a mystery of psychology. Or, rather, it is a mystery of two psychologies. In that Brazilian business two of the most famous men of modern history acted flat against their characters. Mind you, Olivier and St Clare were both heroes – the old thing, and no mistake; it was like the fight between Hector and Achilles. Now, what would you say to an affair in which Achilles was timid and Hector was treacherous?'

'Go on,' said the large man impatiently as the other bit his finger again.

'Sir Arthur St Clare was a soldier of the old religious type – the type that saved us during the Mutiny,' continued Brown. 'He was always more for duty than for dash; and with all his personal courage was decidedly a prudent commander, particularly indignant at any needless waste of soldiers. Yet, in this last battle, he attempted something that a baby could see was absurd. One need not be a strategist to see it was as wild as wind; just as one need not be a strategist to keep out of the way of a motorbus. Well, that is the first mystery; what had become of the English general's head? The second riddle is, what had become of the Brazilian general's heart? President Olivier might be called a visionary or a nuisance; but even his enemies admitted that he was magnanimous to the point of knight errantry. Almost every other prisoner he had ever captured had been set free, or even loaded with benefits. Men who had really wronged him came away touched by his simplicity and sweetness. Why the deuce should he diabolically revenge himself only once in his life; and then for the one particular blow that could not have hurt him? Well, there you have it. One of the wisest men in the world acted like an idiot for no reason. One of the best men in the world acted like a fiend for no reason. That's the long and short of it; and I leave it to you, my boy.'

'No, you don't,' said the other with a snort. 'I leave it to you; and you jolly well tell me all about it.'

'Well,' resumed Father Brown, 'it's not fair to say that the public impression is just what I've said, without adding that two things have happened since. I can't say they threw a new light, for nobody can make sense of them. But they threw a new kind of darkness, they threw the darkness in new directions. The first was this. The family physician of the St Clares quarrelled with that family and began publishing a violent series of articles, in which he said that the late general was a religious maniac; but as far as the tale went, this seemed to mean little more than a religious man. Anyhow, the story fizzled out. Everyone knew, of course, that St Clare had some of the eccentricities of puritan piety. The second incident was much more arresting. In the luckless and unsupported regiment which made that rash attempt at the Black River there was a certain Captain Keith, who was at that time engaged to St Clare's daughter, and who afterwards married her. He was one of those who were captured by Olivier, and, like all the rest except the general, appears to have been bounteously treated and promptly set free. Some twenty years afterwards this man, then Lieutenant-Colonel Keith, published a sort of autobiography called "A British Officer in Burma and Brazil". In the place where the reader looks eagerly for some account of the mystery of St Clare's disaster may be found the following words: "Everywhere else in this book I have narrated things exactly as they occurred, holding as I do the old-fashioned opinion that the glory of England is old enough to take care of itself. The exception I shall make is in this matter of the defeat by the Black River; and my reasons, though private, are honourable and compelling. I will, however, add this in justice to the memories of two distinguished men. General St Clare has been accused of incapacity on this occasion; I can at least testify that this action, properly understood, was one of the most brilliant and sagacious of his life. President Olivier by similar report is charged with savage injustice. I think it due to the honour of an enemy to say that he acted on this occasion with even more than his characteristic good feeling. To put the matter popularly, I can assure my countrymen that St Clare was by no means such a fool, nor Olivier such a brute as he looked. This is all I have to say; nor shall any earthly consideration induce me to add a word." '

A large frozen moon like a lustrous snowball began

to show through the tangle of twigs in front of them, and by its light the narrator had been able to refresh his memory of Captain Keith's text from a scrap of printed paper. As he folded it up and put it back in his pocket Flambeau threw up his hand with a French gesture.

'Wait a bit, wait a bit,' he cried excitedly. 'I believe I can guess it at the first go.'

He strode on, breathing hard, his black head and bull neck forward, like a man winning a walking race. The little priest, amused and interested, had some trouble in trotting beside him. Just before them the trees fell back a little to left and right, and the road swept downwards across a clear, moonlit valley, till it dived again like a rabbit into the wall of another wood. The entrance to the farther forest looked small and round, like the black hole of a remote railway tunnel. But it was within some hundred yards, and gaped like a cavern before Flambeau spoke again.

'I've got it,' he cried at last, slapping his thigh with his great hand. 'Four minutes' thinking, and I can tell you the whole story myself.'

'All right,' assented his friend. 'You tell it.'

Flambeau lifted his head, but lowered his voice. 'General Sir Arthur St Clare,' he said, 'came of a family in which madness was hereditary; and his whole aim was to keep this from his daughter, and even, if possible, from his future son-in-law. Rightly or wrongly, he thought the final collapse was close, and resolved on suicide. Yet ordinary suicide would blazon the very idea he dreaded. As the campaign approached the clouds came thicker on his brain, and at last in a mad moment he sacrificed his public duty to his private. He rushed rashly into battle, hoping to fall by the first shot. When he found that he had only attained capture and discredit, the sealed bomb in his brain burst, and he broke his own sword and hanged himself.'

He stared firmly at the grey façade of forest in front of him, with the one black gap in it, like the mouth of the grave, into which their path plunged. Perhaps something menacing in the road thus suddenly swallowed reinforced his vivid vision of the tragedy, for he shuddered.

'A horrid story,' repeated the priest with bent head; 'but not the real story.'

Then he threw back his head with a sort of despair and cried: 'Oh, I wish it had been.'

The tall Flambeau faced round and stared at him.

'Yours is a clean story,' cried Father Brown, deeply moved. 'A sweet, pure, honest story, as open and white as that moon. Madness and despair are innocent enough. There are worse things, Flambeau.'

Flambeau looked up wildly at the moon thus invoked; and from where he stood one black tree-bough curved across it exactly like a devil's horn.

'Father – Father,' cried Flambeau with the French gesture and stepping yet more rapidly forward, 'do you mean it was worse than that?'

'Worse than that,' said the other like a grave echo. And they plunged into the black cloister of the woodland, which ran by them in a dim tapestry of trunks, like one of the dark corridors in a dream.

They were soon in the most secret entrails of the wood, and felt close about them the foliage that they could not see, when the priest said again: 'Where does a wise man hide a leaf? In the forest. But what does he do if there is no forest?'

'Well – well,' cried Flambeau irritably, 'what does he do?'

'He grows a forest to hide it in,' said the priest in an obscure voice. 'A fearful sin.'

'Look here,' cried his friend impatiently, for the dark wood and the dark sayings got a little on his nerves; 'will you tell me this story or not? What other evidence is there to go on?'

'There are three more bits of evidence,' said the other, 'that I have dug up in holes and corners, and I will give them in logical rather than chronological order. First of all, of course, our authority for the issue and event of the battle is in Olivier's own despatches, which are lucid enough. He was entrenched with two or three regiments on the heights that swept down to the Black River, on the other side of which was lower and more marshy ground. Beyond this again was gently rising country, on which was the first English outpost, supported by others which lay, however, considerably in its rear. The British forces as a whole were greatly superior in numbers; but this particular regiment was just far enough from its base to make Olivier consider the project of crossing the river to cut it off. By sunset, however, he had decided to retain his own position, which was a specially strong one. At daybreak next morning he was thunderstruck to see that this stray handful of English, entirely unsupported from their rear, had flung themselves across the river, half by the bridge to the right, and the other half by a ford higher up, and were massed upon the marshy bank below him.

'That they should attempt an attack with such numbers against such a position was incredible enough; but Olivier noticed something yet more extraordinary. For instead of attempting to seize more solid ground, this mad regiment, having put the river in its rear by one wild charge, did nothing more, but stuck there in the mire like flies in treacle. Needless to say, the Brazilians blew great gaps in them with artillery, which they could only return with spirited but lessening rifle fire. Yet they never broke; and Olivier's curt account ends with a strong tribute of admiration for the mystic valour of these imbeciles. "Our line then advanced finally," writes Olivier, "and drove them into the river; we captured General St Clare himself and several other officers. The colonel and the major had both fallen in the battle. I cannot resist saying that few finer sights can have been seen in history than the last stand of this extraordinary regiment; wounded officers picking up the rifles of dead soldiers, and the general himself facing us on horseback bareheaded and with a broken sword." On what happened to the general afterwards Olivier is as silent as Captain Keith.'

'Well,' grunted Flambeau, 'get on to the next bit of evidence.'

'The next evidence,' said Father Brown, 'took some time to find, but it will not take long to tell. I found at last, in an almshouse down in the Lincolnshire Fens, an old soldier who not only was wounded at the Black River, but had actually knelt beside the colonel of the regiment when he died. This latter was a certain Colonel Clancy, a big bull of an Irishman; and it would seem that he died almost as much of rage as of bullets. He, at any rate, was not responsible for that ridiculous raid; it must have been imposed on him by the general. His last edifying words, according to my informant, were these: "And there goes the damned old donkey with the end of his sword knocked off. I wish it was his head." You will remark that everyone seems to have noticed this detail about the broken sword blade, though most people regard it somewhat more reverently than did the late Colonel Clancy. And now for the third fragment.'

Their path through the woodland began to go upward, and the speaker paused a little for breath before he went on. Then he continued in the same businesslike tone: 'Only a month or two ago a certain Brazilian official died in England, having quarrelled with Olivier and left his country. He was a well-known figure both here and on the Continent, a Spaniard named Espado; I knew him myself, a yellow-faced old dandy, with a hooked nose. For various private reasons I had permission to see the documents he had left; he was a Catholic, of course, and I had been with him towards the end. There was nothing of his that lit up any corner of the black St Clare business, except five or six common exercise books filled with the diary of some English soldier. I can only suppose that it was found by the Brazilians on one of those that fell. Anyhow, it stopped abruptly the night before the battle.

'But the account of that last day in the poor fellow's life was certainly worth reading. I have it on me; but it's too dark to read it here, and I will give you a résumé. The first part of that entry is full of jokes, evidently flung about among the men, about somebody called the Vulture. It does not seem as if this person, whoever he was, was one of themselves, nor even an Englishman; neither is he exactly spoken of as one of the enemy. It sounds rather as if he were some local go-between and non-combatant; perhaps a guide or a journalist. He has been closeted with old Colonel Clancy; but is more often seen talking to the major. Indeed, the major is somewhat prominent in this soldier's narrative; a lean, dark-haired man, apparently, of the name of Murray – a north of Ireland man and a Puritan. There are continual jests about the contrast between this Ulsterman's austerity and the conviviality of Colonel Clancy. There is also some joke about the Vulture wearing bright-coloured clothes.

'But all these levities are scattered by what may well be called the note of a bugle. Behind the English camp, and almost parallel to the river, ran one of the few great roads of that district. Westward the road curved round towards the river, which it crossed by the bridge before mentioned. To the east the road swept backwards into the wilds, and some two miles along it was the next English outpost. From this direction there came along the road that evening a glitter and clatter of light cavalry, in which even the simple diarist could recognise with astonishment the general with his staff. He rode the great white horse which you have seen so often in illustrated papers and Academy pictures; and you may be sure that the salute they gave him was not merely ceremonial. He, at least, wasted no time on ceremony, but, springing from the saddle immediately, mixed with the group of officers, and fell into emphatic though confidential speech. What struck our friend the diarist most was his special disposition to discuss matters with Major Murray; but, indeed, such a selection, so long as it was not marked, was in no way unnatural. The two men were made for sympathy; they were men who "read their Bibles"; they were both the old Evangelical type of officer. However this may be, it is certain that when the general mounted again he was still talking earnestly to Murray; and that as he walked his horse slowly down the road towards the river, the tall Ulsterman still walked by his bridle-rein in earnest debate. The soldiers watched the two until they vanished behind a clump of trees where the road turned towards the river. The colonel had gone back to his tent, and the men to their pickets; the man with the diary lingered for another four minutes, and saw a marvellous sight.

'The great white horse which had marched slowly down the road, as it had marched in so many processions, flew back, galloping up the road towards them as if it were mad to win a race. At first they thought it had run away with the man on its back; but they soon saw that the general, a fine rider, was himself urging it to full speed. Horse and man swept up to them like a whirlwind; and then, reining up the reeling charger, the general turned on them a face like flame, and called for the colonel like the trumpet that wakes the dead.

'I conceive that all the earthquake events of that catastrophe tumbled on top of each other rather like lumber in the minds of men such as our friend with the diary. With the dazed excitement of a dream, they found themselves falling – literally falling – into their ranks, and learned that an attack was to be led at once across the river. The general and the major, it was said, had found out something at the bridge, and there was only just time to strike for life. The major had gone back at once to call up the reserve along the road behind; it was doubtful if even with that prompt appeal help could reach them in time. But they must pass the stream that night, and seize the heights by morning. It is with the very stir and throb of that romantic nocturnal march that the diary suddenly ends.'

Father Brown had mounted ahead; for the woodland path grew smaller, steeper, and more twisted, till they felt as if they were ascending a winding staircase. The priest's voice came from above out of the darkness.

'There was one other little and enormous thing. When the general urged them to their chivalric charge he drew half his sword from the scabbard; and then, as if ashamed of such melodrama, thrust it back again. The sword again, you see.'

A half-light broke through the network of boughs above them, flinging the ghost of a net about their feet; for they were mounting again to the faint luminosity of the naked light. Flambeau felt truth all round him as an atmosphere, but not as an idea. He answered with bewildered brain: 'Well, what's the matter with the sword? Officers generally have swords, don't they?'

'They are not often mentioned in modern war,' said the other dispassionately; 'but in this affair one falls over the blessed sword everywhere.'

'Well, what is there in that?' growled Flambeau; 'it was a twopence coloured sort of incident; the old man's blade breaking in his last battle. Anyone might bet the papers would get hold of it, as they have. On all these tombs and things it's shown broken at the point. I hope you haven't dragged me through this Polar expedition merely because two men with an eye for a picture saw St Clare's broken sword.'

'No,' cried Father Brown, with a sharp voice like a pistol shot; 'but who saw his unbroken sword?'

'What do you mean?' cried the other, and stood still

under the stars. They had come abruptly out of the grey gates of the wood.

'I say, who saw his unbroken sword?' repeated Father Brown obstinately. 'Not the writer of the diary, anyhow; the general sheathed it in time.'

Flambeau looked about him in the moonlight, as a man struck blind might look in the sun; and his friend went on for the first time with eagerness: 'Flambeau,' he cried, 'I cannot prove it, even after hunting through the tombs. But I am sure of it. Let me add just one more tiny fact that tips the whole thing over. The colonel, by a strange chance, was one of the first struck by a bullet. He was struck long before the troops came to close quarters. But he saw St Clare's sword broken. Why was it broken? How was it broken? My friend, it was broken before the battle.'

'Oh!' said his friend, with a sort of forlorn jocularity; 'and pray where is the other piece?'

'I can tell you,' said the priest promptly. 'In the northeast corner of the cemetery of the Protestant Cathedral at Belfast.'

'Indeed?' enquired the other. 'Have you looked for it?'

'I couldn't,' replied Brown, with frank regret. 'There's a great marble monument on top of it; a monument to the heroic Major Murray, who fell fighting gloriously at the famous Battle of the Black River.'

Flambeau seemed suddenly galvanised into existence. 'You mean,' he cried hoarsely, 'that General St Clare hated Murray, and murdered him on the field of battle because –'

'You are still full of good and pure thoughts,' said the other. 'It was worse than that.'

'Well,' said the large man, 'my stock of evil imagination is used up.'

The priest seemed really doubtful where to begin, and at last he said again: 'Where would a wise man hide a leaf? In the forest.'

The other did not answer.

'If there were no forest, he would make a forest. And if he wished to hide a dead leaf, he would make a dead forest.'

There was still no reply, and the priest added still more mildly and quietly: 'And if a man had to hide a dead body, he would make a field of dead bodies to hide it in.'

Flambeau began to stamp forward with an intolerance of delay in time or space; but Father Brown went on as if he were continuing the last sentence: 'Sir Arthur St Clare, as I have already said, was a man who read his Bible. That was what was the matter with *him*. When will people understand that it is useless for a man to read his bible unless he also reads everybody else's Bible? A printer reads a Bible for misprints. A Mormon reads his Bible and finds polygamy; a Christian Scientist reads his and finds we have no arms and legs. St Clare was an old Anglo-Indian Protestant soldier. Now, just think what that might mean; and, for Heaven's sake, don't cant about it. It might mean a man physically formidable living under a tropic sun in an Oriental society, and soaking himself without sense or guidance in an Oriental book. Of course, he read the Old Testament rather than the New. Of course, he found in the Old Testament anything that he wanted – lust, tyranny, treason. Oh, I dare say he was honest, as you call it. But what is the good of a man being honest in his worship of dishonesty?

'In each of the hot and secret countries to which that man went he kept a harem, he tortured witnesses, he amassed shameful gold; but certainly he would have said with steady eyes that he did it to the glory of the Lord. My own theology is sufficiently expressed by asking which Lord? Anyhow, there is this about such evil, that it opens door after door in hell, and always into smaller and smaller chambers. This is the real case against crime, that a man does not become wilder and wilder, but only meaner and meaner. St Clare was soon suffocated by difficulties of bribery and blackmail; and needed more and more cash. And by the time of the battle of the Black River he had fallen from world to world to that place which Dante makes the lowest floor of the universe.'

'What do you mean?' asked his friend again.

'I mean *that*,' retorted the cleric, and suddenly pointed at a puddle sealed with ice that shone in the moon. 'Do you remember whom Dante put in the last circle of ice?'

'The traitors,' said Flambeau, and shuddered. As he looked round at the inhuman landscape of trees, with taunting and almost obscene outlines, he could almost fancy he was Dante, and the priest with the rivulet of a voice was, indeed, a Virgil leading him through a land of eternal sins.

The voice went on: 'Olivier, as you know, was quixotic, and would not permit a secret service and spies. The thing, however, was done, like many other things, behind his back. It was managed by my old friend Espado; he was the bright-clad fop, whose hook nose got him called the Vulture. Posing as a sort of philanthropist at the front, he felt his way through the English Army, and at last got his fingers on its one corrupt man – please God! – and that man at the top. St Clare was in foul need of money, and mountains of it. The discredited family doctor was threatening those extraordinary exposures that afterwards began and were broken off; tales of monstrous and prehistoric things in Park Lane; things done by an English Evangelical that smelt like human sacrifice and hordes of slaves. Money was wanted, too, for his daughter's dowry; for to him the fame of wealth was as sweet as wealth itself. He snapped the last thread, whispered the word to Brazil, and wealth poured in from the enemies of England. But another man had talked to Espado the Vulture as well as he. Somehow the dark, grim young major from Ulster had guessed the hideous truth; and when they walked slowly together down that road towards the bridge Murray was telling the general that he must resign instantly, or be court-martialled and shot. The general temporised with him till they came to the fringe of tropic trees by the bridge; and there by the singing river and the sunlit palms (for I can see the picture) the general drew his sabre and plunged it through the body of the major.'

The wintry road curved over a ridge in cutting frost, with cruel black shapes of bush and thicket; but Flambeau fancied that he saw beyond it faintly the edge of an aureole that was not starlight and moonlight, but some fire such as is made by men. He watched it as the tale drew to its close.

'St Clare was a hell-hound, but he was a hound of breed. Never, I'll swear, was he so lucid and so strong as when poor Murray lay a cold lump at his feet. Never in all his triumphs, as Captain Keith said truly, was the great man so great as he was in this last world-despised defeat. He looked coolly at his weapon to wipe off the blood; he saw the point he had planted between his victim's shoulders had broken off in the body. He saw quite calmly, as through a club windowpane, all that must follow. He saw that men must find the unaccountable corpse; must extract the unaccountable sword-point; must notice the unaccountable broken sword – or absence of sword. He had killed, but not silenced. But his imperious intellect rose against the facer – there was one way yet. He could make the corpse less unaccountable. He could create a hill of corpses to cover this one. In twenty minutes eight hundred English soldiers were marching down to their death.'

The warmer glow behind the black winter wood grew richer and brighter, and Flambeau strode on to reach it. Father Brown also quickened his stride; but he seemed merely absorbed in his tale.

'Such was the valour of that English thousand, and such the genius of their commander, that if they had at once attacked the hill, even their mad march might have met some luck. But the evil mind that played with them like pawns had other aims and reasons. They must remain in the marshes by the bridge at least till British corpses should be a common sight there. Then for the last grand scene: the silver-haired soldier-saint would give up his shattered sword to save further slaughter. Oh, it was well organised for an impromptu. But I think (I cannot prove), I think that it was while they stuck there in the bloody mire that someone doubted – and someone guessed.'

He was mute a moment, and then said: 'There is a voice from nowhere that tells me the man who guessed was the lover . . . the man to wed the old man's child.'

'But what about Olivier and the hanging?' asked Flambeau.

'Olivier, partly from chivalry, partly from policy, seldom encumbered his march with captives,' explained the narrator. 'He released everybody in most cases. He released everybody in this case.'

'Everybody but the general,' said the tall man.

'Everybody,' said the priest.

Flambeau knitted his black brows. 'I don't grasp it all yet,' he said.

'There is another picture, Flambeau,' said Brown in his more mystical undertone. 'I can't prove it; but I can do more – I can see it. There is a camp breaking up on the bare, torrid hills at morning, and Brazilian uniforms massed in blocks and columns to march. There is the red shirt and long black beard of Olivier, which blows as he stands, his broad-brimmed hat in his hand. He is saying farewell to the great enemy he is setting free – the simple, snow-headed English veteran, who thanks him in the name of his men. The English remnant stand behind at attention; beside them are stores and vehicles for the retreat. The drums roll; the Brazilians are moving; the English are still like statues. So they abide till the last hum and flash of the enemy have faded from the tropic horizon. Then they alter their postures all at once, like dead men coming to life; they turn their fifty faces upon the general – faces not to be forgotten.'

Flambeau gave a great jump. 'Ah,' he cried. 'You don't mean – '

'Yes,' said Father Brown in a deep, moving voice. 'It was an English hand that put the rope round St Clare's neck; I believe the hand that put the ring on his daughter's finger. They were English hands that dragged him up to the tree of shame; the hands of men that had adored him and followed him to victory. And they were English souls (God pardon and endure us all!) who stared at him swinging in that foreign sun on the green gallows of palm, and prayed in their hatred that he might drop off it into hell.'

As the two topped the ridge there burst on them the strong scarlet light of a red-curtained English inn. It stood sideways in the road, as if standing aside in the amplitude of hospitality. Its three doors stood open with invitation; and even where they stood they could hear the hum and laughter of humanity happy for a night.

'I need not tell you more,' said Father Brown. 'They tried him in the wilderness and destroyed him; and then, for the honour of England and of his daughter, they took an oath to seal up for ever the story of the traitor's purse and the assassin's sword blade. Perhaps – Heaven help them – they tried to forget it. Let us try to forget it, anyhow; here is our inn.'

'With all my heart,' said Flambeau, and was just striding into the bright, noisy bar when he stepped back and almost fell on the road.

'Look there, in the devil's name!' he cried, and pointed rigidly at the square wooden sign that overhung the road. It showed dimly the crude shape of a sabre hilt and a shortened blade; and was inscribed in false archaic lettering, 'The Sign of the Broken Sword.'

'Were you not prepared?' asked Father Brown gently. 'He is the god of this country; half the inns and parks and streets are named after him and his story.'

'I thought we had done with the leper,' cried Flambeau, and spat on the road.

'You will never have done with him in England,' said the priest, looking down, 'while brass is strong and stone abides. His marble statues will erect the souls of proud, innocent boys for centuries, his village tomb will smell of loyalty as of lilies. Millions who never knew him shall love him like a father – this man whom the last few that knew him dealt with like dung. He shall be a saint; and the truth shall never be told of him, because I have made up my mind at last. There is so much good and evil in breaking secrets, that I put my conduct to a test. All these newspapers will perish; the anti-Brazil boom is already over; Olivier is already honoured everywhere. But I told myself that if anywhere, by name, in metal or marble that will endure like the pyramids, Colonel Clancy, or Captain Keith, or President Olivier, or any innocent man was wrongly blamed, then I would speak. If it were only that St Clare was wrongly praised, I would be silent. And I will.'

They plunged into the red-curtained tavern, which was not only cosy, but even luxurious inside. On a table stood a silver model of the tomb of St Clare, the silver head bowed, the silver sword broken. On the walls were coloured photographs of the same scene, and of the system of wagonettes that took tourists to see it. They sat down on the comfortable padded benches.

'Come, it's cold,' cried Father Brown; 'let's have some wine or beer.'

'Or brandy,' said Flambeau.

The Paradise of Thieves

The great Muscari, most original of the young Tuscan poets, walked swiftly into his favourite restaurant, which overlooked the Mediterranean, was covered by an awning and fenced by little lemon and orange trees. Waiters in white aprons were already laying out on white tables the insignia of an early and elegant lunch; and this seemed to increase a satisfaction that already touched the top of swagger. Muscari had an eagle nose like Dante; his hair and neckerchief were dark and flowing; he carried a black cloak, and might almost have carried a black mask, so much did he bear with him a sort of Venetian melodrama. He acted as if a troubadour had still a definite social office, like a bishop. He went as near as his century permitted to walking the world literally like Don Juan, with rapier and guitar.

For he never travelled without a case of swords, with which he had fought many brilliant duels, or without a corresponding case for his mandolin, with which he had actually serenaded Miss Ethel Harrogate, the highly-conventional daughter of a Yorkshire banker on a holiday. Yet he was neither a charlatan nor a child; but a hot, logical Latin who liked a certain thing and was it. His poetry was as straightforward as anyone else's prose. He desired fame or wine or the beauty of women with a torrid directness inconceivable among the cloudy ideals or cloudy compromises of the north; to vaguer races his intensity smelt of danger or even crime. Like fire or the sea, he was too simple to be trusted.

The banker and his beautiful English daughter

were staying at the hotel attached to Muscari's restaurant; that was why it was his favourite restaurant. A glance flashed round the room told him at once, however, that the English party had not descended. The restaurant was glittering, but still comparatively empty. Two priests were talking at a table in a corner, but Muscari (an ardent Catholic) took no more notice of them than of a couple of crows. But from a yet farther seat, partly concealed behind a dwarf tree golden with oranges, there rose and advanced towards the poet a person whose costume was the most aggressively opposite to his own.

This figure was clad in tweeds of a piebald check, with a pink tie, a sharp collar and protuberant yellow boots. He contrived, in the true tradition of 'Arry at Margate, to look at once startling and commonplace. But as the Cockney apparition drew nearer, Muscari was astounded to observe that the head was distinctly different from the body. It was an Italian head: fuzzy, swarthy and very vivacious, that rose abruptly out of the standing collar like cardboard and the comic pink tie. In fact it was a head he knew. He recognised it, above all the dire erection of English holiday array, as the face of an old but forgotten friend named Ezza. This youth had been a prodigy at college, and European fame was promised him when he was barely fifteen; but when he appeared in the world he failed, first publicly as a dramatist and a demagogue, and then privately for years on end as an actor, a traveller, a commission agent or a journalist. Muscari had known him last behind the footlights; he was but too well attuned to the excitements of that profession, and it was believed that some moral calamity had swallowed him up.

'Ezza!' cried the poet, rising and shaking hands in a pleasant astonishment. 'Well! I've seen you in many costumes in the green room; but I never expected to see you dressed up as an Englishman.'

'This,' answered Ezza gravely: 'is not the costume of an Englishman, but of the Italian of the future.'

'In that case,' remarked Muscari, 'I confess I prefer the Italian of the past.'

'That is your old mistake, Muscari,' said the man in tweeds, shaking his head; 'and the mistake of Italy. In the sixteenth century we Tuscans made the morning: we had the newest steel, the newest carving, the newest chemistry. Why should we not now have the newest factories, the newest motors, the newest finance – and the newest clothes?'

'Because they are not worth having,' answered Muscari. 'You cannot make Italians really progressive; they are too intelligent. Men who see the short cut to good living will never go by the new elaborate roads.'

'Well, to me Marconi, or D'Annunzio, is the star of Italy,' said the other. 'That is why I have become a Futurist – and a courier.'

'A courier!' cried Muscari, laughing. 'Is that the last of your list of trades? And whom are you conducting?'

'Oh, a man of the name of Harrogate, and his family, I believe.'

'Not the banker in this hotel?' enquired the poet, with some eagerness.

'That's the man,' answered the courier.

'Does it pay well?' asked the troubadour innocently.

'It will pay me,' said Ezza, with a very enigmatic smile. 'But I am a rather curious sort of courier.' Then, as if changing the subject, he said abruptly: 'He has a daughter – and a son.'

'The daughter is divine,' affirmed Muscari, 'the father and son are, I suppose, human. But granted his harmless qualities, doesn't that banker strike you as a splendid instance of my argument? Harrogate has millions in his safes, and I have – the hole in my pocket. But you daren't say – you can't say – that he's cleverer than I, or bolder than I, or even more energetic. He's not clever; he's got eyes like blue buttons; he's not energetic, he moves from chair to chair like a paralytic. He's a conscientious, kindly old blockhead; but he's got money simply because he collects money, as a boy collects stamps. You're too strong-minded for business, Ezza. You won't get on. To be clever enough to get all that money, one must be stupid enough to want it.'

'I'm stupid enough for that,' said Ezza gloomily. 'But I should suggest a suspension of your critique of the banker, for here he comes.'

Mr Harrogate, the great financier, did indeed enter the room, but nobody looked at him. He was a massive elderly man with a boiled blue eye and faded grey-sandy moustaches; but for his heavy stoop he might have been a colonel. He carried several unopened letters in his hand. His son Frank was a really fine lad, curly-haired, sunburnt and strenuous; but nobody looked at him either. All eyes, as usual, were riveted, for the moment at least, upon Ethel Harrogate, whose golden Greek head and colour of the dawn seemed set purposely above that sapphire sea, like a goddess's. The poet Muscari drew a deep breath as if he were drinking something, as indeed he was. He was drinking the Classic; which his fathers made. Ezza studied her with a gaze equally intense and far more baffling.

Miss Harrogate was specially radiant and ready for conversation on this occasion; and her family had fallen into the easier Continental habit, allowing the stranger Muscari and even the courier Ezza to share their table and their talk. In Ethel Harrogate conventionality crowned itself with a perfection and splendour of its own. Proud of her father's prosperity, fond of her fashionable pleasures, a fond daughter but an arrant flirt, she was all these things with a sort of golden good nature that made her very pride pleasing and her worldly respectability a fresh and hearty thing.

They were in an eddy of excitement about some alleged peril in the mountain path they were to attempt that week. The danger was not from rock and avalanche, but from something yet more romantic. Ethel had been earnestly assured that brigands, the true cut-throats of the modern legend, still haunted that ridge and held that pass of the Apennines.

'They say,' she cried, with the awful relish of a schoolgirl, 'that all that country isn't ruled by the King of Italy, but by the King of Thieves. Who is the King of Thieves?'

'A great man,' replied Muscari, 'worthy to rank with your own Robin Hood, signorina. Montano, the King of Thieves, was first heard of in the mountains some ten years ago, when people said brigands were extinct. But his wild authority spread with the swiftness of a silent revolution. Men found his fierce proclamations nailed in every mountain village; his sentinels, gun in hand, in every mountain ravine. Six times the Italian Government tried to dislodge him, and was defeated in six pitched battles as if by Napoleon.'

'Now that sort of thing,' observed the banker weightily, 'would never be allowed in England;

perhaps, after all, we had better choose another route. But the courier thought it perfectly safe.'

'It is perfectly safe,' said the courier contemptuously, 'I have been over it twenty times. There may have been some old jailbird called a King in the time of our grandmothers; but he belongs to history if not to fable. Brigandage is utterly stamped out.'

'It can never be utterly stamped out,' Muscari answered; 'because armed revolt is a reaction natural to southerners. Our peasants are like their mountains, rich in grace and green gaiety, but with the fires beneath. There is a point of human despair where the northern poor take to drink – and our own poor take to daggers.'

'A poet is privileged,' replied Ezza, with a sneer. 'If Signor Muscari were English he would still be looking for highwaymen in Wandsworth. Believe me, there is no more danger of being captured in Italy than of being scalped in Boston.'

'Then you propose to attempt it?' asked Mr Harrogate, frowning.

'Oh, it sounds rather dreadful,' cried the girl, turning her glorious eyes on Muscari. 'Do you really think the pass is dangerous?'

Muscari threw back his black mane. 'I know it is dangerous,' he said. 'I am crossing it tomorrow.'

The young Harrogate was left behind for a moment emptying a glass of white wine and lighting a cigarette, as the beauty retired with the banker, the courier and the poet, distributing peals of silvery satire. At about the same instant the two priests in the corner rose; the taller, a white-haired Italian, taking his leave. The shorter priest turned and walked towards the banker's son, and the latter was astonished to realise that though a Roman priest the man was an Englishman. He vaguely remembered meeting him at the social crushes of some of his Catholic friends. But the man spoke before his memories could collect themselves.

'Mr Frank Harrogate, I think,' he said. 'I have had an introduction, but I do not mean to presume on it. The odd thing I have to say will come far better from a stranger. Mr Harrogate, I say one word and go: take care of your sister in her great sorrow.'

Even for Frank's truly fraternal indifference the radiance and derision of his sister still seemed to sparkle and ring; he could hear her laughter still from the garden of the hotel, and he stared at his sombre adviser in puzzledom.

'Do you mean the brigands?' he asked; and then, remembering a vague fear of his own, 'or can you be thinking of Muscari?'

'One is never thinking of the real sorrow,' said the strange priest. 'One can only be kind when it comes.'

And he passed promptly from the room, leaving the other almost with his mouth open.

A day or two afterwards a coach containing the company was really crawling and staggering up the spurs of the menacing mountain range. Between Ezza's cheery denial of the danger and Muscari's boisterous defiance of it, the financial family were firm in their original purpose; and Muscari made his mountain journey coincide with theirs. A more surprising feature was the appearance at the coast-town station of the little priest of the restaurant; he alleged merely that business led him also to cross the mountains of the midland. But young Harrogate could not but connect his presence with the mystical fears and warnings of yesterday.

The coach was a kind of commodious wagonette, invented by the modernist talent of the courier, who dominated the expedition with his scientific activity and breezy wit. The theory of danger from thieves was banished from thought and speech; though so far conceded in formal act that some slight protection was employed. The courier and the young banker carried loaded revolvers, and Muscari (with much boyish gratification) buckled on a kind of cutlass under his black cloak.

He had planted his person at a flying leap next to the lovely Englishwoman; on the other side of her sat the priest, whose name was Brown and who was fortunately a silent individual; the courier and the father and son were on the *banc* behind. Muscari was in towering spirits, seriously believing in the peril, and his talk to Ethel might well have made her think him a maniac. But there was something in the crazy and gorgeous ascent, amid crags like peaks loaded with woods like orchards, that dragged her spirit up alone with his into purple preposterous heavens with wheeling suns. The white road climbed like a white cat; it spanned sunless chasms like a tightrope; it was flung round far-off headlands like a lasso.

And yet, however high they went, the desert still blossomed like the rose. The fields were burnished in sun and wind with the colour of kingfisher and parrot and hummingbird; the hues of a hundred flowering flowers. There are no lovelier meadows and woodlands than the English; no nobler crests or chasms than those of Snowdon and Glencoe. But Ethel Harrogate had never before seen the southern parks tilted on the splintered northern peaks; the gorge of Glencoe laden with the fruits of Kent. There was nothing here of that chill and desolation that in Britain one associates with high and wild scenery. It was rather like a mosaic palace, rent with earthquakes; or like a Dutch tulip garden blown to the stars with dynamite.

'It's like Kew Gardens on Beachy Head,' said Ethel.

'It is our secret,' answered he, 'the secret of the volcano; that is also the secret of the revolution – that a thing can be violent and yet fruitful.'

'You are rather violent yourself,' and she smiled at him.

'And yet rather fruitless,' he admitted; 'if I die tonight I die unmarried and a fool.'

'It is not my fault if you have come,' she said after a difficult silence.

'It is never your fault,' answered Muscari; 'it was not your fault that Troy fell.'

As he spoke they came under overwhelming cliffs that spread almost like wings above a corner of peculiar peril. Shocked by the big shadow on the narrow ledge, the horses stirred doubtfully. The driver leapt to the earth to hold their heads, and they became ungovernable. One horse reared up to his full height – the titanic and terrifying height of a horse when he becomes a biped. It was just enough to alter the equilibrium; the whole coach heeled over like a ship and crashed through the fringe of bushes over the cliff. Muscari threw an arm round Ethel, who clung to him, and shouted aloud. It was for such moments that he lived.

At the moment when the gorgeous mountain walls went round the poet's head like a purple windmill a thing happened which was superficially even more startling. The elderly and lethargic banker sprang erect in the coach and leapt over the precipice before the tilted vehicle could take him there. In the first flash it looked as wild as suicide; but in the second it was as sensible as a safe investment. The Yorkshireman had evidently more promptitude, as well as more sagacity, than Muscari had given him credit for; for he landed in a lap of land which might have been specially padded with turf and clover to receive him. As it happened, indeed, the whole company were equally lucky, if less dignified in their form of ejection. Immediately under this abrupt turn of the road was a grassy and flowery hollow like a sunken meadow; a sort of green velvet pocket in the long, green, trailing garments of the hills. Into this they were all tipped or tumbled with little damage, save that their smallest baggage and even the contents of their pockets were scattered in the grass around them. The wrecked coach still hung above, entangled in the tough hedge, and the horses plunged painfully down the slope. The first to sit up was the little priest, who scratched his head with a face of foolish wonder. Frank Harrogate heard him say to himself: 'Now why on earth have we fallen just here?'

He blinked at the litter around him, and recovered his own very clumsy umbrella. Beyond it lay the broad sombrero fallen from the head of Muscari, and beside it a sealed business letter which, after a glance at the address, he returned to the elder Harrogate. On the other side of him the grass partly hid Miss Ethel's sunshade, and just beyond it lay a curious little glass bottle hardly two inches long. The priest picked it up; in a quick, unobtrusive manner he uncorked and sniffed it, and his heavy face turned the colour of clay.

'Heaven deliver us!' he muttered; 'it can't be hers! Has her sorrow come on her already?' He slipped it into his own waistcoat pocket. 'I think I'm justified,' he said, 'till I know a little more.'

He gazed painfully at the girl, at that moment being raised out of the flowers by Muscari, who was saying: 'We have fallen into heaven; it is a sign. Mortals climb up and they fall down; but it is only gods and goddesses who can fall upwards.'

And indeed she rose out of the sea of colours so beautiful and happy a vision that the priest felt his suspicion shaken and shifted. 'After all,' he thought, 'perhaps the poison isn't hers; perhaps it's one of Muscari's melodramatic tricks.'

Muscari set the lady lightly on her feet, made her an absurdly theatrical bow, and then, drawing his cutlass, hacked hard at the taut reins of the horses, so that they scrambled to their feet and stood in the grass trembling. When he had done so, a most remarkable thing occurred. A very quiet man, very poorly dressed and extremely sunburnt, came out of the bushes and took hold of the horses' heads. He had a queer-shaped knife, very broad and crooked, buckled on his belt; there was nothing else remarkable about him, except his sudden and silent appearance. The poet asked him who he was, and he did not answer.

Looking around him at the confused and startled group in the hollow, Muscari then perceived that another tanned and tattered man, with a short gun under his arm, was looking at them from the ledge just below, leaning his elbows on the edge of the turf. Then he looked up at the road from which they had fallen and saw, looking down on them, the muzzles of four other carbines and four other brown faces with bright but quite motionless eyes.

'The brigands!' cried Muscari, with a kind of

monstrous gaiety. 'This was a trap. Ezza, if you will oblige me by shooting the coachman first, we can cut our way out yet. There are only six of them.'

'The coachman,' said Ezza, who was standing grimly with his hands in his pockets, 'happens to be a servant of Mr Harrogate's.'

'Then shoot him all the more,' cried the poet impatiently; 'he was bribed to upset his master. Then put the lady in the middle, and we will break the line up there – with a rush.'

And, wading in wild grass and flowers, he advanced fearlessly on the four carbines; but finding that no one followed except young Harrogate, he turned, brandishing his cutlass to wave the others on. He beheld the courier still standing slightly astride in the centre of the grassy ring, his hands in his pockets; and his lean, ironical Italian face seemed to grow longer and longer in the evening light.

'You thought, Muscari, I was the failure among our schoolfellows,' he said, 'and you thought you were the success. But I have succeeded more than you and fill a bigger place in history. I have been acting epics while you have been writing them.'

'Come on, I tell you!' thundered Muscari from above. 'Will you stand there talking nonsense about yourself with a woman to save and three strong men to help you? What do you call yourself?'

'I call myself Montano,' cried the strange courier in a voice equally loud and full. 'I am the King of Thieves, and I welcome you all to my summer palace.'

And even as he spoke five more silent men with weapons ready came out of the bushes, and looked towards him for their orders. One of them held a large paper in his hand.

'This pretty little nest where we are all picnicking,' went on the courier-brigand, with the same easy yet sinister smile, 'is, together with some caves underneath it, known by the name of the Paradise of Thieves. It is my principal stronghold on these hills; for (as you have doubtless noticed) the eyrie is invisible both from the road above and from the valley below. It is something better than impregnable; it is unnoticeable. Here I mostly live, and here I shall certainly die, if the gendarmes ever track me here. I am not the kind of criminal that "reserves his defence", but the better kind that reserves his last bullet.'

All were staring at him thunderstruck and still, except Father Brown, who heaved a huge sigh as of relief and fingered the little phial in his pocket. 'Thank God!' he muttered; 'that's much more probable. The poison belongs to this robber-chief, of course. He carries it so that he may never be captured, like Cato.'

The King of Thieves was, however, continuing his address with the same kind of dangerous politeness. 'It only remains for me,' he said, 'to explain to my guests the social conditions upon which I have the pleasure of entertaining them. I need not expound the quaint old ritual of ransom, which it is incumbent upon me to keep up; and even this only applies to a part of the company. The Reverend Father Brown and the celebrated Signor Muscari I shall release tomorrow at dawn and escort to my outposts. Poets and priests, if you will pardon my simplicity of speech, never have any money. And so (since it is impossible to get anything out of them), let us seize the opportunity to show our admiration for classic literature and our reverence for Holy Church.'

He paused with an unpleasing smile; and Father Brown blinked repeatedly at him, and seemed suddenly to be listening with great attention. The brigand captain took the large paper from the attendant brigand and, glancing it over, continued: 'My other intentions are clearly set forth in this public document, which I will hand round in a moment; and which after that will be posted on a tree by every village in the valley, and every cross-road in the hills. I will not weary you with the verbalism, since you will be able to check it; the substance of my proclamation is this: I announce first that I have captured the English millionaire, the colossus of finance, Mr Samuel Harrogate. I next announce that I have found on his person notes and bonds for two thousand pounds, which he has given up to me. Now since it would be really immoral to announce such a thing to a credulous public if it had not occurred, I suggest it should occur without further delay. I suggest that Mr Harrogate senior should now give me the two thousand pounds in his pocket.'

The banker looked at him under lowering brows, red-faced and sulky, but seemingly cowed. That leap from the falling carriage seemed to have used up his last virility. He had held back in a hangdog style when his son and Muscari had made a bold movement to break out of the brigand trap. And now his red and trembling hand went reluctantly to his breast-pocket, and passed a bundle of papers and envelopes to the brigand.

'Excellent!' cried that outlaw gaily; 'so far we are all cosy. I resume the points of my proclamation, so soon to be published to all Italy. The third item is that of ransom. I am asking from the friends of the Harrogate family a ransom of three thousand pounds, which I am sure is almost insulting to that family in its moderate estimate of their importance. Who would not pay triple this sum for another day's association with such a domestic circle? I will not conceal from you that the document ends with certain legal phrases about the unpleasant things that may happen if the money is not paid; but meanwhile ladies and gentlemen, let me assure you that I am comfortably off here for accommodation, wine and cigars, and bid you for the present a sportsman-like welcome to the luxuries of the Paradise of Thieves.'

All the time that he had been speaking, the dubious-looking men with carbines and dirty slouch hats had been gathering silently in such preponderating numbers that even Muscari was compelled to recognise his sally with the sword as hopeless. He glanced around him; but the girl had already gone over to soothe and comfort her father, for her natural affection for his person was as strong or stronger than her somewhat snobbish pride in his success. Muscari, with the illogicality of a lover, admired this filial devotion, and yet was irritated by it. He slapped his sword back in the scabbard and went and flung himself somewhat sulkily on one of the green banks. The priest sat down within a yard or two, and Muscari turned his aquiline eye and nose on him in an instantaneous irritation.

'Well,' said the poet tartly, 'do people still think me too romantic? Are there, I wonder, any brigands left in the mountains?'

'There may be,' said Father Brown agnostically.

'What do you mean?' asked the other sharply.

'I mean I am puzzled,' replied the priest. 'I am

puzzled about Ezza or Montano, or whatever his name is. He seems to me much more inexplicable as a brigand even than he was as a courier.'

'But in what way?' persisted his companion. 'Santa Maria! I should have thought the brigand was plain enough.'

'I find three curious difficulties,' said the priest in a quiet voice. 'I should like to have your opinion on them. First of all I must tell you I was lunching in that restaurant at the seaside. As four of you left the room, you and Miss Harrogate went ahead, talking and laughing; the banker and the courier came behind, speaking sparely and rather low. But I could not help hearing Ezza say these words – "Well, let her have a little fun; you know the blow may smash her any minute." Mr Harrogate answered nothing; so the words must have had some meaning. On the impulse of the moment I warned her brother that she might be in peril; I said nothing of its nature, for I did not know. But if it meant this capture in the hills, the thing is nonsense. Why should the brigand-courier warn his patron, even by a hint, when it was his whole purpose to lure him into the mountain-mousetrap? It could not have meant that. But if not, what is this other disaster, known both to courier and banker, which hangs over Miss Harrogate's head?'

'Disaster to Miss Harrogate!' ejaculated the poet, sitting up with some ferocity. 'Explain yourself; go on.'

'All my riddles, however, revolve round our bandit chief,' resumed the priest reflectively. 'And here is the second of them. Why did he put so prominently in his demand for ransom the fact that he had taken two thousand pounds from his victim on the spot? It had no faintest tendency to evoke the ransom. Quite the other way, in fact. Harrogate's friends would be far likelier to fear for his fate if they thought the thieves were poor and desperate. Yet the spoliation on the spot was emphasised and even put first in the demand. Why should Ezza Montano want so specially to tell all Europe that he had picked the pocket before he levied the blackmail?'

'I cannot imagine,' said Muscari, rubbing up his black hair for once with an unaffected gesture. 'You may think you enlighten me, but you are leading me deeper in the dark. What may be the third objection to the King of the Thieves?'

'The third objection,' said Father Brown, still in meditation, 'is this bank we are sitting on. Why does our brigand-courier call this his chief fortress and the Paradise of Thieves? It is certainly a soft spot to fall on and a sweet spot to look at. It is also quite true, as he says, that it is invisible from valley and peak, and is therefore a hiding-place. But it is not a fortress. It never could be a fortress. I think it would be the worst fortress in the world. For it is actually commanded from above by the common highroad across the mountains – the very place where the police would most probably pass. Why, five shabby short guns held us helpless here about half an hour ago. The quarter of a company of any kind of soldiers could have blown us over the precipice. Whatever is the meaning of this odd little nook of grass and flowers, it is not an entrenched position. It is something else; it has some other strange sort of importance: some value that I do not understand. It is more like an accidental theatre or a natural green-room; it is like the scene for some romantic comedy; it is like . . . '

As the little priest's words lengthened and lost

themselves in a dull and dreamy sincerity, Muscari, whose animal senses were alert and impatient, heard a new noise in the mountains. Even for him the sound was as yet very small and faint; but he could have sworn the evening breeze bore with it something like the pulsation of horses' hoofs and a distant hallooing.

At the same moment, and long before the vibration had touched the less-experienced English ears, Montano the brigand ran up the bank above them and stood in the broken hedge, steadying himself against a tree and peering down the road. He was a strange figure as he stood there, for he had assumed a flapped fantastic hat and swinging baldric and cutlass in his capacity of bandit king, but the bright prosaic tweed of the courier showed through in patches all over him.

The next moment he turned his olive, sneering face and made a movement with his hand. The brigands scattered at the signal, not in confusion, but in what was evidently a kind of guerilla discipline. Instead of occupying the road along the ridge, they sprinkled themselves along the side of it behind the trees and the hedge, as if watching unseen for an enemy. The noise beyond grew stronger, beginning to shake the mountain road, and a voice could be clearly heard calling out orders. The brigands swayed and huddled, cursing and whispering, and the evening air was full of little metallic noises as they cocked their pistols, or loosened their knives, or trailed their scabbards over the stones. Then the noises from both quarters seemed to meet on the road above; branches broke, horses neighed, men cried out.

'A rescue!' cried Muscari, springing to his feet and waving his hat; 'the gendarmes are on them! Now for freedom and a blow for it! Now to be rebels against robbers! Come, don't let us leave everything to the police; that is so dreadfully modern. Fall on the rear of these ruffians. The gendarmes are rescuing us; come, friends, let us rescue the gendarmes!'

And throwing his hat over the trees, he drew his cutlass once more and began to escalade the slope up to the road. Frank Harrogate jumped up and ran across to help him, revolver in hand, but was astounded to hear himself imperatively recalled by the raucous voice of his father, who seemed to be in great agitation.

'I won't have it,' said the banker in a choking voice; 'I command you not to interfere.'

'But, father,' said Frank very warmly, 'an Italian gentleman has led the way. You wouldn't have it said that the English hung back.'

'It is useless,' said the older man, who was trembling violently, 'it is useless. We must submit to our lot.'

Father Brown looked at the banker; then he put his hand instinctively as if on his heart, but really on the little bottle of poison; and a great light came into his face like the light of the revelation of death.

Muscari meanwhile, without waiting for support, had crested the bank up to the road, and struck the brigand king heavily on the shoulder, causing him to stagger and swing round, Montano also had his cutlass unsheathed, and Muscari, without further speech, sent a slash at his head which he was compelled to catch and parry. But even as the two short blades crossed and clashed the King of Thieves deliberately dropped his point and laughed.

'What's the good, old man?' he said in spirited Italian slang; 'this damned farce will soon be over.'

'What do you mean, you shuffler?' panted the

fire-eating poet. 'Is your courage a sham as well as your honesty?'

'Everything about me is a sham,' responded the ex-courier in complete good-humour. 'I am an actor; and if I ever had a private character, I have forgotten it. I am no more a genuine brigand than I am a genuine courier. I am only a bundle of masks, and you can't fight a duel with that.' And he laughed with boyish pleasure and fell into his old straddling attitude, with his back to the skirmish up the road.

Darkness was deepening under the mountain walls, and it was not easy to discern much of the progress of the struggle, save that tall men were pushing their horses' muzzles through a clinging crowd of brigands, who seemed more inclined to harass and hustle the invaders than to kill them. It was more like a town crowd preventing the passage of the police than anything the poet had ever pictured as the last stand of doomed and outlawed men of blood. Just as he was rolling his eyes in bewilderment he felt a touch on his elbow, and found the odd little priest standing there like a small Noah with a large hat, and requesting the favour of a word or two.

'Signor Muscari,' said the cleric, 'in this queer crisis personalities may be pardoned. I may tell you without offence of a way in which you will do more good than by helping the gendarmes, who are bound to break through in any case. You will permit me the impertinent intimacy; but do you care about that girl? Care enough to marry her and make her a good husband, I mean?'

'Yes,' said the poet quite simply.

'Does she care about you?'

'I think so,' was the equally grave reply.

'Then go over there and offer yourself,' said the priest: 'offer her everything you can; offer her heaven and earth if you've got them. The time is short.'

'Why?' asked the astonished man of letters.

'Because,' said Father Brown, 'her Doom is coming up the road.'

'Nothing is coming up the road,' argued Muscari, 'except the rescue.'

'Well, you go over there,' said his adviser, 'and be ready to rescue her from the rescue.'

Almost as he spoke the hedges were broken all along the ridge by a rush of the escaping brigands. They dived into bushes and thick grass like defeated men pursued; and the great cocked hats of the mounted gendarmerie were seen passing along above the broken hedge. Another order was given; there was a noise of dismounting, and a tall officer with a cocked hat, a grey imperial, and a paper in his hand appeared in the gap that was the gate of the Paradise of Thieves. There was a momentary silence, broken in an extraordinary way by the banker, who cried out in a hoarse and strangled voice: 'Robbed! I've been robbed!'

'Why, that was hours ago,' cried his son in astonishment: 'when you were robbed of two thousand pounds.'

'Not of two thousand pounds,' said the financier, with an abrupt and terrible composure, 'only of a small bottle.'

The policeman with the grey imperial was striding across the green hollow. Encountering the King of the Thieves in his path, he clapped him on the shoulder with something between a caress and a buffet and gave him a push that sent him staggering away. 'You'll get into trouble, too,' he said, 'if you play these tricks.'

Again to Muscari's artistic eye it seemed scarcely like the capture of a great outlaw at bay. Passing on, the policeman halted before the Harrogate group and said: 'Samuel Harrogate, I arrest you in the name of the law for embezzlement of the funds of the Hull and Huddersfield Bank.'

The great banker nodded with an odd air of business assent, seemed to reflect a moment, and before they could interpose took a half turn and a step that brought him to the edge of the outer mountain wall. Then, flinging up his hands, he leapt exactly as he leapt out of the coach. But this time he did not fall into a little meadow just beneath; he fell a thousand feet below, to become a wreck of bones in the valley.

The anger of the Italian policeman, which he expressed volubly to Father Brown, was largely mixed with admiration. 'It was like him to escape us at last,' he said. '*He* was a great brigand if you like. This last trick of his I believe to be absolutely unprecedented. He fled with the company's money to Italy, and actually got himself captured by sham brigands in his own pay, so as to explain both the disappearance of the money and the disappearance of himself. That demand for ransom was really taken seriously by most of the police. But for years he's been doing things as good as that, quite as good as that. He will be a serious loss to his family.'

Muscari was leading away the unhappy daughter, who held hard to him, as she did for many a year after. But even in that tragic wreck he could not help having a smile and a hand of half-mocking friendship for the indefensible Ezza Montano. 'And where are you going next?' he asked him over his shoulder.

'Birmingham,' answered the actor, puffing a

cigarette. 'Didn't I tell you I was a Futurist? I really do believe in those things if I believe in anything. Change, bustle, and new things every morning. I am going to Manchester, Liverpool, Leeds, Hull, Huddersfield, Glasgow, Chicago – in short, to enlightened, energetic, civilised society!'

'In short,' said Muscari, 'to the real Paradise of Thieves.'

The Mistake of the Machine

Flambeau and his friend the priest were sitting in the Temple Gardens about sunset; and their neighbourhood or some such accidental influence had turned their talk to matters of legal process. From the problem of the licence in cross-examination, their talk strayed to Roman and mediaeval torture, to the examining magistrate in France and the Third Degree in America.

'I've been reading,' said Flambeau, 'of this new psychometric method they talk about so much, especially in America. You know what I mean; they put a pulsometer on a man's wrist and judge by how his heart goes at the pronunciation of certain words. What do you think of it?'

'I think it very interesting,' replied Father Brown; 'it reminds me of that interesting idea in the Dark Ages that blood would flow from a corpse if the murderer touched it.'

'Do you really mean,' demanded his friend, 'that you think the two methods equally valuable?'

'I think them equally valueless,' replied Brown. 'Blood flows, fast or slow, in dead folk or living, for so many more million reasons than we can ever know. Blood will have to flow very funnily; blood will have to flow up the Matterhorn, before I will take it as a sign that I am to shed it.'

'The method,' remarked the other, 'has been guaranteed by some of the greatest American men of science.'

'What sentimentalists men of science are!' exclaimed Father Brown, 'and how much more sentimental must American men of science be! Who but a Yankee would think of proving anything from heart-throbs? Why, they must be as sentimental as a man who thinks a woman is in love with him if she blushes. That's a test from the circulation of the blood, discovered by the immortal Harvey; and a jolly rotten test, too.'

'But surely,' insisted Flambeau, 'it might point pretty straight at something or other.'

'There's a disadvantage in a stick pointing straight,' answered the other. 'What is it? Why, the other end of the stick always points the opposite way. It depends whether you get hold of the stick by the right end. I saw the thing done once and I've never believed in it since.' And he proceeded to tell the story of his disillusionment.

It happened nearly twenty years before, when he was chaplain to his co-religionists in a prison in Chicago – where the Irish population displayed a capacity both for crime and penitence which kept him tolerably busy. The official second-in-command under the Governor was an ex-detective named Greywood Usher, a cadaverous, careful-spoken Yankee philosopher, occasionally varying a very rigid visage with an odd apologetic grimace. He liked Father Brown in a slightly patronising way; and Father Brown liked him, though he heartily disliked his theories. His theories were extremely complicated and were held with extreme simplicity.

One evening he had sent for the priest, who, according to his custom, took a seat in silence at a table piled and littered with papers, and waited. The official selected from the papers a scrap of newspaper cutting, which he handed across to the cleric, who read it gravely. It appeared to be an extract from one of the pinkest of American Society papers, and ran as follows:

> Society's brightest widower is once more on the Freak Dinner stunt. All our exclusive citizens will recall the Perambulator Parade Dinner, in which Last-Trick Todd, at his palatial home at Pilgrim's Pond, caused so many of our prominent *débutantes* to look even younger than their years. Equally elegant and more miscellaneous and large-hearted in social outlook was Last-Trick's show the year previous, the popular Cannibal Crush Lunch, at which the confections handed round were sarcastically moulded in the forms of human arms and legs, and during which more than one of our gayest mental gymnasts was heard offering to eat his partner. The witticism which will inspire this evening is as yet in Mr Todd's pretty reticent intellect, or locked in the jewelled bosoms of our city's gayest leaders; but there is talk of a pretty parody of the simple manners and customs at the other end of Society's scale. This would be all the more telling, as hospitable Todd is entertaining in Lord Falconroy, the famous traveller, a true-blooded aristocrat fresh from England's oak-groves. Lord Falconroy's travels began before his ancient feudal title was resurrected; he was in the Republic in his youth, and fashion murmurs a sly reason for his return. Miss Etta Todd is one of our deep-souled New Yorkers, and comes into an income of nearly twelve hundred million dollars.

'Well,' asked Usher, 'does that interest you?'

'Why, words rather fail me,' answered Father Brown. 'I cannot think at this moment of anything in this world that would interest me less. And, unless the just anger of the Republic is at last going to electrocute journalists for writing like that, I don't quite see why it should interest you either.'

'Ah!' said Mr Usher dryly, and handing across another scrap of newspaper. 'Well, does *that* interest you?'

The Paragraph was headed 'Savage Murder of a Warder. Convict Escapes', and ran:

> Just before dawn this morning a shout for help was heard in the Convict Settlement at Sequah in this State. The authorities, hurrying in the direction of the cry, found the corpse of the warder who patrols the top of the north wall of the prison, the steepest and most difficult exit, for which one man has always been found sufficient. The unfortunate officer had, however, been hurled from the high wall, his brains beaten out as with a club, and his gun was missing. Further enquiries showed that one of the cells was empty; it had been occupied by a rather sullen ruffian giving his name as Oscar Rian. He was only temporarily detained for some comparatively trivial assault; but he gave everyone the impression of a man with a black past and a dangerous future. Finally, when daylight had fully revealed the scene of murder, it was found that he had written on the wall above the body a fragmentary sentence, apparently with a finger dipped in blood: 'This was self-defence and he had the gun. I meant no harm to him or any man but one. I am

keeping the bullet for Pilgrim's Pond – O. R.'
A man must have used most fiendish treachery or most savage and amazing bodily daring to have stormed such a wall in spite of an armed man.

'Well, the literary style is somewhat improved,' admitted the priest cheerfully, 'but still I don't see what I can do for you. I should cut a poor figure, with my short legs, running about this State after an athletic assassin of that sort. I doubt whether anybody could find him. The convict settlement at Sequah is thirty miles from here; the country between is wild and tangled enough, and the country beyond, where he will surely have the sense to go, is a perfect no-man's land tumbling away to the prairies. He may be in any hole or up any tree.'

'He isn't in any hole,' said the governor; 'he isn't up any tree.'

'Why, how do you know?' asked Father Brown, blinking.

'Would you like to speak to him?' enquired Usher.

Father Brown opened his innocent eyes wide. 'He is here?' he exclaimed. 'Why, how did your men get hold of him?'

'I got hold of him myself,' drawled the American, rising and lazily stretching his lanky legs before the fire. 'I got hold of him with the crooked end of a walking-stick. Don't look so surprised. I really did. You know I sometimes take a turn in the country lanes outside this dismal place; well, I was walking early this evening up a steep lane with dark hedges and grey-looking ploughed fields on both sides; and a young moon was up and silvering the road. By the light of it I saw a man running across the field towards the road; running with his body bent and at a good mile-race trot. He appeared to be much exhausted; but when he came to the thick black hedge he went through it as if it were made of spiders' webs; or rather (for I heard the strong branches breaking and snapping like bayonets) as if he himself were made of stone. In the instant in which he appeared up against the moon, crossing the road, I slung my hooked cane at his legs, tripping him and bringing him down. Then I blew my whistle long and loud, and our fellows came running up to secure him.'

'It would have been rather awkward,' remarked Brown, 'if you had found he was a popular athlete practising a mile race.'

'He was not,' said Usher grimly. 'We soon found out who he was; but I had guessed it with the first glint of the moon on him.'

'You thought it was the runaway convict,' observed the priest simply, 'because you had read in the newspaper cutting that morning that a convict had run away.'

'I had somewhat better grounds,' replied the governor coolly. 'I pass over the first as too simple to be emphasised – I mean that fashionable athletes do not run across ploughed fields or scratch their eyes out in bramble hedges. Nor do they run all doubled up like a crouching dog. There were more decisive details to a fairly well-trained eye. The man was clad in coarse and ragged clothes, but they were something more than merely coarse and ragged. They were so ill-fitting as to be quite grotesque; even as he appeared in black outline against the moonrise, the coat-collar in which his head was buried made him look like a hunchback, and the long loose sleeves looked as if he had no hands. It at once occurred to me that he had somehow managed to change his convict clothes for some confederate's clothes which did not fit him. Second, there was a pretty stiff wind against which he was running; so that I must have seen the streaky look of blowing hair, if the hair had not been very short. Then I remembered that beyond these ploughed fields he was crossing lay Pilgrim's Pond, for which (you will remember) the convict was keeping his bullet; and I sent my walking-stick flying.'

'A brilliant piece of rapid deduction,' said Father Brown; 'but had he got a gun?'

As Usher stopped abruptly in his walk the priest added apologetically: 'I've been told a bullet is not half so useful without it.'

'He had no gun,' said the other gravely; 'but that was doubtless due to some very natural mischance or change of plans. Probably the same policy that made him change the clothes made him drop the gun; he began to repent the coat he had left behind him in the blood of his victim.'

'Well, that is possible enough,' answered the priest.

'And it's hardly worth speculating on,' said Usher, turning to some other papers, 'for we know it's the man by this time.'

His clerical friend asked faintly: 'But how?' And Greywood Usher threw down the newspapers and took up the two press-cuttings again.

'Well, since you are so obstinate,' he said, 'let's begin at the beginning. You will notice that these two cuttings have only one thing in common, which is the mention of Pilgrim's Pond, the estate, as you know, of the millionaire Ireton Todd. You also know that he is a remarkable character; one of those that rose on stepping-stones –'

'Of our dead selves to higher things,' assented his companion. 'Yes; I know that, Petroleum, I think.'

'Anyhow,' said Usher, 'Last-Trick Todd counts for a great deal in this rum affair.'

He stretched himself once more before the fire and continued talking in his expansive, radiantly explanatory style.

'To begin with, on the face of it, there is no mystery here at all. It is not mysterious, it is not even odd, that a jailbird should take his gun to Pilgrim's Pond. Our people aren't like the English, who will forgive a man for being rich if he throws away money on hospitals or horses. Last-Trick Todd has made himself big by his own considerable abilities; and there's no doubt that many of those on whom he has shown his abilities would like to show theirs on him with a shotgun. Todd might easily get dropped by some man he'd never even heard of; some labourer he'd locked out, or some clerk in a business he'd busted. Last-Trick is a man of mental endowments and a high public character; but in this country the relations of employers and employed are considerably strained.

'That's how the whole thing looks supposing this Rian made for Pilgrim's Pond to kill Todd. So it looked to me, till another little discovery woke up what I have of the detective in me. When I had my prisoner safe, I picked up my cane again and strolled down the two or three turns of country road that brought me to one of the side entrances of Todd's grounds, the one nearest to the pool or lake after which the place is named. It was some two hours ago, about seven by this time; the moonlight was more luminous, and I could see the long white streaks of it lying on the mysterious mere with its grey, greasy, half-liquid shores in which they say our fathers used to make witches walk until they sank. I'd forgotten the exact tale; but you know the place I mean; it lies north of Todd's house towards the wilderness, and has two queer wrinkled trees, so dismal that they look more like huge fungoids than decent foliage. As I stood peering at this misty pool, I fancied I saw the faint figure of a man moving from the house towards it, but it was all too dim and distant for one to be certain of the fact, and still less of the details. Besides, my attention was very sharply arrested by something much closer. I crouched behind the fence which ran not more than two hundred yards from one wing of the great mansion, and which was fortunately split in places, as if specially for the application of a cautious eye. A door had opened in the dark bulk of the left wing, and a figure appeared black against the illuminated interior – a muffled figure bending forward, evidently peering out into the night. It closed the door behind it, and I saw it was carrying a lantern, which threw a patch of imperfect light on the dress and figure of the wearer. It seemed to be the figure of a woman, wrapped up in a ragged cloak and evidently disguised to avoid notice; there was something very strange both about the rags and the furtiveness in a person coming out of those rooms lined with gold. She took cautiously the curved garden path which brought her within half a hundred yards of me; then she stood up for an instant on the terrace of turf that looks towards the slimy lake, and holding her flaming lantern above her head she deliberately swung it three times to and fro as for a signal. As she swung it the second time a flicker of its light fell for a moment on her own face, a face that I knew. She was unnaturally pale, and her head was bundled in her borrowed plebeian shawl; but I am certain it was Etta Todd, the millionaire's daughter.

'She retraced her steps in equal secrecy and the door closed behind her again. I was about to climb the fence and follow, when I realised that the detective fever that had lured me into the adventure was rather undignified; and that in a more authoritative capacity I already held all the cards in my hand. I was just turning away when a new noise broke on the night. A window was thrown up in one of the upper floors, but just round the corner of the house so that I could not see it; and a voice of terrible distinctness was heard shouting across the dark garden to know where Lord Falconroy was, for he was missing from every room in the house. There was no mistaking that voice. I have heard it on many a political platform or meeting of directors; it was Ireton Todd himself. Some of the others seemed to have gone to the lower windows or on to the steps, and were calling up to him that Falconroy had gone for a stroll down to the Pilgrim's Pond an hour before, and could not be traced since. Then Todd cried "Mighty Murder!" and shut down the window violently; and I could hear him plunging down the stairs inside. Repossessing myself of my former and wiser purpose, I whipped out of the way of the general search that must follow; and returned here not later than eight o'clock.

'I now ask you to recall that little Society paragraph which seemed to you so painfully lacking in interest. If the convict was not keeping the shot for Todd, as he evidently wasn't, it is most likely that he was keeping it for Lord Falconroy; and it looks as if he had delivered the goods. No more handy place to shoot a man than in the curious geological surroundings of that pool, where a body thrown down would sink through thick slime to a depth practically unknown. Let us suppose, then, that our friend with the cropped hair came to kill Falconroy and not Todd. But, as I have pointed out, there are many reasons why people in America might want to kill Todd. There is no reason why anybody in America should want to kill an English lord newly landed, except for the one reason mentioned in the pink paper – that the lord is paying his attentions to the millionaire's daughter. Our crop-haired friend, despite his ill-fitting clothes, must be an aspiring lover.

'I know the notion will seem to you jarring and even comic; but that's because you are English. It sounds to you like saying the Archbishop of Canterbury's daughter will be married in St George's, Hanover Square, to a crossing-sweeper on ticket-of-leave. You don't do justice to the climbing and aspiring power of our more remarkable citizens. You see a good-looking grey-haired man in evening-dress with a sort of authority about him, you know he is a pillar of the State, and you fancy he had a father. You are in error. You do not realise that a comparatively few years ago he may have been in a tenement or (quite likely) in a jail. You don't allow for our national buoyancy and uplift. Many of our most influential citizens have not only risen recently, but risen comparatively late in life. Todd's daughter was fully eighteen when her father first made his pile; so there isn't really anything impossible in her having a hanger-on in low life; or even in her hanging on to him, as I think she must be doing, to judge by the lantern business. If so, the hand that held the lantern may not be unconnected with the hand that held the gun. This case, sir, will make a noise.'

'Well,' said the priest patiently, 'and what did you do next?'

'I reckon you'll be shocked,' replied Greywood Usher, 'as I know you don't cotton to the march of science in these matters. I am given a good deal of discretion here, and perhaps take a little more than I'm given; and I thought it was an excellent opportunity to test that Psychometric Machine I told you about. Now, in my opinion, that machine can't lie.'

'No machine can lie,' said Father Brown; 'nor can it tell the truth.'

'It did in this case, as I'll show you,' went on Usher positively. 'I sat the man in the ill-fitting clothes in a comfortable chair, and simply wrote words on a blackboard; and the machine simply recorded the variations of his pulse; and I simply observed his manner. The trick is to introduce some word connected with the supposed crime in a list of words connected with something quite different, yet a list in which it occurs quite naturally. Thus I wrote "heron" and "eagle" and "owl", and when I wrote "falcon" he was tremendously agitated; and when I began to make an "r" at the end of the word, that machine just bounded. Who else in this republic has any reason to jump at the name of a newly-arrived Englishman like Falconroy except the man who's shot him? Isn't that better evidence than a lot of gabble from witnesses – the evidence of a reliable machine?'

'You always forget,' observed his companion, 'that the reliable machine always has to be worked by an unreliable machine.'

'Why, what do you mean?' asked the detective.'

'I mean Man,' said Father Brown, 'the most unreliable machine I know of. I don't want to be rude;

and I don't think you will consider Man to be an offensive or inaccurate description of yourself. You say you observed his manner; but how do you know you observed it right? You say the words have to come in a natural way; but how do you know that you did it naturally? How do you know, if you come to that, that he did not observe your manner? Who is to prove that you were not tremendously agitated? There was no machine tied on to your pulse.'

'I tell you,' cried the American in the utmost excitement, 'I was as cool as a cucumber.'

'Criminals also can be as cool as cucumbers,' said Brown with a smile. 'And almost as cool as you.'

'Well, this one wasn't,' said Usher, throwing the papers about. 'Oh, you make me tired!'

'I'm sorry,' said the other. 'I only point out what seems a reasonable possibility. If you could tell by his manner when the word that might hang him had come, why shouldn't he tell from your manner that the words that might hang him was coming? I should ask for more than words myself before I hanged anybody.'

Usher smote the table and rose in a sort of angry triumph.

'And that,' he cried, 'is just what I'm going to give you. I tried the machine first just in order to test the thing in other ways afterwards and the machine, sir, is right.'

He paused a moment and resumed with less excitement. 'I rather want to insist, if it comes to that, that so far I had very little to go on except the scientific experiment. There was really nothing against the man at all. His clothes were ill-fitting, as I've said, but they were rather better, if anything, than those of the submerged class to which he evidently belonged.

Moreover, under all the stains of his plunging through ploughed fields or bursting through dusty hedges, the man was comparatively clean. This might mean, of course, that he had only just broken prison; but it reminded me more of the desperate decency of the comparatively respectable poor. His demeanour was, I am bound to confess, quite in accordance with theirs. He was silent and dignified as they are; he seemed to have a big, but buried, grievance, as they do. He professed total ignorance of the crime and the whole question; and showed nothing but a sullen impatience for something sensible that might come to take him out of his meaningless scrape. He asked me more than once if he could telephone for a lawyer who had helped him a long time ago in a trade dispute, and in every sense acted as you would expect an innocent man to act. There was nothing against him in the world except that little finger on the dial that pointed to the change of his pulse.

'Then, sir, the machine was on its trial; and the machine was right. By the time I came with him out of the private room into the vestibule where all sorts of other people were awaiting examination, I think he had already more or less made up his mind to clear things up by something like a confession. He turned to me and began to say in a low voice: 'Oh, I can't stick this any more. If you must know all about me – '

'At the same instant one of the poor women sitting on the long bench stood up, screaming aloud and pointing at him with her finger. I have never in my life heard anything more demoniacally distinct. Her lean finger seemed to pick him out as if it were a peashooter. Though the word was a mere howl, every syllable was as clear as a separate stroke on the clock.

' "Drugger Davis!" she shouted. "They've got Drugger Davis!"

'Among the wretched women, mostly thieves and streetwalkers, twenty faces were turned, gaping with glee and hate. If I had never heard the words, I should have known by the very shock upon his features that the so-called Oscar Rian had heard his real name. But I'm not quite so ignorant, you may be surprised to hear. Drugger Davis was one of the most terrible and depraved criminals that ever baffled our police. It is certain he had done murder more than once long before his last exploit with the warder. But he was never entirely fixed for it, curiously enough because he did it in the same manner as those milder – or meaner – crimes for which he was fixed pretty often. He was a handsome, well-bred-looking brute, as he still is, to some extent; and he used mostly to go about with barmaids or shop-girls and do them out of their money. Very often, though, he went a good deal farther; and they were found drugged with cigarettes or chocolates and their whole property missing. Then came one case where the girl was found dead; but deliberation could not quite be proved, and, what was more practical still, the criminal could not be found. I heard a rumour of his having reappeared somewhere in the opposite character this time, lending money instead of borrowing it; but still to such poor widows as he might personally fascinate, and still with the same bad result for them. Well, there is your innocent man, and there is his innocent record. Even, since then, four criminals and three warders have identified him and confirmed the story. Now what have you got to say to my poor little machine after that? Hasn't the machine done for him? Or do you prefer to say that the woman and I have done for him?'

'As to what you've done for him,' replied Father Brown, rising and shaking himself in a floppy way, 'you've saved him from the electrical chair. I don't think they can kill Drugger Davis on that old vague story of the poison; and as for the convict who killed the warder, I suppose it's obvious that you haven't got him. Mr Davis is innocent of that crime, at any rate.'

'What do you mean?' demanded the other. 'Why should he be innocent of that crime?'

'Why, bless us all!' cried the small man in one of his rare moments of animation, 'why, because he's guilty of the other crimes! I don't know what you people are made of. You seem to think that all sins are kept together in a bag. You talk as if a miser on Monday were always a spendthrift on Tuesday. You tell me this man you have here spent weeks and months wheedling needy women out of small sums of money; that he used a drug at the best, and a poison at the worst; that he turned up afterwards as the lowest kind of money-lender, and cheated most poor people in the same patient and pacific style. Let it be granted – let us admit, for the sake of argument, that he did all this. If that is so, I will tell you what he didn't do. He didn't storm a spiked wall against a man with a loaded gun. He didn't write on the wall with his own hand, to say he had done it. He didn't stop to state that his justification was self-defence. He didn't explain that he had no quarrel with the poor warder. He didn't name the house of the rich man to which he was going with the gun. He didn't write his own initials in a man's blood. Saints alive! Can't you see the whole character is different, in good and evil? Why, you don't seem to be like I am a bit. One would think you'd never had any vices of your own.'

The amazed American had already parted his lips in protest when the door of his private and official room was hammered and rattled in an unceremonious way to which he was totally unaccustomed.

The door flew open. The moment before Greywood Usher had been coming to the conclusion that Father Brown might possibly be mad. The moment after he began to think he was mad himself. There burst and fell into his private room a man in the filthiest rags, with a greasy squash hat still askew on his head, and a shabby green shade shoved up from one of his eyes, both of which were glaring like a tiger's. The rest of his face was almost undiscoverable, being masked with a matted beard and whiskers through which the nose could barely thrust itself, and further buried in a squalid red scarf or handkerchief. Mr Usher prided himself on having seen most of the roughest specimens in the State, but he thought he had never seen such a baboon dressed as a scarecrow as this. But, above all, he had never in all his placid scientific existence heard a man like that speak to him first.

'See here, old man Usher,' shouted the being in the red handkerchief, 'I'm getting tired. Don't you try any of your hide-and-seek on me; I don't get fooled any. Leave go of my guests, and I'll let up on the fancy clockwork. Keep him here for a split instant and you'll feel pretty mean. I reckon I'm not a man with no pull.'

The eminent Usher was regarding the bellowing monster with an amazement which had dried up all other sentiments. The mere shock to his eyes had rendered his ears almost useless. At last he rang a bell with a hand of violence. While the bell was still strong and pealing, the voice of Father Brown fell soft but distinct.

'I have a suggestion to make,' he said, 'but it seems a little confusing. I don't know this gentleman – but – but I think I know him. Now, you know him – you know him quite well – but you don't know him – naturally. Sounds paradoxical, I know.'

'I reckon the cosmos is cracked,' said Usher, and fell asprawl in his round office chair.

'Now, see here,' vociferated the stranger, striking the table, but speaking in a voice that was all the more mysterious because it was comparatively mild and rational though still resounding. 'I won't let you in. I want – '

'Who in hell are you?' yelled Usher, suddenly sitting up straight.

'I think the gentleman's name is Todd,' said the priest.

Then he picked up the pink slip of newspaper.

'I fear you don't read the Society papers properly,' he said, and began to read out in a monotonous voice, ' "Or locked in the jewelled bosoms of our city's gayest leaders; but there is talk of a pretty parody of the manners and customs of the other end of Society's scale." There's been a big Slum Dinner up at Pilgrim's Pond tonight; and a man, one of the guests, disappeared. Mr Ireton Todd is a good host, and has tracked him here, without even waiting to take off his fancy-dress.'

'What man do you mean?'

'I mean the man with the comically ill-fitting clothes you saw running across the ploughed field. Hadn't you better go and investigate him? He will be rather impatient to get back to his champagne, from which he ran away in such a hurry, when the convict with the gun hove in sight.'

'Do you seriously mean – ' began the official.

'Why, look here, Mr Usher,' said Father Brown quietly, 'you said the machine couldn't make a mistake; and in one sense it didn't. But the other machine did; the machine that worked it. You assumed that the man in rags jumped at the name of Lord Falconroy, because he was Lord Falconroy's murderer. He jumped at the name of Lord Falconroy because he *is* Lord Falconroy.'

'Then why the blazes didn't he say so?' demanded the staring Usher.

'He felt his plight and recent panic were hardly patrician,' replied the priest, 'so he tried to keep the name back at first. But he was just going to tell it you, when' – and Father Brown looked down at his boots – 'when a woman found another name for him.'

'But you can't be so mad as to say,' said Greywood Usher, very white, 'that Lord Falconroy was Drugger Davis.'

The priest looked at him very earnestly, but with a baffling and undecipherable face.

'I am not saying anything about it,' he said. 'I leave all the rest to you. Your pink paper says that the title was recently revived for him; but those papers are very unreliable. It says he was in the States in youth; but the whole story seems very strange. Davis and Falconroy are both pretty considerable cowards, but so are lots of other men. I would not hang a dog on my own opinion about this. But I think,' he went on softly and reflectively, 'I think you Americans are too modest. I think you idealise the English aristocracy – even in assuming it to be so aristocratic. You see a good-looking Englishman in evening-dress; you know he's in the House of Lords; and you fancy he has a father. You don't allow for our national buoyancy and uplift. Many of our most influential noblemen have not only risen recently, but – '

'Oh, stop it!' cried Greywood Usher, wringing one lean hand in impatience against a shade of irony in the other's face.

'Don't stay talking to this lunatic!' cried Todd brutally. 'Take me to my friend.'

Next morning Father Brown appeared with the same demure expression, carrying yet another piece of pink newspaper.

'I'm afraid you neglect the fashionable press rather,' he said, 'but this cutting may interest you.'

Usher read the headlines, 'Last-Trick's Strayed Revellers: Mirthful Incident near Pilgrim's Pond'. The paragraph went on: 'A laughable occurrence took place outside Wilkinson's Motor Garage last night. A policeman on duty had his attention drawn by larrikins to a man in prison dress who was stepping with considerable coolness into the steering-seat of a pretty high-toned Panhard; he was accompanied by a girl wrapped in a ragged shawl. On the police interfering, the young woman threw back the shawl, and all recognised Millionaire Todd's daughter, who had just come from the Slum Freak Dinner at the Pond, where all the choicest guests were in a similar *déshabillé*. She and the gentleman who had donned prison uniform were going for the customary joy-ride.'

Under the pink slip Mr Usher found a strip of a later paper, headed, 'Astounding Escape of Millionaire's Daughter with Convict. She had Arranged Freak Dinner. Now Safe in – '

Mr Greenwood Usher lifted his eyes, but Father Brown was gone.

The Perishing of the Pendragons

Father Brown was in no mood for adventures. He had lately fallen ill with over-work, and when he began to recover, his friend Flambeau had taken him on a cruise in a small yacht with Sir Cecil Fanshaw, a young Cornish squire and an enthusiast for Cornish coast scenery. But Brown was still rather weak; he was no very happy sailor; and though he was never of the sort that either grumbles or breaks down, his spirits did not rise above patience and civility. When the other two men praised the ragged violet sunset or the ragged volcanic crags, he agreed with them. When Flambeau pointed out a rock shaped like a dragon, he looked at it and thought it very like a dragon. When Fanshaw more excitedly indicated a rock that was like Merlin, he looked at it, and signified assent. When Flambeau asked whether this rocky gate of the twisted river was not the gate of Fairyland, he said 'Yes.' He heard the most important things and the most trivial with the same tasteless absorption. He heard that the coast was death to all but careful seamen; he also heard that the ship's cat was asleep. He heard that Fanshaw couldn't find his cigar-holder anywhere; he also heard the pilot deliver the oracle 'Both eyes bright, she's all right; one eye winks, down she sinks'. He heard Flambeau say to Fanshaw that no doubt this meant the pilot must keep both eyes open and be spry. And he heard Fanshaw say to Flambeau that, oddly enough, it didn't mean this: it meant that while they saw two of the coast-lights, one near and the other distant, exactly side by side, they were in the right river-channel; but that if one light was hidden behind the other, they were going on the rocks. He heard Fanshaw add that his country was full of such quaint fables and idioms; it was the very home of romance; he even pitted this part of Cornwall against Devonshire, as a claimant to the laurels of Elizabethan seamanship. According to him there had been captains among these coves and islets compared with whom Drake was practically a landsman. He heard Flambeau laugh, and ask if, perhaps, the adventurous title of 'Westward Ho!' only meant that all Devonshire men wished they were living in Cornwall. He heard Fanshaw say there was no need to be silly; that not only had Cornish captains been heroes, but that they were heroes still: that near that very spot there was an old admiral, now retired, who was scarred by thrilling voyages full of adventures; and who had in his youth found the last group of eight Pacific Islands that was added to the chart of the world. This Cecil Fanshaw was, in person, of the kind that commonly urges such crude but pleasing enthusiasms; a very young man, light-haired, high-coloured, with an eager profile; with a boyish bravado of spirits, but an almost girlish delicacy of tint and type. The big shoulders, black brows and black mousquetaire swagger of Flambeau were a great contrast.

All these trivialities Brown heard and saw; but heard them as a tired man hears a tune in the railway wheels, or saw them as a sick man sees the pattern of his wallpaper. No one can calculate the turns of mood in convalescence: but Father Brown's depression must have had a great deal to do with his mere unfamiliarity with the sea. For as the river-mouth narrowed like the neck of a bottle, and the water grew calmer and the air warmer and more earthly, he seemed to wake up and take notice like a baby. They had reached that phase just after sunset when air and water both look bright, but earth and all its growing things look almost black by comparison. About this particular evening, however, there was something exceptional. It was one of those rare atmospheres in which a smoked-glass slide seems to have been slid away from between us and Nature; so that even dark colours on that day look more gorgeous than bright colours on cloudier days. The trampled earth of the river-banks and the peaty stain in the pools did not look drab but glowing umber, and the dark woods astir in the breeze did not look, as usual, dim blue with mere depth or distance, but more like wind-tumbled masses of some vivid violet blossom. This magic clearness and intensity in the colours was further forced on Brown's slowly reviving senses by something romantic and even secret in the very form of the landscape.

The river was still well wide and deep enough for a pleasure boat so small as theirs; but the curves of the countryside suggested that it was closing in on either hand; the woods seemed to be making broken and flying attempts at bridge-building – as if the boat were passing from the romance of a valley to the romance of a hollow and so to the supreme romance of a tunnel. Beyond this mere look of things there was little for Brown's freshening fancy to feed on; he saw no human beings, except some gypsies trailing along the river bank, with faggots and osiers cut in the forest; and one sight no longer unconventional, but in such remote parts still uncommon: a dark-haired lady, bareheaded, and paddling her own canoe. If

Father Brown ever attached any importance to either of these, he certainly forgot them at the next turn of the river which brought in sight a singular object.

The water seemed to widen and split, being cloven by the dark wedge of a fish-shaped and wooded islet. With the rate at which they went, the islet seemed to swim towards them like a ship; a ship with a very high prow – or, to speak more strictly, a very high funnel. For at the extreme point nearest them stood up an odd-looking building, unlike anything they could remember or connect with any purpose. It was not specially high, but it was too high for its breadth to be called anything but a tower. Yet it appeared to be built entirely of wood, and that in a most unequal and eccentric way. Some of the planks and beams were of good, seasoned oak; some of such wood cut raw and recent; some again of white pinewood, and a great deal more of the same sort of wood painted black with tar. These black beams were set crooked or crisscross at all kinds of angles, giving the whole a most patchy and puzzling appearance. There were one or two windows, which appeared to be coloured and leaded in an old-fashioned but more elaborate style. The travellers looked at it with that paradoxical feeling we have when something reminds us of something, and yet we are certain it is something very different.

Father Brown, even when he was mystified, was clever in analysing his own mystification. And he found himself reflecting that the oddity seemed to consist in a particular shape cut out in an incongruous material; as if one saw a top-hat made of tin, or a frock-coat cut out of tartan. He was sure he had seen timbers of different tints arranged like that somewhere, but never in such architectural proportions.

The next moment a glimpse through the dark trees told him all he wanted to know, and he laughed. Through a gap in the foliage there appeared for a moment one of those old wooden houses, faced with black beams, which are still to be found here and there in England, but which most of us see imitated in some show called 'Old London' or 'Shakespeare's England.' It was in view only long enough for the priest to see that, however old-fashioned, it was a comfortable and well-kept country-house, with flower beds in front of it. It had none of the piebald and crazy look of the tower that seemed made out of its refuse.

'What on earth's this?' said Flambeau, who was still staring at the tower.

Fanshaw's eyes were shining, and he spoke triumphantly. 'Aha! You've not seen a place quite like this before, I fancy; that's why I've brought you here, my friend. Now you shall see whether I exaggerate about the mariners of Cornwall. This place belongs to Old Pendragon, whom we call the admiral; though he retired before getting the rank. The spirit of Raleigh and Hawkins is a memory with the Devon folk; it's a modern fact with the Pendragons. If Queen Elizabeth were to rise from the grave and come up this river in a gilded barge, she would be received by the admiral in a house exactly such as she was accustomed to, in every corner and casement, in every panel on the wall or plate on the table. And she would find an English Captain still talking fiercely of fresh lands to be found in little ships, as much as if she had dined with Drake.'

'She'd find a rum sort of thing in the garden,' said Father Brown, 'which would not please her Renaissance eye. That Elizabethan domestic architecture is charming in its way; but it's against the very nature of it to break out into turrets.'

'And yet,' answered Fanshaw, 'that's the most romantic and Elizabethan part of the business. It was built by the Pendragons in the very days of the Spanish wars; and though it's needed patching and even rebuilding for another reason, it's always been rebuilt in the old way. The story goes that the lady of Sir Peter Pendragon built it in this place and to this height, because from the top you can just see the corner where vessels turn into the river mouth; and she wished to be the first to see her husband's ship, as he sailed home from the Spanish Main.'

'For what other reason,' asked Father Brown, 'do you mean that it has been rebuilt?'

'Oh, there's a strange story about that, too,' said the young squire with relish. 'You are really in a land of strange stories. King Arthur was here and Merlin and the fairies before him. The story goes that Sir Peter Pendragon, who (I fear) had some of the faults of the pirates as well as the virtues of the sailor, was bringing home three Spanish gentlemen in honourable captivity, intending to escort them to Elizabeth's court. But he was a man of flaming and tigerish temper, and coming to high words with one of them, he caught him by the throat and flung him, by accident or design, into the sea. A second Spaniard, who was the brother of the first, instantly drew his sword and flew at Pendragon, and after a short but furious combat in which both got three wounds in as many minutes, Pendragon drove his blade through the other's body and the second Spaniard was accounted for. As it happened the ship had already turned into the river mouth and was close to comparatively shallow water. The third Spaniard sprang over the side of the ship, struck out for the shore, and was soon near enough to it to stand up to his waist in water. And turning again to face the ship, and holding up both arms to Heaven – like a prophet calling plagues upon a wicked city – he called out to Pendragon in a piercing and terrible voice, that he at least was yet living, that he would go on living, that he would live for ever; and that generation after generation the house of Pendragon should never see him or his, but should know by very certain signs that he and his vengeance were alive. With that he dived under the wave, and was either drowned or swam so long under water that no hair of his head was seen afterwards.'

'There's that girl in the canoe again,' said Flambeau irrelevantly, for good-looking young women would call him off any topic. 'She seems bothered by the queer tower just as we were.'

Indeed, the black-haired young lady was letting her canoe float slowly and silently past the strange islet; and was looking intently up at the strange tower, with a strong glow of curiosity on her oval and olive face.

'Never mind girls,' said Fanshaw impatiently; 'there are plenty of them in the world, but not many things like the Pendragon Tower. As you may easily suppose, plenty of superstitions and scandals have followed in the track of the Spaniard's curse; and no doubt, as you would put it, any accident happening to this Cornish family would be connected with it by rural credulity. But it is perfectly true that this tower has been burnt down two or three times; and the family can't be called lucky, for more than two, I think, of the admiral's near kin have perished by shipwreck; and one at least, to my own knowledge, on practically the same spot where Sir Peter threw the Spaniard overboard.'

'What a pity!' exclaimed Flambeau. 'She's going.'

'When did your friend the admiral tell you this family history?' asked Father Brown, as the girl in the canoe paddled off, without showing the least intention of extending her interest from the tower to the yacht, which Fanshaw had already caused to lie alongside the island.

'Many years ago,' replied Fanshaw; 'he hasn't been to sea for some time now, though he is as keen on it as ever. I believe there's a family compact or something. Well, here's the landing-stage; let's come ashore and see the old boy.'

They followed him on to the island, just under the tower, and Father Brown, whether from the mere touch of dry land, or the interest of something on the other bank of the river (which he stared at very hard for some seconds), seemed singularly improved in briskness. They entered a wooded avenue between two fences of thin greyish wood, such as often enclose parks or gardens, and over the top of which the dark trees tossed to and fro like black and purple plumes upon the hearse of a giant. The tower, as they left it behind, looked all the quainter, because such entrances are usually flanked by two towers; and this one looked lopsided. But for this, the avenue had the usual appearance of the entrance to a gentleman's grounds; and, being so curved that the house was now out of sight, somehow looked a much larger park than any plantation on such an island could really be. Father Brown was, perhaps, a little fanciful in his fatigue, but he almost thought the whole place must be growing larger, as things do in a nightmare. Anyhow, a mystical monotony was the only character of their march, until Fanshaw suddenly stopped, and pointed to something sticking out through the grey fence – something that looked at first rather like the imprisoned horn of some beast. Closer observation showed that it was a slightly curved blade of metal that shone faintly in the fading light.

Flambeau, who like all Frenchmen had been a soldier, bent over it and said in a startled voice. 'Why, it's a sabre! I believe I know the sort, heavy and curved, but shorter than the cavalry; they used to have them in artillery and the – '

As he spoke the blade plucked itself out of the crack it had made and came down again with a more ponderous slash, splitting the fissiparous fence to the bottom with a rending noise. Then it was pulled out again, flashed above the fence some feet farther along, and again split it halfway down with the first stroke; and after waggling a little to extricate itself (accompanied with curses in the darkness) split it down to the ground with a second. Then a kick of devilish energy sent the whole loosened square of thin wood flying into the pathway, and a great gap of dark coppice gaped in the paling.

Fanshaw peered into the dark opening and uttered an exclamation of astonishment. 'My dear admiral!' he exclaimed, 'do you – er – do you generally cut out a new front door whenever you want to go for a walk?'

The voice in the gloom swore again, and then broke into a jolly laugh. 'No,' it said; 'I've really got to cut down this fence somehow; it's spoiling all the plants, and no one else here can do it. But I'll only carve another bit off the front door, and then come out and welcome you.'

And sure enough, he heaved up his weapon once more, and, hacking twice, brought down another and similar strip of fence, making the opening about fourteen feet wide in all. Then through this larger forest gateway he came out into the evening light, with a chip of grey wood sticking to his sword-blade.

He momentarily fulfilled all Fanshaw's fable of an old piratical admiral; though the details seemed afterwards to decompose into accidents. For instance, he wore a broad-brimmed hat as protection against the sun; but the front flap of it was turned up straight to the sky, and the two corners pulled down lower than the ears, so that it stood across his forehead in a crescent like the old cocked hat worn by Nelson. He wore an ordinary dark-blue jacket, with nothing special about the buttons, but the combination of it with white linen trousers somehow had a sailorish look. He was tall and loose, and walked with a sort of swagger, which was not a sailor's roll, and yet somehow suggested it; and he held in his hand a short sabre which was like a navy cutlass, bat about twice as big. Under the bridge of the hat his eagle face looked eager, all the more because it was not only clean-shaven, but without eyebrows. It seemed almost as if all the hair had come off his face from his thrusting it through a throng of elements. His eyes were prominent and piercing. His colour was curiously attractive, while partly tropical; it reminded one vaguely of a blood-orange. That is, that while it was ruddy and sanguine, there was a yellow in it that was in no way sickly, but seemed rather to glow like gold apples of the Hesperides. Father Brown thought he had never seen a figure so expressive of all the romances about the countries of the Sun.

When Fanshaw had presented his two friends to their host he fell again into a tone of rallying the latter about his wreckage of the fence and his apparent rage of profanity. The admiral pooh-poohed it at first as a piece of necessary but annoying garden work; but at length the ring of real energy came back into his laughter, and he cried with a mixture of impatience and good humour: 'Well, perhaps I do go at it a bit rabidly, and feel a kind of pleasure in smashing anything. So would you if your only pleasure was in cruising about to find some new Cannibal Islands, and you had to stick on this muddy little rockery in a sort of rustic pond. When I remember how I've cut down a mile and a half of green poisonous jungle with an old cutlass half as sharp as this; and then remember I must stop here and chop this matchwood, because of some confounded old bargain scribbled in a family Bible, why, I – '

He swung up the heavy steel again; and this time sundered the wall of wood from top to bottom at one stroke.

'I feel like that,' he said laughing, but furiously flinging the sword some yards down the path, 'and now let's go up to the house; you must have some dinner.'

The semicircle of lawn in front of the house was varied by three circular garden beds, one of red tulips, a second of yellow tulips, and the third of some white, waxen-looking blossoms that the visitors did not know and presumed to be exotic. A heavy, hairy and rather sullen-looking gardener was hanging up a heavy coil of garden hose. The corners of the expiring sunset which seemed to cling about the corners of the house gave glimpses here and there of the colours of remoter flower beds; and in a treeless space on one side of the house opening upon the river stood a tall brass tripod on which was tilted a big brass telescope. Just outside the steps of the porch stood a little painted green garden table, as if someone had just had tea there. The entrance was flanked with two of those half-featured lumps of stone with holes for eyes that are said to be South Sea idols; and on the brown oak beam across the doorway were some confused carvings that looked almost as barbaric.

As they passed indoors, the little cleric hopped suddenly on to the table, and standing on it peered unaffectedly through his spectacles at the mouldings in the oak. Admiral Pendragon looked very much astonished, though not particularly annoyed; while Fanshaw was so amused with what looked like a performing pigmy on his little stand, that he could not control his laughter. But Father Brown was not likely to notice either the laughter or the astonishment.

He was gazing at three carved symbols, which, though very worn and obscure, seemed still to convey some sense to him. The first seemed to be the outline of some tower or other building, crowned with what looked like curly-pointed ribbons. The second was clearer: an old Elizabethan galley with decorative waves beneath it, but interrupted in the middle by a curious jagged rock, which was either a fault in the wood or some conventional representation of the water coming in. The third represented the upper half of a human figure, ending in an escalloped line like the waves; the face was rubbed and featureless, and both arms were held very stiffly up in the air.

'Well,' muttered Father Brown, blinking, 'here is the legend of the Spaniard plain enough. Here he is holding up his arms and cursing in the sea; and here are the two curses: the wrecked ship and the burning of Pendragon Tower.'

Pendragon shook his head with a kind of venerable amusement. 'And how many other things might it not be?' he said. 'Don't you know that that sort of half-man, like a half-lion or half-stag, is quite common in heraldry? Might not that line through the ship be one of those *parti-per-pale* lines, *indented*, I think they call it? And though the third thing isn't so very heraldic, it would be more heraldic to suppose it a tower crowned with laurel than with fire; and it looks just as like it.'

'But it seems rather odd,' said Flambeau, 'that it should exactly confirm the old legend.'

'Ah,' replied the sceptical traveller, 'but you don't know how much of the old legend may have been made up from the old figures. Besides, it isn't the only old legend. Fanshaw, here, who is fond of such things, will tell you there are other versions of the tale, and much more horrible ones. One story credits my unfortunate ancestor with having had the Spaniard cut in two; and that will fit the pretty picture also. Another obligingly credits our family with the possession of a tower full of snakes and explains those little, wriggly things in that way. And a third theory supposes the crooked line on the ship to be a conventionalised thunderbolt; but that alone, if seriously examined, would show what a very little way these unhappy coincidences really go.'

'Why, how do you mean?' asked Fanshaw.

'It so happens,' replied his host coolly, 'that there was no thunder and lightning at all in the two or three shipwrecks I know of in our family.'

'Oh!' said Father Brown, and jumped down from the little table.

There was another silence in which they heard the continuous murmur of the river; then Fanshaw said, in a doubtful and perhaps disappointed tone: 'Then you don't think there is anything in the tales of the tower in flames?'

'There are the tales, of course,' said the admiral, shrugging his shoulders; 'and some of them, I don't deny, on evidence as decent as one ever gets for such things. Someone saw a blaze hereabout, don't you know, as he walked home through a wood; someone keeping sheep on the uplands inland thought he saw a flame hovering over Pendragon Tower. Well, a damp dab of mud like this confounded island seems the last place where one would think of fires.'

'What is that fire over there?' asked Father Brown with a gentle suddenness, pointing to the woods on the left river-bank. They were all thrown a little off their balance, and the more fanciful Fanshaw had even some difficulty in recovering his, as they saw a long, thin stream of blue smoke ascending silently into the end of the evening light.

Then Pendragon broke into a scornful laugh again. 'Gypsies!' he said; 'they've been camping about here for a week. Gentlemen, you want your dinner,' and he turned as if to enter the house.

But the antiquarian superstition in Fanshaw was still quivering, and he said hastily: 'But, admiral, what's that hissing noise quite near the island? It's very like fire.'

'It's more like what it is,' said the admiral, laughing as he led the way; 'it's only some canoe going by.'

Almost as he spoke, the butler, a lean man in black,

with very black hair and a very long, yellow face, appeared in the doorway and told him that dinner was served.

The dining-room was as nautical as the cabin of a ship; but its note was rather that of the modern than the Elizabethan captain. There were, indeed, three antiquated cutlasses in a trophy over the fireplace, and one brown sixteenth-century map with tritons and little ships dotted about a curly sea. But such things were less prominent on the white panelling than some cases of quaint-coloured South American birds, very scientifically stuffed, fantastic shells from the Pacific, and several instruments so rude and queer in shape that savages might have used them either to kill their enemies or to cook them. But the alien colour culminated in the fact that, besides the butler, the admiral's only servants were two negroes, somewhat quaintly clad in tight uniforms of yellow. The priest's instinctive trick of analysing his own impressions told him that the colour and the little neat coat-tails of these bipeds had suggested the word 'Canary', and so by a mere pun connected them with southward travel. Towards the end of the dinner they took their yellow clothes and black faces out of the room, leaving only the black clothes and yellow face of the butler.

'I'm rather sorry you take this so lightly,' said Fanshaw to the host; 'for the truth is, I've brought these friends of mine with the idea of their helping you, as they know a good deal of these things. Don't you really believe in the family story at all?'

'I don't believe in anything,' answered Pendragon very briskly, with a bright eye cocked at a red tropical bird. 'I'm a man of science.'

Rather to Flambeau's surprise, his clerical friend, who seemed to have entirely woken up, took up the digression and talked natural history with his host with a flow of words and much unexpected information, until the dessert and decanters were set down and the last of the servants vanished.

Then he said, without altering his tone: 'Please don't think me impertinent, Admiral Pendragon. I don't ask for curiosity, but really for my guidance and your convenience. Have I made a bad shot if I guess you don't want these old things talked of before your butler?'

The admiral lifted the hairless arches over his eyes and exclaimed. 'Well, I don't know where you got it, but the truth is I can't stand the fellow, though I've no excuse for discharging a family servant. Fanshaw, with his fairy tales, would say my blood moved against men with that black, Spanish-looking hair.'

Flambeau struck the table with his heavy fist. 'By Jove!' he cried; 'and so had that girl!'

'I hope it'll all end tonight,' continued the admiral, 'when my nephew comes back safe from his ship. You looked surprised. You won't understand, I suppose, unless I tell you the story. You see, my father had two sons; I remained a bachelor, but my elder brother married, and had a son who became a sailor like all the rest of us, and will inherit the proper estate. Well, my father was a strange man; he somehow combined Fanshaw's superstition with a good deal of my scepticism; they were always fighting in him; and after my first voyages, he developed a notion which he thought somehow would settle finally whether the curse was truth or trash. If all the Pendragons sailed about anyhow, he thought there would be too much chance of natural catastrophes to prove anything. But if we went to sea one at a time in strict order of succession to the property, he thought it might show whether any connected fate followed the family as a family. It was a silly notion, I think, and I quarrelled with my father pretty heartily; for I was an ambitious man and was left to the last, coming, by succession, after my own nephew.'

'And your father and brother,' said the priest, very gently, 'died at sea, I fear.'

'Yes,' groaned the admiral; 'by one of those brutal accidents on which are built all the lying mythologies of mankind, they were both shipwrecked. My father, coming up this coast out of the Atlantic, was washed up on these Cornish rocks. My brother's ship was sunk, no one knows where, on the voyage home from Tasmania. His body was never found. I tell you it was from perfectly natural mishap; lots of other people besides Pendragons were drowned; and both disasters are discussed in a normal way by navigators. But, of course, it set this forest of superstition on fire; and men saw the flaming tower everywhere. That's why I say it will be all right when Walter returns. The girl he's engaged to was coming today; but I was so afraid of some chance delay frightening her that I wired her not to come till she heard from me. But he's practically sure to be here sometime tonight, and then it'll all end in smoke – tobacco smoke. We'll crack that old lie when we crack a bottle of this wine.'

'Very good wine,' said Father Brown, gravely lifting his glass, 'but, as you see, a very bad wine bibber. I most sincerely beg your pardon': for he had spilt a small spot of wine on the tablecloth. He drank and put down the glass with a composed face; but his hand had started at the exact moment when he became conscious of a face looking in through the garden window just behind the admiral – the face of a woman, swarthy, with southern hair and eyes, and young, but like a mask of tragedy.

After a pause the priest spoke again in his mild manner. 'Admiral,' he said, 'will you do me a favour? Let me, and my friends if they like, stop in that tower of yours just for tonight? Do you know that in my business you're an exorcist almost before anything else?'

Pendragon sprang to his feet and paced swiftly to and fro across the window, from which the face had instantly vanished. 'I tell you there is nothing in it,' he cried, with ringing violence. 'There is one thing I know about this matter. You may call me an atheist. I am an atheist.' Here he swung round and fixed Father Brown with a face of frightful concentration. 'This business is perfectly natural. There is no curse in it at all.'

Father Brown smiled. 'In that case,' he said, 'there can't be any objection to my sleeping in your delightful summerhouse.'

'The idea is utterly ridiculous,' replied the admiral, beating a tattoo on the back of his chair.

'Please forgive me for everything,' said Brown in his most sympathetic tone, 'including spilling the wine. But it seems to me you are not quite so easy about the flaming tower as you try to be.'

Admiral Pendragon sat down again as abruptly as he had risen; but he sat quite still, and when he spoke again it was in a lower voice. 'You do it at your own peril,' he said; 'but wouldn't *you* be an atheist to keep sane in all this devilry?'

* * *

Some three hours afterwards Fanshaw, Flambeau and the priest were still dawdling about the garden in the dark; and it began to dawn on the other two that Father Brown had no intention of going to bed either in the tower or the house.

'I think the lawn wants weeding,' said he dreamily. 'If I could find a spud or something I'd do it myself.'

They followed him, laughing and half remonstrating; but he replied with the utmost solemnity, explaining to them, in a maddening little sermon, that one can always find some small occupation that is helpful to others. He did not find a spud; but he found an old broom made of twigs, with which he began energetically to brush the fallen leaves off the grass.

'Always some little thing to be done,' he said with idiotic cheerfulness; 'as George Herbert says: "Who sweeps an admiral's garden in Cornwall as for Thy laws makes that and the action fine." And now,' he added, suddenly slinging the broom away, 'let's go and water the flowers.'

With the same mixed emotions they watched him uncoil some considerable lengths of the large garden hose, saying with an air of wistful discrimination: 'The red tulips before the yellow, I think. Look a bit dry, don't you think?'

He turned the little tap on the instrument, and the water shot out straight and solid as a long rod of steel.

'Look out, Samson,' cried Flambeau; 'why, you've cut off the tulip's head.'

Father Brown stood ruefully contemplating the decapitated plant.

'Mine does seem to be a rather kill or cure sort of watering,' he admitted, scratching his head. 'I suppose it's a pity I didn't find the spud. You should have seen me with the spud! Talking of tools, you've got that sword-stick, Flambeau, you always carry? That's right; and Sir Cecil could have that sword the admiral threw away by the fence here. How grey everything looks!'

'The mist's rising from the river,' said the staring Flambeau.

Almost as he spoke the huge figure of the hairy gardener appeared on a higher ridge of the trenched and terraced lawn, hailing them with a brandished rake and a horribly bellowing voice. 'Put down that hose,' he shouted; 'put down that hose and go to your – '

'I am fearfully clumsy,' replied the reverend gentleman weakly; 'do you know, I upset some wine at dinner.' He made a wavering half-turn of apology towards the gardener, with the hose still spouting in his hand. The gardener caught the cold crash of the water full in his face like the crash of a cannonball; staggered, slipped and went sprawling with his boots in the air.

'How very dreadful!' said Father Brown, looking round in a sort of wonder. 'Why, I've hit a man!'

He stood with his head forward for a moment as if looking or listening; and then set off at a trot towards the tower, still trailing the hose behind him. The tower was quite close, but its outline was curiously dim.

'Your river mist,' he said, 'has a rum smell.'

'By the Lord it has,' cried Fanshaw, who was very white. 'But you can't mean – '

'I mean,' said Father Brown, 'that one of the admiral's scientific predictions is coming true tonight. This story is going to end in smoke.'

As he spoke a most beautiful rose-red light seemed to burst into blossom like a gigantic rose;

but accompanied with a crackling and rattling noise that was like the laughter of devils.

'My God! What is this?' cried Sir Cecil Fanshaw.

'The sign of the flaming tower,' said Father Brown, and sent the driving water from his hose into the heart of the red patch.

'Lucky we hadn't gone to bed!' ejaculated Fanshaw. 'I suppose it can't spread to the house.'

'You may remember,' said the priest quietly, 'that the wooden fence that might have carried it was cut away.'

Flambeau turned electrified eyes upon his friend, but Fanshaw only said rather absently: 'Well, nobody can be killed, anyhow.'

'This is rather a curious kind of tower,' observed Father Brown; 'when it takes to killing people, it always kills people who are somewhere else.'

At the same instant the monstrous figure of the gardener with the streaming beard stood again on the green ridge against the sky, waving others to come on; but now waving not a rake but a cutlass. Behind him came the two negroes, also with the old crooked cutlasses out of the trophy. But in the blood-red glare, with their black faces and yellow figures, they looked like devils carrying instruments of torture. In the dim garden behind them a distant voice was heard calling out brief directions. When the priest heard the voice, a terrible change came over his countenance.

But he remained composed; and never took his eye off the patch of flame which had begun by spreading, but now seemed to shrink a little as it hissed under the torch of the long silver spear of water. He kept his finger along the nozzle of the pipe to ensure the aim, and attended to no other business, knowing only by the noise and that semi-conscious corner of the eye, the exciting incidents that began to tumble themselves about the island garden. He gave two brief directions to his friends. One was: 'Knock these fellows down somehow and tie them up, whoever they are; there's some rope down by those faggots. They want to take away my nice hose.' The other was: 'As soon as you get a chance, call out to that canoeing girl; she's over on the bank with the gypsies. Ask her if they could get some buckets across and fill them from the river.' Then he closed his mouth and continued to water the new red flower as ruthlessly as he had watered the red tulip.

He never turned his head to look at the strange fight that followed between the foes and friends of the mysterious fire. He almost felt the island shake when Flambeau collided with the huge gardener; he merely imagined how it would whirl round them as they wrestled. He heard the crashing fall; and his friend's gasp of triumph as he dashed on to the first negro; and the cries of both the blacks as Flambeau and Fanshaw bound them. Flambeau's enormous strength more than redressed the odds in the fight, especially as the fourth man still hovered near the house, only a shadow and a voice. He heard also the water broken by the paddles of a canoe; the girl's voice giving orders, the voices of gypsies answering and coming nearer, the plumping and sucking noise of empty buckets plunged into a full stream; and finally the sound of many feet around the fire. But all this was less to him than the fact that the red rent, which had lately once more increased, had once more slightly diminished.

Then came a cry that very nearly made him turn

his head. Flambeau and Fanshaw, now reinforced by some of the gypsies, had rushed after the mysterious man by the house; and he heard from the other end of the garden the Frenchman's cry of horror and astonishment. It was echoed by a howl not to be called human, as the being broke from their hold and ran along the garden. Three times at least it raced round the whole island, in a way that was as horrible as the chase of a lunatic, both in the cries of the pursued and the ropes carried by the pursuers; but was more horrible still, because it somehow suggested one of the chasing games of children in a garden. Then, finding them closing in on every side, the figure sprang upon one of the higher river banks and disappeared with a splash into the dark and driving river.

'You can do no more, I fear,' said Brown in a voice cold with pain. 'He has been washed down to the rocks by now, where he has sent so many others. He knew the use of a family legend.'

'Oh, don't talk in these parables,' cried Flambeau impatiently. 'Can't you put it simply in words of one syllable?'

'Yes,' answered Brown, with his eye on the hose. ' "Both eyes bright, she's all right; one eye blinks, down she sinks." '

The fire hissed and shrieked more and more, like a strangled thing, as it grew narrower and narrower under the flood from the pipe and buckets, but Father Brown still kept his eye on it as he went on speaking: 'I thought of asking this young lady, if it were morning yet, to look through that telescope at the river mouth and the river. She might have seen something to interest her: the sign of the ship, or Mr Walter

Pendragon coming home, and perhaps even the sign of the half-man, for though he is certainly safe by now, he may very well have waded ashore. He has been within a shave of another shipwreck; and would never have escaped it, if the lady hadn't had the sense to suspect the old admiral's telegram and come down to watch him. Don't let's talk about the old admiral. Don't let's talk about anything. It's enough to say that whenever this tower, with its pitch and resin-wood, really caught fire, the spark on the horizon always looked like the twin light to the coast lighthouse.'

'And that,' said Flambeau, 'is how the father and brother died. The wicked uncle of the legends very nearly got his estate after all.'

Father Brown did not answer; indeed, he did not speak again, save for civilities, till they were all safe round a cigar-box in the cabin of the yacht. He saw that the frustrated fire was extinguished; and then refused to linger, though he actually heard young Pendragon, escorted by an enthusiastic crowd, come tramping up the river bank; and might (had he been moved by romantic curiosities) have received the combined thanks of the man from the ship and the girl from the canoe. But his fatigue had fallen on him once more, and he only started once, when Flambeau abruptly told him he had dropped cigar-ash on his trousers.

'That's no cigar-ash,' he said rather wearily. 'That's from the fire, but you don't think so because you're all smoking cigars. That's just the way I got my first faint suspicion about the chart.'

'Do you mean Pendragon's chart of his Pacific Islands?' asked Fanshaw.

'You thought it was a chart of the Pacific Islands,'

answered Brown. 'Put a feather with a fossil and a bit of coral and everyone will think it's a specimen. Put the same feather with a ribbon and an artificial flower and everyone will think it's for a lady's hat. Put the same feather with an ink-bottle, a book, and a stack of writing-paper, and most men will swear they've seen a quill pen. So you saw that map among tropic birds and shells and thought it was a map of Pacific Islands. It was the map of this river.'

'But how do you know?' asked Fanshaw.

'I saw the rock you thought was like a dragon, and the one like Merlin, and – '

'You seem to have noticed a lot as we came in,' cried Fanshaw. 'We thought you were rather abstracted.'

'I was seasick,' said Father Brown simply. 'I felt simply horrible. But feeling horrible has nothing to do with not seeing things.' And he closed his eyes.

'Do you think most men would have seen that?' asked Flambeau. He received no answer: Father Brown was asleep.

The Strange Crime of John Boulnois

Mr Calhoun Kidd was a very young gentleman with a very old face, a face dried up with its own eagerness, framed in blue-black hair and a black butterfly tie. He was the emissary in England of the colossal American daily called the *Western Sun* – also humorously described as the 'Rising Sunset'. This was in allusion to a great journalistic declaration (attributed to Mr Kidd himself) that 'he guessed the sun would rise in the west yet, if American citizens did a bit more hustling'. Those, however, who mock American journalism from the standpoint of somewhat mellower traditions forget a certain paradox which partly redeems it. For while the journalism of the States permits a pantomimic vulgarity long past anything English, it also shows a real excitement about the most earnest mental problems, of which English papers are innocent, or rather incapable. The *Sun* was full of the most solemn matters treated in the most farcical way. William James figured there as well as 'Weary Willie', and pragmatists alternated with pugilists in the long procession of its portraits.

Thus, when a very unobtrusive Oxford man named John Boulnois wrote in a very unreadable review called the *Natural Philosophy Quarterly* a series of articles on alleged weak points in Darwinian evolution, it fluttered no corner of the English papers; though Boulnois's theory (which was that of a comparatively stationary universe visited occasionally by convulsions of change) had some rather faddy fashionableness at Oxford, and got so far as to be named 'Catastrophism'. But many American papers seized on the challenge as a great event; and the *Sun* threw the shadow of Mr Boulnois quite gigantically across its pages. By the paradox already noted, articles of valuable intelligence and enthusiasm were presented with headlines apparently written by an illiterate maniac; headlines such as 'Darwin chews dirt; critic Boulnois says he jumps the shocks' – or 'Keep catastrophic, says thinker Boulnois'. And Mr Calhoun Kidd, of the *Western Sun*, was bidden to take his butterfly tie and lugubrious visage down to the little house outside Oxford where Thinker Boulnois lived in happy ignorance of such a title.

That fated philosopher had consented, in a somewhat dazed manner, to receive the interviewer, and had named the hour of nine that evening. The last of a summer sunset clung about Cumnor and the low wooded hills; the romantic Yankee was both doubtful of his road and inquisitive about his surroundings; and seeing the door of a genuine feudal old-country inn, the Champion Arms, standing open, he went in to make enquiries.

In the bar parlour he rang the bell, and had to wait some little time for a reply to it. The only other person present was a lean man with close red hair and loose, horsey-looking clothes, who was drinking very bad whisky, but smoking a very good cigar. The whisky, of course, was the choice brand of the Champion Arms; the cigar he had probably brought with him from London. Nothing could be more different than his cynical *négligé* from the dapper dryness of the young American; but something in his pencil and open notebook, and perhaps in the expression of his alert blue eye, caused Kidd to guess, correctly, that he was a brother journalist.

'Could you do me the favour,' asked Kidd, with the courtesy of his nation, 'of directing me to the Grey Cottage, where Mr Boulnois lives as I understand?'

'It's a few yards down the road,' said the red-haired man, removing his cigar; 'I shall be passing it myself in a minute, but I'm going on to Pendragon Park to try and see the fun.'

'What is Pendragon Park?' asked Calhoun Kidd.

'Sir Claude Champion's place – haven't you come down for that, too?' asked the other pressman, looking up. 'You're a journalist, aren't you?'

'I have come to see Mr Boulnois,' said Kidd.

'I've come to see Mrs Boulnois,' replied the other. 'But I shan't catch her at home.' And he laughed rather unpleasantly.

'Are you interested in Catastrophism?' asked the wondering Yankee.

'I'm interested in catastrophies; and there are going to be some,' replied his companion gloomily. 'Mine's a filthy trade, and I never pretend it isn't.'

With that he spat on the floor; yet somehow in the very act and instant one could realise that the man had been brought up as a gentleman.

The American pressman considered him with more attention. His face was pale and dissipated, with the promise of formidable passions yet to be loosed; but it was a clever and sensitive face; his clothes were coarse and careless, but he had a good seal ring on one of his long, thin fingers. His name, which came out in the course of talk, was James Dalroy; he was the son of a bankrupt Irish landlord, and attached to a pink paper which he heartily despised, called *Smart Society*, in the capacity of reporter and something painfully like a spy.

Smart Society, I regret to say, felt none of that interest in Boulnois on Darwin which was such a credit to the head and hearts of the *Western Sun*. Dalroy had come down, it seemed, to snuff up the scent of a scandal which might very well end in the Divorce Court, but which was at present hovering between Grey Cottage and Pendragon Park.

Sir Claude Champion was known to the readers of the *Western Sun* as well as Mr Boulnois. So were the Pope and the Derby winner; but the idea of their intimate acquaintanceship would have struck Kidd as equally incongruous. He had heard of (and written about, nay, falsely pretended to know) Sir Claude Champion, as 'one of the brightest and wealthiest of England's Upper Ten'; as the great sportsman who raced yachts round the world; as the great traveller who wrote books about the Himalayas, as the politician who swept constituencies with a startling sort of Tory Democracy, and as the great dabbler in art, music, literature, and, above all, acting. Sir Claude was really rather magnificent in other than American eyes. There was something of the Renascence Prince about his omnivorous culture and restless publicity; he was not only a great amateur, but an ardent one. There was in him none of that antiquarian frivolity that we convey by the word 'dilettante'.

That faultless falcon profile with purple-black Italian eye, which had been snapshot so often both for *Smart Society* and the *Western Sun*, gave everyone the impression of a man eaten by ambition as by a fire, or even a disease. But though Kidd knew a great deal about Sir Claude – a great deal more, in fact, than there was to know – it would never have crossed his wildest dreams to connect so showy an aristocrat with the newly-unearthed founder of Catastrophism, or to guess that Sir Claude Champion and John Boulnois could be intimate friends. Such, according to Dalroy's account, was nevertheless the fact. The two had hunted in couples at school and college, and, though their social destinies had been very different (for Champion was a great landlord and almost a millionaire, while Boulnois was a poor scholar and, until just lately, an unknown one), they still kept in very close touch with each other. Indeed, Boulnois's cottage stood just outside the gates of Pendragon Park.

But whether the two men could be friends much longer was becoming a dark and ugly question. A year or two before, Boulnois had married a beautiful and not unsuccessful actress, to whom he was devoted in his own shy and ponderous style; and the proximity of the household to Champion's had given that flighty celebrity opportunities for behaving in a way that could not but cause painful and rather base excitement. Sir Claude had carried the arts of publicity to perfection; and he seemed to take a crazy pleasure in being equally ostentatious in an intrigue that could do him no sort of honour. Footmen from Pendragon were perpetually leaving bouquets for Mrs Boulnois; carriages and motorcars were perpetually calling at the cottage for Mrs Boulnois; balls and masquerades perpetually filled the grounds in which the baronet paraded Mrs Boulnois, like the Queen of Love and Beauty at a tournament. That very evening, marked by Mr Kidd for the exposition of Catastrophism, had been marked by Sir Claude Champion for an open-air rendering of *Romeo and Juliet*, in which he was to play Romeo to a Juliet it was needless to name.

'I don't think it can go on without a smash,' said the young man with red hair, getting up and shaking himself. 'Old Boulnois may be squared – or he may be square. But if he's square he's thick – what you might call cubic. But I don't believe it's possible.'

'He is a man of grand intellectual powers,' said Calhoun Kidd in a deep voice.

'Yes,' answered Dalroy; 'but even a man of grand intellectual powers can't be such a blighted fool as all that. Must you be going on? I shall be following myself in a minute or two.'

But Calhoun Kidd, having finished a mill and soda, betook himself smartly up the road towards the Grey Cottage, leaving his cynical informant to his whisky and tobacco. The last of the daylight had faded; the skies were of a dark, green-grey, like slate, studded here and there with a star, but lighter on the left side of the sky, with the promise of a rising moon.

The Grey Cottage, which stood entrenched, as it were, in a square of stiff, high thorn-hedges, was so close under the pines and palisades of the Park that Kidd at first mistook it for the Park Lodge. Finding the name on the narrow wooden gate, however, and seeing by his watch that the hour of the 'Thinker's' appointment had just struck, he went in and knocked at the front door. Inside the garden hedge, he could see that the house, though unpretentious enough, was larger and more luxurious than it looked at first, and was quite a different kind of place from a porter's lodge. A dog-kennel and a beehive stood outside, like symbols of old English country-life: the moon was rising behind a plantation of prosperous pear trees: the dog that came out of the kennel was reverend-looking and reluctant to bark: and the plain, elderly manservant who opened the door was brief but dignified.

'Mr Boulnois asked me to offer his apologies, sir,' he said, 'but he has been obliged to go out suddenly.'

'But see here, I had an appointment,' said the interviewer, with a rising voice. 'Do you know where he went to?'

'To Pendragon Park, sir,' said the servant, rather sombrely, and began to close the door.

Kidd started a little.

'Did he go with Mrs – with the rest of the party?' he asked rather vaguely.

'No, sir,' said the man shortly; 'he stayed behind, and then went out alone.' And he shut the door, brutally, but with an air of duty not done.

The American, that curious compound of impudence and sensitiveness, was annoyed. He felt a strong desire to hustle them all along a bit and teach them business habits; the hoary old dog and the grizzled, heavy-faced old butler with his prehistoric shirt-front, and the drowsy old moon, and above all the scatter-brained old philosopher who couldn't keep an appointment.

'If that's the way he goes on he deserves to lose his wife's purest devotion,' said Mr Calhoun Kidd. 'But perhaps he's gone over to make a row. In that case I reckon a man from the *Western Sun* will be on the spot.'

And turning the corner by the open lodge-gates, he set off, stumping up the long avenue of black pine-woods that pointed in abrupt perspective towards the inner gardens of Pendragon Park. The trees were as black and orderly as plumes upon a hearse; there were still a few stars. He was a man with more literary than direct natural associations; the word 'Ravenswood' came into his head repeatedly. It was partly the raven colour of the pine-woods; but partly also an indescribable atmosphere almost described in Scott's great tragedy; the smell of something that died in the eighteenth century; the smell of dank gardens and broken urns, of wrongs that will never now be righted; of something that is none the less incurably sad because it is strangely unreal.

More than once, as he went up that trim, black road of tragic artifice, he stopped startled, thinking he heard steps in front of him. He could see nothing in front but the twin sombre walls of pine and the wedge of starlit sky above them. At first he thought he must have fancied it or been mocked by a mere echo of his own tramp. But as he went on he was more and more inclined to conclude, with the remains of his reason, that there really were other feet upon the road. He thought hazily of ghosts; and was surprised how swiftly he could see the image of an appropriate and local ghost, one with a face as white as Pierrot's, but patched with black. The apex of the triangle of dark-blue sky was growing brighter and bluer, but he did not realise as yet that this was because he was coming nearer to the lights of the great house and garden. He only felt that the atmosphere was growing more intense; there was in the sadness more violence and secrecy – more – he hesitated for the word, and then said it with a jerk of laughter – Catastrophism.

More pines, more pathway slid past him, and then he stood rooted as by a blast of magic. It is vain to say that he felt as if he had got into a dream; but this time he felt quite certain that he had got into a book. For we human beings are used to inappropriate things; we are accustomed to the clatter of the incongruous; it is a tune to which we can go to sleep. If one appropriate thing happens, it wakes us up like the pang of a perfect chord. Something happened such as would have happened in such a place in a forgotten tale.

Over the black pinewood came flying and flashing in the moon a naked sword – such a slender and sparkling rapier as may have fought many an unjust duel in that ancient park. It fell on the pathway far in front of him and lay there glistening like a large needle. He ran like a hare and bent to look at it. Seen at close quarters it had rather a showy look: the big red jewels in the hilt and guard were a little dubious. But there were other red drops upon the blade which were not dubious.

He looked round wildly in the direction from which the dazzling missile had come, and saw that at this point the sable façade of fir and pine was interrupted by a smaller road at right angles; which, when he turned it, brought him in full view of the long, lighted house, with a lake and fountains in front of it. Nevertheless, he did not look at this, having something more interesting to look at.

Above him, at the angle of the steep green bank of the terraced garden, was one of those small picturesque surprises common in the old landscape gardening; a kind of small round hill or dome of grass, like a giant molehill, ringed and crowned with three concentric fences of roses, and having a sundial in the highest point in the centre. Kidd could see the finger of the dial stand up dark against the sky like the dorsal fin of a shark, and the vain moonlight clinging to that idle clock. But he saw something else clinging to it also, for one wild moment – the figure of a man.

Though he saw it there only for a moment, though it

was outlandish and incredible in costume, being clad from neck to heel in tight crimson, with glints of gold, yet he knew in one flash of moonlight who it was. That white face flung up to heaven, clean-shaven and so unnaturally young, like Byron with a Roman nose, those black curls already grizzled – he had seen the thousand public portraits of Sir Claude Champion. The wild red figure reeled an instant against the sundial; the next it had rolled down the steep bank and lay at the American's feet, faintly moving one arm. A gaudy, unnatural gold ornament on the arm suddenly reminded Kidd of *Romeo and Juliet*; of course the tight crimson suit was part of the play. But there was a long red stain down the bank from which the man had rolled – that was no part of the play. He had been run through the body.

Mr Calhoun Kidd shouted and shouted again. Once more he seemed to hear phantasmal footsteps, and started to find another figure already near him. He knew the figure, and yet it terrified him. The dissipated youth who had called himself Dalroy had a horribly quiet way with him; if Boulnois failed to keep appointments that had been made, Dalroy had a sinister air of keeping appointments that hadn't. The moonlight discoloured everything; against Dalroy's red hair his wan face looked not so much white as pale green.

All this morbid impressionism must be Kidd's excuse for having cried out, brutally and beyond all reason: 'Did you do this, you devil?'

James Dalroy smiled his unpleasing smile; but before he could speak, the fallen figure made another movement of the arm, waving vaguely towards the place where the sword fell; then came a moan, and then it managed to speak.

'Boulnois . . . Boulnois, I say . . . Boulnois did it . . . jealous of me . . . he was jealous, he was, he was . . .'

Kidd bent his head down to hear more, and just managed to catch the words: 'Boulnois . . . with my own sword . . he threw it . . . '

Again the failing hand waved towards the sword, and then fell rigid with a thud. In Kidd rose from its depth all that acrid humour that is the strange salt of the seriousness of his race.

'See here,' he said sharply and with command, 'you must fetch a doctor. This man's dead.'

'And a priest, too, I suppose,' said Dalroy in an undecipherable manner. 'All these Champions are papists.'

The American knelt down by the body, felt the heart, propped up the head and used some last efforts at restoration: but before the other journalist re-appeared, followed by a doctor and a priest, he was already prepared to assert they were too late.

'Were you too late also?' asked the doctor, a solid prosperous-looking man, with conventional moustache and whiskers, but a lively eye, which darted over Kidd dubiously.

'In one sense,' drawled the representative of the *Sun*. 'I was too late to save the man, but I guess I was in time to hear something of importance. I heard the dead man denounce his assassin.'

'And who was the assassin?' asked the doctor, drawing his eyebrows together.

'Boulnois,' said Calhoun Kidd, and whistled softly.

The doctor stared at him gloomily with a reddening brow; but he did not contradict. Then the priest, a shorter figure in the background, said mildly: 'I understood that Mr Boulnois was not coming to Pendragon Park this evening.'

'There again,' said the Yankee grimly, 'I may be in a position to give the old country a fact or two. Yes, *sir*, John Boulnois was going to stay in all this evening; he fixed up a real good appointment there with me. But John Boulnois changed his mind; John Boulnois left his home abruptly and all alone, and came over to this derned Park an hour or so ago. His butler told me so. I think we hold what the all-wise police call a clue – have you sent for them?'

'Yes,' said the doctor; 'but we haven't alarmed anyone else yet.'

'Does Mrs Boulnois know?' asked James Dalroy; and again Kidd was conscious of an irrational desire to hit him on his curling mouth.

'I have not told her,' said the doctor gruffly; 'but here come the police.'

The little priest had stepped out into the main avenue, and now returned with the fallen sword, which looked ludicrously large and theatrical when attached to his dumpy figure, at once clerical and commonplace. 'Just before the police come,' he said apologetically, 'has anyone got a light?'

The Yankee journalist took an electric torch from his pocket, and the priest held it close to the middle part of the blade, which he examined with blinking care. Then, without glancing at the point or pommel, he handed the long weapon to the doctor.

'I fear I'm no use here,' he said, with a brief sigh. 'I'll say good-night to you, gentlemen.' And he walked away up the dark avenue towards the house, his hands clasped behind him and his big head bent in cogitation.

The rest of the group made increased haste towards the lodge-gates, where an inspector and two constables could already be seen in consultation with the lodge-keeper. But the little priest only walked slower and slower in the dim cloister of pine, and at last stopped dead, on the steps of the house. It was his silent way of acknowledging an equally silent approach; for there came towards him a presence that might have satisfied even Calhoun Kidd's demands for a lovely and aristocratic ghost. It was a young woman in silvery satins of a Renaissance design; she had golden hair in two long shining ropes, and a face so startlingly pale between them that she might have been chryselephantine – made, that is, like some old Greek statues, out of ivory and gold. But her eyes were very bright, and her voice, though low, was confident.

'Father Brown?' she said.

'Mrs Boulnois?' he replied gravely. Then he looked at her and immediately said: 'I see you know about Sir Claude.'

'How do you know I know?' she asked steadily.

He did not answer the question, but asked another: 'Have you seen your husband?'

'My husband is at home,' she said. 'He has nothing to do with this.'

Again he did not answer; and the woman drew nearer to him, with a curiously intense expression on her face.

'Shall I tell you something more?' she said, with a rather fearful smile. 'I don't think he did it, and *you* don't either.'

Father Brown returned her gaze with a long, grave stare, and then nodded, yet more gravely.

'Father Brown,' said the lady, 'I am going to tell you

all I know, but I want you to do me a favour first. Will you tell me *why* you haven't jumped to the conclusion of poor John's guilt, as all the rest have done? Don't mind what you say: I – I know about the gossip and the appearances that are against him.'

Father Brown looked honestly embarrassed, and passed his hand across his forehead. 'Two very little things,' he said. 'At least, one's very trivial and the other very vague. But such as they are, they don't fit in with Mr Boulnois being the murderer.'

He turned his blank, round face up to the stars and continued absent-mindedly: 'To take the vague idea first. I attach a good deal of importance to vague ideas. All those things that "aren't evidence" are what convince me. I think a moral impossibility the biggest of all impossibilities. I know your husband only slightly, but I think this crime of his, as generally conceived, something very like a moral impossibility. Please do not think I mean that Boulnois could not be so wicked. Anybody can be wicked – as wicked as he chooses. We can direct our moral wills; but we can't generally change our instinctive tastes and ways of doing things. Boulnois might commit a murder, but not this murder. He would not snatch Romeo's sword from its romantic scabbard; or slay his foe on the sundial as on a kind of altar; or leave his body among the roses; or fling the sword away among the pines. If Boulnois killed anyone he'd do it quietly and heavily, as he'd do any other doubtful thing – take a tenth glass of port, or read a loose Greek poet. No, the romantic setting is not like Boulnois. It's more like Champion.'

'Ah!' she said, and looked at him with eyes like diamonds.

'And the trivial thing was this,' said Brown. 'There

were fingerprints on that sword; fingerprints can be detected quite a time after they are made if they're on some polished surface like glass or steel. These were on a polished surface. They were halfway down the blade of the sword. Whose prints they were I have no earthly clue; but why should anybody hold a sword halfway down? It was a long sword, but length is an advantage in lunging at an enemy. At least, at most enemies. At all enemies except one.'

'Except one!' she repeated.

'There is only one enemy,' said Father Brown, 'whom it is easier to kill with a dagger than a sword.'

'I know,' said the woman. 'Oneself.'

There was a long silence, and then the priest said quietly but abruptly: 'Am I right, then? Did Sir Claude kill himself?'

'Yes,' she said, with a face like marble. 'I saw him do it.'

'He died,' said Father Brown, 'for love of you?'

An extraordinary expression flashed across her face, very different from pity, modesty, remorse, or anything her companion had expected: her voice became suddenly strong and full. 'I don't believe,' she said, 'he ever cared about me a rap. He hated my husband.'

'Why?' asked the other, and turned his round face from the sky to the lady.

'He hated my husband because . . . it is so strange I hardly know how to say it . . . because . . .'

'Yes?' said Brown patiently.

'Because my husband wouldn't hate him.'

Father Brown only nodded, and seemed still to be listening; he differed from most detectives in fact and fiction in a small point – he never pretended not to understand when he understood perfectly well.

Mrs Boulnois drew near once more with the same contained glow of certainty. 'My husband,' she said, 'is a great man. Sir Claude Champion was not a great man: he was a celebrated and successful man. My husband has never been celebrated or successful; and it is the solemn truth that he has never dreamed of being so. He no more expects to be famous for thinking than for smoking cigars. On all that side he has a sort of splendid stupidity. He has never grown up. He still liked Champion exactly as he liked him at school; he admired him as he would admire a conjuring trick done at the dinner-table. But he couldn't be got to conceive the notion of *envying* Champion. *And Champion wanted to be envied.* He went mad and killed himself for that.'

'Yes,' said Father Brown; 'I think I begin to understand.'

'Oh, don't you see?' she cried; 'the whole picture is made for that – the place is planned for it. Champion put John in a little house at his very door, like a dependant – to make him *feel* a failure. He never felt it. He thinks no more about such things than – than an absent-minded lion. Champion would burst in on John's shabbiest hours or homeliest meals with some dazzling present or announcement or expedition that made it like the visit of Haroun Alraschid, and John would accept or refuse amiably with one eye off, so to speak, like one lazy schoolboy agreeing or disagreeing with another. After five years of it John had not turned a hair; and Sir Claude Champion was a monomaniac.'

'And Haman began to tell them,' said Father Brown, 'of all the things wherein the king had honoured him; and he said: "All these things profit me nothing while I see Mordecai the Jew sitting in the gate." '

'The crisis came,' Mrs Boulnois continued, 'when I

persuaded John to let me take down some of his speculations and send them to a magazine. They began to attract attention, especially in America, and one paper wanted to interview him. When Champion (who was interviewed nearly every day) heard of this late little crumb of success falling to his unconscious rival, the last link snapped that held back his devilish hatred. Then he began to lay that insane siege to my own love and honour which has been the talk of the shire. You will ask me why I allowed such atrocious attentions. I answer that I could not have declined them except by explaining to my husband, and there are some things the soul cannot do, as the body cannot fly. Nobody could have explained to my husband. Nobody could do it now. If you said to him in so many words, "Champion is stealing your wife", he would think the joke a little vulgar: that it could be anything but a joke – that notion could find no crack in his great skull to get in by. Well, John was to come and see us act this evening, but just as we were starting he said he wouldn't; he had got an interesting book and a cigar. I told this to Sir Claude, and it was his death-blow. The monomaniac suddenly saw despair. He stabbed himself, crying out like a devil that Boulnois was slaying him; he lies there in the garden dead of his own jealousy to produce jealousy; and John is sitting in the dining-room reading a book.'

There was another silence, and then the little priest said: 'There is only one weak point, Mrs Boulnois, in all your very vivid account. Your husband is not sitting in the dining-room reading a book. That American reporter told me he had been to your house, and your butler told him Mr Boulnois had gone to Pendragon Park after all.'

Her bright eyes widened to an almost electric glare; and yet it seemed rather bewilderment than confusion or fear. 'Why, what *can* you mean?' she cried. 'All the servants were out of the house, seeing the theatricals. And we don't keep a butler, thank goodness!'

Father Brown started and spun half round like an absurd teetotum. 'What, what?' he cried seeming galvanised into sudden life. 'Look here – I say – can I make your husband hear if I go to the house?'

'Oh, the servants will be back by now,' she said, wondering.

'Right, right!' rejoined the cleric energetically, and set off scuttling up the path towards the Park gates. He turned once to say: 'Better get hold of that Yankee, or "Crime of John Boulnois" will be all over the Republic in large letters.'

'You don't understand,' said Mrs Boulnois. 'He wouldn't mind. I don't think he imagines that America really is a place.'

When Father Brown reached the house with the beehive and the drowsy dog, a small and neat maidservant showed him into the dining-room, where Boulnois sat reading by a shaded lamp, exactly as his wife described him. A decanter of port and a wineglass were at his elbow; and the instant the priest entered he noted the long ash stand out unbroken on his cigar.

'He has been here for half an hour at least,' thought Father Brown. In fact, he had the air of sitting where he had sat when his dinner was cleared away.

'Don't get up, Mr Boulnois,' said the priest in his pleasant, prosaic way. 'I shan't interrupt you a moment. I fear I break in on some of your scientific studies.'

'No,' said Boulnois; 'I was reading "The Bloody

Thumb".' He said it with neither frown nor smile, and his visitor was conscious of a certain deep and virile indifference in the man which his wife had called greatness. He laid down a gory yellow 'shocker' without even feeling its incongruity enough to comment on it humorously. John Boulnois was a big, slow-moving man with a massive head, partly grey and partly bald, and blunt, burly features. He was in shabby and very old-fashioned evening-dress, with a narrow triangular opening of shirt-front: he had assumed it that evening in his original purpose of going to see his wife act Juliet.

'I won't keep you long from "The Bloody Thumb" or any other catastrophic affairs,' said Father Brown, smiling. 'I only came to ask you about the crime you committed this evening.'

Boulnois looked at him steadily, but a red bar began to show across his broad brow; and he seemed like one discovering embarrassment for the first time.

'I know it was a strange crime,' assented Brown in a low voice. 'Stranger than murder perhaps – to you. The little sins are sometimes harder to confess than the big ones – but that's why it's so important to confess them. Your crime is committed by every fashionable hostess six times a week: and yet you find it stick to your tongue like a nameless atrocity.'

'It makes one feel,' said the philosopher slowly, 'such a damned fool.'

'I know,' assented the other, 'but one often has to choose between feeling a damned fool and being one.'

'I can't analyse myself well,' went on Boulnois; 'but sitting in that chair with that story I was as happy as a schoolboy on a half-holiday. It was security, eternity – I can't convey it . . . the cigars were within reach ... the matches were within reach ... the *Thumb* had four more appearances to ... it was not only a peace, but a plenitude. Then that bell rang, and I thought for one long, mortal minute that I couldn't get out of that chair – literally, physically, muscularly couldn't. Then I did it like a man lifting the world, because I knew all the servants were out. I opened the front door, and there was a little man with his mouth open to speak and his notebook open to write in. I remembered the Yankee interviewer I had forgotten. His hair was parted in the middle, and I tell you that murder – '

'I understand,' said Father Brown. 'I've seen him.'

'I didn't commit murder,' continued the Catastrophist mildly, 'but only perjury. I said I had gone across to Pendragon Park and shut the door in his face. That is my crime, Father Brown, and I don't know what penance you would inflict for it.'

'I shan't inflict any penance,' said the clerical gentleman, collecting his heavy hat and umbrella with an air of some amusement; 'quite the contrary. I came here specially to let you off the little penance which would otherwise have followed your little offence.'

'And what,' asked Boulnois, smiling, 'is the little penance I have so luckily been let off?'

'Being hanged,' said Father Brown.

The Oracle of the Dog

'Yes,' said Father Brown, 'I always like a dog, so long as he isn't spelt backwards.'

Those who are quick in talking are not always quick in listening. Sometimes even their brilliancy produces a sort of stupidity. Father Brown's friend and companion was a young man with a stream of ideas and stories, an enthusiastic young man named Fiennes, with eager blue eyes and blond hair that seemed to be brushed back, not merely with a hairbrush but with the wind of the world as he rushed through it. But he stopped in the torrent of his talk in a momentary bewilderment before he saw the priest's very simple meaning.

'You mean that people make too much of them?' he said. 'Well, I don't know. They're marvellous creatures. Sometimes I think they know a lot more than we do.'

Father Brown said nothing, but continued to stroke the head of the big retriever in a half-abstracted but apparently soothing fashion.

'Why,' said Fiennes, warming again to his monologue, 'there was a dog in the case I've come to see you about: what they call the "Invisible Murder Case", you know. It's a strange story, but from my point of view the dog is about the strangest thing in it. Of course, there's the mystery of the crime itself, and how old Druce can have been killed by somebody else when he was all alone in the summerhouse –'

The hand stroking the dog stopped for a moment in

its rhythmic movement, and Father Brown said calmly: 'Oh, it was a summerhouse, was it?'

'I thought you'd read all about it in the papers,' answered Fiennes. 'Stop a minute; I believe I've got a cutting that will give you all the particulars.' He produced a strip of newspaper from his pocket and handed it to the priest, who began to read it, holding it close to his blinking eyes with one hand while the other continued its half-conscious caresses of the dog. It looked like the parable of a man not letting his right hand know what his left hand did.

Many mystery stories, about men murdered behind locked doors and windows, and murderers escaping without means of entrance and exit, have come true in the course of the extraordinary events at Cranston on the coast of Yorkshire, where Colonel Druce was found stabbed from behind by a dagger that has entirely disappeared from the scene, and apparently even from the neighbourhood.

The summerhouse in which he died was indeed accessible at one entrance, the ordinary doorway which looked down the central walk of the garden towards the house. But, by a combination of events almost to be called a coincidence, it appears that both the path and the entrance were watched during the crucial time, and there is a chain of witnesses who confirm each other. The summerhouse stands at the extreme end of the garden, where there is no exit or entrance of any kind. The central garden path is a lane between two ranks of tall delphiniums, planted so close that any stray step off the path would leave its traces; and both path and plants run right up to the very mouth of the summerhouse, so that no straying from that straight path could fail to be observed, and no other mode of entrance can be imagined.

Patrick Floyd, secretary of the murdered man, testified that he had been in a position to overlook the whole garden from the time when Colonel Druce last appeared alive in the doorway to the time when he was found dead; as he, Floyd, had been on the top of a stepladder clipping the garden hedge. Janet Druce, the dead man's daughter, confirmed this, saying that she had sat on the terrace of the house throughout that time and had seen Floyd at his work. Touching some part of the time, this is again supported by Donald Druce, her brother – who overlooked the garden – standing at his bedroom window in his dressing-gown, for he had risen late. Lastly, the account is consistent with that given by Dr Valentine, a neighbour, who called for a time to talk with Miss Druce on the terrace, and by the Colonel's solicitor, Mr Aubrey Traill, who was apparently the last to see the murdered man alive – presumably with the exception of the murderer.

All are agreed that the course of events was as follows: about half-past three in the afternoon, Miss Druce went down the path to ask her father when he would like tea; but he said he did not want any and was waiting to see Traill, his lawyer, who was to be sent to him in the summerhouse. The girl then came away and met Traill coming down the path; she directed him to her father and he went in as directed. About half an hour afterwards he came out again, the Colonel coming with him to the door and showing himself to all appearance in health and even high spirits. He had been somewhat annoyed earlier in the day by his son's irregular hours, but seemed to recover his temper in a perfectly normal fashion, and had been rather markedly genial in receiving other visitors, including two of his nephews, who came over for the day. But as these were out walking during the whole period of the tragedy, they had no evidence to give. It is said, indeed, that the Colonel was not on very good terms with Dr Valentine, but that gentleman only had a brief interview with the daughter of the house, to whom he is supposed to be paying serious attentions.

Traill, the solicitor, says he left the Colonel entirely alone in the summerhouse, and this is confirmed by Floyd's bird's-eye view of the garden, which showed nobody else passing the only entrance. Ten minutes later, Miss Druce again went down the garden and had not reached the end of the path when she saw her father, who was conspicuous by his white linen coat, lying in a heap on the floor. She uttered a scream which brought others to the spot, and on entering the place they found the Colonel lying dead beside his basket-chair, which was also upset. Dr Valentine, who was still in the immediate neighbourhood, testified that the wound was made by some sort of stiletto, entering under the shoulder-blade and piercing the heart. The police have searched the neighbourhood for such a weapon, but no trace of it can be found.

'So Colonel Druce wore a white coat, did he?' said Father Brown as he put down the paper.

'Trick he learnt in the tropics,' replied Fiennes, with some wonder. 'He'd had some queer adventures there, by his own account; and I fancy his dislike of

Valentine was connected with the doctor coming from the tropics, too. But it's all an infernal puzzle. The account there is pretty accurate; I didn't see the tragedy, in the sense of the discovery; I was out walking with the young nephews and the dog – the dog I wanted to tell you about. But I saw the stage set for it as described; the straight lane between the blue flowers right up to the dark entrance, and the lawyer going down it in his blacks and his silk hat, and the red head of the secretary showing high above the green hedge as he worked on it with his shears. Nobody could have mistaken that red head at any distance; and if people say they saw it there all the time, you may be sure they did. This red-haired secretary, Floyd, is quite a character; a breathless bounding sort of fellow, always doing everybody's work as he was doing the gardener's. I think he is an American; he's certainly got the American view of life – what they call the viewpoint, bless 'em.'

'What about the lawyer?' asked Father Brown.

There was a silence, and then Fiennes spoke quite slowly for him. 'Traill struck me as a singular man. In his fine black clothes he was almost foppish, yet you can hardly call him fashionable. For he wore a pair of long, luxuriant black whiskers such as haven't been seen since Victorian times. He had rather a fine grave face and a fine grave manner, but every now and then he seemed to remember to smile. And when he showed his white teeth he seemed to lose a little of his dignity, and there was something faintly fawning about him. It may have been only embarrassment, for he would also fidget with his cravat and his tie-pin, which were at once handsome and unusual, like himself. If I could think of anybody – but what's the good, when the whole thing's impossible? Nobody knows who did it. Nobody knows how it could be done. At least there's only one exception I'd make, and that's why I really mentioned the whole thing. The dog knows.'

Father Brown sighed and then said absently: 'You were there as a friend of young Donald, weren't you? He didn't go on your walk with you?'

'No,' replied Fiennes smiling. 'The young scoundrel had gone to bed that morning and got up that afternoon. I went with his cousins, two young officers from India, and our conversation was trivial enough. I remember the elder, whose name I think is Herbert Druce and who is an authority on horse-breeding, talked about nothing but a mare he had bought and the moral character of the man who sold her; while his brother Harry seemed to be brooding on his bad luck at Monte Carlo. I only mention it to show you, in the light of what happened on our walk, that there was nothing psychic about us. The dog was the only mystic in our company.'

'What sort of a dog was he?' asked the priest.

'Same breed as that one,' answered Fiennes. 'That's what started me off on the story, your saying you didn't believe in believing in a dog. He's a big black retriever, named Nox, and a suggestive name, too; for I think what he did a darker mystery than the murder. You know Druce's house and garden are by the sea; we walked about a mile from it along the sands and then turned back, going the other way. We passed a rather curious rock called the Rock of Fortune, famous in the neighbourhood because it's one of those examples of one stone barely balanced on another, so that a touch would knock it over. It is not really very high but the hanging outline of it makes it look a little wild and sinister; at least it made it look so to me, for I don't imagine my jolly young companions were afflicted with the picturesque. But it may be that I was beginning to feel an atmosphere; for just then the question arose of whether it was time to go back to tea, and even then I think I had a premonition that time counted for a good deal in the business. Neither Herbert Druce nor I had a watch, so we called out to his brother, who was some paces behind, having stopped to light his pipe under the hedge. Hence it happened that he shouted out the hour, which was twenty-past four, in his big voice through the growing twilight; and somehow the loudness of it made it sound like the proclamation of something tremendous. His unconsciousness seemed to make it all the more so; but that was always the way with omens; and particular ticks of the clock were really very ominous things that afternoon. According to Dr Valentine's testimony, poor Druce had actually died just about half-past four.

'Well, they said we needn't go home for ten minutes, and we walked a little farther along the sands, doing nothing in particular – throwing stones for the dog and throwing sticks into the sea for him to swim after. But to me the twilight seemed to grow oddly oppressive, and the very shadow of the top-heavy Rock of Fortune lay on me like a load. And then the curious thing happened. Nox had just brought back Herbert's walking-stick out of the sea and his brother had thrown his in also. The dog swam out again, but just about what must have been the stroke of the half-hour, he stopped swimming. He came back again on to the shore and stood in front of us. Then he suddenly threw up his head and sent up a howl or wail of woe – if ever I heard one in the world.

'What the devil's the matter with the dog?' asked Herbert; but none of us could answer. There was a long silence after the brute's wailing and whining died away on the desolate shore; and then the silence was broken. As I live, it was broken by a faint and far-off shriek, like the shriek of a woman from beyond the hedges inland. We didn't know what it was then; but we knew afterwards. It was the cry the girl gave when she first saw the body of her father.'

'You went back, I suppose,' said Father Brown patiently. 'What happened then?'

'I'll tell you what happened then,' said Fiennes with a grim emphasis. 'When we got back into that garden the first thing we saw was Traill, the lawyer; I can see him now with his black hat and black whiskers relieved against the perspective of the blue flowers stretching down to the summerhouse, with the sunset and the strange outline of the Rock of Fortune in the distance. His face and figure were in shadow against the sunset; but I swear the white teeth were showing in his head and he was smiling.

'The moment Nox saw that man the dog dashed forward and stood in the middle of the path barking at him madly, murderously, volleying out curses that were almost verbal in their dreadful distinctness of hatred. And the man doubled up and fled along the path between the flowers.'

Father Brown sprang to his feet with a startling impatience.

'So the dog denounced him, did he?' he cried. 'The oracle of the dog condemned him. Did you see what birds were flying, and are you sure whether they were on the right hand or the left? Did you consult the augurs about the sacrifices? Surely you didn't omit to cut open the dog and examine his entrails. That is the sort of scientific test you heathen humanitarians seem to trust when you are thinking of taking away the life and honour of a man.'

Fiennes sat gaping for an instant before he found breath to say: 'Why, what's the matter with you? What have I done now?'

A sort of anxiety came back into the priest's eyes – the anxiety of a man who has run against a post in the dark and wonders for a moment whether he has hurt it.

'I'm most awfully sorry,' he said with sincere distress. 'I beg your pardon for being so rude; pray forgive me.'

Fiennes looked at him curiously. 'I sometimes think you are more of a mystery than any of the mysteries,' he said. 'But anyhow, if you don't believe in the mystery of the dog, at least you can't get over the mystery of the man. You can't deny that at the very moment when the beast came back from the sea and bellowed, his master's soul was driven out of his body by the blow of some unseen power that no mortal man can trace or even imagine. And as for the lawyer – I don't go only by the dog – there are other curious details, too. He struck me as a smooth, smiling, equivocal sort of person; and one of his tricks seemed like a sort of hint. You know the doctor and the police were on the spot very quickly; Valentine was brought back when walking away from the house, and he telephoned instantly. That, with the secluded house, small numbers, and enclosed space, made it pretty possible to search everybody who could have been near; and everybody was thoroughly searched – for a weapon. The whole house, garden, and shore were combed for a weapon. The disappearance of the dagger is almost as crazy as the disappearance of the man.'

'The disappearance of the dagger,' said Father Brown, nodding. He seemed to have become suddenly attentive.

'Well,' continued Fiennes, 'I told you that man Traill had a trick of fidgeting with his tie and tie-pin – especially his tie-pin. His pin, like himself, was at once showy and old-fashoned. It had one of those stones with concentric coloured rings that look like an eye; and his own concentration on it got on my nerves, as if he had been a Cyclops with one eye in the middle of his body. But the pin was not only large but long; and it occurred to me that his anxiety about its adjustment was because it was even longer than it looked; as long as a stiletto in fact.'

Father Brown nodded thoughtfully. 'Was any other instrument ever suggested?' he asked.

'There was another suggestion,' answered Fiennes, 'from one of the young Druces – the cousins, I mean. Neither Herbert nor Harry Druce would have struck one at first as likely to be of assistance in scientific detection; but while Herbert was really the traditional type of heavy dragoon, caring for nothing but horses and being an ornament to the Horse Guards, his younger brother Harry had been in the Indian Police and knew something about such things. Indeed, in his own way he was quite clever; and I rather fancy he had been too clever; I mean he had left the police through breaking some red-tape regulations and taking some sort of risk and responsibility of his own. Anyhow, he was in some sense a detective out of work, and threw himself into this business with more than the ardour of an amateur. And it was with him that I had an argument about the weapon – an argument that led to something new. It began by his countering my description of the dog barking at Traill; and he said that a dog at his worst didn't bark, but growled.'

'He was quite right there,' observed the priest.

'This young fellow went on to say that, if it came to that, he'd heard Nox growling at other people before then; and among others at Floyd, the secretary. I retorted that his own argument answered itself; for the crime couldn't be brought home to two or three people, and least of all to Floyd, who was as innocent as a harum-scarum schoolboy, and had been seen by everybody all the time perched above the garden hedge with his fan of red hair as conspicuous as a scarlet cockatoo. "I know there's difficulties anyhow," said my colleague; "but I wish you'd come with me down the garden a minute. I want to show you something I don't think anyone else has seen." This was on the very day of the discovery, and the garden was just as it had been. The stepladder was still standing by the hedge, and just under the hedge my guide stopped and disentangled something from the deep grass. It was the shears used for clipping the hedge, and on the point of one of them was a smear of blood.'

There was a short silence, and then Father Brown said suddenly. 'What was the lawyer there for?'

'He told us the Colonel sent for him to alter his will,' answered Fiennes. 'And, by the way, there was another thing about the business of the will that I ought to mention. You see, the will wasn't actually signed in the summerhouse that afternoon.'

'I suppose not,' said Father Brown; 'there would have to be two witnesses.'

'The lawyer actually came down the day before and it was signed then; but he was sent for again next day because the old man had a doubt about one of the witnesses and had to be reassured.'

'Who were the witnesses?' asked Father Brown.

'That's just the point,' replied his informant eagerly, 'the witnesses were Floyd, the secretary, and this Dr Valentine, the foreign sort of surgeon or whatever he is; and the two have a quarrel. Now I'm bound to say that the secretary is something of a busybody. He's one of those hot and headlong people whose warmth of temperament has unfortunately turned mostly to pugnacity and bristling suspicion; to distrusting people instead of to trusting them. That sort of red-haired red-hot fellow is always either universally credulous or universally incredulous; and sometimes both. He was not only a jack-of-all-trades, but he knew better than all tradesmen. He not only knew everything, but he warned everybody against everybody. All that must be taken into account in his suspicions about Valentine; but in that particular case there seems to have been something behind it. He said the name of Valentine was not really Valentine. He said he had seen him elsewhere known by the name of De Villon. He said it would invalidate the will; of course he was kind enough to explain to the lawyer what the law was on that point. They were both in a frightful wax.'

Father Brown laughed. 'People often are when they are to witness a will,' he said; 'for one thing, it means that they can't have any legacy under it. But what did Dr Valentine say? No doubt the universal secretary knew more about the doctor's name than the doctor did. But even the doctor might have some information about his own name.'

Fiennes paused a moment before he replied.

'Dr Valentine took it in a curious way. Dr Valentine is a curious man. His appearance is rather striking but very foreign. He is young but wears a beard cut square; and his face is very pale, dreadfully pale and dreadfully serious. His eyes have a sort of ache in them, as if he ought to wear glasses, or had given himself a headache with thinking; but he is quite handsome and always very formally dressed, with a top hat and a dark coat and a little red rosette. His manner is rather cold and haughty, and he has a way of staring at you which is very disconcerting. When thus charged with having changed his name, he merely stared like a sphinx and then said with a little laugh that he supposed Americans had no names to change. At that I think the Colonel also got into a fuss and said all sorts of angry things to the doctor; all the more angry because of the doctor's pretensions to a future place in his family. But I shouldn't have thought much of that but for a few words that I happened to hear later, early in the afternoon of the tragedy. I don't want to make a lot of them, for they weren't the sort of words on which one would like, in the ordinary way, to play the eavesdropper. As I was passing out towards the front gate with my two companions and the dog, I heard voices which told me that Dr Valentine and Miss Druce had withdrawn for a moment into the shadow of the house, in an angle behind a row of flowering plants, and were talking to each other in passionate whisperings – sometimes almost like hissings; for it was something of a lovers' quarrel as well as a lovers' tryst. Nobody repeats the sort of things they said for the most part; but in an unfortunate business like this I'm bound to say that there was repeated more than once a phrase about killing somebody. In fact, the girl seemed to be begging him not to kill somebody, or saying that no provocation could justify killing anybody; which seems an unusual sort of talk to address to a gentleman who has dropped in to tea.'

'Do you know,' asked the priest, 'whether Dr Valentine seemed to be very angry after the scene with the secretary and the Colonel – I mean about witnessing the will?'

'By all accounts,' replied the other, 'he wasn't half so angry as the secretary was. It was the secretary who went away raging after witnessing the will.'

'And now,' said Father Brown, 'what about the will itself?'

'The Colonel was a very wealthy man, and his will was important. Traill wouldn't tell us the alteration at that stage, but I have since heard – only this morning in fact – that most of the money was transferred from the son to the daughter. I told you that Druce was wild with my friend Donald over his dissipated hours.'

'The question of motive has been rather overshadowed by the question of method,' observed Father Brown thoughtfully. 'At that moment, apparently, Miss Druce was the immediate gainer by the death.'

'Good God! What a cold-blooded way of talking,' cried Fiennes, staring at him. 'You don't really mean to hint that she – '

'Is she going to marry that Dr Valentine?' asked the other.

'Some people are against it,' answered his friend.

'But he is liked and respected in the place and is a skilled and devoted surgeon.'

'So devoted a surgeon,' said Father Brown, 'that he had surgical instruments with him when he went to call on the young lady at teatime. For he must have used a lancet or something, and he never seems to have gone home.'

Fiennes sprang to his feet and looked at him in a heat of enquiry. 'You suggest he might have used the very same lancet – '

Father Brown shook his head. 'All these suggestions are fancies just now,' he said. 'The problem is not who did it or what did it, but how it was done. We might find many men and even many tools – pins and shears and lancets. But how did a man get into the room? How did even a pin get into it?'

He was staring reflectively at the ceiling as he spoke, but as he said the last words his eye cocked in an alert fashion as if he had suddenly seen a curious fly on the ceiling.

'Well, what would you do about it?' asked the young man. 'You have a lot of experience; what would you advise now?'

'I'm afraid I'm not much use,' said Father Brown with a sigh. 'I can't suggest very much without having ever been near the place or the people. For the moment you can only go on with local enquiries. I gather that your friend from the Indian Police is more or less in charge of your enquiry down there. I should run down and see how he is getting on. See what he's been doing in the way of amateur detection. There may be news already.'

As his guests, the biped and the quadruped, disappeared, Father Brown took up his pen and went back to his interrupted occupation of planning a course of lectures on the Encyclical *Rerum Novarum*. The subject was a large one and he had to re-cast it more than once, so that he was somewhat similarly employed some two days later when the big black dog again came bounding into the room and sprawled all over him with enthusiasm and excitement. The master who followed the dog shared the excitement if not the enthusiasm. He had been excited in a less pleasant fashion, for his blue eyes seemed to start from his head and his eager face was even a little pale.

'You told me,' he said abruptly and without preface, 'to find out what Harry Druce was doing. Do you know what he's done?'

The priest did not reply, and the young man went on in jerky tones: 'I'll tell you what he's done. He's killed himself.'

Father Brown's lips moved only faintly, and there was nothing practical about what he was saying – nothing that has anything to do with this story or this world.

'You give me the creeps sometimes,' said Fiennes. 'Did you – did you expect this?'

'I thought it possible,' said Father Brown; 'that was why I asked you to go and see what he was doing. I hoped you might not be too late.'

'It was I who found him,' said Fiennes rather huskily. 'It was the ugliest and most uncanny thing I ever knew. I went down that old garden again, and I knew there was something new and unnatural about it besides the murder. The flowers still tossed about in blue masses on each side of the black entrance into the old grey summerhouse; but to me the blue flowers looked like blue devils dancing before some dark cavern of the underworld. I looked all round, everything seemed to be in its ordinary place. But the queer notion grew on me that there was something wrong with the very shape of the sky. And then I saw what it was. The Rock of Fortune always rose in the background beyond the garden hedge and against the sea. And the Rock of Fortune was gone.'

Father Brown had lifted his head and was listening intently.

'It was as if a mountain had walked away out of a landscape or a moon fallen from the sky; though I knew, of course, that a touch at any time would have tipped the thing over. Something possessed me and I rushed down that garden path like the wind and went crashing through that hedge as if it were a spider's web. It was a thin hedge really, though its undisturbed trimness had made it serve all the purposes of a wall. On the shore I found the loose rock fallen from its pedestal; and poor Harry Druce lay like a wreck underneath it. One arm was thrown round it in a sort of embrace as if he had pulled it down on himself; and on the broad brown sands beside it, in large crazy lettering, he had scrawled the words: "The Rock of Fortune falls on the Fool".'

'It was the Colonel's will that did that,' observed Father Brown. 'The young man had staked everything on profiting himself by Donald's disgrace, especially when his uncle sent for him on the same day as the lawyer, and welcomed him with so much warmth. Otherwise he was done; he'd lost his police job; he was beggared at Monte Carlo. And he killed himself when he found he'd killed his kinsman for nothing.'

'Here, stop a minute!' cried the staring Fiennes. 'You're going too fast for me.'

'Talking about the will, by the way,' continued Father Brown calmly, 'before I forget it, or we go on to bigger things, there was a simple explanation, I think, of all that business about the doctor's name. I rather fancy I have heard both names before somewhere. The doctor is really a French nobleman with the title of the Marquis de Villon. But he is also an ardent Republican and has abandoned his title and fallen back on the forgotten family surname. "With your Citizen Riquetti you have puzzled Europe for ten days".'

'What is that?' asked the young man blankly.

'Never mind,' said the priest. 'Nine times out of ten it is a rascally thing to change one's name; but this was a piece of fine fanaticism. That's the point of his sarcasm about Americans having no names – that is, no titles. Now in England the Marquis of Hartington is never called Mr Hartington; but in France the Marquis de Villon is called M. de Villon. So it might well look like a change of name. As for the talk about killing, I fancy that also was a point of French etiquette. The doctor was talking about challenging Floyd to a duel, and the girl was trying to dissuade him.

'Oh, I *see*,' cried Fiennes slowly. 'Now I understand what she meant.'

'And what is that about?' asked his companion, smiling.

'Well,' said the young man, 'it was something that happened to me just before I found that poor fellow's body; only the catastrophe drove it out of my head. I suppose it's hard to remember a little romantic idyll when you've just come on top of a tragedy. But as I went down the lanes leading to the Colonel's old place I met his daughter walking with Dr Valentine. She was in mourning, of course, and he always wore black as if he were going to a funeral; but I can't say that their faces were very funereal. Never have I seen two people looking in their own way more respectably radiant and cheerful. They stopped and saluted me, and then she told me they were married and living in a little house on the outskirts of the town, where the doctor was continuing his practice. This rather surprised me, because I knew that her old father's will had left her his property; and I hinted at it delicately by saying I was going along to her father's old place and had half expected to meet her there. But she only laughed and said: "Oh, we've given up all that. My husband doesn't like heiresses." And I discovered with some astonishment they really had insisted on restoring the property to poor Donald; so I hope he's had a healthy shock and will treat it sensibly. There was never much really the matter with him; he was very young and his father was not very wise. But it was in connection with that that she said something I didn't understand at the time; but now I'm sure it must be as you say. She said with a sort of sudden and splendid arrogance that was entirely altruistic: "I hope it'll stop that red-haired fool from fussing any more about the will. Does he think my husband, who has given up a crest and a coronet as old as the Crusades for his principles, would kill an old man in a summerhouse for a legacy like that?" Then she laughed again and said, "My husband isn't killing anybody except in the way of business. Why, he didn't even ask his friends to call on the secretary." Now, of course, I see what she meant.'

'I see part of what she meant, of course,' said Father

Brown. 'What did she mean exactly by the secretary fussing about the will?'

Fiennes smiled as he answered. 'I wish you knew the secretary, Father Brown. It would be a joy to you to watch him make things hum, as he calls it. He made the house of mourning hum. He filled the funeral with all the snap and zip of the brightest sporting event. There was no holding him, after something had really happened. I've told you how he used to oversee the gardener as he did the garden, and how he instructed the lawyer in the law. Needless to say, he also instructed the surgeon in the practice of surgery; and as the surgeon was Dr Valentine, you may be sure it ended in accusing him of something worse than bad surgery. The secretary got it fixed in his red head that the doctor had committed the crime, and when the police arrived he was perfectly sublime. Need I say that he became, on the spot, the greatest of all amateur detectives? Sherlock Holmes never towered over Scotland Yard with more titanic intellectual pride and scorn than Colonel Druce's private secretary over the police investigating Colonel Druce's death. I tell you it was a joy to see him. He strode about with an abstracted air, tossing his scarlet crest of hair and giving curt impatient replies. Of course it was his demeanour during these days that made Druce's daughter so wild with him. Of course he had a theory. It's just the sort of theory a man would have in a book; and Floyd is the sort of man who ought to be in a book. He'd be better fun and less bother in a book.'

'What was his theory?' asked the other.

'Oh, it was full of pep,' replied Fiennes gloomily. 'It would have been glorious copy if it could have held together for ten minutes longer. He said the Colonel was still alive when they found him in the summer-house, and the doctor killed him with the surgical instrument on pretence of cutting the clothes.'

'I see,' said the priest. 'I suppose he was lying flat on his face on the mud floor as a form of siesta.'

'It's wonderful what hustle will do,' continued his informant. 'I believe Floyd would have got his great theory into the papers at any rate, and perhaps had the doctor arrested, when all these things were blown sky high as if by dynamite by the discovery of that dead body lying under the Rock of Fortune. And that's what we come back to after all. I suppose the suicide is almost a confession. But nobody will ever know the whole story.'

There was a silence, and then the priest said modestly: 'I rather think I know the whole story.'

Fiennes stared. 'But look here,' he cried; 'how do you come to know the whole story, or to be sure it's the true story? You've been sitting here a hundred miles away writing a sermon; do you mean to tell me you really know what happened already? If you've really come to the end, where in the world do you begin? What started you off with your own story?'

Father Brown jumped up with a very unusual excitement and his first exclamation was like an explosion.

'The dog!' he cried. 'The dog, of course! You had the whole story in your hands in the business of the dog on the beach, if you'd only noticed the dog properly.'

Fiennes stared still more. 'But you told me before that my feelings about the dog were all nonsense, and the dog had nothing to do with it.'

'The dog had everything to do with it,' said Father Brown, 'as you'd have found out if you'd only treated the dog as a dog, and not as God Almighty judging the souls of men.'

He paused in an embarrassed way for a moment, and then said, with a rather pathetic air of apology: 'The truth is, I happen to be awfully fond of dogs. And it seemed to me that in all this lurid halo of dog superstitions nobody was really thinking about the poor dog at all. To begin with a small point, about his barking at the lawyer or growling at the secretary. You asked how I could guess things a hundred miles away; but honestly it's mostly to your credit, for you described people so well that I know the types. A man like Traill, who frowns usually and smiles suddenly, a man who fiddles with things, especially at his throat, is a nervous, easily embarrassed man. I shouldn't wonder if Floyd the efficient secretary, is nervy and jumpy, too; those Yankee hustlers often are. Otherwise he wouldn't have cut his fingers on the shears and dropped them when he heard Janet Druce scream.

'Now dogs hate nervous people. I don't know whether they make the dog nervous, too; or whether, being after all a brute, he is a bit of a bully; or whether his canine vanity (which is colossal) is simply offended at not being liked. But anyhow there was nothing in poor Nox protesting against those people, except that he disliked them for being afraid of him. Now I know you're awfully clever, and nobody of sense sneers at cleverness. But I sometimes fancy, for instance, that you are too clever to understand animals. Sometimes you are too clever to understand men, especially when they act almost as simply as animals. Animals are very literal; they live in a world of truisms. Take this case: a dog barks at a man and a man runs away from a dog. Now you do not seem to be quite simple enough to see the fact: that the dog barked because he disliked the man and the man fled because he was frightened of the dog. They had no other motives and they needed none; but you must read psychological mysteries into it and suppose the dog had super-normal vision, and was a mysterious mouthpiece of doom. You must suppose the man was running away, not from the dog but from the hangman. And yet, if you come to think of it, all this deeper psychology is exceedingly improbable. If the dog really could completely and consciously realise the murderer of his master he wouldn't stand yapping as he might at a curate at a tea-party; he's much more likely to fly at his throat. And on the other hand, do you really think a man who had hardened his heart to murder an old friend and then walk about smiling at the old friend's family, under the eyes of his old friend's daughter and post-mortem doctor – do you think a man like that would be doubled up by mere remorse because a dog barked? He might feel the tragic irony of it; it might shake his soul, like any other tragic trifle. But he wouldn't rush madly the length of a garden to escape from the only witness whom he knew to be unable to talk. People have a panic like that when they are frightened, not of tragic ironies, but of teeth. The whole thing is simpler than you can understand.

'But when we come to that business by the seashore, things are much more interesting. As you stated them, they were much more puzzling. I didn't understand that tale of the dog going in and out of the water;

it didn't seem to me a doggy thing to do. If Nox had been very much upset about something else, he might possibly have refused to go after the stick at all. He'd probably go off nosing in whatever direction he suspected the mischief. But when once a dog is actually chasing a thing, a stone or a stick or a rabbit, my experience is that he won't stop for anything but the most peremptory command, and not always for that. That he should turn round because his mood changed seems to me unthinkable.'

'But he did turn round,' insisted Fiennes; 'and came back without the stick.'

'He came back without the stick for the best reason in the world,' replied the priest. 'He came back because he couldn't find it. He whined because he couldn't find it. That's the sort of thing a dog really does whine about. A dog is a devil of a ritualist. He is as particular about the precise routine of a game as a child about the precise repetition of a fairytale. In this case something had gone wrong with the game. He came back to complain seriously of the conduct of the stick. Never had such a thing happened before. Never had an eminent and distinguished dog been so treated by a rotten old walking-stick.'

'Why, what had the walking-stick done?' enquired the young man.

'It had sunk,' said Father Brown.

Fiennes said nothing, but continued to stare; and it was the priest who continued: 'It had sunk because it was not really a stick, but a rod of steel with a very thin shell of cane and a sharp point. In other words, it was a sword-stick. I suppose a murderer never gets rid of a bloody weapon so oddly and yet so naturally as by throwing it into the sea for a retriever.'

'I begin to see what you mean,' admitted Fiennes; 'but even if a sword-stick was used, I have no guess of how it was used.'

'I had a sort of guess,' said Father Brown, 'right at the beginning when you said the word summerhouse. And another when you said that Druce wore a white coat. As long as everybody was looking for a short dagger, nobody thought of it; but if we admit a rather long blade like a rapier, it's not so impossible.'

He was leaning back, looking at the ceiling, and began like one going back to his own first thoughts and fundamentals.

'All that discussion about detective stories like the Yellow Room, about a man found dead in sealed chambers which no one could enter, does not apply to the present case, because it is a summerhouse. When we talk of a Yellow Room, or any room, we imply walls that are really homogeneous and impenetrable. But a summerhouse is not made like that; it is often made, as it was in this case, of closely interlaced but separate boughs and strips of wood, in which there are chinks here and there. There was one of them just behind Druce's back as he sat in his chair up against the wall. But just as the room was a summerhouse, so the chair was a basket-chair. That also was a lattice of loopholes. Lastly, the summerhouse was close up under the hedge; and you have just told me that it was really a thin hedge. A man standing outside it could easily see, amid a network of twigs and branches and canes, one white spot of the Colonel's coat as plain as the white of a target.

'Now, you left the geography a little vague; but it was possible to put two and two together. You said the Rock of Fortune was not really high; but you also said it could be seen dominating the garden like a mountain-peak. In other words, it was very near the end of the garden, though your walk had taken you a long way round to it. Also, it isn't likely the young lady really howled so as to be heard half a mile. She gave an ordinary involuntary cry, and yet you heard it on the shore. And among other interesting things that you told me, may I remind you that you said Harry Druce had fallen behind to light his pipe under a hedge.'

Fiennes shuddered slightly. 'You mean he drew his blade there and sent it through the hedge at the white spot. But surely it was a very odd chance and a very sudden choice. Besides, he couldn't be certain the old man's money had passed to him, and as a fact it hadn't.'

Father Brown's face became animated.

'You misunderstand the man's character,' he said, as if he himself had known the man all his life. 'A curious but not unknown type of character. If he had really *known* the money would come to him, I seriously believe he wouldn't have done it. He would have seen it as the dirty thing it was.'

'Isn't that rather paradoxical?' asked the other.

'This man was a gambler,' said the priest, 'and a man in disgrace for having taken risks and anticipated orders. It was probably for something pretty unscrupulous, for every imperial police is more like a Russian secret police than we like to think. But he had gone beyond the line and failed. Now, the temptation of that type of man is to do a mad thing precisely because the risk will be wonderful in retrospect. He wants to say, "Nobody but I could have seized that chance or seen that it was then or never. What a wild and wonderful guess it was, when I put all those things together; Donald in disgrace; and the lawyer being sent for; and Herbert and I sent for at the same time – and then nothing more but the way the old man grinned at me and shook hands. Anybody would say I was mad to risk it; but that is how fortunes are made, by the man mad enough to have a little foresight." In short, it is the vanity of guessing. It is the megalomania of the gambler. The more incongruous the coincidence, the more instantaneous the decision, the more likely he is to snatch the chance. The accident, the very triviality of the white speck and the hole in the hedge intoxicated him like a vision of the world's desire. Nobody clever enough to see such a combination of accidents could be cowardly enough not to use them! That is how the devil talks to the gambler. But the devil himself would hardly have induced that unhappy man to go down in a dull, deliberate way and kill an old uncle from whom he'd always had expectations. It would be too respectable.'

He paused a moment, and then went on with a certain quiet emphasis.

'And now try to call up the scene, even as you saw it yourself. As he stood there, dizzy with his diabolical opportunity, he looked up and saw that strange outline that might have been the image of his own tottering soul; the one great crag poised perilously on the other like a pyramid on its point, and remembered that it was called the Rock of Fortune. Can you guess how such a man at such a moment would read such a signal? I think it strung him up to action and even to vigilance. He who would be a tower must not fear to be a toppling tower. Anyhow, he acted; his next difficulty was to cover his tracks. To be found with a sword-stick, let alone a bloodstained sword-stick, would be fatal in the search that was certain to follow. If he left it anywhere, it would be found and probably traced. Even if he threw it into the sea the action might be noticed, and thought noticeable – unless indeed he could think of some more natural way of covering the action. As you know, he did think of one, and a very good one. Being the only one of you with a watch, he told you it was not yet time to return, strolled a little farther and started the game of throwing in sticks for the retriever. But how his eyes must have rolled darkly over all that desolate seashore before they alighted on the dog!'

Fiennes nodded, gazing thoughtfully into space. His mind seemed to have drifted back to a less practical part of the narrative.

'It's queer,' he said, 'that the dog really was in the story after all.'

'The dog could almost have told you the story, if he could talk,' said the priest. 'All I complain of is that because he couldn't talk, you made up his story for him, and made him talk with the tongues of men and angels. It's part of something I've noticed more and more in the modern world, appearing in all sorts of newspaper rumours and conversational catchwords; something that's arbitrary without being authoritative. People readily swallow the untested claims of this, that, or the other. It's drowning all your old rationalism and scepticism, it's coming in like a sea; and the name of it is superstition.' He stood up abruptly, his face heavy with a sort of frown, and went on talking almost as if he were alone. 'It's the first effect of not believing in God that you lose your common sense and can't see things as they are. Anything that anybody talks about, and says there's a good deal in it, extends itself indefinitely like a vista in a nightmare. And a dog is an omen, and a cat is a mystery, and a pig is a mascot and a beetle is a scarab, calling up all the menagerie of polytheism from Egypt and old India; Dog Anubis and great green-eyed Pasht and all the holy howling Bulls of Bashan; reeling back to the bestial gods of the beginning, escaping into elephants and snakes and crocodiles; and all because you are frightened of four words: "He was made Man".'

The young man got up with a little embarrassment, almost as if he had overheard a soliloquy. He called to the dog and left the room with vague but breezy farewells. But he had to call the dog twice, for the dog had remained behind quite motionless for a moment, looking up steadily at Father Brown as the wolf looked at St Francis.

The Dagger with Wings

Father Brown, at one period of his life, found it difficult to hang his hat on a hat-peg without repressing a slight shudder. The origin of this idiosyncrasy was indeed a mere detail in much more complicated events; but it was perhaps the only detail that remained to him in his busy life to remind him of the whole business. Its remote origin was to be found in the facts which led Dr Boyne, the medical officer attached to the police force, to send for the priest on a particular frosty morning in December.

Dr Boyne was a big dark Irishman, one of those rather baffling Irishmen to be found all over the world, who will talk scientific scepticism, materialism and cynicism at length and at large, but who never dream of referring anything touching the ritual of religion to anything except the traditional religion of their native land. It would be hard to say whether their creed is a very superficial varnish or a very fundamental substratum; but most probably it is both, with a mass of materialism in between. Anyhow, when he thought that matters of that sort might be involved, he asked Father Brown to call, though he made no pretence of preference for that aspect of them.

'I'm not sure I want you, you know,' was his greeting. I'm not sure about anything yet. I'm hanged if I can make out whether it's a case for a doctor, or a policeman, or a priest.'

'Well,' said Father Brown with a smile, 'as I suppose

you're both a policeman and a doctor, I seem to be rather in a minority.'

'I admit you're what politicians call an instructed minority,' replied the doctor. 'I mean, I know you've had to do a little in our line as well as your own. But it's precious hard to say whether this business is in your line or ours, or merely in the line of the Commissioners in Lunacy. We've just had a message from a man living near here, in that white house on the hill, asking for protection against a murderous persecution. We've gone into the facts as far as we could, and perhaps I'd better tell you the story, as it is supposed to have happened, from the beginning.

'It seems that a man named Aylmer, who was a wealthy landowner in the West Country, married rather late in life and had three sons, Philip, Stephen and Arnold. But in his bachelor days, when he thought he would have no heir, he had adopted a boy whom he thought very brilliant and promising, who went by the name of John Strake. His origin seems to be vague; they say he was a foundling; some say he was a gypsy. I think the last notion is mixed up with the fact that Aylmer in his old age dabbled in all sorts of dingy occultism, including palmistry and astrology, and his three sons say that Strake encouraged him in it. But they said a great many other things besides that. They said Strake was an amazing scoundrel, and especially an amazing liar; a genius in inventing lies on the spur of the moment, and telling them so as to deceive a detective. But that might very well be a natural prejudice, in the light of what happened. Perhaps you can more or less imagine what happened. The old man left practically everything to the adopted son; and when he died the three real sons disputed the will. They said their father had been frightened into surrender and, not to put too fine a point on it, into gibbering idiocy. They said Strake had the strangest and most cunning ways of getting at him, in spite of the nurses and the family, and terrorising him on his deathbed. Anyhow, they seemed to have proved something about the dead man's mental condition, for the courts set aside the will and the sons inherited. Strake is said to have broken out in the most dreadful fashion, and sworn he would kill all three of them, one after another, and that nothing could hide them from his vengeance. It is the third or last of the brothers, Arnold Aylmer, who is asking for police protection.'

'Third and last,' said the priest, looking at him gravely.

'Yes,' said Boyne. 'The other two are dead.'

There was a silence before he continued. 'That is where the doubt comes in. There is no proof they were murdered, but they might possibly have been. The eldest, who took up his position as squire, was supposed to have committed suicide in his garden. The second, who went into trade as a manufacturer, was knocked on the head by the machinery in his factory; he might very well have taken a false step and fallen. But if Strake did kill them, he is certainly very cunning in his way of getting to work and getting away. On the other hand, it's more than likely that the whole thing is a mania of conspiracy founded on a coincidence. Look here, what I want is this. I want somebody of sense, who isn't an official, to go up and have a talk to this Mr Arnold Aylmer, and form an impression of him. You know what a man with a delusion is like, and how a man looks when he is telling the truth. I want you to be the advance guard, before we take the matter up.'

'It seems rather odd,' said Father Brown, 'that you haven't had to take it up before. If there is anything in this business, it seems to have been going on for a good time. Is there any particular reason why he should send for you just now, any more than any other time?'

'That had occurred to me, as you may imagine,' answered Dr Boyne. 'He does give a reason, but I confess it is one of the things that make me wonder whether the whole thing isn't only the whim of some half-witted crank. He declared that all his servants have suddenly gone on strike and left him, so that he is obliged to call on the police to look after his house. And on making enquiries, I certainly do find that there has been a general exodus of servants from that house on the hill; and of course the town is full of tales, very one-sided tales I dare say. Their account of it seems to be that their employer had become quite impossible in his fidgets and fears and exactions; that he wanted them to guard the house like sentries, or sit up like night nurses in a hospital; that they could never be left alone because he must never be left alone. So they all announced in a loud voice that he was a lunatic, and left. Of course that does not prove he is a lunatic; but it seems rather rum nowadays for a man to expect his valet or his parlourmaid to act as an armed guard.'

'And so,' said the priest with a smile, 'he wants a policeman to act as his parlourmaid because his parlourmaid won't act as a policeman.'

'I thought that rather thick, too,' agreed the doctor; 'but I can't take the responsibility of a flat refusal till

I've tried a compromise. You are the compromise.'

'Very well,' said Father Brown simply. 'I'll go and call on him now if you like.'

The rolling country round the little town was sealed and bound with frost, and the sky was as clear and cold as steel, except in the northeast where clouds with lurid haloes were beginning to climb up the sky. It was against these darker and more sinister colours that the house on the hill gleamed with a row of pale pillars, forming a short colonnade of the classical sort. A winding road led up to it across the curve of the down and plunged into a mass of dark bushes. Just before it reached the bushes the air seemed to grow colder and colder, as if he were approaching an ice-house or the North Pole. But he was a highly practical person, never entertaining such fancies except as fancies. And he merely cocked his eye at the great livid cloud crawling up over the house, and remarked cheerfully: 'It's going to snow.'

Through a low ornamental iron gateway of the Italianate pattern he entered a garden having something of that desolation which only belongs to the disorder of orderly things. Deep-green growths were grey with the faint powder of the frost, large weeds had fringed the fading pattern of the flower-beds as if in a ragged frame; and the house stood as if waist-high in a stunted forest of shrubs and bushes. The vegetation consisted largely of evergreens or very hardy plants; and though it was thus thick and heavy, it was too northern to be called luxuriant. It might be described as an Arctic jungle. So it was in some sense with the house itself, which had a row of columns and a classical façade, which might have looked out on the Mediterranean; but which seemed now to be withering in the wind of the North Sea. Classical ornament here and there accentuated the contrast; caryatides and carved masks of comedy or tragedy looked down from corners of the building upon the grey confusion of the garden paths; but the faces seemed to be frostbitten. The very volutes of the capitals might have curled up with the cold.

Father Brown went up the grassy steps to a square porch flanked by big pillars and knocked at the door. About four minutes afterwards he knocked again. Then he stood still patiently waiting with his back to the door and looked out on the slowly darkening landscape. It was darkening under the shadow of that one great continent of cloud that had come flying out of the north; and even as he looked out beyond the pillars of the porch, which seemed huge and black above him in the twilight, he saw the opalescent crawling rim of the great cloud as it sailed over the roof and bowed over the porch like a canopy. The grey canopy with its faintly coloured fringes seemed to sink lower and lower upon the garden beyond, until what had recently been a clear and pale-hued winter sky was left in a few silver ribbons and rags like a sickly sunset. Father Brown waited, and there was no sound within.

Then he betook himself briskly down the steps and round the house to look for another entrance. He eventually found one, a side door in the flat wall, and on this also he hammered and outside this also he waited. Then he tried the handle and found the door apparently bolted or fastened in some fashion; and then he moved along that side of the house, musing on the possibilities of the position, and wondering whether the eccentric Mr Aylmer had barricaded himself too deep in the house to hear any kind of summons; or whether perhaps he would barricade himself all the more, on the assumption that any summons must be the challenge of the avenging Strake. It might be that the decamping servants had only unlocked one door when they left in the morning, and that their master had locked that; but whatever he might have done it was unlikely that they, in the mood of that moment, had looked so carefully to the defences. He continued his prowl round the place; it was not really a large place, though perhaps a little pretentious; and in a few moments he found he had made the complete circuit. A moment after he found what he suspected and sought. The french window of one room, curtained and shadowed with creeper, stood open by a crack, doubtless accidentally left ajar, and he found himself in a central room, comfortably upholstered in a rather old-fashioned way, with a staircase leading up from it on one side and a door leading out of it on the other. Immediately opposite him was another door with red glass let into it, a little gaudily for later tastes; something that looked like a red-robed figure in cheap stained glass. On a round table to the right stood a sort of aquarium – a great bowl full of greenish water, in which fishes and similar things moved about as in a tank; and just opposite it a plant of the palm variety with very large green leaves. All this looked so very dusty and Early Victorian that the telephone, visible in the curtained alcove, was almost a surprise.

'Who is that?' a voice called out sharply and rather suspiciously from behind the stained-glass door.

'Could I see Mr Aylmer?' asked the priest apologetically.

The door opened and a gentleman in a peacock-green dressing-gown came out with an enquiring look. His hair was rather rough and untidy, as if he had been in bed or lived in a state of slowly getting up, but his eyes were not only awake but alert, and some would have said alarmed. Father Brown knew that the contradiction was likely enough in a man who had rather run to seed under the shadow either of a delusion or a danger. He had a fine aquiline face when seen in profile, but when seen full face the first impression was of the untidiness and even the wilderness of his loose brown beard.

'I am Mr Aylmer,' he said, 'but I have got out of the way of expecting visitors.'

Something about Mr Aylmer's unrestful eye prompted the priest to go straight to the point. If the man's persecution was only a monomania, he would be the less likely to resent it.

'I was wondering,' said Father Brown softly, 'whether it is quite true that you never expect visitors.'

'You are right,' replied his host steadily. 'I always expect one visitor. And he may be the last.'

'I hope not,' said Father Brown, 'but at least I am relieved to infer that I do not look very like him.'

Mr Aylmer shook himself with a sort of savage laugh. 'You certainly do not,' he said.

'Mr Aylmer,' said Father Brown frankly, 'I apologise for the liberty, but some friends of mine have told me about your trouble, and asked me to see if I could do anything for you. The truth is, I have some little experience in affairs like this.'

'There are no affairs like this,' said Aylmer.

'You mean,' observed Father Brown, 'that the tragedies in your unfortunate family were not normal deaths?'

'I mean they were not even normal murders,' answered the other. 'The man who is hounding us all to death is a hell-hound, and his power is from hell.'

'All evil has one origin,' said the priest gravely. 'But how do you know they were not normal murders?'

Aylmer answered with a gesture which offered his guest a chair; then he seated himself slowly in another, frowning, with his hands on his knees; but when he looked up his expression had grown milder and more thoughtful, and his voice was quite cordial and composed.

'Sir,' he said, 'I don't want you to imagine that I'm in the least an unreasonable person. I have come to these conclusions by reason, because unfortunately reason really leads there. I have read a great deal on these subjects; for I was the only one who inherited my father's scholarship in somewhat obscure matters, and I have since inherited his library. But what I tell you does not rest on what I have read but on what I have seen.'

Father Brown nodded, and the other proceeded, as if picking his words: 'In my elder brother's case I was not certain at first. There were no marks or footprints where he was found shot, and the pistol was left beside him. But he had just received a threatening letter, certainly from our enemy, for it was marked with a sign like a winged dagger, which was one of his infernal cabalistic tricks. And a servant said she had seen something moving along the garden wall in the twilight that was much too large to be a cat. I leave it there; all I can say is that if the murderer came, he managed to leave no traces of his coming. But when my brother Stephen died it was different; and since then I have known. A machine was working in an open scaffolding under the factory tower; I scaled the platform a moment after he had fallen under the iron hammer that struck him; I did not see anything else strike him, but I saw what I saw.

'A great drift of factory smoke was rolling between me and the factory tower; but through a rift of it I saw on the top of it a dark human figure wrapped in what looked like a black cloak. Then the sulphurous smoke drove between us again; and when it cleared I looked up at the distant chimney – there was nobody there. I am a rational man, and I will ask all rational men how he had reached that dizzy unapproachable turret, and how he left it.'

He stared across at the priest with a sphinx-like challenge; then after a silence he said abruptly: 'My brother's brains were knocked out, but his body was not much damaged. And in his pocket we found one of those warning messages dated the day before and stamped with the flying dagger.

'I am sure,' he went on gravely, 'that the symbol of the winged dagger is not merely arbitrary or accidental. Nothing about that abominable man is accidental. He is all design; though it is indeed a most dark and intricate design. His mind is woven not only out of elaborate schemes but out of all sorts of secret languages and signs, and dumb signals and wordless pictures which are the names of nameless things. He is the worst sort of man that the world knows: he is the wicked mystic. Now, I don't pretend to penetrate all that is conveyed by this symbol; but it seems surely that it must have a relation to all that was most remarkable, or even incredible, in his movements as he had hovered round my unfortunate family. Is there no connection between the idea of a winged weapon and the mystery by which Philip was struck dead on his own lawn without the lightest touch of any footprint having disturbed the dust or grass? Is there no connection between the plumed poignard flying like a feathered arrow and that figure which hung on the far top of the toppling chimney, clad in a cloak for pinions?'

'You mean,' said Father Brown thoughtfully, 'that he is in a perpetual state of levitation.'

'Simon Magus did it,' replied Aylmer, 'and it was one of the commonest predictions of the Dark Ages that Antichrist would be able to fly. Anyhow, there was the flying dagger on the document; and whether or no it could fly, it could certainly strike.'

'Did you notice what sort of paper it was on?' asked Father Brown. 'Common paper?'

The sphinx-like face broke abruptly into a harsh laugh.

'You can see what they're like,' said Aylmer grimly, 'for I got one myself this morning.'

He was leaning back in his chair now, with his long legs thrust out from under the green dressing-gown, which was a little short for him, and his bearded chin pillowed on his chest. Without moving otherwise, he thrust his hand deep in the dressing-gown pocket and held out a fluttering scrap of paper at the end of a rigid arm. His whole attitude was suggestive of a sort of paralysis, that was both rigidity and collapse. But the next remark of the priest had a curious effect of rousing him.

Father Brown was blinking in his short-sighted way at the paper presented to him. It was a singular sort of paper, rough without being common, as from an artist's sketchbook; and on it was drawn boldly in red ink a dagger decorated with wings like the rod of Hermes, with the written words, 'Death comes the day after this, as it came to your brothers.'

Father Brown tossed the paper on the floor and sat bolt upright in his chair.

'You mustn't let that sort of stuff stupefy you,' he said sharply. 'These devils always try to make us helpless by making us hopeless.'

Rather to his surprise, an awakening wave went over the prostrate figure, which sprang from its chair as if startled out of a dream.

'You're right, you're right!' cried Aylmer with a rather uncanny animation; 'and the devils shall find I'm not so hopeless after all, nor so helpless either. Perhaps I have more hope and better help than you fancy.'

He stood with his hands in his pockets, frowning down at the priest, who had a momentary doubt, during that strained silence, about whether the man's long peril had not touched his brain. But when he spoke it was quite soberly.

'I believe my unfortunate brothers failed because they used the wrong weapons. Philip carried a revolver, and that was how his death came to be called suicide. Stephen had police protection, but he also had a sense of what made him ridiculous; and he could not allow a policeman to climb up a ladder after him to a scaffolding where he stood only a moment. They were both scoffers, reacting into scepticism from the strange mysticism of my father's last days. But I always knew there was more in my father than they understood. It is true that by studying magic he fell at last under the blight of black magic; the black magic of this scoundrel Strake. But my brothers were wrong about the antidote. The antidote to black magic is not brute materialism or worldly wisdom. The antidote to black magic is white magic.'

'It rather depends,' said Father Brown, 'what you mean by white magic.'

'I mean silver magic,' said the other, in a low voice, like one speaking of a secret revelation. Then after a silence, he said: 'Do you know what I mean by silver magic? Excuse me a moment.'

He turned and opened the central door with the red glass and went into a passage beyond it. The house had less depth than Brown had supposed; instead of the door opening into interior rooms, the corridor it revealed ended in another door on the garden. The door of one room was on one side of the passage; doubtless, the priest told himself, the proprietor's bedroom whence he had rushed out in his dressing-gown. There was nothing else on that side but an ordinary hat-stand with the ordinary dingy cluster of old hats and overcoats; but on the other side was something more interesting: a very dark old oak sideboard laid out with some old silver, and overhung by a trophy or ornament of old weapons. It was by that that Arnold Aylmer halted, looking up at a long, antiquated pistol with a bell-shaped mouth.

The door at the end of the passage was barely open, and through the crack came a streak of white daylight. The priest had very quick instincts about natural things, and something in the unusual brilliancy of that white line told him what had happened outside. It was indeed what he had prophesied when he was approaching the house. He ran past his rather startled host and opened the door, to face something that was at once a blank and a blaze. What he had seen shining through the crack was not only the most negative whiteness of daylight but the positive whiteness of snow. All round, the sweeping fall of the country was covered with that shining pallor that seems at once hoary and innocent.

'Here is white magic anyhow,' said Father Brown in his cheerful voice. Then, as he turned back into the hall, he murmured, 'And silver magic too, I suppose,' for the white lustre touched the silver with splendour and lit up the old steel here and there in the darkling armoury. The shaggy head of the brooding Aylmer seemed to have a halo of silver fire, as he turned with his face in shadow and the outlandish pistol in his hand.

'Do you know why I choose this sort of old blunderbuss?' he asked. 'Because I can load it with this sort of bullet.'

He had picked up a small apostle spoon from the sideboard, and by sheer violence broke off the small figure at the top. 'Let us go back into the other room,' he added.

'Did you ever read about the death of Dundee?' he asked when they had re-seated themselves. He had recovered from his momentary annoyance at the priest's restlessness. 'Graham of Claverhouse, you know, who persecuted the Covenanters and had a black horse that could ride straight up a precipice. Don't you know he could only be shot with a silver bullet, because he had sold himself to the Devil? That's one comfort about you; at least you know enough to believe in the Devil.'

'Oh, yes,' replied Father Brown, 'I believe in the Devil. What I don't believe in is the Dundee. I mean the Dundee of Covenanting legends, with his nightmare of a horse. John Graham was simply a seventeenth-century professional soldier, rather better than most. If he dragooned them it was because he was a dragoon, but not a dragon. Now my experience is that it's not that sort of swaggering blade who sells himself to the Devil. The devil-worshippers I've known were quite different. Not to mention names, which might cause a social flutter, I'll take a man in Dundee's own day. Have you ever heard of Dalrymple of Stair?'

'No,' replied the other gruffly.

'You've heard of what he did,' said Father Brown, 'and it was worse than anything Dundee ever did; yet he escapes the infamy by oblivion. He was the man who made the Massacre of Glencoe. He was a very learned man and lucid lawyer, a statesman with very serious and enlarged ideas of statesmanship, a quiet man with a very refined and intellectual face. That's the sort of man who sells himself to the Devil.'

Aylmer half started from his chair with an enthusiasm of eager assent.

'By God! you are right,' he cried. 'A refined intellectual face! That is the face of John Strake.'

Then he raised himself and stood looking at the priest with a curious concentration. 'If you will wait here a little while,' he said, 'I will show you something.'

He went back through the central door, closing it after him; going, the priest presumed, to the old sideboard or possibly to his bedroom. Father Brown remained seated, gazing abstractedly at the carpet, where a faint red glimmer shone from the glass in the doorway. Once it seemed to brighten like a ruby and then darkened again, as if the sun of that stormy day had passed from cloud to cloud. Nothing moved except the aquatic creatures which floated to and fro in the dim green bowl. Father Brown was thinking hard.

A minute or two afterwards he got up and slipped quietly to the alcove of the telephone, where he rang up his friend Dr Boyne, at the official headquarters. 'I wanted to tell you about Aylmer and his affairs,' he said quietly. 'It's a queer story, but I rather think there's something in it. If I were you I'd send some men up here straight away; four or five men, I think, and surround the house. If anything does happen there'll probably be something startling in the way of an escape.'

Then he went back and sat down again, staring at the dark carpet, which again glowed blood-red with the light from the glass door. Something in that filtered light set his mind drifting on certain borderlands of thought, with the first white daybreak before the coming of colour, and all that mystery which is alternately veiled and revealed in the symbol of windows and of doors.

An inhuman howl in a human voice came from beyond the closed doors, almost simultaneously with the noise of firing. Before the echoes of the shot had died away the door was violently flung open and his host staggered into the room, the dressing-gown half torn from his shoulder and the long pistol smoking in his hand. He seemed to be shaking in every limb, yet he was shaken in part with an unnatural laughter.

'Glory be to the White Magic!' he cried; 'Glory be to the silver bullet! The hell-hound has hunted once too often, and my brothers are avenged at last.'

He sank into a chair and the pistol slid from his hand and fell on the floor. Father Brown darted past him, slipped through the glass door and went down the passage. As he did so he put his hand on the handle of the bedroom door, as if half intending to enter; then he stooped a moment, as if examining something – and then he ran to the outer door and opened it.

On the field of snow, which had been so blank a little while before, lay one black object. At the first glance it looked a little like an enormous bat. A second glance showed that it was, after all, a human figure; fallen on its face, the whole head covered by a broad black hat having something of a Latin-American look; while the appearance of black-wings came from the two flaps or loose sleeves of a very vast black cloak spread out, perhaps by accident, to their utmost length on either side. Both the hands were hidden, though Father Brown thought he could detect the position of one of them, and saw close to it, under the edge of the cloak, the glimmer of some metallic weapon. The main effect, however, was curiously like that of the simple extravagances of heraldry; like a black eagle displayed on a white ground. But by walking round it and peering under the hat the priest got a glimpse of the face, which was indeed what his host had called refined and intellectual; even sceptical and austere: the face of John Strake.

'Well, I'm jiggered,' muttered Father Brown. 'It really does look like some vast vampire that has swooped down like a bird.'

'How else could he have come?' came a voice from the doorway, and Father Brown looked up to see Aylmer once more standing there.

'Couldn't he have walked?' replied Father Brown evasively.

Aylmer stretched out his arm and swept the white landscape with a gesture.

'Look at the snow,' he said in a deep voice that had a sort of roll and thrill in it. 'Is not the snow unspotted – pure as the white magic you yourself called it? Is there a speck on it for miles, save that one foul black blot that has fallen there? There are no footprints, but a few of yours and mine; there are none approaching the house from anywhere.'

Then he looked at the little priest for a moment with a concentrated and curious expression, and said: 'I will tell you something else. That cloak he flies with is too long to walk with. He was not a very tall man, and it would trail behind him like a royal train. Stretch it out over his body, if you like, and see.'

'What happened to you both?' asked Father Brown abruptly.

'It was too swift to describe,' answered Aylmer. 'I had looked out of the door and was turning back when there came a kind of rushing of wind all around me, as if I were being buffeted by a wheel revolving in mid-air. I spun round somehow and fired blindly; and then I saw nothing but what you see now. But I am morally certain you wouldn't see it if I had not had a silver shot in my gun. It would have been a different body lying there in the snow.'

'By the way,' remarked Father Brown, 'shall we leave it lying there in the snow? Or would you like it taken into your room – I suppose that's your bedroom in the passage?'

'No, no,' replied Aylmer hastily; 'we must leave it there till the police have seen it. Besides, I've had as much of such things as I can stand for the moment. Whatever else happens, I'm going to have a drink. After that, they can hang me if they like.'

Inside the central apartment, between the palm

plant and the bowl of fishes, Aylmer tumbled into a chair. He had nearly knocked the bowl over as he lurched into the room, but he had managed to find the decanter of brandy after plunging his hand rather blindly into several cupboards and corners. He did not at any time look like a methodical person, but at this moment his distraction must have been extreme. He drank with a long gulp and began to talk rather feverishly, as if to fill up a silence.

'I see you are still doubtful,' he said, 'though you have seen the thing with your own eyes. Believe me, there was something more behind the quarrel between the spirit of Strake and the spirit of the house of Aylmer. Besides, you have no business to be an unbeliever. You ought to stand for all the things these stupid people call superstitions. Come now, don't you think there's a lot in those old wives' tales about luck and charms and so on, silver bullets included? What do you say about them as a Catholic?'

'I say I'm an agnostic,' replied Father Brown, smiling.

'Nonsense,' said Aylmer impatiently. 'It's your business to believe things.'

'Well, I do believe some things, of course,' conceded Father Brown; 'and therefore, of course, I don't believe other things.'

Aylmer was leaning forward, and looking at him with a strange intensity that was almost like that of a mesmerist.

'You do believe it,' he said. 'You do believe everything. We all believe everything, even when we deny everything. The deniers believe. The unbelievers believe. Don't you feel in your heart that these contradictions do not really contradict: that there is a cosmos that contains them all? The soul goes round upon a wheel of stars and all things return; perhaps Strake and I have striven in many shapes, beast against beast and bird against bird, and perhaps we shall strive for ever. But since we seek and need each other, even that eternal hatred is an eternal love. Good and evil go round in a wheel that is one thing and not many. Do you not realise in your heart, do you not believe behind all your beliefs, that there is but one reality and we are its shadows; and that all things are but aspects of one thing: a centre where men melt into Man and Man into God?'

'No,' said Father Brown.

Outside, twilight had begun to fall, in that phase of such a snow-laden evening when the land looks brighter than the sky. In the porch of the main entrance, visible through a half-curtained window, Father Brown could dimly see a bulky figure standing. He glanced casually at the french windows through which he had originally entered, and saw they were darkened with two equally motionless figures. The inner door with the coloured glass stood slightly ajar; and he could see in the short corridor beyond, the ends of two long shadows, exaggerated and distorted by the level light of evening, but still like grey caricatures of the figures of men. Dr Boyne had already obeyed his telephone message. The house was surrounded.

'What is the good of saying no?' insisted his host, still with the same hypnotic stare. 'You have seen part of that eternal drama with your own eyes. You have seen the threat of John Strake to slay Arnold Aylmer by black magic. You have seen Arnold Aylmer slay John Strake by white magic. You see Arnold Aylmer alive and talking to you now. And yet you do not believe it.'

'No, I do not believe it,' said Father Brown, and rose from his chair like one terminating a visit.

'Why not?' asked the other.

The priest only lifted his voice a little, but it sounded in every corner of the room like a bell.

'Because you are not Arnold Aylmer,' he said. 'I know who you are. Your name is John Strake; and you have murdered the last of the brothers, who is lying outside in the snow.'

A ring of white showed round the iris of the other man's eyes; he seemed to be making, with bursting eyeballs, a last effort to mesmerise and master his companion. Then he made a sudden movement sideways; and even as he did so the door behind him opened and a big detective in plain clothes put one hand quietly on his shoulder. The other hand hung down, but it held a revolver. The man looked wildly round, and saw plain-clothes men in all corners of the quiet room.

That evening Father Brown had another and longer conversation with Dr Boyne about the tragedy of the Aylmer family. By that time there was no longer any doubt of the central fact of the case, for John Strake had confessed his identity and even confessed his crimes; only it would be truer to say that he boasted of his victories. Compared to the fact that he had rounded off his life's work with the last Aylmer lying dead, everything else, including existence itself, seemed to be indifferent to him.

'The man is a sort of monomaniac,' said Father Brown. 'He is not interested in any other matter; not even in any other murder. I owe him something for that; for I had to comfort myself with the reflection a good many times this afternoon. As has doubtless occurred to you, instead of weaving all that wild but ingenious romance about winged vampires and silver bullets, he might have put an ordinary leaden bullet into me, and walked out of the house. I assure you it occurred quite frequently to me.'

'I wonder why he didn't,' observed Boyne. 'I don't understand it; but I don't understand anything yet. How on earth did you discover it, and what in the world did you discover?'

'Oh, you provided me with very valuable information,' replied Father Brown modestly, 'especially the one piece of information that really counted. I mean the statement that Strake was a very inventive and imaginative liar, with great presence of mind in producing his lies. This afternoon he needed it; but he rose to the occasion. Perhaps his only mistake was in choosing a preternatural story; he had the notion that because I am a clergyman I should believe anything. Many people have little notions of that kind.'

'But I can't make head or tail of it,' said the doctor. 'You must really begin at the beginning.'

'The beginning of it was a dressing-gown,' said Father Brown simply. 'It was the one really good disguise I've ever known. When you meet a man in a house with a dressing-gown on, you assume quite automatically that he's in his own house. I assumed it myself; but afterwards queer little things began to happen. When he took the pistol down he clicked it at arm's length, as a man does to make sure a strange weapon isn't loaded; of course he would know whether the pistols in his own hall were loaded or not. I didn't like the way he looked for the brandy, or the way he nearly barged into the bowl of fishes. For a man who has a fragile thing of that sort as a fixture in his rooms gets a quite mechanical habit of avoiding it. But these things might possibly have been fancies; the first real point was this. He came out from the little passage between the two doors; and in that passage there's only one other door leading to a room; so I assumed it was the bedroom he had just come from. I tried the handle; but it was locked. I thought this odd; and looked through the keyhole. It was an utterly bare room, obviously deserted; no bed, no anything. Therefore he had not come from inside any room, but from outside the house. And when I saw that, I think I saw the whole picture.

'Poor Arnold Aylmer doubtless slept and perhaps lived upstairs, and came down in his dressing-gown and passed through the red glass door. At the end of the passage, black against the winter daylight, he saw the enemy of his house. He saw a tall bearded man in a broad-brimmed black hat and a large flapping black cloak. He did not see much more in this world. Strake sprang on him, throttling or stabbing him; we cannot be sure till the inquest. Then Strake, standing in the narrow passage between the hat-stand and the old sideboard, and looking down in triumph on the last of his foes, heard something he had not expected. He heard footsteps in the parlour beyond. It was myself entering by the french windows.

'His masquerade was a miracle of promptitude. It involved not only a disguise but a romance – an impromptu romance. He took off his big black hat and cloak and put on the dead man's dressing-gown. Then he did a rather grisly thing; at least a thing that affects my fancy as more grisly than the rest. He hung the corpse like a coat on one of the hat-pegs. He draped it in his own long cloak, and found it hung well below the heels; he covered the head entirely with his own wide hat. It was the only possible way of hiding it in that little passage with the locked door; but it was really a very clever one. I myself walked past the hat-stand once without knowing it was anything but a hat-stand. I think that unconsciousness of mine will always give me a shiver.

'He might perhaps have left it at that; but I might have discovered the corpse at any minute; and, hung where it was, it was a corpse calling for what you might call an explanation. He adopted the bolder stroke of discovering it himself and explaining it himself.

'Then there dawned on this strange and frightfully fertile mind the conception of a story of substitution; the reversal of the parts. He had already assumed the part of Arnold Aylmer. Why should not his dead enemy assume the part of John Strake? there must have been something in that topsy-turvydom to take the fancy of that darkly fanciful man. It was like some frightful fancy-dress ball to which the two mortal enemies were to go dressed up as each other. Only, the fancy-dress ball was to be a dance of death: and one of the dancers would be dead. That is why I can imagine that man putting it in his own mind, and I can imagine him smiling.'

Father Brown was gazing into vacancy with his large grey eyes, which, when not blurred by his trick of blinking, were the one notable thing in his face. He went on speaking simply and seriously: 'All things are from God; and above all, reason and imagination and the great gifts of the mind. They are good in themselves; and we must not altogether forget their origin even in their perversion. Now this man had in him a very noble power to be perverted; the power of telling stories. He was a great novelist; only he had twisted his fictive power to practical and to evil ends; to deceiving men with false fact instead of with true fiction. It began with his deceiving old Aylmer with elaborate excuses and ingeniously detailed lies; but even that may have been, at the beginning, little more than the tall stories and tarradiddles of the child who may say equally he has seen the King of England or the King of the Fairies. It grew strong in him through the vice that perpetuates all vices, pride; he grew more and more vain of his promptitude in producing stories of his originality, and subtlety in developing them. That is what the young Aylmers meant by saying that he could always cast a spell over their father; and it was true. It was the sort of spell that the storyteller cast over the tyrant in the Arabian Nights. And to the last he walked the world with the pride of a poet, and with the false yet unfathomable courage of a great liar. He could always produce more Arabian Nights if ever his neck was in danger. And today his neck was in danger.

'But I am sure, as I say, that he enjoyed it as a fantasy as well as a conspiracy. He set about the task of telling the true story the wrong way round: of treating the dead man as living and the live man as dead. He had already got into Aylmer's dressing-gown; he proceeded to get into Aylmer's body and soul. He looked at the corpse as if it were his own corpse lying cold in the snow. Then he spread-eagled it in that strange fashion to suggest the sweeping descent of a bird of prey, and decked it out not only in his own dark and flying garments but in a whole dark fairytale about the black bird that could only fall by the silver bullet. I do not know whether it was the silver glittering on the sideboard or the snow shining beyond the door that suggested to his intensely artistic temperament the theme of white magic and the white metal used against magicians. But whatever its origin, he made it his own like a poet; and did it very promptly, like a practical man. He completed the exchange and reversal of parts by flinging the corpse out on to the snow as the corpse of Strake. He did his best to work up a creepy conception of Strake as something hovering in the air everywhere, a harpy with wings of speed and claws of death; to explain the absence of footprints and other things. For one piece of artistic impudence I hugely admire him. He actually turned one of the contradictions in his case into an argument for it; and said that the man's cloak being too long for him proved that he never walked on the ground like an ordinary mortal. But he looked at me very hard while he said that; and something told me that he was at that moment trying a very big bluff.'

Dr Boyne looked thoughtful. 'Had you discovered the truth by then?' he asked. 'There is something very queer and close to the nerves, I think, about notions affecting identity. I don't know whether it would be more weird to get a guess like that swiftly or slowly. I wonder when you suspected and when you were sure.'

'I think I really suspected when I telephoned to you,' replied his friend. 'And it was nothing more than the red light from the closed door brightening and darkening on the carpet. It looked like a splash of blood that grew vivid as it cried for vengeance. Why should it change like that? I knew the sun had not come out; it could only be because the second door behind it had been opened and shut on the garden.

But if he had gone out and seen his enemy then, he would have raised the alarm then; and it was some time afterwards that the fracas occurred. I began to feel he had gone out to do something . . . to prepare something . . . but as to when I was certain, that is a different matter. I knew that right at the end he was trying to hypnotise me, to master me by the black art of eyes like talismans and a voice like an incantation. That's what he used to do with old Aylmer, no doubt. But it wasn't only the way he said it, it was what he said. It was the religion and philosophy of it.'

'I'm afraid I'm a practical man,' said the doctor with gruff humour, 'and I don't bother much about religion and philosophy.'

'You'll never be a practical man till you do,' said Father Brown. 'Look here, doctor; you know me pretty well; I think you know I'm not a bigot. You know I know there are all sorts in all religions; good men in bad ones and bad men in good ones. But there's just one little fact I've learned simply as a practical man, an entirely practical point, that I've picked up by experience, like the tricks of an animal or the trademark of a good wine. I've scarcely ever met a criminal who philosophised at all, who didn't philosophise along those lines of orientalism and recurrence and reincarnation, and the wheel of destiny and the serpent biting its own tail. I have found merely in practice that there is a curse on the servants of that serpent; on their belly shall they go and the dust shall they eat; and there was never a blackguard or a profligate born who could not talk that sort of spirituality. It may not be like that in its real religious origins; but here in our working world it is the religion of rascals; and I knew it was a rascal who was speaking.'

'Why,' said Boyne, 'I should have thought that a rascal could pretty well profess any religion he chose.'

'Yes,' assented the other; 'he could profess any religion; that is he could pretend to any religion, if it was all a pretence. If it was mere mechanical hypocrisy and nothing else, no doubt it could be done by a mere mechanical hypocrite. Any sort of mask can be put on any sort of face. Anybody can learn certain phrases or state verbally that he holds certain views. I can go out into the street and state that I am a Wesleyan Methodist or a Sandemanian, though I fear in no very convincing accent. But we are talking about an artist; and for the enjoyment of the artist the mask must be to some extent moulded on the face. What he makes outside him must correspond to something inside him; he can only make his effects out of some of the materials of his soul. I suppose he could have said he was a Wesleyan Methodist; but he could never be an eloquent Methodist as he can be an eloquent mystic and fatalist. I am talking of the sort of ideal such a man thinks of if he really tries to be idealistic. It was his whole game with me to be as idealistic as possible; and whenever that is attempted by that sort of man, you will generally find it is that sort of ideal. That sort of man may be dripping with gore; but he will always be able to tell you quite sincerely that Buddhism is better than Christianity. Nay, he will tell you quite sincerely that Buddhism is more Christian than Christianity. That alone is enough to throw a hideous and ghastly ray of light on his notion of Christianity.'

'Upon my soul,' said the doctor, laughing, 'I can't make out whether you're denouncing or defending him.'

'It isn't defending a man to say he is a genius,' said Father Brown. 'Far from it. And it is simply a psychological fact that an artist will betray himself by some sort of sincerity. Leonardo da Vinci cannot draw as if he couldn't draw. Even if he tried, it will always be a strong parody of a weak thing. This man would have made something much too fearful and wonderful out of the Wesleyan Methodist.'

When the priest went forth again and set his face homeward, the cold had grown more intense and yet was somehow intoxicating. The trees stood up like silver candelabra of some incredible cold candlemas of purification. It was a piercing cold, like that silver sword of pure pain that once pierced the very heart of purity. But it was not a killing cold, save in the sense of seeming to kill all the mortal obstructions to our immortal and immeasurable vitality. The pale green sky of twilight, with one star like the star of Bethlehem, seemed by some strange contradiction to be a cavern of clarity. It was as if there could be a green furnace of cold which wakened all things to life like warmth, and that the deeper they went into those cold crystalline colours the more were they light like winged creatures and clear like coloured glass. It tingled with truth and it divided truth from error with a blade like ice; but all that was left had never felt so much alive. It was as if all joy were a jewel in the heart of an iceberg. The priest hardly understood his own mood as he advanced deeper and deeper into the green gloaming, drinking deeper and deeper draughts of that virginal vivacity of the air. Some forgotten muddle and morbidity seemed to be left behind, or wiped out as the snow had painted out the footprints of the man of blood. As he shuffled homewards through the snow, he muttered to himself: 'And yet he is right enough about there being a white magic, if he only knows where to look for it.'

The Mirror of the Magistrate

James Bagshaw and Wilfred Underhill were old friends, and were fond of rambling through the streets at night, talking interminably as they turned corner after corner in the silent and seemingly lifeless labyrinth of the large suburb in which they lived. The former, a big, dark, good-humoured man with a strip of black moustache, was a professional police detective; the latter, a sharp-faced, sensitive-looking gentleman with light hair, was an amateur interested in detection. It will come as a shock to the readers of the best scientific romance to learn that it was the policeman who was talking and the amateur who was listening, even with a certain respect.

'Ours is the only trade,' said Bagshaw, 'in which the professional is always supposed to be wrong. After all, people don't write stories in which hairdressers can't cut hair and have to be helped by a customer; or in which a cabman can't drive a cab until his fare explains to him the philosophy of cab-driving. For all that, I'd never deny that we often tend to get into a rut; or, in other words, have the disadvantages of going by a rule. Where the romancers are wrong is, that they don't allow us even the advantages of going by a rule.'

'Surely,' said Underhill, 'Sherlock Holmes would say that he went by a logical rule.'

'He may be right,' answered the other; 'but I mean a collective rule. It's like the staff work of an army. We pool our information.'

'And you don't think detective stories allow for that?' asked his friend.

'Well, let's take any imaginary case of Sherlock Holmes, and Lestrade, the official detective. Sherlock Holmes, let us say, can guess that a total stranger crossing the street is a foreigner, merely because he seems to look for the traffic to go to the right instead of the left. I'm quite ready to admit that Holmes might guess that. I'm quite sure Lestrade wouldn't guess anything of the kind. But what they leave out is the fact that the policeman, who couldn't guess, might very probably know. Lestrade might know the man was a foreigner merely because his department has to keep an eye on all foreigners; some would say on all natives, too. As a policeman I'm glad the police know so much; for every man wants to do his own job well. But as a citizen, I sometimes wonder whether they don't know too much.'

'You don't seriously mean to say,' cried Underhill incredulously, 'that you know anything about strange people in a strange street. That if a man walked out of that house over there, you would know anything about him?'

'I should if he was the householder,' answered Bagshaw. 'That house is rented by a literary man of Anglo-Roumanian extraction, who generally lives in Paris, but is over here in connection with some poetical play of his. His name's Osric Orm, one of the new poets, and pretty steep to read, I believe.'

'But I mean all the people down the road,' said his companion. 'I was thinking how strange and new and nameless everything looks, with these high blank walls and these houses lost in large gardens. You can't know all of them.'

'I know a few,' answered Bagshaw. 'This garden wall we're walking under is at the end of the grounds of Sir

Humphrey Gwynne, better known as Mr Justice Gwynne, the old judge who made such a row about spying during the war. The house next door to it belongs to a wealthy cigar merchant. He comes from Spanish-America and looks very swarthy and Spanish himself; but he bears the very English name of Buller. The house beyond that – did you hear that noise?'

'I heard something,' said Underhill, 'but I really don't know what it was.'

'I know what it was,' replied the detective, 'it was a rather heavy revolver, fired twice, followed by a cry for help. And it came straight out of the back garden of Mr Justice Gwynne, that paradise of peace and legality.'

He looked up and down the street sharply and then added: 'And the only gate of the back garden is half a mile round on the other side. I wish this wall were a little lower, or I were a little lighter; but it's got to be tried.'

'It is lower a little farther on,' said Underhill, 'and there seems to be a tree that looks helpful.'

They moved hastily along and found a place where the wall seemed to stoop abruptly, almost as if it had half-sunk into the earth; and a garden tree, flamboyant with the gayest garden blossom, straggled out of the dark enclosure and was gilded by the gleam of a solitary street-lamp. Bagshaw caught the crooked branch and threw one leg over the low wall; and the next moment they stood knee-deep amid the snapping plants of a garden border.

The garden of Mr Justice Gwynne by night was rather a singular spectacle. It was large and lay on the empty edge of the suburb, in the shadow of a tall, dark house that was the last in its line of houses. The house was literally dark, being shuttered and unlighted, at least on the side overlooking the garden. But the garden itself, which lay in its shadow and should have been a tract of absolute darkness, showed a random glitter, like that of fading fireworks; as if a giant rocket had fallen in fire among the trees. As they advanced they were able to locate it as the light of several coloured lamps, entangled in the trees like the jewel fruits of Aladdin, and especially as the light from a small, round lake or pond, which gleamed with pale colours as if a lamp were kindled under it.

'Is he having a party?' asked Underhill. 'The garden seems to be illuminated.'

'No,' answered Bagshaw. 'It's a hobby of his, and I believe he prefers to do it when he's alone. He likes playing with a little plant of electricity that he works from that bungalow or hut over there, where he does his work and keeps his papers. Buller, who knows him very well, says the coloured lamps are rather more often a sign he's not to be disturbed.'

'Sort of red danger signals,' suggested the other.

'Good Lord! I'm afraid they are danger signals!' and he began suddenly to run.

A moment after Underhill saw that he had seen. The opalescent ring of light, like the halo of the moon, round the sloping sides of the pond, was broken by two black stripes or streaks which soon proved themselves to be the long, black legs of a figure fallen head downwards into the hollow, with the head in the pond.

'Come on,' cried the detective sharply, 'that looks to me like – '

His voice was lost, as he ran on across the wide lawn, faintly luminous in the artificial light, making a bee-line across the big garden for the pool and the fallen figure. Underhill was trotting steadily in that straight track, when something happened that startled him for the moment. Bagshaw, who was travelling as steadily as a bullet towards the black figure by the luminous pool, suddenly turned at a sharp angle and began to run even more rapidly towards the shadow of the house. Underhill could not imagine what he meant by the altered direction. The next moment, when the detective had vanished into the shadow of the house, there came out of that obscurity the sound of a scuffle and a curse; and Bagshaw returned lugging with him a little struggling man with red hair. The captive had evidently been escaping under the shelter of the building, when the quicker ears of the detective had heard him rustling like a bird among the bushes.

'Underhill,' said the detective, 'I wish you'd run on and see what's up by the pool. And now, who are you?' he asked, coming to a halt. 'What's your name?'

'Michael Flood,' said the stranger in a snappy fashion. He was an unnaturally lean little man, with a hooked nose too large for his face, which was colourless, like parchment, in contrast with the ginger colour of his hair. 'I've got nothing to do with this. I found him lying dead and I was scared; but I only came to interview him for a paper.'

'When you interview celebrities for the Press,' said Bagshaw, 'do you generally climb over the garden wall?'

And he pointed grimly to a trail of footprints coming and going along the path towards the flower bed.

The man calling himself Flood wore an expression equally grim.

'An interviewer might very well get over the wall,' he

said, 'for I couldn't make anybody hear at the front door. The servant had gone out.'

'How do you know he'd gone out?' asked the detective suspiciously.

'Because,' said Flood, with an almost unnatural calm, 'I'm not the only person who gets over garden walls. It seems just possible that you did it yourself. But, anyhow, the servant did; for I've just this moment seen him drop over the wall, away on the other side of the garden, just by the garden door.'

'Then why didn't he use the garden door?' demanded the cross-examiner.

'How should I know?' retorted Flood. 'Because it was shut, I suppose. But you'd better ask him, not me; he's coming towards the house at this minute.'

There was, indeed, another shadowy figure beginning to be visible through the fire-shot gloaming, a squat, square-headed figure, wearing a red waistcoat as the most conspicuous part of a rather shabby livery. He appeared to be making with unobtrusive haste towards a side-door in the house, until Bagshaw halloed to him to halt. He drew nearer to them very reluctantly, revealing a heavy, yellow face, with a touch of something Asiatic which was consonant with his flat, blue-black hair.

Bagshaw turned abruptly to the man called Flood. 'Is there anybody in this place,' he said, 'who can testify to your identity?'

'Not many, even in this country,' growled Flood. 'I've only just come from Ireland; the only man I know round here is the priest at St Dominic's Church – Father Brown.'

'Neither of you must leave this place,' said Bagshaw, and then added to the servant: 'But you can go into the house and ring up St Dominic's Presbytery and ask Father Brown if he would mind coming round here at once. No tricks, mind.'

While the energetic detective was securing the potential fugitives, his companion, at his direction, had hastened on to the actual scene of the tragedy. It was a strange enough scene; and, indeed, if the tragedy had not been tragic it would have been highly fantastic. The dead man (for the briefest examination proved him to be dead) lay with his head in the pond, where the glow of the artificial illumination encircled the head with something of the appearance of an unholy halo. The face was gaunt and rather sinister, the brow bald, and the scanty curls dark grey, like iron rings; and, despite the damage done by the bullet wound in the temple, Underhill had no difficulty in recognising the features he had seen in the many portraits of Sir Humphrey Gwynne. The dead man was in evening-dress, and his long, black legs, so thin as to be almost spidery, were sprawling at different angles up the steep bank from which he had fallen. As by some weird whim of diabolical arabesque, blood was eddying out, very slowly, into the luminous water in snaky rings, like the transparent crimson of sunset clouds.

Underhill did not know how long he stood staring down at this macabre figure, when he looked up and saw a group of four figures standing above him on the bank. He was prepared for Bagshaw and his Irish captive, and he had no difficulty in guessing the status of the servant in the red waistcoat. But the fourth figure had a sort of grotesque solemnity that seemed strangely congruous to that incongruity. It was a stumpy figure with a round face and a hat like a black halo. He realised that it was, in fact, a priest; but there was something about it that reminded him of some quaint old black woodcut at the end of a Dance of Death.

Then he heard Bagshaw saying to the priest: 'I'm glad you can identify this man; but you must realise that he's to some extent under suspicion. Of course, he may be innocent; but he did enter the garden in an irregular fashion.'

'Well, I think he's innocent myself,' said the little priest in a colourless voice. 'But, of course, I may be wrong.'

'Why do you think he is innocent?'

'Because he entered the garden in an irregular fashion,' answered the cleric. 'You see, I entered it in a regular fashion myself. But I seem to be almost the only person who did. All the best people seem to get over garden walls nowadays.'

'What do you mean by a regular fashion?' asked the detective.

'Well,' said Father Brown, looking at him with limpid gravity, 'I came in by the front door. I often come into houses that way.'

'Excuse me,' said Bagshaw, 'but does it matter very much how you came in, unless you propose to confess to the murder?'

'Yes, I think it does,' said the priest mildly. 'The truth is, that when I came in at the front door I saw something I don't think any of the rest of you have seen. It seems to me it might have something to do with it.'

'What did you see?'

'I saw a sort of general smash-up,' said Father Brown in his mild voice. 'A big looking-glass broken, and a small palm tree knocked over, and the pot smashed all over the floor. Somehow, it looked to me as if something had happened.'

'You are right,' said Bagshaw after a pause. 'If you saw that, it certainly looks as if it had something to do with it.'

'And if it had anything to do with it,' said the priest very gently, 'it looks as if there was one person who had nothing to do with it; and that is Mr Michael Flood, who entered the garden over the wall in an irregular fashion, and then tried to leave it in the same irregular fashion. It is his irregularity that makes me believe in his innocence.'

'Let us go into the house,' said Bagshaw abruptly.

As they passed in at the side-door, the servant leading the way, Bagshaw fell back a pace or two and spoke to his friend.

'Something odd about that servant,' he said. 'Says his name is Green, though he doesn't look it; but there seems no doubt he's really Gwynne's servant, apparently the only regular servant he had. But the queer thing is, that he flatly denied that his master was in the garden at all, dead or alive. Said the old judge had gone out to a grand legal dinner and couldn't be home for hours, and gave that as his excuse for slipping out.'

'Did he,' asked Underhill, 'give any excuse for his curious way of slipping in?'

'No, none that I can make sense of,' answered the detective. 'I can't make him out. He seems to be scared of something.'

Entering by the side-door, they found themselves at the inner end of the entrance hall, which ran along the side of the house and ended with the front door, surmounted by a dreary fanlight of the old-fashioned pattern. A faint, grey light was beginning to outline its radiation upon the darkness, like some dismal and discoloured sunrise; but what light there was in the hall came from a single, shaded lamp, also of an antiquated sort, that stood on a bracket in a corner. By the light of this Bagshaw could distinguish the debris of which Brown had spoken. A tall palm, with long sweeping leaves, had fallen full length, and its dark red pot was shattered into shards. They lay littered on the carpet, along with pale and gleaming fragments of a broken mirror, of which the almost empty frame hung behind them on the wall at the end of the vestibule. At right angles to this entrance, and directly opposite the side-door as they entered, was another and similar passage leading into the rest of the house. At the other end of it could be seen the telephone which the servant had used to summon the priest; and a half-open door, showing, even through the crack, the serried ranks of great leather-bound books, marked the entrance to the judge's study.

Bagshaw stood looking down at the fallen pot and the mingled fragments at his feet.

'You're quite right,' he said to the priest; 'there's been a struggle here. And it must have been a struggle between Gwynne and his murderer.'

'It seemed to me,' said Father Brown modestly, 'that something had happened here.'

'Yes; it's pretty clear what happened,' assented the detective. 'The murderer entered by the front door and found Gwynne; probably Gwynne let him in. There was a death grapple, possibly a chance shot, that hit the glass, though they might have broken it with a stray kick or anything. Gwynne managed to free himself and fled into the garden, where he was pursued and shot finally by the pond. I fancy that's the whole story of the crime itself; but, of course, I must look round the other rooms.'

The other rooms, however, revealed very little, though Bagshaw pointed significantly to the loaded automatic pistol that he found in a drawer of the library desk.

'Looks as if he was expecting this,' he said; 'yet it seems queer he didn't take it with him when he went out into the hall.'

Eventually they returned to the hall, making their way towards the front door, Father Brown letting his eye rove around in a rather absent-minded fashion. The two corridors, monotonously papered in the same grey and faded pattern, seemed to emphasise the dust and dingy floridity of the few early Victorian ornaments, the green rust that devoured the bronze of the lamp, the dull gold that glimmered in the frame of the broken mirror.

'They say it's bad luck to break a looking-glass,' he said. 'This looks like the very house of ill-luck. There's something about the very furniture – '

'That's rather odd,' said Bagshaw sharply. 'I thought the front door would be shut, but it's left on the latch.'

There was no reply; and they passed out of the front door into the front garden, a narrower and more formal plot of flowers, having at one end a curiously clipped hedge with a hole in it, like a green cave, under the shadow of which some broken steps peeped out.

Father Brown strolled up to the hole and ducked his head under it. A few moments after he had disappeared they were astonished to hear his quiet voice in conversation above their heads, as if he were talking to somebody at the top of a tree. The detective followed, and found that the curious covered stairway led to what looked like a broken bridge, overhanging the darker and emptier spaces of the garden. It just curled round the corner of the house, bringing in sight the field of coloured lights beyond and beneath. Probably it was the relic of some abandoned architectural fancy of building a sort of terrace on arches across the lawn. Bagshaw thought it a curious cul-de-sac in which to find anybody in the small hours between night and morning; but he was not looking at the details of it just then. He was looking at the man who was found.

As the man stood with his back turned – a small man in light grey clothes – the one outstanding feature about him was a wonderful head of hair, as yellow and radiant as the head of a huge dandelion. It was literally outstanding like a halo, and something in that association made the face, when it was slowly and sulkily turned on them, rather a shock of contrast. That halo should have enclosed an oval face of the mildly angelic sort; but the face was crabbed and elderly with a powerful jowl and a short nose that somehow suggested the broken nose of a pugilist.

'This is Mr Orm, the celebrated poet, I understand,' said Father Brown, as calmly as if he were introducing two people in a drawing-room.

'Whoever he is,' said Bagshaw, 'I must trouble him to come with me and answer a few questions.'

Mr Osric Orm, the poet, was not a model of self-expression when it came to the answering of questions. There, in that corner of the old garden, as the grey twilight before dawn began to creep over the heavy hedges and the broken bridge, and afterwards in a succession of circumstances and stages of legal enquiry that grew more and more ominous, he refused to say anything except that he had intended to call on Sir Humphrey Gwynne, but had not done so because he could not get anyone to answer the bell. When it was pointed out that the door was practically open, he snorted. When it was hinted that the hour was somewhat late, he snarled. The little that he said was obscure, either because he really knew hardly any English, or because he knew better than to know any. His opinions seemed to be of a nihilistic and destructive sort, as was indeed the tendency of his poetry for those who could follow it; and it seemed possible that his business with the judge, and perhaps his quarrel with the judge, had been something in the anarchist line. Gwynne was known to have had something of a mania about Bolshevist spies, as he had about German spies. Anyhow, one coincidence, only a few moments after his capture, confirmed Bagshaw in the impression that the case must be taken seriously. As they went out of the front gate into the street, they so happened to encounter yet another neighbour, Buller, the cigar merchant from next door, conspicuous by his brown, shrewd face and the unique orchid in his buttonhole; for he had a name in that branch of horticulture. Rather to the surprise of the rest, he hailed his neighbour, the poet, in a matter-of-fact manner, almost as if he had expected to see him.

'Hallo, here we are again,' he said. 'Had a long talk with old Gwynne, I suppose?'

'Sir Humphrey Gwynne is dead,' said Bagshaw. 'I am investigating the case and I must ask you to explain.'

Buller stood as still as the lamppost beside him, possibly stiffened with surprise. The red end of his cigar brightened and darkened rhythmically, but his brown face was in shadow; when he spoke it was with quite a new voice.

'I only mean,' he said, 'that when I passed two hours ago Mr Orm was going in at this gate to see Sir Humphrey.'

'He says he hasn't seen him yet,' observed Bagshaw, 'or even been into the house.'

'It's a long time to stand on the doorstep,' observed Buller.

'Yes,' said Father Brown; 'it's rather a long time to stand in the street.'

'I've been home since then,' said the cigar merchant. 'Been writing letters and came out again to post them.'

'You'll have to tell all that later,' said Bagshaw. 'Good-night – or good-morning.'

The trial of Osric Orm for the murder of Sir Humphrey Gwynne, which filled the newspapers for so many weeks, really turned entirely on the same crux as that little talk under the lamp-post, when the grey-green dawn was breaking about the dark streets and gardens. Everything came back to the enigma of those two empty hours between the time when Buller saw Orm going in at the garden gate, and the time when Father Brown found him apparently still lingering in the garden. He had certainly had the time to commit six murders, and might almost have committed them for want of something to do; for he could give no coherent account of what he was doing. It was argued by the prosecution that he had also the opportunity, as the front door was unlatched, and the side-door into the larger garden left standing open. The court followed, with considerable interest, Bagshaw's clear reconstruction of the struggle in the passage, of which the traces were so evident; indeed, the police had since found the shot that had shattered the glass. Finally, the hole in the hedge to which he had been tracked, had very much the appearance of a hiding-place. On the other hand, Sir Matthew Blake, the very able counsel for the defence, turned this last argument the other way: asking why any man should entrap himself in a place without possible exit, when it would obviously be much more sensible to slip out into the street. Sir Matthew Blake also made effective use of the mystery that still rested upon the motive for the murder. Indeed, upon this point, the passages between Sir Matthew Blake and Sir Arthur Travers, the equally brilliant advocate for the prosecution, turned rather to the advantage of the prisoner. Sir Arthur could only throw out suggestions about a Bolshevist conspiracy which sounded a little thin. But when it came to investigating the facts of Orm's mysterious behaviour that night he was considerably more effective.

The prisoner went into the witness-box, chiefly because his astute counsel calculated that it would create a bad impression if he did not. But he was almost as uncommunicative to his own counsel as to the prosecuting counsel. Sir Arthur Travers made all possible capital out of his stubborn silence, but did not succeed in breaking it. Sir Arthur was a long, gaunt man, with a long, cadaverous face, in striking contrast to the sturdy figure and bright, birdlike eye of Sir Matthew Blake. But if Sir Matthew suggested a very cocksure sort of cock-sparrow, Sir Arthur might more truly have been compared to a crane or stork; as he leaned forward, prodding the poet with questions, his long nose might have been a long beak.

'Do you mean to tell the jury,' he asked, in tones of grating incredulity, 'that you never went in to see the deceased gentleman at all?'

'No!' replied Orm shortly.

'You wanted to see him, I suppose. You must have been very anxious to see him. Didn't you wait two whole hours in front of his front door?'

'Yes,' replied the other.

'And yet you never even noticed the door was open?'

'No,' said Orm.

'What in the world were you doing for two hours in somebody else's front garden?' insisted the barrister. 'You were doing something I suppose?'

'Yes.'

'Is it a secret?' asked Sir Arthur, with adamantine jocularity.

'It's a secret from you,' answered the poet.

It was upon this suggestion of a secret that Sir Arthur seized in developing his line of accusation. With a boldness which some thought unscrupulous, he turned the very mystery of the motive, which was the strongest part of his opponent's case, into an argument for his own. He gave it as the first fragmentary hint of some far-flung and elaborate conspiracy, in which a patriot had perished like one caught in the coils of an octopus.

'Yes,' he cried in a vibrating voice, 'my learned friend is perfectly right! We do not know the exact reason why this honourable public servant was murdered. We shall not know the reason why the next public servant is murdered. If my learned friend himself falls a victim to his eminence, and the hatred which the hellish powers of destruction feel for the guardians of law, he will be murdered, and he will not know the reason. Half the decent people in this court will be butchered in their beds, and we shall not know the reason. And we shall never know the reason and never arrest the massacre, until it has depopulated our country, so long as the defence is permitted to stop all proceedings with this stale tag about "motive", when every other fact in the case, every glaring incongruity, every gaping silence, tells us that we stand in the presence of Cain.'

'I never knew Sir Arthur so excited,' said Bagshaw to his group of companions afterwards. 'Some people are saying he went beyond the usual limit and that the prosecutor in a murder case oughtn't to be so vindictive. But I must say there was something downright creepy about that little goblin with the yellow hair, that seemed to play up to the impression. I was vaguely recalling, all the time, something that De Quincey says about Mr Williams, that ghastly criminal who slaughtered two whole families almost in silence. I think he says that Williams had hair of a vivid unnatural yellow; and that he thought it had been dyed by a trick learned in India, where they dye horses green or blue. Then there was his queer, stony silence, like a troglodyte's; I'll never deny that it all worked me up until I felt there was a sort of monster in the dock. If that was only Sir Arthur's eloquence, then he certainly took a heavy responsibility in putting so much passion into it.'

'He was a friend of poor Gwynne's, as a matter of fact,' said Underhill, more gently; 'a man I know saw them hobnobbing together after a great legal dinner lately. I dare say that's why he feels so strongly in this case. I suppose it's doubtful whether a man ought to act in such a case on mere personal feeling.'

'He wouldn't,' said Bagshaw. 'I bet Sir Arthur Travers wouldn't act only on feeling, however strongly he felt. He's got a very stiff sense of his own professional position. He's one of those men who are ambitious even when they've satisfied their ambition. I know nobody who'd take more trouble to keep his position in the world. No; you've got hold of the wrong moral to his rather thundering sermon. If he lets himself go like that, it's because he thinks he can get a conviction anyhow, and wants to put himself at the head of some political movement against the conspiracy he talks about. He must have some very good reason for wanting to convict Orm and some very good reason for thinking he can do it. That means that the facts will support him. His confidence doesn't look well for the prisoner.' He became conscious of an insignificant figure in the group.

'Well, Father Brown,' he said with a smile; 'what do you think of our judicial procedure?'

'Well,' replied the priest rather absently, 'I think the thing that struck me most was how different men look in their wigs. You talk about the prosecuting barrister being so tremendous. But I happened to see him take his wig off for a minute, and he really looks quite a different man. He's quite bald, for one thing.'

'I'm afraid that won't prevent his being tremendous,' answered Bagshaw. 'You don't propose to found the defence on the fact that the prosecuting counsel is bald, do you?'

'Not exactly,' said Father Brown good-humouredly. 'To tell the truth, I was thinking how little some kinds of people know about other kinds of people. Suppose I went among some remote people who had never even heard of England. Suppose I told them that there is a man in my country who won't ask a question of life and death, until he has put an erection made of horsehair on the top of his head, with little tails behind, and grey corkscrew curls at the side, like an Early Victorian old woman. They would think he must be rather eccentric; but he isn't at all eccentric, he's only conventional. They would think so, because they don't know anything about English barristers; because they don't know what a barrister is. Well, that barrister doesn't know what a poet is. He doesn't understand that a poet's eccentricities wouldn't seem eccentric to other poets. He thinks it odd that Orm should walk about in a beautiful garden for two hours, with nothing to do. God bless my soul! A poet would think nothing of walking about in the same backyard for ten hours if he had a poem to do. Orm's own counsel was quite as stupid. It never occurred to him to ask Orm the obvious question.'

'What question do you mean?' asked the other.

'Why, what poem he was making up, of course,' said Father Brown rather impatiently.

'What line he was stuck at, what epithet he was looking for, what climax he was trying to work up to. If there were any educated people in court, who know what literature is, they would have known well enough whether he had had anything genuine to do. You'd have asked a manufacturer about the conditions of his factory; but nobody seems to consider the conditions under which poetry is manufactured. It's done by doing nothing.'

'That's all very well,' replied the detective; 'but why did he hide? Why did he climb up that crooked little stairway and stop there; it led nowhere.'

'Why, because it led nowhere, of course,' cried Father

Brown explosively. 'Anybody who clapped eyes on that blind alley ending in mid-air might have known an artist would want to go there, just as a child would.'

He stood blinking for a moment, and then said apologetically: 'I beg your pardon; but it seems odd that none of them understand these things. And then there was another thing. Don't you know that everything has, for an artist, one aspect or angle that is exactly *right*? A tree, a cow, and a cloud, in a certain relation only, mean something; as three letters, in one order only, mean a word. Well, the view of that illuminated garden from that unfinished bridge was the right view of it. It was as unique as the fourth dimension. It was a sort of fairy foreshortening; it was like looking *down* at heaven and seeing all the stars growing on trees and that luminous pond like a moon fallen flat on the fields in some happy nursery tale. He could have looked at it for ever. If you told him the path led nowhere, he would tell you it had led him to the country at the end of the world. But do you expect him to tell you that in the witness-box? What would you say to him if he did? You talk about a man having a jury of his peers. Why don't you have a jury of poets?'

'You talk as if you were a poet yourself,' said Bagshaw.

'Thank your stars I'm not,' said Father Brown. 'Thank your lucky stars a priest has to be more charitable than a poet. Lord have mercy on us, if you knew what a crushing, what a cruel contempt he feels for the lot of you, you'd feel as if you were under Niagara.'

'You may know more about the artistic temperament than I do,' said Bagshaw after a pause; 'but, after all, the answer is simple. You can only show that he might have done what he did, without committing the crime. But it's equally true that he might have committed the crime. And who else could have committed it?'

'Have you thought about the servant, Green?' asked Father Brown, reflectively. 'He told a rather queer story.'

'Ah,' cried Bagshaw quickly, 'you think Green did it, after all.'

'I'm quite sure he didn't,' replied the other. 'I only asked if you'd thought about his queer story. He only went out for some trifle, a drink or an assignation or what not. But he went out by the garden door and came back over the garden wall. In other words, he left the door open, but he came back to find it shut. Why? Because Somebody Else had already passed out that way.'

'The murderer,' muttered the detective doubtfully. 'Do you know who he was?'

'I know what he looked like,' answered Father Brown quietly. 'That's the only thing I do know. I can almost see him as he came in at the front door, in the gleam of the hall lamp; his figure, his clothes, even his face!'

'What's all this?'

'He looked like Sir Humphrey Gwynne,' said the priest.

'What the devil do you mean?' demanded Bagshaw. 'Gwynne was lying dead with his head in the pond.'

'Oh, yes,' said Father Brown.

After a moment he went on: 'Let's go back to that theory of yours, which was a very good one, though I don't quite agree with it. You suppose the murderer came in at the front door, met the judge in the front hall, struggling with him and breaking the mirror; that the judge then retreated into the garden, where he was finally shot. Somehow, it doesn't sound natural to me. Granted he retreated down the hall, there are two exits at the end, one into the garden and one into the house. Surely, he would be more likely to retreat into the house? His gun was there; his telephone was there; his servant, so far as he knew, was there. Even the nearest neighbours were in that direction. Why should he stop to open the garden door and go out alone on the deserted side of the house?'

'But we know he did go out of the house,' replied his companion, puzzled. 'We know he went out of the house, because he was found in the garden.'

'He never went out of the house, because he never was in the house,' said Father Brown. 'Not that evening, I mean. He was sitting in that bungalow. I read *that* lesson in the dark, at the beginning, in red and golden stars across the garden. They were worked from the hut; they wouldn't have been burning at all if he hadn't been in the hut. He was trying to run across to the house and the telephone, when the murderer shot him beside the pond.'

'But what about the pot and the palm and the broken mirror?' cried Bagshaw. 'Why, it was you who found them! It was you yourself who said there must have been a struggle in the hall.'

The priest blinked rather painfully. 'Did I?' he muttered. 'Surely, I didn't say that. I never thought that. What I think I said, was that something had happened in the hall. And something did happen; but it wasn't a struggle.'

'Then what broke the mirror?' asked Bagshaw shortly.

'A bullet broke the mirror,' answered Father Brown gravely; 'a bullet fired by the criminal. The big fragments of falling glass were quite enough to knock over the pot and the palm.'

'Well, what else could he have been firing at except Gwynne?' asked the detective.

'It's rather a fine metaphysical point,' answered his clerical companion almost dreamily. 'In one sense, of course, he was firing at Gwynne. But Gwynne wasn't there to be fired at. The criminal was alone in the hall.'

He was silent for a moment, and then went on quietly. 'Imagine the looking-glass at the end of the passage, before it was broken, and the tall palm arching over it. In the half-light, reflecting these monochrome walls, it would look like the end of the passage. A man reflected in it would look like a man coming from inside the house. It would look like the master of the house – if only the reflection were a little like him.'

'Stop a minute,' cried Bagshaw. 'I believe I begin – '

'You begin to see,' said Father Brown. 'You begin to see why all the suspects in this case must be innocent. Not one of them could possibly have mistaken his own reflection for old Gwynne. Orm would have known at once that his bush of yellow hair was not a bald head. Flood would have seen his own red head, and Green his own red waistcoat. Besides, they're all short and shabby; none of them could have thought his own image was a tall, thin, old gentleman in evening-dress. We want another, equally tall and thin, to match him. That's what I meant by saying that I knew what the murderer looked like.'

'And what do you argue from that?' asked Bagshaw, looking at him steadily.

The priest uttered a sort of sharp, crisp laugh, oddly different from his ordinary mild manner of speech.

'I am going to argue,' he said, 'the very thing that you said was so ludicrous and impossible.'

'What do you mean?'

'I'm going to base the defence,' said Father Brown, 'on the fact that the prosecuting counsel has a bald head.'

'Oh, my God!' said the detective quietly, and got to his feet, staring.

Father Brown had resumed his monologue in an unruffled manner.

'You've been following the movements of a good many people in this business; you policemen were prodigiously interested in the movements of the poet, and the servant, and the Irishman. The man whose movements seem to have been rather forgotten is the dead man himself. His servant was quite honestly astonished at finding his master had returned. His master had gone to a great dinner of all the leaders of the legal profession, but had left it abruptly and come home. He was not ill, for he summoned no assistance; he had almost certainly quarrelled with some leader of the legal profession. It's among the leaders of that profession that we should have looked first for his enemy. He returned, and shut himself up in the bungalow, where he kept all his private documents about treasonable practices. But the leader of the legal profession, who knew there was something against him in those documents, was thoughtful enough to follow his accuser home; he also being in evening-dress, but with a pistol in his pocket. That is all; and nobody could ever have guessed it except for the mirror.'

He seemed to be gazing into vacancy for a moment, and then added: 'A queer thing is a mirror; a picture frame that holds hundreds of different pictures, all vivid and all vanished for ever. Yet, there was something specially strange about the glass that hung at the end of that grey corridor under that green palm. It is as if it was a magic glass and had a different fate from others, as if its picture could somehow survive it, hanging in the air of that twilight house like a spectre; or at least like an abstract diagram, the skeleton of an argument. We could, at least, conjure out of the void the thing that Sir Arthur Travers saw. By the way, there was one very true thing that you said about him.'

'I'm glad to hear it,' said Bagshaw with grim good nature. 'And what was it?'

'You said,' observed the priest, 'that Sir Arthur must have some good reason for wanting to get Orm hanged.'

A week later the priest met the police detective once more, and learned that the authorities had already been moving on the new lines of enquiry when they were interrupted by a sensational event.

'Sir Arthur Travers,' began Father Brown.

'Sir Arthur Travers is dead,' said Bagshaw, briefly.

'Ah!' said the other, with a little catch in his voice; 'you mean that he – '

'Yes,' said Bagshaw, 'he shot at the same man again, but not in a mirror.'

The Blast of the Book

Professor Openshaw always lost his temper, with a loud bang, if anybody called him a spiritualist; or a believer in spiritualism. This, however, did not exhaust his explosive elements; for he also lost his temper if anybody called him a disbeliever in spiritualism. It was his pride to have given his whole life to investigating psychic phenomena; it was also his pride never to have given a hint of whether he thought they were really psychic or merely phenomenal. He enjoyed nothing so much as to sit in a circle of devout spiritualists and give devastating descriptions of how he had exposed medium after medium and detected fraud after fraud: for indeed he was a man of much detective talent and insight, when once he had fixed his eye on an object, and he always fixed his eye on a medium, as a highly suspicious object. There was a story of his having spotted the same spiritualist mountebank under three different disguises: dressed as a woman, a white-bearded old man, and a Brahmin of a rich chocolate brown. These recitals made the true believers rather restless, as indeed they were intended to do; but they could hardly complain, for no spiritualist denies the existence of fraudulent mediums; only the professor's flowing narrative might well seem to indicate that all mediums were fraudulent.

But woe to the simple-minded and innocent materialist (and materialists as a race are rather innocent and simple-minded) who, presuming on this narrative tendency, should advance the thesis that ghosts were against the laws of nature, or that such things were only old superstitions; or that it was all tosh, or, alternately, bunk. Him would the professor, suddenly reversing all his scientific batteries, sweep from the field with a cannonade of unquestionable cases and unexplained phenomena, of which the wretched rationalist had never heard in his life, giving all the dates and details, stating all the attempted and abandoned natural explanations; stating everything, indeed, except whether he, John Oliver Openshaw, did or did not believe in spirits; and that neither spiritualist nor materialist could ever boast of finding out.

Professor Openshaw, a lean figure with pale leonine hair and hypnotic blue eyes, stood exchanging a few words with Father Brown, who was a friend of his, on the steps outside the hotel where both had been breakfasting that morning and sleeping the night before. The professor had come back rather late from one of his grand experiments, in general exasperation, and was still tingling with the fight that he always waged alone and against both sides.

'Oh, I don't mind you,' he said laughing. 'You don't believe in it even if it's true. But all these people are perpetually asking me what I'm trying to prove. They don't seem to understand that I'm a man of science. A man of science isn't trying to prove anything. He's trying to find out what will prove itself.'

'But he hasn't found out yet,' said Father Brown.

'Well, I have some little notions of my own, that are not quite so negative as most people think,' answered the professor, after an instant of frowning silence; 'anyhow, I've begun to fancy that if there is something to be found, they're looking for it along the wrong line.

It's all too theatrical; it's showing off, all their shiny ectoplasm and trumpets and voices and the rest; all on the model of old melodramas and mouldy historical novels about the family ghost. If they'd go to history instead of historical novels, I'm beginning to think they'd really find something. But not apparitions.'

'After all,' said Father Brown, 'Apparitions are only appearances. I suppose you'd say the family ghost is only keeping up appearances.'

The professor's gaze, which had commonly a fine abstracted character, suddenly fixed and focused itself as it did on a dubious medium. It had rather the air of a man screwing a strong magnifying-glass into his eye. Not that he thought the priest was in the least like a dubious medium; but he was startled into attention by his friend's thought following so closely on his own.

'Appearances!' he muttered, 'crikey, but it's odd you should say that just now. The more I learn, the more I fancy they lose by merely looking for appearances. Now if they'd look a little into disappearances – '

'Yes,' said Father Brown, 'after all, the real fairy legends weren't so very much about the appearance of famous fairies; calling up Titania or exhibiting Oberon by moonlight. But there were no end of legends about people *disappearing*, because they were stolen by the fairies. Are you on the track of Kilmeny or Thomas the Rhymer?'

'I'm on the track of ordinary modern people you've read of in the newspapers,' answered Openshaw. 'You may well stare; but that's my game just now; and I've been on it for a long time. Frankly, I think a lot of psychic appearances could be explained away. It's the disappearances I can't explain, unless they're psychic. These people in the newspapers who vanish and are never found – if you knew the details as I do . . . and now only this morning I got confirmation; an extraordinary letter from an old missionary, quite a respectable old boy. He's coming to see me at my office this morning. Perhaps you'd lunch with me or something; and I'd tell the results – in confidence.'

'Thanks; I will – unless,' said Father Brown modestly, 'the fairies have stolen me by then.'

With that they parted and Openshaw walked round the corner to a small office he rented in the neighbourhood; chiefly for the publication of a small periodical, of psychical and psychological notes of the driest and most agnostic sort. He had only one clerk, who sat at a desk in the outer office, totting up figures and facts for the purposes of the printed report; and the professor paused to ask if Mr Pringle had called. The clerk answered mechanically in the negative and went on mechanically adding up figures; and the professor turned towards the inner room that was his study. 'Oh, by the way, Berridge,' he added, without turning round, 'if Mr Pringle comes, send him straight in to me. You needn't interrupt your work; I rather want those notes finished tonight if possible. You might leave them on my desk tomorrow, if I am late.'

And he went into his private office, still brooding on the problem which the name of Pringle had raised; or rather, perhaps, had ratified and confirmed in his mind. Even the most perfectly balanced of agnostics is partially human; and it is possible that the missionary's letter seemed to have greater weight as promising to support his private and still tentative hypothesis. He sat down in his large and comfortable chair, opposite the engraving of Montaigne; and read once more the short letter from the Revd Luke Pringle, making the appointment for that morning. No man knew better than Professor Openshaw the marks of the letter of the crank: the crowded details; the spidery handwriting; the unnecessary length and repetition. There were none of these things in this case; but a brief and businesslike typewritten statement that the writer had encountered some curious case of disappearance, which seemed to fall within the province of the professor as a student of psychic problems. The professor was favourably impressed; nor had he any unfavourable impression, in spite of a slight movement of surprise, when he looked up and saw that the Revd Luke Pringle was already in the room.

'Your clerk told me I was to come straight in,' said Mr Pringle apologetically, but with a broad and rather agreeable grin. The grin was partly masked by masses of reddish-grey beard and whiskers; a perfect jungle of a beard, such as is sometimes grown by white men living in the jungles; but the eyes above the snub nose had nothing about them in the least wild or outlandish. Openshaw had instantly turned on them that concentrated spotlight or burning-glass of sceptical scrutiny which he turned on many men to see if they were mountebanks or maniacs; and, in this case, he had a rather unusual sense of reassurance. The wild beard might have belonged to a crank, but the eyes completely contradicted the beard; they were full of that quite frank and friendly laughter which is never found in the faces of those who are serious frauds or serious lunatics. He would have expected a man with those eyes to be a philistine, a jolly sceptic, a man who shouted out shallow but hearty contempt for ghosts and spirits; but anyhow, no professional humbug could afford to look as frivolous as that. The man was buttoned up to the throat in a shabby old cape, and only his broad limp hat suggested the cleric; but missionaries from wild places do not always bother to dress like clerics.

'You probably think all this is another hoax, professor,' said Mr Pringle, with a sort of abstract enjoyment, 'and I hope you will forgive my laughing at your very natural air of disapproval. All the same, I've got to tell my story to somebody who knows, because it's true. And, all joking apart, it's tragic as well as true. Well, to cut it short, I was missionary in Nya-Nya, a station in West Africa, in the thick of the forests, where almost the only other white man was the officer in command of the district, Captain Wales; and he and I grew rather thick. Not that he liked missions; he was, if I may say so, thick in many ways; one of those square-headed, square-shouldered men of action who hardly need to think, let alone believe. That's what makes it all the queerer. One day he came back to his tent in the forest, after a short leave, and said he had gone through a jolly rum experience, and didn't know what to do about it. He was holding a rusty old book in a leather binding, and he put it down on a table beside his revolver and an old Arab sword he kept, probably as a curiosity. He said this book had belonged to a man on the boat he had just come off; and the man swore that nobody must open the book, or look inside it; or else they would be carried off by the devil, or disappear, or something. Wales said this was all nonsense, of course; and they had a quarrel; and the upshot seems to have been that this man, taunted with cowardice or superstition, actually did look into the book; and instantly dropped it; walked to the side of the boat –'

'One moment,' said the professor, who had made one or two notes. 'Before you tell me anything else. Did this man tell Wales where he had got the book, or who it originally belonged to?'

'Yes,' replied Pringle, now entirely grave. 'It seems he said he was bringing it back to Dr Hankey, the Oriental traveller now in England, to whom it originally belonged, and who had warned him of its strange properties. Well, Hankey is an able man and a rather crabbed and sneering sort of man; which makes it queerer still. But the point of Wales's story is much simpler. It is that the man who had looked into the book walked straight over the side of the ship, and was never seen again.'

'Do you believe it yourself?' asked Openshaw, after a pause.

'Well, I do,' replied Pringle. 'I believe it for two reasons. First, that Wales was an entirely unimaginative man; and he added one touch that only an imaginative man could have added. He said that the man walked straight over the side on a still and calm day; but there was no splash.'

The professor looked at his notes for some seconds in silence; and then said: 'And your other reason for believing it?'

'My other reason,' answered the Revd Luke Pringle, 'is what I saw myself.'

There was another silence; until he continued in the same matter-of-fact way. Whatever he had, he had nothing of the eagerness with which the crank, or even the believer, tried to convince others.

'I told you that Wales put down the book on the table beside the sword. There was only one entrance to the tent; and it happened that I was standing in it, looking out into the forest, with my back to my companion. He was standing by the table grumbling and growling about the whole business; saying it was tomfoolery in the twentieth century to be frightened of opening a book; asking why the devil he shouldn't open it himself. Then some instinct stirred in me and I said that he had better not do that, it had better be returned to Dr Hankey. "What harm could it do?" he said restlessly. "What harm did it do?" I answered obstinately. "What happened to your friend on the boat?" He didn't answer, indeed I didn't know what he could answer; but I pressed my logical advantage in mere vanity. "If it comes to that," I said, "what is your version of what really happened on the boat?" Still he didn't answer; and I looked round and saw that he wasn't there.

'The tent was empty. The book was lying on the table; open, but on its face, as if he had turned it downwards. But the sword was lying on the ground near the other side of the tent; and the canvas of the tent showed a great slash, as if somebody had hacked his way out with the sword. The gash in the tent gaped at me; but showed only the dark glimmer of the forest outside. And when I went across and looked through the rent I could not be certain whether the tangle of the tall plants and the undergrowth had been bent or broken; at least not farther than a few feet. I have never seen or heard of Captain Wales from that day.

'I wrapped the book up in brown paper, taking good care not to look at it; and I brought it back to England, intending at first to return it to Dr Hankey. Then I saw some notes in your paper suggesting a hypothesis about such things; and I decided to stop on the way and put the matter before you; as you have a name for being balanced and having an open mind.'

Professor Openshaw laid down his pen and looked steadily at the man on the other side of the table; concentrating in that single stare all his long experience of many entirely different types of humbug, and even some eccentric and extraordinary types of honest men. In the ordinary way, he would have begun with the healthy hypothesis that the story was a pack of lies. On the whole he did incline to assume that it was a pack of lies. And yet he could not fit the man into his story; if it were only that he could not see that sort of liar telling that sort of lie. The man was not trying to look honest on the surface, as most quacks and impostors do; somehow, it seemed all the other way; as if the man *was* honest, in spite of something else that was merely on the surface. He thought of a good man with one innocent delusion; but again the symptoms were not the same; there was even a sort of virile indifference; as if the man did not care much about his delusion, if it was a delusion.

'Mr Pringle,' he said sharply, like a barrister making a witness jump, 'where is this book of yours now?'

The grin reappeared on the bearded face which had grown grave during the recital.

'I left it outside,' said Mr Pringle. 'I mean in the outer office. It was a risk, perhaps; but the less risk of the two.'

'What do you mean?' demanded the professor. 'Why didn't you bring it straight in here?'

'Because,' answered the missionary, 'I knew that as soon as you saw it, you'd open it – before you had heard the story. I thought it possible you might think twice about opening it – after you'd heard the story.'

Then after a silence he added: 'There was nobody out there but your clerk; and he looked a stolid steady-going specimen, immersed in business calculations.'

Openshaw laughed unaffectedly. 'Oh, Babbage,' he cried, 'your magic tomes are safe enough with him, I assure you. His name's Berridge – but I often call him Babbage; because he's so exactly like a calculating machine. No human being, if you can call him a human being, would be less likely to open other people's brown-paper parcels. Well, we may as well go and bring it in now; though I assure you I will consider seriously the course to be taken with it. Indeed, I tell you frankly,' and he stared at the man again, 'that I'm not quite sure whether we ought to open it here and now, or send it to this Dr Hankey.'

The two had passed together out of the inner into the outer office: and even as they did so, Mr Pringle gave a cry and ran forward towards the clerk's desk. For the clerk's desk was there; but not the clerk. On the clerk's desk lay a faded old leather book, torn out of its brown-paper wrappings, and lying closed, but as if it had just been opened. The clerk's desk stood against the wide window that looked out into the street; and the window was shattered with a huge ragged hole in the glass; as if a human body had been shot through it into the world without. There was no other trace of Mr Berridge.

Both the two men left in the office stood as still as statues; and then it was the professor who slowly came to life. He looked even more judicial than he had ever looked in his life, as he slowly turned and held out his hand to the missionary.

'Mr Pringle,' he said, 'I beg your pardon. I beg your pardon only for thoughts that I have had; and half-thoughts at that. But nobody could call himself a scientific man and not face a fact like this.'

'I suppose,' said Pringle doubtfully, 'that we ought to make some enquiries. Can you ring up his house and find out if he has gone home?'

'I don't know that he's on the telephone,' answered Openshaw, rather absently; 'he lives somewhere up Hampstead way, I think. But I suppose somebody will enquire here, if his friends or family miss him.'

'Could we furnish a description,' asked the other, 'if the police want it?'

'The police!' said the professor, starting from his reverie. 'A description . . . Well, he looked awfully like everybody else, I'm afraid, except for goggles. One of those clean-shaven chaps. But the police . . . look here, what *are* we to do about this mad business?'

'I know what I ought to do,' said the Revd Mr Pringle firmly, 'I am going to take this book straight to the only original Dr Hankey, and ask him what the devil it's all about. He lives not very far from here, and I'll come straight back and tell you what he says.'

'Oh, very well,' said the professor at last, as he sat down rather wearily; perhaps relieved for the moment to be rid of the responsibility. But long after the brisk and ringing footsteps of the little missionary had died away down the street, the professor sat in the same posture, staring into vacancy like a man in a trance.

He was still in the same seat and almost in the same attitude, when the same brisk footsteps were heard on the pavement without and the missionary entered, this time, as a glance assured him, with empty hands.

'Dr Hankey,' said Pringle gravely, 'wants to keep the book for an hour and consider the point. Then he asks us both to call, and he will give us his decision.

He specially desired, professor, that you should accompany me on the second visit.'

Openshaw continued to stare in silence; then he said, suddenly: 'Who the devil is Dr Hankey?'

'You sound rather as if you meant he was the devil,' said Pringle, smiling, 'and I fancy some people have thought so. He had quite a reputation in your own line; but he gained it mostly in India, studying local magic and so on, so perhaps he's not so well known here. He is a yellow skinny little devil with a lame leg, and a doubtful temper; but he seems to have set up in an ordinary respectable practice in these parts, and I don't know anything definitely wrong about him – unless it's wrong to be the only person who can possibly know anything about all this crazy affair.'

Professor Openshaw rose heavily and went to the telephone; he rang up Father Brown, changing the luncheon engagement to a dinner, that he might hold himself free for the expedition to the house of the Anglo-Indian doctor; after that he sat down again, lit a cigar and sank once more into his own unfathomable thoughts.

Father Brown went round to the restaurant appointed for dinner, and kicked his heels for some time in a vestibule full of mirrors and palms in pots; he had been informed of Openshaw's afternoon engagement, and, as the evening closed in dark and stormy round the glass and the green plants, guessed that it had produced something unexpected and unduly prolonged. He even wondered for a moment whether the professor would turn up at all; but when the professor eventually did, it was clear that his own more general guesses had been justified. For it was a very wild-eyed and even wild-haired professor who eventually drove back with Mr Pringle from the expedition to the North of London, where suburbs are still fringed with heathy wastes and scraps of common, looking more sombre under the rather thunderstorm sunset. Nevertheless, they had apparently found the house, standing a little apart though within hail of other houses; they had verified the brass-plate duly engraved: 'J. I. Hankey, MD, MRCS'. Only they did not find J. I. Hankey, MD, MRCS. They found only what a nightmare whisper had already subconsciously prepared them to find: a commonplace parlour with the accused volume lying on the table, as if it had just been read; and beyond, a backdoor burst open and a faint trail of footsteps that ran a little way up so steep a garden-path that it seemed that no lame man could have run up so lightly. But it was a lame man who had run; for in those few steps there was the misshapen unequal mark of some sort of surgical boot; then two marks of that boot alone (as if the creature had hopped) and then nothing. There was nothing further to be learnt from Dr J. I. Hankey, except that he had made his decision. He had read the oracle and received the doom.

When the two came into the entrance under the palms, Pringle put the book down suddenly on a small table, as if it burned his fingers. The priest glanced at it curiously; there was only some rude lettering on the front with a couplet:

They that looked into this book
Them the Flying Terror took;

and underneath, as he afterwards discovered, similar warnings in Greek, Latin and French. The other two had turned away with a natural impulsion towards drinks, after their exhaustion and bewilderment; and Openshaw had called to the waiter, who brought cocktails on a tray.

'You will dine with us, I hope,' said the professor to the missionary; but Mr Pringle amiably shook his head.

'If you'll forgive me,' he said, 'I'm going off to wrestle with this book and this business by myself somewhere. I suppose I couldn't use your office for an hour or so?'

'I suppose – I'm afraid it's locked,' said Openshaw in some surprise.

'You forget there's a hole in the window.' The Revd Luke Pringle gave the very broadest of all his broad grins and vanished into the darkness without.

'A rather odd fellow, that, after all,' said the professor, frowning.

He was rather surprised to find Father Brown talking to the waiter who had brought the cocktails, apparently about the waiter's most private affairs; for there was some mention of a baby who was now out of danger. He commented on the fact with some surprise, wondering how the priest came to know the man; but the former only said, 'Oh, I dine here every two or three months, and I've talked to him now and then.'

The professor, who himself dined there about five times a week, was conscious that he had never thought of talking to the man; but his thoughts were interrupted by a strident ringing and a summons to the telephone. The voice on the telephone said it was Pringle; it was rather a muffled voice, but it might well be muffled in all those bushes of beard and whisker. Its message was enough to establish identity.

'Professor,' said the voice, 'I can't stand it any longer. I'm going to look for myself. I'm speaking from your office and the book is in front of me. If anything happens to me, this is to say goodbye. No – it's no good trying to stop me. You wouldn't be in time anyhow. I'm opening the book now. I . . .'

Openshaw thought he heard something like a sort of thrilling or shivering yet almost soundless crash; then he shouted the name of Pringle again and again; but he heard no more. He hung up the receiver, and, restored to a superb academic calm, rather like the calm of despair, went back and quietly took his seat at the dinner-table. Then, as coolly as if he were describing the failure of some small silly trick at a séance, he told the priest every detail of this monstrous mystery.

'Five men have now vanished in this impossible way,' he said. 'Every one is extraordinary; and yet the one case I simply can't get over is my clerk, Berridge. It's just because he was the quietest creature that he's the queerest case.'

'Yes,' replied Father Brown, 'it was a queer thing for Berridge to do, anyway. He was awfully conscientious. He was always so jolly careful to keep all the office business separate from any fun of his own. Why, hardly anybody knew he was quite a humorist at home and – '

'Berridge!' cried the professor. 'What on earth are you talking about? Did you know him?'

'Oh no,' said Father Brown carelessly, 'only as you say I know the waiter. I've often had to wait in your office, till you turned up; and of course I passed the time of day with poor Berridge. He was rather a card. I remember he once said he would like to collect valueless things, as collectors did the silly things they thought valuable. You know the old story about the woman who collected valueless things.'

'I'm not sure I know what you're talking about,' said Openshaw. 'But even if my clerk was eccentric (and I never knew a man I should have thought less so), it wouldn't explain what happened to him; and it certainly wouldn't explain the others.'

'What others?' asked the priest.

The professor stared at him and spoke distinctly, as if to a child.

'My dear Father Brown, five men have disappeared.'

'My dear Professor Openshaw, no men have disappeared.'

Father Brown gazed back at his host with equal steadiness and spoke with equal distinctness. Nevertheless, the professor required the words repeated, and they were repeated as distinctly.

'I say that no men have disappeared.'

After a moment's silence, he added, 'I suppose the hardest thing is to convince anybody that 0+0+0=0. Men believe the oddest things if they are in a series; that is why Macbeth believed the three words of the three witches; though the first was something he knew himself; and the last something he could only bring about himself. But in your case the middle term is the weakest of all.'

'What do you mean?'

'You saw nobody vanish. You did not see the man vanish from the boat. You did not see the man vanish from the tent. All that rests on the word of Mr Pringle, which I will not discuss just now. But you'll admit this; you would never have taken his word yourself, *unless* you had seen it confirmed by your clerk's disappearance; just as Macbeth would never have believed he would be king, if he had not been confirmed in believing he would be Cawdor.'

'That may be true,' said the professor, nodding slowly. 'But *when* it was confirmed, I knew it was the truth. You say I saw nothing myself. But I did; I saw my own clerk disappear. Berridge did disappear.'

'Berridge did not disappear,' said Father Brown. 'On the contrary.'

'What the devil do you mean by "on the contrary"?'

'I mean,' said Father Brown, 'that he never disappeared. He appeared.'

Openshaw stared across at his friend, but the eyes had already altered in his head, as they did when they concentrated on a new presentation of a problem. The priest went on: 'He appeared in your study, disguised in a bushy red beard and buttoned up in a clumsy cape, and announced himself as the Revd Luke Pringle. And you had never noticed your own clerk enough to know him again, when he was in so rough-and-ready a disguise.'

'But surely,' began the professor.

'Could you describe him for the police?' asked Father Brown. 'Not you. You probably knew he was clean-shaven and wore tinted glasses; and merely taking off those glasses was a better disguise than putting on anything else. You had never seen his eyes any more than his soul; jolly laughing eyes. He had planted his absurd book and all the properties; then he calmly smashed the window, put on the beard and cape and walked into your study; knowing that you had never looked at him in your life.'

'But why should he play me such an insane trick?' demanded Openshaw.

'Why, *because* you had never looked at him in your

life,' said Father Brown; and his hand slightly curled and clinched, as if he might have struck the table, if he had been given to gesture. 'You called him the calculating-machine, because that was all you ever used him for. You never found out even what a stranger strolling into your office could find out, in five minutes' chat: that he was a character; that he was full of antics; that he had all sorts of views on you and your theories and your reputation for "spotting" people. Can't you understand his itching to prove that you couldn't spot your own clerk? He has nonsense notions of all sorts. About collecting useless things, for instance. Don't you know the story of the woman who bought the two most useless things: an old doctor's brass-plate and a wooden leg? With those your ingenious clerk created the character of the remarkable Dr Hankey; as easily as the visionary Captain Wales. Planting them in his own house – '

'Do you mean that place we visited beyond Hampstead was Berridge's own house?' asked Openshaw.

'Did *you* know his house – or even his address?' retorted the priest. 'Look here, don't think I'm speaking disrespectfully of you or your work. You are a great servant of truth and you know I could never be disrespectful to that. You've seen through a lot of liars, when you put your mind to it. But don't *only* look at liars. Do, just occasionally, look at honest men – like the waiter.'

'Where is Berridge now?' asked the professor, after a long silence.

'I haven't the least doubt,' said Father Brown, 'that he is back in your office. In fact, he came back into your office at the exact moment when the Revd Luke Pringle read the awful volume and faded into the void.'

There was another long silence and then Professor Openshaw laughed; with the laugh of a great man who is great enough to look small. Then he said abruptly: 'I suppose I do deserve it; for not noticing the nearest helpers I have. But you must admit the accumulation of incidents was rather formidable. Did you *never* feel just a momentary awe of the awful volume?'

'Oh, that,' said Father Brown. 'I opened it as soon as I saw it lying there. It's all blank pages. You see, I am not superstitious.'

The Green Man

A young man in knickerbockers, with an eager sanguine profile, was playing golf against himself on the links that lay parallel to the sand and sea, which were all growing grey with twilight. He was not carelessly knocking a ball about, but rather practising particular strokes with a sort of microscopic fury; like a neat and tidy whirlwind. He had learned many games quickly, but he had a disposition to learn them a little more quickly than they can be learnt. He was rather prone to be a victim of those remarkable invitations by which a man may learn the violin in six lessons – or acquire a perfect French accent by a correspondence course. He lived in the breezy atmosphere of such hopeful advertisement and adventure. He was at present the private secretary of Admiral Sir Michael Craven, who owned the big house behind the park abutting on the links. He was ambitious, and had no intention of continuing indefinitely to be private secretary to anybody. But he was also reasonable; and he knew that the best way of ceasing to be a secretary was to be a good secretary. Consequently he was a very good secretary; dealing with the ever-accumulating arrears of the admiral's correspondence with the same swift centripetal concentration with which he addressed the golf-ball. He had to struggle with the correspondence alone and at his own discretion at present; for the admiral had been with his ship for the last six months; and, though now returning, was not expected for hours, or possibly days.

With an athletic stride, the young man, whose name was Harold Harker, crested the rise of turf that was the rampart of the links and, looking out across the sands to the sea, saw a strange sight. He did not see it very clearly; for the dusk was darkening every minute under stormy clouds; but it seemed to him, by a sort of momentary illusion, like a dream of days long past or a drama played by ghosts, out of another age in history.

The last of the sunset lay in long bars of copper and gold above the last dark strip of sea that seemed rather black than blue. But blacker still against this gleam in the west, there passed in sharp outline, like figures in a shadow pantomime, two men with three-cornered cocked hats and swords; as if they had just landed from one of the wooden ships of Nelson. It was not at all the sort of hallucination that would have come natural to Mr Harker, had he been prone to hallucinations. He was of the type that is at once sanguine and scientific; and would be more likely to fancy the flying-ships of the future than the fighting-ships of the past. He therefore very sensibly came to the conclusion that even a futurist can believe his eyes.

His illusion did not last more than a moment. On the second glance, what he saw was unusual but not incredible. The two men who were striding in single file across the sands, one some fifteen yards behind the other, were ordinary modern naval officers; but naval officers wearing that almost extravagant full-dress uniform which naval officers never do wear if they can possibly help it; only on great ceremonial occasions such as the visits of royalty. In the man walking in front, who seemed more or less unconscious of the man walking behind, Harker recognised at once the high-bridged nose and spike-shaped beard of his own employer the admiral. The other man following in his tracks he did not know. But he did know something about the circumstances connected with the ceremonial occasion. He knew that when the admiral's ship put in at the adjacent port, it was to be formally visited by a great personage; which was enough, in that sense, to explain the officers being in full dress. But he did also know the officers; or at any rate the admiral. And what could have possessed the admiral to come on shore in that rig-out, when one could swear he would seize five minutes to change into mufti or at least into undress uniform, was more than his secretary could conceive. It seemed somehow to be the very last thing he would do. It was indeed to remain for many weeks one of the chief mysteries of this mysterious business. As it was, the outline of these fantastic court uniforms against the empty scenery, striped with dark sea and sand, had something suggestive of comic opera; and reminded the spectator of *Pinafore*.

The second figure was much more singular; somewhat singular in appearance, despite his correct lieutenant's uniform, and still more extraordinary in behaviour. He walked in a strangely irregular and uneasy manner; sometimes quickly and sometimes slowly; as if he could not make up his mind whether to overtake the admiral or not. The admiral was rather deaf and certainly heard no footsteps behind him on the yielding sand; but the footsteps behind him, if traced in the detective manner, would have given rise to twenty conjectures from a limp to a dance. The man's face was swarthy as well as darkened with shadow and every now and then the eyes in it shifted and shone, as if to accent his agitation. Once he began to run and then abruptly relapsed into a swaggering slowness and carelessness. Then he did something which Mr Harker could never have conceived any normal officer in His Britannic Majesty's Service doing, even in a lunatic asylum. He drew his sword.

It was at this bursting-point of the prodigy that the two passing figures disappeared behind a headland on the shore. The staring secretary had just time to notice the swarthy stranger, with a resumption of carelessness, knock off a head of sea-holly with his glittering blade. He seemed then to have abandoned all idea of catching the other man up. But Mr Harold Harker's face became very thoughtful indeed; and he stood there ruminating for some time before he gravely took himself inland, towards the road that ran past the gates of the great house and so by a long curve down to the sea.

It was up this curving road from the coast that the admiral might be expected to come, considering the direction in which he had been walking, and making the natural assumption that he was bound for his own door. The path along the sands, under the links, turned inland just beyond the headland and solidifying itself into a road, returned towards Craven House. It was down this road, therefore, that the secretary darted, with characteristic impetuosity, to meet his patron returning home. But the patron was apparently not returning home. What was still more peculiar, the secretary was not returning home either; at least not until many hours later; a delay quite long enough to arouse alarm and mystification at Craven House.

Behind the pillars and palms of that rather too palatial country house, indeed, there was expectancy gradually changing to uneasiness. Gryce the butler, a big bilious man abnormally silent below as well as above stairs, showed a certain restlessness as he moved about the main front-hall and occasionally looked out of the side windows of the porch, on the white road that swept towards the sea. The admiral's sister Marion, who kept house for him, had her brother's high nose with a more sniffy expression; she was voluble, rather rambling, not without humour, and capable of sudden emphasis as shrill as a cockatoo. The admiral's daughter Olive was dark, dreamy, and as a rule abstractedly silent, perhaps melancholy; so that her aunt generally conducted most of the conversation, and that without reluctance. But the girl also had a gift of sudden laughter that was very engaging.

'I can't think why they're not here already,' said the elder lady. 'The postman distinctly told me he'd seen the admiral coming along the beach; along with that dreadful creature Rook. Why in the world they call him Lieutenant Rook –'

'Perhaps,' suggested the melancholy young lady, with a momentary brightness, 'perhaps they call him Lieutenant because he is a lieutenant.'

'I can't think why the admiral keeps him,' snorted her aunt, as if she were talking of a housemaid. She was very proud of her brother and always called him the admiral; but her notions of a commission in the Senior Service were inexact.

'Well, Roger Rook is sulky and unsociable and all that,' replied Olive, 'but of course that wouldn't prevent him being a capable sailor.'

'Sailor!' cried her aunt with one of her rather startling cockatoo notes, 'he isn't my notion of a sailor. The Lass that Loved a Sailor, as they used to sing when I was young . . . Just think of it! He's not gay and free and whatsitsname. He doesn't sing shanties or dance a hornpipe.'

'Well,' observed her niece with gravity. 'The admiral doesn't very often dance a hornpipe.'

'Oh, you know what I mean – he isn't bright or breezy or anything,' replied the old lady. 'Why, that secretary fellow could do better than that.'

Olive's rather tragic face was transfigured by one of her good and rejuvenating waves of laughter.

'I'm sure Mr Harker would dance a hornpipe for you,' she said, 'and say he had learnt it in half an hour from the book of instructions. He's always learning things of that sort.'

She stopped laughing suddenly and looked at her aunt's rather strained face.

'I can't think why Mr Harker doesn't come,' she added.

'I don't care about Mr Harker,' replied the aunt, and rose and looked out of the window.

The evening light had long turned from yellow to grey and was now turning almost to white under the widening moonlight, over the large flat landscape by the coast; unbroken by any features save a clump of sea-twisted trees round a pool and beyond, rather gaunt and dark against the horizon, the shabby fishermen's tavern on the shore that bore the name of the Green Man. And all that road and landscape was empty of any living thing. Nobody had seen the figure in the cocked hat that had been observed, earlier in the evening, walking by the sea; or the other and stranger figure that had been seen trailing after him. Nobody had even seen the secretary who saw them.

It was after midnight when the secretary at last burst

in and aroused the household; and his face, white as a ghost, looked all the paler against the background of the stolid face and figure of a big inspector of police. Somehow that red, heavy, indifferent face looked, even more than the white and harassed one, like a mask of doom. The news was broken to the two women with such consideration or concealments as were possible. But the news was that the body of Admiral Craven had been eventually fished out of the foul weeds and scum of the pool under the trees; and that he was drowned and dead.

Anybody acquainted with Mr Harold Harker, secretary, will realize that, whatever his agitation, he was by morning in a mood to be tremendously on the spot. He hustled the inspector, whom he had met the night before on the road down by the Green Man, into another room for private and practical consultation. He questioned the inspector rather as the inspector might have questioned a yokel. But Inspector Burns was a stolid character; and was either too stupid or too clever to resent such trifles. It soon began to look as if he were by no means so stupid as he looked; for he disposed of Harker's eager questions in a manner that was slow but methodical and rational.

'Well,' said Harker (his head full of many manuals with titles like 'Be a detective in ten days'). 'Well, it's the old triangle, I suppose. Accident, suicide or murder.'

'I don't see how it could be accident,' answered the policeman. 'It wasn't even dark yet and the pool's fifty yards from the straight road that he knew like his own doorstep. He'd no more have got into that pond than he'd go and carefully lie down in a puddle in the street. As for suicide, it's rather a responsibility to suggest it, and rather improbable too. The admiral was a pretty spry and successful man and frightfully rich, nearly a millionaire in fact; though of course that doesn't prove anything. He seemed to be pretty normal and comfortable in his private life too; he's the last man I should suspect of drowning himself.'

'So that we come,' said the secretary, lowering his voice with the thrill, 'I suppose we come to the third possibility.'

'We won't be in too much of a hurry about that,' said the inspector, to the annoyance of Harker, who was in a hurry about everything. 'But naturally there are one or two things one would like to know. One would like to know about his property, for instance. Do you know who's likely to come in for it? You're his private secretary; do you know anything about his will?'

'I'm not so private a secretary as all that,' answered the young man. 'His solicitors are Messrs Willis, Hardman and Dyke, over in Suttford High Street; and I believe the will is in their custody.'

'Well, I'd better get round and see them pretty soon,' said the inspector.

'Let's get round and see them at once,' said the impatient secretary.

He took a turn or two restlessly up and down the room and then exploded in a fresh place.

'What have you done about the body, inspector?' he asked.

'Dr Straker is examining it now at the police station. His report ought to be ready in an hour or so.'

'It can't be ready too soon,' said Harker. 'It would save time if we could meet him at the lawyer's.' Then he stopped and his impetuous tone changed abruptly to one of some embarrassment.

'Look here,' he said, 'I want . . . we want to consider the young lady, the poor admiral's daughter, as much as possible just now. She's got a notion that may be all nonsense; but I wouldn't like to disappoint her. There's some friend of hers she wants to consult, staying in the town at present. Man of the name of Brown; priest or parson of some sort; she's given me his address. I don't take much stock in priests or parsons, but – '

The inspector nodded. 'I don't take any stock in priests or parsons; but I take a lot of stock in Father Brown,' he said. 'I happened to have to do with him in a queer sort of society jewel case. He ought to have been a policeman instead of a parson.'

'Oh, all right,' said the breathless secretary as he vanished from the room. 'Let him come to the lawyer's too.'

Thus it happened that, when they hurried across to the neighbouring town to meet Dr Straker at the solicitor's office, they found Father Brown already seated there, with his hands folded on his heavy umbrella, chatting pleasantly to the only available member of the firm. Dr Straker also had arrived, but apparently only at that moment, as he was carefully placing his gloves in his top-hat and his top-hat on a side-table. And the mild and beaming expression of the priest's moonlike face and spectacles, together with the silent chuckles of the jolly old grizzled lawyer, to whom he was talking, were enough to show that the doctor had not yet opened his mouth to bring the news of death.

'A beautiful morning after all,' Father Brown was saying. 'That storm seems to have passed over us. There were some big black clouds, but I notice that not a drop of rain fell.'

'Not a drop,' agreed the solicitor, toying with a pen; he was the third partner, Mr Dyke; 'there's not a cloud in the sky now. It's the sort of day for a holiday.' Then he realized the newcomers and looked up, laying down the pen and rising. 'Ah, Mr Harker, how are you? I hear the admiral is expected home soon.' Then Harker spoke, and his voice rang hollow in the room.

'I am sorry to say we are the bearers of bad news. Admiral Craven was drowned before reaching home.'

There was a change in the very air of the still office, though not in the attitudes of the motionless figures; both were staring at the speaker as if a joke had been frozen on their lips. Both repeated the word 'drowned' and looked at each other, and then again at their informant. Then there was a small hubbub of questions.

'When did this happen?' asked the priest.

'Where was he found?' asked the lawyer.

'He was found,' said the inspector, 'in that pool by the coast, not far from the Green Man, and dragged out all covered with green scum and weeds so as to be almost unrecognisable. But Dr Straker here has – What is the matter, Father Brown? Are you ill?'

'The Green Man,' said Father Brown with a shudder. 'I'm so sorry . . . I beg your pardon for being upset.'

'Upset by what?' asked the staring officer.

'By his being covered with green scum, I suppose,' said the priest, with a rather shaky laugh. Then he added rather more firmly, 'I thought it might have been seaweed.'

By this time everybody was looking at the priest, with a not unnatural suspicion that he was mad; and yet the next crucial surprise was not to come from him. After a dead silence, it was the doctor who spoke.

Dr Straker was a remarkable man, even to look at. He was very tall and angular, formal and professional in his dress; yet retaining a fashion that has hardly been known since mid-Victorian times. Though comparatively young, he wore his brown beard very long and spreading over his waistcoat; in contrast with it, his features, which were both harsh and handsome, looked singularly pale. His good looks were also diminished by something in his deep eyes that was not squinting, but like the shadow of a squint. Everybody noticed these things about him, because the moment he spoke, he gave forth an indescribable air of authority. But all he said was: 'There is one more thing to be said, if you come to details, about Admiral Craven being drowned.' Then he added reflectively, 'Admiral Craven was not drowned.'

The inspector turned with quite a new promptitude and shot a question at him.

'I have just examined the body,' said Dr Straker, 'the cause of death was a stab through the heart with some pointed blade like a stiletto. It was after death, and even some little time after, that the body was hidden in the pool.'

Father Brown was regarding Dr Straker with a very lively eye, such as he seldom turned upon anybody; and when the group in the office began to break up, he managed to attach himself to the medical man for a little further conversation, as they went back down the street. There had not been very much else to detain them except the rather formal question of the will. The impatience of the young secretary had been somewhat tried by the professional etiquette of the old lawyer.

But the latter was ultimately induced, rather by the tact of the priest than the authority of the policeman, to refrain from making a mystery where there was no mystery at all. Mr Dyke admitted, with a smile, that the admiral's will was a very normal and ordinary document, leaving everything to his only child Olive; and that there really was no particular reason for concealing the fact.

The doctor and the priest walked slowly down the street that struck out of the town in the direction of Craven House. Harker had plunged on ahead of him with all his native eagerness to get somewhere; but the two behind seemed more interested in their discussion than their direction. It was in rather an enigmatic tone that the tall doctor said to the short cleric beside him: 'Well, Father Brown, what do you think of a thing like this?'

Father Brown looked at him rather intently for an instant and then said: 'Well, I've begun to think of one or two things; but my chief difficulty is that I only knew the admiral slightly; though I've seen something of his daughter.'

'The admiral,' said the doctor with a grim immobility of feature, 'was the sort of man of whom it is said that he had not an enemy in the world.'

'I suppose you mean,' answered the priest, 'that there's something else that will not be said.'

'Oh, it's no affair of mine,' said Straker hastily but rather harshly. 'He had his moods, I suppose. He once threatened me with a legal action about an operation; but I think he thought better of it. I can imagine his being rather rough with a subordinate.'

Father Brown's eyes were fixed on the figure of the secretary striding far ahead; and as he gazed he realised the special cause of his hurry. Some fifty yards farther ahead the admiral's daughter was dawdling along the road towards the admiral's house. The secretary soon came abreast of her; and for the remainder of the time Father Brown watched the silent drama of two human backs as they diminished into the distance. The secretary was evidently very much excited about something; but if the priest guessed what it was, he kept it to himself. When he came to the corner leading to the doctor's house, he only said briefly: 'I don't know if you have anything more to tell us.'

'Why should I?' answered the doctor very abruptly; and striding off, left it uncertain whether he was asking why he should have anything to tell, or why he should tell it.

Father Brown went stumping on alone, in the track of the two young people; but when he came to the entrance and avenues of the admiral's park, he was arrested by the action of the girl, who turned suddenly and came straight towards him; her face unusually pale and her eyes bright with some new and as yet nameless emotion.

'Father Brown,' she said in a low voice, 'I must talk to you as soon as possible. You must listen to me, I can't see any other way out.'

'Why, certainly,' he replied, as coolly as if a gutter-boy had asked him the time. 'Where shall we go and talk?'

The girl led him at random to one of the rather tumbledown arbours in the grounds; and they sat down behind a screen of large ragged leaves. She began instantly, as if she must relieve her feelings or faint.

'Harold Harker,' she said, 'has been talking to me about things. Terrible things.'

The priest nodded and the girl went on hastily. 'About Roger Rook. Do you know about Roger?'

'I've been told,' he answered, 'that his fellow-seamen call him the Jolly Roger, because he is never jolly; and looks like the pirate's skull and cross-bones.'

'He was not always like that,' said Olive in a low voice. 'Something very queer must have happened to him. I knew him well when we were children; we used to play over there on the sands. He was harum-scarum and always talking about being a pirate; I dare say he was the sort they say might take to crime through reading shockers; but there was something poetical in his way of being piratical. He really was a Jolly Roger then. I suppose he was the last boy who kept up the old legend of really running away to sea; and at last his family had to agree to his joining the navy. Well . . . '

'Yes,' said Father Brown patiently.

'Well,' she admitted, caught in one of her rare moments of mirth. 'I suppose poor Roger found it disappointing. Naval officers so seldom carry knives in their teeth or wave bloody cutlasses and black flags. But that doesn't explain the change in him. He just stiffened; grew dull and dumb, like a dead man walking about. He always avoids me; but that doesn't matter. I supposed some great grief that's no business of mine had broken him up. And now – well, if what Harold says is true, the grief is neither more nor less than going mad; or being possessed of a devil.'

'And what does Harold say?' asked the priest.

'It's so awful I can hardly say it,' she answered. 'He swears he saw Roger creeping behind my father that night; hesitating and then drawing his sword . . . and the doctor says father was stabbed with a steel point . . . I *can't* believe Roger Rook had anything to do with it. His sulks and my father's temper sometimes led to quarrels; but what are quarrels? I can't exactly say I'm standing up for an old friend; because he isn't even friendly. But you can't help feeling sure of some things, even about an old acquaintance. And yet Harold swears that he – '

'Harold seems to swear a great deal,' said Father Brown.

There was a sudden silence; after which she said in a different tone: 'Well, he does swear other things too. Harold Harker proposed to me just now.'

'Am I to congratulate you, or rather him?' enquired her companion.

'I told him he must wait. He isn't good at waiting.' She was caught again in a ripple of her incongruous sense of the comic: 'He said I was his ideal and his ambition and so on. He has lived in the States; but somehow I never remember it when he is talking about dollars; only when he is talking about ideals.'

'And I suppose,' said Father Brown very softly, 'that it is because you have to decide about Harold that you want to know the truth about Roger.'

She stiffened and frowned, and then equally abruptly smiled, saying: 'Oh, you know too much.'

'I know very little, especially in this affair,' said the priest gravely. 'I only know who murdered your father.' She started up and stood staring down at him stricken white. Father Brown made a wry face as he went on: 'I made a fool of myself when I first realised it; when they'd just been asking where he was found, and went on talking about green scum and the Green Man.'

Then he also rose; clutching his clumsy umbrella with a new resolution, he addressed the girl with a new gravity.

'There is something else that I know, which is the key to all these riddles of yours; but I won't tell you yet. I suppose it's bad news; but it's nothing like so bad as the things you have been fancying.' He buttoned up his coat and turned towards the gate. 'I'm going to see this Mr Rook of yours. In a shed by the shore, near where Mr Harker saw him walking. I rather think he lives there.' And he went bustling off in the direction of the beach.

Olive was an imaginative person; perhaps too imaginative to be safely left to brood over such hints as her friend had thrown out; but he was in rather a hurry to find the best relief for her broodings. The mysterious connection between Father Brown's first shock of enlightenment and the chance language about the pool and the inn, hag-rode her fancy in a hundred forms of ugly symbolism. The Green Man became a ghost trailing loathsome weeds and walking the countryside under the moon; the sign of the Green Man became a human figure hanging as from a gibbet; and the tarn itself became a tavern, a dark sub-aqueous tavern for the dead sailors. And yet he had taken the most rapid method to overthrow all such nightmares, with a burst of blinding daylight which seemed more mysterious than the night.

For before the sun had set, something had come back into her life that turned her whole world topsy-turvy once more; something she had hardly known that she desired until it was abruptly granted; something that was, like a dream, old and familiar, and yet remained incomprehensible and incredible. For

Roger Rook had come striding across the sands, and even when he was a dot in the distance, she knew he was transfigured; and as he came nearer and nearer, she saw that his dark face was alive with laughter and exultation. He came straight towards her, as if they had never parted, and seized her shoulders saying: 'Now I can look after you, thank God.'

She hardly knew what she answered; but she heard herself questioning rather wildly why he seemed so changed and so happy.

'Because I am happy,' he answered. 'I have heard the bad news.'

All parties concerned, including some who seemed rather unconcerned, found themselves assembled on the garden path leading to Craven House, to hear the formality, now truly formal, of the lawyer's reading of the will: and the probable, and more practical, sequel of the lawyer's advice upon the crisis. Besides the grey-haired solicitor himself, armed with the testamentary document, there was the inspector armed with more direct authority touching the crime, and Lieutenant Rook in undisguised attendance on the lady; some were rather mystified on seeing the tall figure of the doctor, some smiled a little on seeing the dumpy figure of the priest. Mr Harker, that flying Mercury, had shot down to the lodge-gates to meet them, led them back on to the lawn, and then dashed ahead of them again to prepare their reception. He said he would be back in a jiffy; and anyone observing his piston-rod of energy could well believe it; but, for the moment, they were left rather stranded on the lawn outside the house.

'Reminds me of somebody making runs at cricket,' said the Lieutenant.

'That young man,' said the lawyer, 'is rather annoyed that the law cannot move quite so quickly as he does. Fortunately Miss Craven understands our professional difficulties and delays. She has kindly assured me that she still has confidence in my slowness.'

'I wish,' said the doctor, suddenly, 'that I had as much confidence in his quickness.'

'Why, what do you mean?' asked Rook, knitting his brows; 'do you mean that Harker is too quick?'

'Too quick and too slow,' said Dr Straker, in his rather cryptic fashion. 'I know one occasion at least when he was not so very quick. Why was he hanging about half the night by the pond and the Green Man, before the inspector came down and found the body? Why did he meet the inspector? Why should he expect to meet the inspector outside the Green Man?'

'I don't understand you,' said Rook. 'Do you mean that Harker wasn't telling the truth?'

Dr Straker was silent. The grizzled lawyer laughed with grim good humour.

'I have nothing more serious to say against the young man,' he said, 'than that he made a prompt and praiseworthy attempt to teach me my own business.'

'For that matter, he made an attempt to teach me mine,' said the inspector, who had just joined the group in front. 'But that doesn't matter. If Dr Straker means anything by his hints, they do matter. I must ask you to speak plainly, doctor. It may be my duty to question him at once.'

'Well, here he comes,' said Rook, as the alert figure of the secretary appeared once more in the doorway.

At this point Father Brown, who had remained silent and inconspicuous at the tail of the procession, astonished everybody very much; perhaps especially those who knew him. He not only walked rapidly to the front, but turned facing the whole group with an arresting and almost threatening expression, like a sergeant bringing soldiers to the halt.

'Stop!' he said almost sternly. 'I apologise to everybody; but it's absolutely necessary that I should see Mr Harker first. I've got to tell him something I know; and I don't think anybody else knows; something he's got to hear. It may save a very tragic misunderstanding with somebody later on.'

'What on earth do you mean?' asked old Dyke the lawyer.

'I mean the bad news,' said Father Brown.

'Here, I say,' began the inspector indignantly; and then suddenly caught the priest's eye and remembered strange things he had seen in other days. 'Well, if it were anyone in the world but you I should say of all the infernal cheek – '

But Father Brown was already out of hearing, and a moment afterwards was plunged in talk with Harker in the porch. They walked to and fro together for a few paces and then disappeared into the dark interior. It was about twelve minutes afterwards that Father Brown came out alone.

To their surprise he showed no disposition to re-enter the house, now that the whole company were at last about to enter it. He threw himself down on the rather rickety seat in the leafy arbour, and as the procession disappeared through the doorway, lit a pipe and proceeded to stare vacantly at the long ragged leaves about his head and to listen to the birds. There was no man who had a more hearty and enduring appetite for doing nothing.

* * *

He was apparently in a cloud of smoke and a dream of abstraction, when the front doors were once more flung open and two or three figures came out helter-skelter, running towards him, the daughter of the house and her young admirer Mr Rook being easily winners in the race. Their faces were alight with astonishment; and the face of Inspector Burns, who advanced more heavily behind them, like an elephant shaking the garden, was inflamed with some indignation as well.

'What *can* all this mean?' cried Olive, as she came panting to a halt. 'He's gone!'

'Bolted!' said the Lieutenant explosively. 'Harker's just managed to pack a suitcase and bolted! Gone clean out of the back door and over the garden-wall to God knows where. What *did* you say to him?'

'Don't be silly!' said Olive, with a more worried expression. 'Of course you told him you'd found him out, and now he's gone. I never could have believed he was wicked like that!'

'Well!' gasped the inspector, bursting into their midst. 'What have you done now? What have you let me down like this for?'

'Well,' repeated Father Brown, 'what have I done?'

'You have let a murderer escape,' cried Burns, with a decision that was like a thunderclap in the quiet garden; 'you have *helped* a murderer to escape. Like a fool I let you warn him; and now he is miles away.'

'I have helped a few murderers in my time, it is true,' said Father Brown; then he added, in careful distinction, 'not, you will understand, helped them to commit the murder.'

'But you knew all the time,' insisted Olive. 'You guessed from the first that it must be he. That's what you meant about being upset by the business of finding the body. That's what the doctor meant by saying my father might be disliked by a subordinate.'

'That's what I complain of,' said the official indignantly. 'You knew even then that he was the – '

'You knew even then,' insisted Olive, 'that the murderer was – '

Father Brown nodded gravely. 'Yes,' he said. 'I knew even then that the murderer was old Dyke.'

'Was *who*?' repeated the inspector and stopped amid a dead silence; punctuated only by the occasional pipe of birds.

'I mean Mr Dyke, the solicitor,' explained Father Brown, like one explaining something elementary to an infant class. 'That gentleman with grey hair who's supposed to be going to read the will.'

They all stood like statues staring at him, as he carefully filled his pipe again and struck a match. At last Burns rallied his vocal powers to break the strangling silence with an effort resembling violence.

'But, in the name of heaven, *why*?'

'Ah, why?' said the priest and rose thoughtfully, puffing at his pipe. 'As to why he did it . . . Well, I suppose the time has come to tell you, or those of you who don't know, the fact that is the key of all this business. It's a great calamity; and it's a great crime; but it's not the murder of Admiral Craven.'

He looked Olive full in the face and said very seriously: 'I tell you the bad news bluntly and in few words; because I think you are brave enough, and perhaps happy enough, to take it well. You have the chance, and I think the power, to be something like a great woman. You are not a great heiress.'

Amid the silence that followed it was he who resumed his explanation.

'Most of your father's money, I am sorry to say, has gone. It went by the financial dexterity of the grey-haired gentleman named Dyke, who is (I grieve to say) a swindler. Admiral Craven was murdered to silence him about the way in which he was swindled. The fact that he was ruined and you were disinherited is the single simple clue, not only to the murder, but to all the other mysteries in this business.' He took a puff or two and then continued.

'I told Mr Rook you were disinherited and he rushed back to help you. Mr Rook is a rather remarkable person.'

'Oh, chuck it,' said Mr Rook with a hostile air.

'Mr Rook is a monster,' said Father Brown with scientific calm. 'He is an anachronism, an atavism, a brute survival of the Stone Age. If there was one barbarous superstition we all supposed to be utterly extinct and dead in these days, it was that notion about honour and independence. But then I get mixed up with so many dead superstitions. Mr Rook is an extinct animal. He is a plesiosaurus. He did not want to live on his wife or have a wife who could call him a fortune-hunter. Therefore he sulked in a grotesque manner and only came to life again when I brought him the good news that you were ruined. He wanted to work for his wife and not be kept by her. Disgusting, isn't it? Let us turn to the brighter topic of Mr Harker.

'I told Mr Harker you were disinherited and he rushed away in a sort of panic. Do not be too hard on Mr Harker. He really had better as well as worse enthusiasms; but he had them all mixed up. There is no harm in having ambitions; but he had ambitions and called them ideals. The old sense of honour taught men to suspect success; to say, "This is a benefit; it may be a bribe". The new nine-times-accursed nonsense about Making Good teaches men to identify being good with making money. That was all that was the matter with him; in every other way he was a thoroughly good fellow, and there are thousands like him. Gazing at the stars and rising in the world were all uplift. Marrying a good wife and marrying a rich wife were all Making Good. But he was not a cynical scoundrel; or he would simply have come back and jilted or cut you as the case might be. He could not face you; while you were there, half of his broken ideal was left.

'I did not tell the admiral; but somebody did. Word came to him somehow, during the last grand parade on board, that his friend the family lawyer had betrayed him. He was in such a towering passion that he did what he could never have done in his senses; came straight on shore in his cocked hat and gold lace to catch the criminal; he wired to the police station, and that was why the inspector was wandering round the Green Man. Lieutenant Rook followed him on shore because he suspected some family trouble and had half a hope he might help and put himself right. Hence his hesitating behaviour. As for his drawing his sword when he dropped behind and thought he was alone, well that's a matter of imagination. He was a romantic person who had dreamed of swords and run away to sea; and found himself in a service where he wasn't even allowed to wear a sword except about once in three years. He thought he was quite alone on the sands where he played as a boy. If you don't understand what he did, I can only say, like Stevenson, "you will never be a pirate". Also you will never be a poet; and you have never been a boy.'

'I never have,' answered Olive gravely, 'and yet I think I understand.'

'Almost every man,' continued the priest musing, 'will play with anything shaped like a sword or dagger, even if it is a paper-knife. That is why I thought it so odd when the lawyer didn't.'

'What do you mean?' asked Burns, 'didn't what?'

'Why, didn't you notice,' answered Brown, 'at that first meeting in the office, the lawyer played with a pen and not with a paperknife; though he had a beautiful bright steel paperknife in the pattern of a stiletto? The pens were dusty and splashed with ink; but the knife had just been cleaned. But he did not play with it. There are limits to the irony of assassins.'

After a silence the inspector said, like one waking from a dream: 'Look here . . . I don't know whether I'm on my head or my heels; I don't know whether you think you've got to the end; but I haven't got to the beginning. Where do you get all this lawyer stuff from? What started you out on that trail?'

Father Brown laughed curtly and without mirth.

'The murderer made a slip at the start,' he said, 'and I can't think why nobody else noticed it. When you brought the first news of the death to the solicitor's office, nobody was supposed to know anything there, except that the admiral was expected home. When you said he was drowned, I asked when it happened and Mr Dyke asked where the corpse was found.'

He paused a moment to knock out his pipe and resumed reflectively: 'Now when you are simply told of a seaman, returning from the sea, that he has been drowned, it is natural to assume that he has been drowned at sea. At any rate, to allow that he may have been drowned at sea. If he had been washed overboard, or gone down with his ship, or had his body "committed to the deep", there would be no reason to expect his body to be found at all. The moment that man asked where it was found, I was sure he knew where it was found. Because he had put it there. Nobody but the murderer need have thought of anything so unlikely as a seaman being drowned in a landlocked pool a few hundred yards from the sea. That is why I suddenly felt sick and turned green, I dare say; as green as the Green Man. I never *can* get used to finding myself suddenly sitting beside a murderer. So I had to turn it off by talking in parables; but the parable meant something, after all. I said that the body was covered with green scum, but it might just as well have been seaweed.'

It is fortunate that tragedy can never kill comedy and that the two can run side by side; and that while the only acting partner of the business of Messrs Willis, Hardman and Dyke blew his brains out when the inspector entered the house to arrest him, Olive and Roger were calling to each other across the sands at evening, as they did when they were children together.

The Point of a Pin

Father Brown always declared that he solved this problem in his sleep. And this was true, though in rather an odd fashion; because it occurred at a time when his sleep was rather disturbed. It was disturbed very early in the morning by the hammering that began in the huge building, or half-building, that was in process of erection opposite to his rooms; a colossal pile of flats still mostly covered with scaffolding and with boards announcing Messrs Swindon & Sand as the builders and owners. The hammering was renewed at regular intervals and was easily recognisable, because Messrs Swindon & Sand specialised in some new American system of cement flooring which, in spite of its subsequent smoothness, solidity, impenetrability and permanent comfort (as described in the advertisements) had to be clamped down at certain points with heavy tools. Father Brown endeavoured, however, to extract exiguous comfort from it; saying that it always woke him up in time for the very earliest Mass, and was therefore something almost in the nature of a carillon. After all, he said, it was almost as poetic that Christians should be awakened by hammers as by bells. As a fact, however, the building operations were a little on his nerves, for another reason. For there was hanging like a cloud over the half-built skyscraper the possibility of a labour crisis, which the newspapers doggedly insisted on describing as a strike. As a matter of fact, if ever it happened, it would be a lock-out. But he worried a good deal about whether it would happen. And it might be questioned whether hammering is more of a strain on the attention because it may go on for ever, or because it may stop at any minute.

'As a mere matter of taste and fancy,' said Father Brown, staring up at the edifice with his owlish spectacles, 'I rather wish it would stop. I wish all houses would stop while they still have the scaffolding up. It seems almost a pity that houses are ever finished. They look so fresh and hopeful with all that fairy filigree of white wood, all light and bright in the sun; and a man so often only finishes a house by turning it into a tomb.'

As he turned away from the object of his scrutiny, he nearly ran into a man who had just darted across the road towards him. It was a man whom he knew slightly, but sufficiently to regard him (in the circumstances) as something of a bird of ill-omen. Mr Mastyk was a squat man with a square head that looked hardly European, dressed with a heavy dandyism that seemed rather too consciously Europeanised. But Brown had seen him lately talking to young Sand of the building firm: and he did not like it. This man Mastyk was the head of an organisation rather new in English industrial politics; produced by extremes at both ends; a definite army of non-Union and largely alien labour hired out in gangs to various firms; and he was obviously hovering about in the hope of hiring it out to this one. In short, he might negotiate some way of outmanoeuvring the trade union and flooding the works with blacklegs. Father Brown had been drawn into some of the debates, being in some sense called in on both sides. And as the capitalists all reported that, to their positive knowledge, he was a Bolshevist; and as the Bolshevists all testified that he was a reactionary rigidly attached to bourgeois ideologies, it may be inferred that he talked a certain amount of sense without any appreciable effect on anybody. The news brought by Mr Mastyk, however, was calculated to jerk everybody out of the ordinary rut of the dispute.

'They want you to go over there at once,' said Mr Mastyk, in awkwardly accented English. 'There is a threat to murder.'

Father Brown followed his guide in silence up several stairways and ladders to a platform of the unfinished building, on which were grouped the more or less familiar figures of the heads of the building business. They included even what had once been the head of it; though the head had been for some time rather a head in the clouds. It was at least a head in a coronet, that hid it from human sight like a cloud. Lord Stanes, in other words, had not only retired from the business but been caught up into the House of Lords and disappeared. His rare reappearances were languid and somewhat dreary; but this one, in conjunction with that of Mastyk, seemed none the less menacing. Lord Stanes was a lean, longheaded, hollow-eyed man with very faint fair hair fading into baldness; and he was the most evasive person the priest had ever met. He was unrivalled in the true Oxford talent of saying, 'No doubt you're right', so as to sound like, 'No doubt you think you're right', or of merely remarking, 'You think so?' so as to imply the acid addition, 'You would'. But Father Brown fancied that the man was not merely bored but faintly embittered, though whether at being called down from Olympus to control such trade squabbles, or merely at not being really any longer in control of them, it was difficult to guess.

On the whole, Father Brown rather preferred the more bourgeois group of partners, Sir Hubert Sand and his nephew Henry; though he doubted privately whether they really had very many ideologies. True, Sir Hubert Sand had obtained considerable celebrity in the newspapers; both as a patron of sport and as a patriot in many crises during and after the Great War. He had won notable distinction in France, for a man of his years, and had afterwards been featured as a triumphant captain of industry overcoming difficulties among the munition-workers. He had been called a strong man; but that was not his fault. He was in fact a heavy, hearty Englishman; a great swimmer; a good squire; and admirable amateur colonel. Indeed, something that can only be called a military make-up pervaded his appearance. He was growing stout, but he kept his shoulders set back; his curly hair and moustache were still brown while the colours of his face were already somewhat withered and faded. His nephew was a burly youth of the pushing, or rather shouldering, sort with a relatively small head thrust out on a thick neck, as if he went at things with his head down; a gesture somehow rendered rather quaint and boyish by the pince-nez that were balanced on his pugnacious pug-nose.

Father Brown had looked at all these things before; and at that moment everybody was looking at something entirely new. In the centre of the woodwork there was nailed up a large loose flapping piece of paper on which something was scrawled in crude and almost crazy capital letters, as if the writer were either almost illiterate or were affecting or parodying illiteracy. The words actually ran: 'The Council of the Workers warns Hubert Sand that he will lower wages and lock out workmen at his peril. If the notices go out tomorrow, he will be dead by the justice of the people.'

Lord Stanes was just stepping back from his examination of the paper, and, looking across at his partner, he said with rather a curious intonation: 'Well, it's you they want to murder. Evidently I'm not considered worth murdering.'

One of those still electric shocks of fancy that sometimes thrilled Father Brown's mind in an almost meaningless way shot through him at that particular instant. He had a queer notion that the man who was speaking could not now be murdered, because he was already dead. It was, he cheerfully admitted, a perfectly senseless idea. But there was something that always gave him the creeps about the cold disenchanted detachment of the noble senior partner; about his cadaverous colour and inhospitable eyes. 'The fellow,' he thought in the same perverse mood, 'has green eyes and looks as if he had green blood.'

Anyhow, it was certain that Sir Hubert Sand had not got green blood. His blood, which was red enough in every sense, was creeping up into his withered or weather-beaten cheeks with all the warm fullness of life that belongs to the natural and innocent indignation of the good-natured.

'In all my life,' he said, in a strong voice and yet shakily, 'I have never had such a thing said or done about me. I may have differed – '

'We can none of us differ about this,' struck in his nephew impetuously. 'I've tried to get on with them, but this is a bit too thick.'

'You don't really think,' began Father Brown, 'that your workmen – '

'I say we may have differed,' said old Sand, still a

little tremulously. 'God knows I never liked the idea of threatening English workmen with cheaper labour – '

'We none of us liked it,' said the young man, 'but if I know you, uncle, this has about settled it.'

Then after a pause he added, 'I suppose, as you say, we did disagree about details; but as to real policy – '

'My dear fellow,' said his uncle, comfortably. 'I hoped there would never be any real disagreement.' From which anybody who understands the English nation may rightly infer that there had been very considerable disagreement. Indeed the uncle and nephew differed almost as much as an Englishman and an American. The uncle had the English ideal of getting outside the business, and setting up a sort of an alibi as a country gentleman. The nephew had the American ideal of getting inside the business; of getting inside the very mechanism like a mechanic. And, indeed, he had worked with most of the mechanics and was familiar with most of the processes and tricks of the trade. And he was American again, in the fact that he did this partly as an employer to keep his men up to the mark, but in some vague way also as an equal, or at least with a pride in showing himself also as a worker. For this reason he had often appeared almost as a representative of the workers, on technical points which were a hundred miles away from his uncle's popular eminence in politics or sport. The memory of those many occasions, when young Henry had practically come out of the workshop in his shirt-sleeves, to demand some concession about the conditions of the work, lent a peculiar force and even violence to his present reaction the other way.

'Well, they've damned-well locked themselves out this time,' he cried. 'After a threat like that there's simply nothing left but to defy them. There's nothing left but to sack them all now; instanter; on the spot. Otherwise we'll be the laughing-stock of the world.'

Old Sand frowned with equal indignation, but began slowly: 'I shall be very much criticised – '

'Criticised!' cried the young man shrilly. 'Criticised if you defy a threat of murder! Have you any notion how you'll be criticised if you don't defy it? Won't you enjoy the headlines? "Great capitalist terrorised" – "Employer yields to murder threat".'

'Particularly,' said Lord Stanes, with something faintly unpleasant in his tone. 'Particularly when he has been in so many headlines already as "The strong man of steel-building".'

Sand had gone very red again and his voice came thickly from under his thick moustache. 'Of course you're right there. If these brutes think I'm afraid – '

At this point there was an interruption in the conversation of the group; and a slim young man came towards them swiftly. The first notable thing about him was that he was one of those whom men, and women too, think are just a little too nice-looking to look nice. He had beautiful dark curly hair and a silken moustache and he spoke like a gentleman, but with almost too refined and exactly modulated an accent. Father Brown knew him at once as Rupert Rae, the secretary of Sir Hubert, whom he had often seen pottering about in Sir Hubert's house; but never with such impatience in his movements or such a wrinkle on his brow.

'I'm sorry, sir,' he said to his employer, 'but there's a man been hanging about over there. I've done my best to get rid of him. He's only got a letter, but he swears he must give it to you personally.'

'You mean he went first to my house?' said Sand, glancing swiftly at his secretary. 'I suppose you've been there all the morning.'

'Yes, sir,' said Mr Rupert Rae.

There was a short silence; and then Sir Hubert Sand curtly intimated that the man had better be brought along; and the man duly appeared.

Nobody, not even the least fastidious lady, would have said that the newcomer was too nice-looking. He had very large ears and a face like a frog, and he stared before him with an almost ghastly fixity, which Father Brown attributed to his having a glass eye. In fact, his fancy was tempted to equip the man with two glass eyes; with so glassy a stare did he contemplate the company. But the priest's experience, as distinct from his fancy, was able to suggest several natural causes for that unnatural waxwork glare; one of them being an abuse of the divine gift of fermented liquor. The man was short and shabby and carried a large bowler hat in one hand and a large sealed letter in the other.

Sir Hubert Sand looked at him; and then said quietly enough, but in a voice that somehow seemed curiously small, coming out of the fullness of his bodily presence: 'Oh – it's you.'

He held out his hand for the letter; and then looked around apologetically, with poised finger, before ripping it open and reading it. When he had read it, he stuffed it into his inside pocket and said hastily and a little harshly: 'Well, I suppose all this business is over, as you say. No more negotiations possible now; we couldn't pay the wages they want anyhow. But I shall want to see you again, Henry, about – about winding things up generally.'

'All right,' said Henry, a little sulkily perhaps, as if

he would have preferred to wind them up by himself. 'I shall be up in number 188 after lunch; got to know how far they've got up there.'

The man with the glass eye, if it was a glass eye, stumped stiffly away; and the eye of Father Brown (which was by no means a glass eye) followed him thoughtfully as he threaded his way through the ladders and disappeared into the street.

It was on the following morning that Father Brown had the unusual experience of oversleeping himself; or at least of starting from sleep with a subjective conviction that he must be late. This was partly due to his remembering, as a man may remember a dream, the fact of having been half-awakened at a more regular hour and fallen asleep again; a common enough occurrence with most of us, but a very uncommon occurrence with Father Brown. And he was afterwards oddly convinced, with that mystic side of him which was normally turned away from the world, that in that detached dark islet of dreamland, between the two wakings, there lay like buried treasure the truth of this tale.

As it was, he jumped up with great promptitude, plunged into his clothes, seized his big knobby umbrella and bustled out into the street, where the bleak white morning was breaking like splintered ice about the huge black building facing him. He was surprised to find that the streets shone almost empty in the cold crystalline light; the very look of it told him it could hardly be so late as he had feared. Then suddenly the stillness was cloven by the arrowlike swiftness of a long grey car which halted before the big deserted flats. Lord Stanes unfolded himself from within and approached the door, carrying (rather languidly) two large suitcases. At the same moment the door opened, and somebody seemed to step back instead of stepping out into the street. Stanes called twice to the man within, before that person seemed to complete his original gesture by coming out on to the doorstep; then the two held a brief colloquy, ending in the nobleman carrying his suitcases upstairs, and the other coming out into full daylight and revealing the heavy shoulders and peering head of young Henry Sand.

Father Brown made no more of this rather odd meeting, until two days later the young man drove up in his own car, and implored the priest to enter it. 'Something awful has happened,' he said, 'and I'd rather talk to you than Stanes. You know Stanes arrived the other day with some mad idea of camping in one of the flats that's just finished. That's why I had to go there early and open the door to him. But all that will keep. I want you to come up to my uncle's place at once.'

'Is he ill?' enquired the priest quickly.

'I think he's dead,' answered the nephew.

'What do you mean by saying you think he's dead?' asked Father Brown a little briskly. 'Have you got a doctor?'

'No,' answered the other. 'I haven't got a doctor or a patient either . . . It's no good calling in doctors to examine the body; because the body has run away. But I'm afraid I know where it has run to . . . the truth is – we kept it dark for two days; but he's disappeared.'

'Wouldn't it be better,' said Father Brown mildly, 'if you told me what has really happened from the beginning?'

'I know,' answered Henry Sand; 'it's an infernal shame to talk flippantly like this about the poor old boy; but people get like that when they're rattled. I'm not much good at hiding things; the long and the short of it is – well, I won't tell you the long of it now. It's what some people would call rather a long shot; shooting suspicions at random and so on. But the short of it is that my unfortunate uncle has committed suicide.'

They were by this time skimming along in the car through the last fringes of the town and the first fringes of the forest and park beyond it; the lodge gates of Sir Hubert Sand's small estate were about half a mile farther on amid the thickening throng of the beeches. The estate consisted chiefly of a small park and a large ornamental garden, which descended in terraces of a certain classical pomp to the very edge of the chief river of the district. As soon as they arrived at the house, Henry took the priest somewhat hastily through the old Georgian rooms and out upon the other side; where they silently descended the slope, a rather steep slope embanked with flowers, from which they could see the pale river spread out before them almost as flat as in a bird's-eye view. They were just turning the corner of the path under an enormous classical urn crowned with a somewhat incongruous garland of geraniums, when Father Brown saw a movement in the bushes and thin trees just below him, that seemed as swift as a movement of startled birds.

In the tangle of thin trees by the river two figures seemed to divide or scatter; one of them glided swiftly into the shadows and the other came forward to face them; bringing them to a halt and an abrupt and rather unaccountable silence. Then Henry Sand said in his heavy way: 'I think you know Father Brown . . . Lady Sand.'

Father Brown did know her; but at that moment he might almost have said that he did not know her. The pallor and constriction of her face was like a mask of tragedy; she was much younger than her husband, but at that moment she looked somehow older than everything in that old house and garden. And the priest remembered, with a subconscious thrill, that she was indeed older in type and lineage and was the true possessor of the place. For her own family had owned it as impoverished aristocrats, before she had restored its fortunes by marrying a successful business man. As she stood there, she might have been a family picture, or even a family ghost. Her pale face was of that pointed yet oval type seen in some old pictures of Mary Queen of Scots; and its expression seemed almost to go beyond the natural unnaturalness of a situation, in which her husband had vanished under suspicion of suicide. Father Brown, with the same subconscious movement of the mind, wondered who it was with whom she had been talking among the trees.

'I suppose you know all this dreadful news,' she said, with a comfortless composure. 'Poor Hubert must have broken down under all this revolutionary persecution, and been just maddened into taking his own life. I don't know whether you can do anything; or whether these horrible Bolsheviks can be made responsible for hounding him to death.'

'I am terribly distressed, Lady Sand,' said Father Brown. 'And still, I must own, a little bewildered. You speak of persecution; do you think that anybody could hound him to death merely by pinning up that paper on the wall?'

'I fancy,' answered the lady, with a darkening brow, 'that there were other persecutions beside the paper.'

'It shows what mistakes one may make,' said the priest sadly. 'I never should have thought he would be so illogical as to die in order to avoid death.'

'I know,' she answered, gazing at him gravely. 'I should never have believed it, if it hadn't been written with his own hand.'

'What?' cried Father Brown, with a little jump like a rabbit that has been shot at.

'Yes,' said Lady Sand calmly. 'He left a confession of suicide; so I fear there is no doubt about it.' And she passed on up the slope alone, with all the inviolable isolation of the family ghost.

The spectacles of Father Brown were turned in mute enquiry to the eyeglasses of Mr Henry Sand. And the latter gentleman, after an instant's hesitation, spoke again in his rather blind and plunging fashion: 'Yes, you see, it seems pretty clear now what he did. He was always a great swimmer and used to come down in his dressing-gown every morning for a dip in the river. Well, he came down as usual, and left his dressing-gown on the bank; it's lying there still. But he also left a message saying he was going for his last swim and then death, or something like that.'

'Where did he leave the message?' asked Father Brown.

'He scrawled it on that tree there, overhanging the water, I suppose the last thing he took hold of; just below where the dressing-gown's lying. Come and see for yourself.'

Father Brown ran down the last short slope to the shore and peered under the hanging tree, whose plumes were almost dipping in the stream. Sure enough, he saw on the smooth bark the words scratched conspicuously and unmistakably: 'One more swim and then drowning. Goodbye. Hubert Sand.' Father Brown's gaze travelled slowly up the bank till it rested on a gorgeous rag of raiment, all red and yellow with gilded tassels. It was the dressing-gown, and the priest picked it up and began to turn it over. Almost as he did so he was conscious that a figure had flashed across his field of vision; a tall dark figure that slipped from one clump of trees to another, as if following the trail of the vanishing lady. He had little doubt that it was the companion from whom she had lately parted. He had still less doubt that it was the dead man's secretary, Mr Rupert Rae.

'Of course, it might be a final afterthought to leave the message,' said Father Brown, without looking up, his eye riveted on the red and gold garment. 'We've all heard of love-messages written on trees; and I suppose there might be death-messages written on trees too.'

'Well, he wouldn't have anything in the pockets of his dressing-gown, I suppose,' said young Sand. 'And a man might naturally scratch his message on a tree if he had no pens, ink or paper.'

'Sounds like French exercises,' said the priest dismally. 'But I wasn't thinking of that.' Then, after a silence, he said in a rather altered voice: 'To tell the truth, I was thinking whether a man might not naturally scratch his message on a tree, even if he had stacks of pens, and quarts of ink, and reams of paper.'

Henry was looking at him with a rather startled air, his eyeglasses crooked on his pug-nose. 'And what do you mean by that?' he asked sharply.

'Well,' said Father Brown slowly, 'I don't exactly mean that postmen will carry letters in the form of logs, or that you will ever drop a line to a friend by putting a postage stamp on a pine tree. It would have to be a particular sort of position – in fact, it would have to be a particular sort of person, who really preferred this sort of arboreal correspondence. But, given the position and the person, I repeat what I said. He would still write on a tree, as the song says, if all the world were paper and all the sea were ink; if that river flowed with everlasting ink or all these woods were a forest of quills and fountain-pens.'

It was evident that Sand felt something creepy about the priest's fanciful imagery; whether because he found it incomprehensible or because he was beginning to comprehend.

'You see,' said Father Brown, turning the dressing-gown over slowly as he spoke, 'a man isn't expected to write his very best handwriting when he chips it on a tree. And if the man were not the man, if I make myself clear – Hullo!'

He was looking down at the red dressing-gown, and it seemed for the moment as if some of the red had come off on his finger; but both the faces turned towards it were already a shade paler.

'Blood!' said Father Brown; and for the instant there was a deadly stillness save for the melodious noises of the river.

Henry Sand cleared his throat and nose with noises that were by no means melodious. Then he said rather hoarsely: 'Whose blood?'

'Oh, mine,' said Father Brown; but he did not smile.

A moment after he said: 'There was a pin in this thing and I pricked myself. But I don't think you quite appreciate the point . . . the point of the pin, I do'; and he sucked his finger like a child.

'You see,' he said after another silence, 'the gown was folded up and pinned together; nobody could have unfolded it – at least without scratching himself. In plain words, Hubert Sand never *wore* this dressing-gown. Any more than Hubert Sand ever wrote on that tree. Or drowned himself in that river.'

The pince-nez tilted on Henry's enquiring nose fell off with a click; but he was otherwise motionless, as if rigid with surprise.

'Which brings us back,' went on Father Brown cheerfully, 'to somebody's taste for writing his private correspondence on trees, like Hiawatha and his picture-writing. Sand had all the time there was, before drowning himself. Why didn't he leave a note for his wife like a sane man? Or, shall we say . . . Why didn't the other man leave a note for the wife like a sane man? Because he would have had to forge the husband's handwriting; always a tricky thing now that experts are so nosey about it. But nobody can be expected to imitate even his own handwriting, let alone somebody else's, when he carves capital letters in the bark of a tree. This is not a suicide, Mr Sand. If it's anything at all, it's a murder.'

The bracken and bushes of the undergrowth snapped and crackled as the big young man rose out of them like a leviathan, and stood lowering, with his thick neck thrust forward.

'I'm no good at hiding things,' he said, 'and I half-suspected something like this – expected it, you might say, for a long time. To tell the truth, I could hardly be civil to the fellow – to either of them, for that matter.'

'What exactly do you mean?' asked the priest, looking him gravely full in the face.

'I mean,' said Henry Sand, 'that you have shown me the murder and I think I could show you the murderers.'

Father Brown was silent and the other went on rather jerkily.

'You said people sometimes wrote love-messages on trees. Well, as a fact, there are some of them on that tree; there are two sort of monograms twisted together up there under the leaves – I suppose you know that Lady Sand was the heiress of this place long before she married; and she knew that damned dandy of a secretary even in those days. I guess they used to meet here and write their vows upon the trysting tree. They seem to have used the trysting tree for another purpose later on. Sentiment, no doubt, or economy.'

'They must be very horrible people,' said Father Brown.

'Haven't there been any horrible people in history or the police-news?' demanded Sand with some excitement. 'Haven't there been lovers who made love seem more horrible than hate? Don't you know about Bothwell and all the bloody legends of such lovers?'

'I know the legend of Bothwell,' answered the priest. 'I also know it to be quite legendary. But of course it's true that husbands have been sometimes put away like that. By the way, where was he put away? I mean, where did they hide the body?'

'I suppose they drowned him, or threw him in the water when he was dead,' snorted the young man impatiently.

Father Brown blinked thoughtfully and then said: 'A river is a good place to hide an imaginary body. It's a rotten bad place to hide a real one. I mean, it's easy to *say* you've thrown it in, because it *might* be washed away to sea. But if you really did throw it in, it's about a hundred to one it wouldn't; the chances of it going ashore somewhere are enormous. I think they must have had a better scheme for hiding the body than that – or the body would have been found by now. And if there were any marks of violence – '

'Oh, bother hiding the body,' said Henry, with some irritation; 'haven't we witness enough in the writing on their own devilish tree?'

'The body is the chief witness in every murder,' answered the other. 'The hiding of the body, nine times out of ten, is the practical problem to be solved.'

There was a silence; and Father Brown continued to turn over the red dressing-gown and spread it out on the shining grass of the sunny shore; he did not look up. But, for some time past he had been conscious that the whole landscape had been changed for him by the presence of a third party; standing as still as a statue in the garden.

'By the way,' he said, lowering his voice, 'how do you explain that little guy with the glass eye, who brought your poor uncle a letter yesterday? It seemed to me he was entirely altered by reading it; that's why I wasn't surprised at the suicide, when I thought it was a suicide. That chap was a rather lowdown private detective, or I'm much mistaken.'

'Why,' said Henry in a hesitating manner, 'why, he might have been – husbands do sometimes put on detectives in domestic tragedies like this, don't they? I suppose he'd got the proofs of their intrigue; and so they – '

'I shouldn't talk too loud,' said Father Brown, 'because your detective is detecting us at this moment, from about a yard beyond those bushes.'

They looked up, and sure enough the goblin with the glass eye was fixing them with that disagreeable optic, looking all the more grotesque for standing among the white and waxen blooms of the classical garden.

Henry Sand scrambled to his feet again with a rapidity that seemed breathless for one of his bulk, and asked the man very angrily and abruptly what he was doing, at the same time telling him to clear out at once.

'Lord Stanes,' said the goblin of the garden, 'would be much obliged if Father Brown would come up to the house and speak to him.'

Henry Sand turned away furiously; but the priest put down his fury to the dislike that was known to exist between him and the nobleman in question. As they mounted the slope, Father Brown paused a moment as if tracing patterns on the smooth tree-trunk, glanced upwards once at the darker and more hidden hieroglyph said to be a record of romance; and then stared at the wider and more sprawling letters of the confession, or supposed confession of suicide.

'Do those letters remind you of anything?' he asked. And when his sulky companion shook his head, he added: 'They remind me of the writing on that placard that threatened him with the vengeance of the strikers.'

'This is the hardest riddle and the queerest tale I have ever tackled,' said Father Brown, a month later, as he sat opposite Lord Stanes in the recently furnished apartment of No. 188, the end flat which was the last to be finished before the interregnum of the industrial dispute and the transfer of work from the Trade Union. It was comfortably furnished; and Lord Stanes was presiding over grog and cigars, when the priest made his confession with a grimace, Lord Stanes had become rather surprisingly friendly, in a cool and casual way.

'I know that is saying a good deal, with your record,' said Stanes, 'but certainly the detectives, including our seductive friend with the glass eye, don't seem at all able to see the solution.'

Father Brown laid down his cigar and said carefully: 'It isn't that they can't see the solution. It is that they can't see the problem.'

'Indeed,' said the other, 'perhaps I can't see the problem either.'

'The problem is unlike all other problems, for this reason,' said Father Brown. 'It seems as if the criminal deliberately did two different things, either of which might have been successful; but which, when done together, could only defeat each other. I am assuming, what I firmly believe, that the same murderer pinned up the proclamation threatening a sort of Bolshevik murder, and also wrote on the tree confessing to an ordinary suicide. Now you may say it is after all possible that the proclamation was a proletarian proclamation; that some extremist workmen wanted to kill their employer, and killed him. Even if that were true, it would still stick at the mystery of why they left, or why anybody left, a contrary trail of private self-destruction. But it certainly isn't true. None of these workmen, however bitter, would have done a thing like that. I know them pretty well; I know their leaders quite well. To suppose that people like Tom Bruce or Hogan would assassinate somebody they could go for in the newspapers, and damage in all sorts of different ways, is the sort of psychology that sensible people call lunacy. No; there was somebody, who was not an indignant workman, who first played the part of an indignant workman, and then played the part of a suicidal employer. But, in the name of wonder, why? If he thought he could pass it off smoothly as a suicide, why did he first spoil it all by publishing a threat of murder? You might say it was an after-thought to fix up the suicide story, as less provocative than the murder story. But it wasn't less provocative *after* the murder story. He must have known he had already turned our thoughts towards murder, when it should have been his whole object to keep our thoughts away from it. If it was an after-thought, it was the after-thought of a very thoughtless person. And I have a notion that this assassin is a very thoughtful person. Can you make anything of it?'

'No; but I see what you mean,' said Stanes, 'by saying that I didn't even see the problem. It isn't merely who killed Sand; it's why anybody should accuse somebody else of killing Sand and then accuse Sand of killing himself.'

Father Brown's face was knotted and the cigar was clenched in his teeth; the end of it glowed and darkened rhythmically like the signal of some burning pulse of the brain. Then he spoke as if to himself: 'We've got to follow very closely and very clearly. It's like separating threads of thought from each other; something like this. Because the murder charge really rather spoilt the suicide charge, he wouldn't normally have made the murder charge. But he did make it; so he had some other reason for making it. It was so strong a reason that perhaps it reconciled him even to weakening his other line of defence: that it was a suicide. In other words, the murder charge wasn't really a murder charge. I mean he wasn't using it as a murder charge; he wasn't doing it so as to shift to somebody else the guilt of murder; he was doing it for some other extraordinary reason of his own. His plan had to contain a proclamation that Sand would be murdered; whether it threw suspicion on other people or not. Somehow or other the mere proclamation itself was necessary. But why?'

He smoked and smouldered away with the same volcanic concentration for five minutes before he spoke again.

'What could a murderous proclamation do, besides suggesting that the strikers were the murderers? What *did* it do? One thing is obvious; it inevitably did the opposite of what it said. It told Sand not to lock out his men; and it was perhaps the only thing in the world that would really have made him do it. You've got to think of the sort of man and the sort of reputation. When a man has been called a strong man in our silly sensational newspapers, when he is fondly regarded as a sportsman by all the most distinguished asses in England, he simply can't back down because he is threatened with a pistol. It would be like walking about at Ascot with a white feather stuck in his absurd white hat. It would break that inner idol or ideal of oneself, which every man not a downright dastard does really prefer to life. And Sand wasn't a dastard; he was courageous; he was also impulsive. It acted instantly like a charm; his nephew, who had been more or less mixed up with the workmen, cried out instantly that the threat must be absolutely and instantly defied.'

'Yes,' said Lord Stanes, 'I noticed that.' They looked at each other for an instant, and then Stanes added carelessly: 'So you think the thing the criminal really wanted was – '

'The lock-out!' cried the priest energetically. 'The strike or whatever you call it; the cessation of work, anyhow. He wanted the work to stop at once; perhaps the blacklegs to come in at once; certainly the trade unionists to go out at once. That is what he really wanted; God knows why. And he brought that off, I think, really without bothering much about its other implication of the existence of Bolshevist assassins. But then . . . then I think something went wrong. I'm only guessing and groping very slowly here; but the only explanation I can think of is that something began to draw attention to the real seat of the trouble; to the reason, whatever it was, of his wanting to bring the building to a halt. And then belatedly, desperately, and rather inconsistently, he tried to lay the other trail that led to the river, simply and solely because it led away from the flats.'

He looked up through his moonlike spectacles, absorbing all the quality of the background and furniture; the restrained luxury of a quiet man of the world; and contrasting it with the two suitcases with which its occupant had arrived so recently in a newly-finished and quite unfurnished flat. Then he said rather abruptly:

'In short, the murderer was frightened of something or somebody in the flats. By the way, why did *you* come to live in the flats? . . . Also by the way, young Henry told me you made an early appointment with him when you moved in. Is that true?'

'Not in the least,' said Stanes, 'I got the key from his uncle the night before. I've no notion why Henry came here that morning.'

'Ah,' said Father Brown, 'then I think I have some notion of why he came . . . I *thought* you startled him by coming in just when he was coming out.'

'And yet,' said Stanes, looking across with a glitter

in his grey-green eyes, 'you do rather think that I also am a mystery.'

'I think you are two mysteries,' said Father Brown. 'The first is why you originally retired from Sand's business. The second is why you have since come back to live in Sand's buildings.'

Stanes smoked reflectively, knocked out his ash, and rang a bell on the table before him. 'If you'll excuse me,' he said, 'I will summon two more to the council. Jackson, the little detective you know of, will answer the bell; and I've asked Henry Sand to come in a little later.'

Father Brown rose from his seat, walked across the room and looked down frowning into the fireplace.

'Meanwhile,' continued Stanes, 'I don't mind answering both your questions. I left the Sand business because I was sure there was some hanky-panky in it and somebody was pinching all the money. I came back to it, and took this flat, because I wanted to watch for the real truth about old Sand's death – on the spot.'

Father Brown faced round as the detective entered the room; he stood staring at the hearth-rug and repeated: 'On the spot.'

'Mr Jackson will tell you,' said Stanes, 'that Sir Hubert commissioned him to find out who was the thief robbing the firm; and he brought a note of his discoveries the day before old Hubert disappeared.'

'Yes,' said Father Brown, 'and I know now where he disappeared to. I know where the body is.'

'Do you mean – ?' began his host hastily.

'It is here,' said Father Brown, and stamped on the hearth-rug. 'Here, under the elegant Persian rug in this cosy and comfortable room.'

'Where in the world did you find that?'

'I've just remembered,' said Father Brown, 'that I found it in my sleep.'

He closed his eyes as if trying to picture a dream, and went on dreamily: 'This is a murder story turning on the problem of how to hide the body; and I found it in my sleep. I was always woken up every morning by hammering from this building. On that morning I half-woke up, went to sleep again and woke once more, expecting to find it late; but it wasn't. Why? Because there *had* been hammering that morning, though all the usual work had stopped; short, hurried hammering in the small hours before dawn. Automatically a man sleeping stirs at such a familiar sound. But he goes to sleep again, because the usual sound is not at the usual hour. Now why did a certain secret criminal want all the work to cease suddenly; and only new workers come in? Because, if the old workers had come in next day, they would have found a new piece of work done in the night. The old workers would have known where they left off; and they would have found the whole flooring of this room already nailed down. Nailed down by a man who knew how to do it; having mixed a good deal with the workmen and learned their ways.'

As he spoke, the door was pushed open and a head poked in with a thrusting motion; a small head at the end of a thick neck and a face that blinked at them through glasses.

'Henry Sand said,' observed Father Brown, staring at the ceiling, 'that he was no good at hiding things. But I think he did himself an injustice.'

Henry Sand turned and moved swiftly away down the corridor.

'He not only hid his thefts from the firm quite

successfully for years,' went on the priest with an air of abstraction, 'but when his uncle discovered them, he hid his uncle's corpse in an entirely new and original manner.'

At the same instant Stanes again rang a bell, with a long strident steady ringing; and the little man with the glass eye was propelled or shot along the corridor after the fugitive, with something of the rotatory motion of a mechanical figure in a zoetrope. At the same moment, Father Brown looked out of the window, leaning over a small balcony, and saw five or six men start from behind bushes and railings in the street below and spread out equally mechanically like a fan or net; opening out after the fugitive who had shot like a bullet out of the front door. Father Brown saw only the pattern of the story; which had never strayed from that room; where Henry had strangled Hubert and hid his body under impenetrable flooring, stopping the whole work on the building to do it. A pinprick had started his own suspicions; but only to tell him he had been led down the long loop of a lie. The point of the pin was that it was pointless.

He fancied he understood Stanes at last, and he liked to collect queer people who were difficult to understand. He realised that this tired gentleman, whom he had once accused of having green blood, had indeed a sort of cold green flame of conscientiousness or conventional honour, that had made him first shift out of a shady business, and then feel ashamed of having shifted it on to others; and come back as a bored laborious detective; pitching his camp on the very spot where the corpse had been buried; so that the murderer, finding him sniffing so near the corpse, had wildly staged the alternative drama of the dressing-gown and the drowned man. All that was plain enough, but, before he withdrew his head from the night air and the stars, Father Brown threw one glance upwards at the vast black bulk of the cyclopean building heaved far up into the night, and remembered Egypt and Babylon, and all that is at once eternal and ephemeral in the work of man.

'I was right in what I said first of all,' he said. 'It reminds one of Coppée's poem about the Pharaoh and the Pyramid. This house is supposed to be a hundred houses; and yet the whole mountain of building is only one man's tomb.'

The Insoluble Problem

This queer incident, in some ways perhaps the queerest of the many that came his way, happened to Father Brown at the time when his French friend Flambeau had retired from the profession of crime and had entered with great energy and success on the profession of crime investigator. It happened that both as a thief and a thief-taker, Flambeau had rather specialised in the matter of jewel thefts, on which he was admitted to be an expert, both in the matter of identifying jewels and the equally practical matter of identifying jewel-thieves. And it was in connection with his special knowledge of this subject, and a special commission which it had won for him, that he rang up his friend the priest on the particular morning on which this story begins.

Father Brown was delighted to hear the voice of his old friend, even on the telephone; but in a general way, and especially at that particular moment, Father Brown was not very fond of the telephone. He was one who preferred to watch people's faces and feel social atmospheres, and he knew well that without these things, verbal messages are apt to be very misleading, especially from total strangers. And it seemed as if, on that particular morning, a swarm of total strangers had been buzzing in his ear with more or less unenlightening verbal messages; the telephone seemed to be possessed of a demon of triviality. Perhaps the most distinctive voice was one which asked him whether he did not issue regular permits for murder and theft upon the payment of a regular tariff hung up in his church; and as the stranger, on being informed that this was not the case, concluded the colloquy with a hollow laugh, it may be presumed that he remained unconvinced. Then an agitated, rather inconsequent female voice rang up requesting him to come round at once to a certain hotel he had heard of some forty-five miles on the road to a neighbouring cathedral town; the request being immediately followed by a contradiction in the same voice, more agitated and yet more inconsequent, telling him that it did not matter and that he was not wanted after all. Then came an interlude of a press agency asking him if he had anything to say on what a film actress had said about moustaches for men; and finally yet a third return of the agitated and inconsequent lady at the hotel, saying that he was wanted, after all. He vaguely supposed that this marked some of the hesitations and panics not unknown among those who are vaguely veering in the direction of Instruction, but he confessed to a considerable relief when the voice of Flambeau wound up the series with a hearty threat of immediately turning up to breakfast.

Father Brown very much preferred to talk to a friend sitting comfortably over a pipe, but it soon appeared that his visitor was on the warpath and full of energy, having every intention of carrying off the little priest captive on some important expedition of his own. It was true that there was a special circumstance involved which might be supposed to claim the priest's attention. Flambeau had figured several times of late as successfully thwarting a theft of famous precious stones; he had torn the tiara of the Duchess of Dulwich out of the very hand of the bandit as he bolted through the garden. He laid so ingenious a trap for the criminal who planned to carry off the celebrated Sapphire Necklace, that the artist in question, actually carried off the copy which he had himself planned to leave as a substitute.

Such were doubtless the reasons that had led to his being specially summoned to guard the delivery of a rather different sort of treasure: perhaps even more valuable in its mere materials, but possessing also another sort of value. A world-famous reliquary, supposed to contain a relic of St Dorothy the martyr, was to be delivered at the Catholic monastery in a cathedral town; and one of the most famous of international jewel-thieves was supposed to have an eye on it; or rather presumably on the gold and rubies of its setting, rather than its purely hagiological importance. Perhaps there was something in this association of ideas which made Flambeau feel that the priest would be a particularly appropriate companion in his adventure; but anyhow, he descended on him, breathing fire and ambition and very voluble about his plans for preventing the theft.

Flambeau indeed bestrode the priest's hearth gigantically and in the old swaggering musketeer attitude, twirling his great moustaches.

'You can't,' he cried, referring to the sixty-mile road to Casterbury. 'You can't allow a profane robbery like that to happen under your very nose.'

The relic was not to reach the monastery till the evening; and there was no need for its defenders to arrive earlier; for indeed a motor journey would take them the greater part of the day. Moreover, Father Brown casually remarked that there was an inn on the road, at which he would prefer to lunch, as he had been already asked to look in there as soon as was convenient.

As they drove along through a densely wooded but sparsely inhabited landscape, in which inns and all other buildings seemed to grow rarer and rarer, the daylight began to take on the character of a stormy twilight even in the heat of noon; and dark purple clouds gathered over the dark grey forests. As is common under the lurid quietude of that kind of light, what colour there was in the landscape gained a sort of secretive glow which is not found in objects under the full sunlight; and ragged red leaves or golden or orange fungi seemed to burn with a dark fire of their own. Under such a half-light they came to a break in the woods like a great rent in a grey wall, and saw beyond, standing above the gap, the tall and rather outlandish-looking inn that bore the name of the Green Dragon.

The two old companions had often arrived together at inns and other human habitations, and found a somewhat singular state of things there; but the signs of singularity had seldom manifested themselves so early. For while their car was still some hundreds of yards from the dark green door, which matched the dark green shutters of the high and narrow building, the door was thrown open with violence and a woman with a wild mop of red hair rushed to meet them, as if she were ready to board the car in full career. Flambeau brought the car to a standstill, but almost before he had done so, she thrust her white and tragic face into the window, crying: 'Are you Father Brown?' and then almost in the same breath; 'who is this man?'

'This gentleman's name is Flambeau,' said Father Brown in a tranquil manner, 'and what can I do for you?'

'Come into the inn,' she said, with extraordinary abruptness even under the circumstances. 'There's been a murder done.'

They got out of the car in silence and followed her to the dark green door which opened inwards on a sort of dark green alley, formed of stakes and wooden pillars, wreathed with vine and ivy, showing square leaves of black and red and many sombre colours. This again led through an inner door into a sort of large parlour hung with rusty trophies of Cavalier arms, of which the furniture seemed to be antiquated and also in great confusion, like the inside of a lumber-room. They were quite startled for the moment; for it seemed as if one large piece of lumber rose and moved towards them; so dusty and shabby and ungainly was the man who thus abandoned what seemed like a state of permanent immobility.

Strangely enough, the man seemed to have a certain agility of politeness, when once he did move; even if it suggested the wooden joints of a courtly stepladder or an obsequious towel-horse. Both Flambeau and Father Brown felt that they had hardly ever clapped eyes on a man who was so difficult to place. He was not what is called a gentleman; yet he had something of the dusty refinement of a scholar; there was something faintly disreputable or *declassé* about him; and yet the smell of him was rather bookish than Bohemian. He was thin and pale, with a pointed nose and a dark pointed beard; his brow was bald, but his hair behind long and lank and stringy; and the expression of his eyes was almost entirely masked by a pair of blue spectacles. Father Brown felt that he had met something of the sort somewhere, and a long time ago; but he could no longer put a name to it. The lumber he sat among was largely literary lumber; especially bundles of seventeenth-century pamphlets.

'Do I understand the lady to say,' asked Flambeau gravely, 'that there is a murder here?'

The lady nodded her red ragged head rather impatiently; except for those flaming elf-locks she had lost some of her look of wildness; her dark dress was of a certain dignity and neatness; her features were strong and handsome; and there was something about her suggesting that double strength of body and mind which makes women powerful, particularly in contrast with men like the man in blue spectacles. Nevertheless, it was he who gave the only articulate answer, intervening with a certain antic gallantry.

'It is true that my unfortunate sister-in-law,' he explained, 'has almost this moment suffered a most appalling shock which we should all have desired to spare her. I only wish that I myself had made the discovery and suffered only the further distress of bringing the terrible news. Unfortunately it was Mrs Flood herself who found her aged grandfather, long sick and bedridden in this hotel, actually dead in the garden; in circumstances which point only too plainly to violence and assault. Curious circumstances, I may say, very curious circumstances indeed.' And he coughed slightly, as if apologising for them.

Flambeau bowed to the lady and expressed his sincere sympathies; then he said to the man: 'I think you said, sir, that you are Mrs Flood's brother-in-law.'

'I am Dr Oscar Flood,' replied the other. 'My brother, this lady's husband, is at present away on the Continent on business, and she is running the hotel. Her grandfather was partially paralysed and very far advanced in years. He was never known to leave his bedroom; so that really these extraordinary circumstances . . . '

'Have you sent for a doctor or the police?' asked Flambeau.

'Yes,' replied Dr Flood, 'we rang up after making the dreadful discovery; but they can hardly be here for some hours. This roadhouse stands so very remote. It is only used by people going to Casterbury or even beyond. So we thought we might ask for your valuable assistance until – '

'If we are to be of any assistance,' said Father Brown, interrupting in too abstracted a manner to seem uncivil; 'I should say we had better go and look at the circumstances at once.'

He stepped almost mechanically towards the door; and almost ran into a man who was shouldering his way in; a big, heavy young man with dark hair unbrushed and untidy, who would nevertheless have been rather handsome save for a slight disfigurement of one eye, which gave him rather a sinister appearance.

'What the devil are you doing?' he blurted out, 'telling every Tom, Dick and Harry – at least you ought to wait for the police.'

'I will be answerable to the police,' said Flambeau with a certain magnificence, and a sudden air of having taken command of everything. He advanced to the doorway, and as he was much bigger than the big young man, and his moustaches were as formidable as the horns of a Spanish bull, the big young man backed before him and had an inconsequent air of being thrown out and left behind, as the group swept out into the garden and up the flagged path towards the mulberry plantation. Only Flambeau heard the little priest say to the doctor: 'He doesn't seem to love us really, does he? By the way, who is he?'

'His name is Dunn,' said the doctor, with a certain restraint of manner. 'My sister-in-law gave him the job of managing the garden, because he lost an eye in the War.'

As they went through the mulberry bushes, the landscape of the garden presented that rich yet ominous effect which is found when the land is actually brighter than the sky. In the broken sunlight from behind, the treetops in front of them stood up like pale green flames against a sky steadily blackening with storm, through every shade of purple and violet. The same light struck strips of the lawn and garden beds; and whatever it illuminated seemed more mysteriously sombre and secret for the light. The garden bed was dotted with tulips that looked like drops of dark blood, and some of which one might have sworn were truly black; and the line ended appropriately with a tulip tree; which Father Brown was disposed, if partly by some confused memory, to identify with what is commonly called the Judas tree. What assisted the association was the fact that there was hanging from one of the branches, like a dried fruit, the dry, thin body of an old man, with a long beard that wagged grotesquely in the wind.

There lay on it something more than the horror of darkness, the horror of sunlight; for the fitful sun painted tree and man in gay colours like a stage property; the tree was in flower and the corpse was hung with a faded peacock-green dressing-gown, and wore on its wagging head a scarlet smoking-cap. Also it had red bedroom-slippers, one of which had fallen off and lay on the grass like a blot of blood.

But neither Flambeau nor Father Brown was looking at these things as yet. They were both staring at a strange object that seemed to stick out of the middle of the dead man's shrunken figure; and which they gradually perceived to be the black but rather rusty iron hilt of a seventeenth-century sword, which had completely transfixed the body. They both remained almost motionless as they gazed at it; until the restless Dr Flood seemed to grow quite impatient with their stolidity.

'What puzzles *me* most,' he said, nervously snapping his fingers, 'is the actual state of the body. And yet it has given me an idea already.'

Flambeau had stepped up to the tree and was studying the sword-hilt through an eyeglass. But for some odd reason, it was at that very instant that the priest in sheer perversity spun round like a teetotum, turned his back on the corpse, and looked peeringly in the very opposite direction. He was just in time to see the red head of Mrs Flood at the remote end of the garden, turned towards a dark young man, too dim with distance to be identified, who was at that moment mounting a motor-bicycle; who vanished, leaving behind him only the dying din of that vehicle. Then the woman turned and began to walk towards them across the garden, just as Father Brown turned also and began a careful inspection of the sword-hilt and the hanging corps.

'I understand you only found him about half an hour ago,' said Flambeau. 'Was there anybody about here just before that? I mean anybody in his bedroom, or that part of the house, or this part of the garden – say for an hour beforehand?'

'No,' said the doctor with precision. 'That is the

very tragic accident. My sister-in-law was in the pantry, which is a sort of outhouse on the other side; this man Dunn was in the kitchen-garden, which is also in that direction; and I myself was poking about among the books, in a room just behind the one you found me in. There are two female servants, but one had gone to the post and the other was in the attic.'

'And were any of these people,' asked Flambeau, very quietly, 'I say *any* of these people, at all on bad terms with the poor old gentleman?'

'He was the object of almost universal affection,' replied the doctor solemnly. 'If there were any misunderstandings, they were mild and of a sort common in modern times. The old man was attached to the old religious habits; and perhaps his daughter and son-in-law had rather wider views. All that can have had nothing to do with a ghastly and fantastic assassination like this.'

'It depends on how wide the modern views were,' said Father Brown, 'or how narrow.'

At this moment they heard Mrs Flood hallooing across the garden as she came, and calling her brother-in-law to her with a certain impatience. He hurried towards her and was soon out of earshot; but as he went he waved his hand apologetically and then pointed with a long finger to the ground.

'You will find the footprints very intriguing,' he said; with the same strange air, as of a funereal showman.

The two amateur detectives looked across at each other. 'I find several other things intriguing,' said Flambeau.

'Oh, yes,' said the priest, staring rather foolishly at the grass.

'I was wondering,' said Flambeau, 'why they should

hang a man by the neck till he was dead, and then take the trouble to stick him with a sword.'

'And I was wondering,' said Father Brown, 'why they should kill a man with a sword thrust through his heart, and then take the trouble to hang him by the neck.'

'Oh, you are simply being contrary,' protested his friend. 'I can see at a glance that they didn't stab him alive. The body would have bled more and the wound wouldn't have closed like that.'

'And I could see at a glance,' said Father Brown, peering up very awkwardly, with his short stature and short sight, 'that they didn't hang him alive. If you'll look at the knot in the noose, you will see it's tied so clumsily that a twist of rope holds it away from the neck, so that it couldn't throttle a man at all. He was dead before they put the rope on him; and he was dead before they put the sword in him. And how was he really killed?'

'I think,' remarked the other, 'that we'd better go back to the house and have a look at his bedroom – and other things.'

'So we will,' said Father Brown. 'But among other things perhaps we had better have a look at these footprints. Better begin at the other end, I think, by his window. Well, there are no footprints on the paved path, as there might be; but then again there mightn't be. Well, here is the lawn just under his bedroom window. And here are his footprints plain enough.'

He blinked ominously at the footprints; and then began carefully retracing his path towards the tree, every now and then ducking in an undignified manner to look at something on the ground. Eventually he returned to Flambeau and said in a chatty manner:

'Well, do you know the story that is written there very plainly? Though it's not exactly a plain story.'

'I wouldn't be content to call it plain,' said Flambeau. 'I should call it quite ugly.'

'Well,' said Father Brown, 'the story that is stamped quite plainly on the earth, with exact moulds of the old man's slippers, is this. The aged paralytic leapt from the window and ran down the beds parallel to the path, quite eager for all the fun of being strangled and stabbed; so eager that he hopped on one leg out of sheer light-heartedness; and even occasionally turned cartwheels – '

'Stop!' cried Flambeau, angrily. 'What the hell is all this hellish pantomime?'

Father Brown merely raised his eyebrows and gestured mildly towards the hieroglyphs in the dust. 'About half the way there's only the mark of one slipper; and in some places the mark of a hand planted all by itself.'

'Couldn't he have limped and then fallen?' asked Flambeau.

Father Brown shook his head. 'At least he'd have tried to use his hands and feet, or knees and elbows, in getting up. There are no other marks there of any kind. Of course the flagged path is quite near, and there are no marks on that; though there might be on the soil between the cracks: it's a crazy pavement.'

'By God, it's a crazy pavement; and a crazy garden; and a crazy story!' And Flambeau looked gloomily across the gloomy and storm-stricken garden, across which the crooked patchwork paths did indeed give a queer aptness to the quaint old English adjective.

'And now,' said Father Brown, 'let us go up and look at his room.' They went in by a door not far from the bedroom window; and the priest paused a moment to look at an ordinary garden broomstick, for sweeping up leaves, that was leaning against the wall. 'Do you see that?'

'It's a broomstick,' said Flambeau, with solid irony.

'It's a blunder,' said Father Brown; 'the first blunder that I've seen in this curious plot.'

They mounted the stairs and entered the old man's bedroom; and a glance at it made fairly clear the main facts, both about the foundation and disunion of the family. Father Brown had felt from the first that he was in what was, or had been, a Catholic household; but was, at least partly, inhabited by lapsed or very loose Catholics. The pictures and images in the grandfather's room made it clear that what positive piety remained had been practically confined to him; and that his kindred had, for some reason or other, gone pagan. But he agreed that this was a hopelessly inadequate explanation even of an ordinary murder; let alone such a very extraordinary murder as this. 'Hang it all,' he muttered, 'the murder is really the least extraordinary part of it.' And even as he used the chance phrase, a slow light began to dawn upon his face.

Flambeau had seated himself on a chair by the little table which stood beside the dead man's bed. He was frowning thoughtfully at three or four white pills or pellets that lay in a small tray beside a bottle of water.

'The murderer or murderess,' said Flambeau, 'has some incomprehensible reason or other for wanting us to think the dead man was strangled or stabbed or both. He was not strangled or stabbed or anything of the kind. Why did they want to suggest it? The most logical explanation is that he died in some particular way which would, in itself, suggest a connection with some particular person. Suppose, for instance, he was poisoned. And suppose somebody is involved who would naturally look more like a poisoner than anybody else.'

'After all,' said Father Brown softly, 'our friend in the blue spectacles is a doctor.'

'I'm going to examine these pills pretty carefully,' went on Flambeau. 'I don't want to lose them, though. They look as if they were soluble in water.'

'It may take you some time to do anything scientific with them,' said the priest, 'and the police doctor may be here before that. So I should certainly advise you not to lose them. That is, if you are going to wait for the police doctor.'

'I am going to stay here till I have solved this problem,' said Flambeau.

'Then you will stay here for ever,' said Father Brown, looking calmly out of the window. 'I don't think I shall stay in this room, anyhow.'

'Do you mean that I shan't solve the problem?' asked his friend. 'Why shouldn't I solve the problem?'

'Because it isn't soluble in water. No, nor in blood,' said the priest; and he went down the dark stairs into the darkening garden. There he saw again what he had already seen from the window.

The heat and weight and obscurity of the thunderous sky seemed to be pressing yet more closely on the landscape; the clouds had conquered the sun which, above, in a narrowing clearance, stood up paler than the moon. There was a thrill of thunder in the air, but now no more stirring of wind or breeze; and even the colours of the garden seemed only like richer shades of darkness. But one colour still glowed with a certain dusky vividness; and that was the red hair of the woman of that house, who was standing with a sort of rigidity, staring, with her hands thrust up into her hair. That scene of eclipse, with something deeper in his own doubts about its significance, brought to the surface the memory of haunting and mystical lines; and he found himself murmuring: 'A secret spot, as savage and enchanted as e'er beneath a waning moon was haunted by woman wailing for her demon lover.' His muttering became more agitated. 'Holy Mary, Mother of God, pray for us sinners . . . that's what it is; that's terribly like what it is; *woman wailing for her demon lover*.'

He was hesitant and almost shaky as he approached the woman; but he spoke with his common composure. He was gazing at her very steadily, as he told her earnestly that she must not be morbid because of the mere accidental accessories of the tragedy, with all their mad ugliness. 'The pictures in your grandfather's room were truer to him than that ugly picture that we saw,' he said gravely. 'Something tells me he was a good man; and it does not matter what his murderers did with his body.'

'Oh, I am sick of his holy pictures and statues!' she said, turning her head away. 'Why don't they defend themselves, if they are what you say they are? But rioters can knock off the Blessed Virgin's head and nothing happens to them. Oh, what's the good? You can't blame us, you daren't blame us, if we've found out that man is stronger than God.'

'Surely,' said Father Brown very gently, 'it is not generous to make even God's patience with us a point against Him.'

'God may be patient and Man impatient,' she answered, 'and suppose we like the impatience better.

You call it sacrilege; but you can't stop it.'

Father Brown gave a curious little jump. 'Sacrilege!' he said; and suddenly turned back to the doorway with a new brisk air of decision. At the same moment Flambeau appeared in the doorway, pale with excitement, with a screw of paper in his hands. Father Brown had already opened his mouth to speak, but his impetuous friend spoke before him.

'I'm on the track at last!' cried Flambeau. 'These pills look the same, but they're really different. And do you know that, at the very moment I spotted them, that one-eyed brute of a gardener thrust his white face into the room; and he was carrying a horse-pistol. I knocked it out of his hand and threw him down the stairs, but I begin to understand everything. If I stay here another hour or two, I shall finish my job.'

'Then you will not finish it,' said the priest, with a ring in his voice very rare in him indeed. 'We shall not stay here another hour. We shall not stay here another minute. We must leave this place at once!'

'What!' cried the astounded Flambeau. 'Just when we are getting near the truth! Why, you can tell that we're getting near the truth because they are afraid of us.'

Father Brown looked at him with a stony and inscrutable face, and said: 'They are not afraid of us when we are here. They will only be afraid of us when we are not here.'

They had both become conscious that the rather fidgety figure of Dr Flood was hovering in the lurid haze; now it precipitated itself forward with the wildest gestures.

'Stop! Listen!' cried the agitated doctor. 'I have discovered the truth!'

'Then you can explain it to your own police,' said Father Brown, briefly. 'They ought to be coming soon. But we must be going.'

The doctor seemed thrown into a whirlpool of emotions, eventually rising to the surface again with a despairing cry. He spread out his arms like a cross, barring their way.

'Be it so!' he cried. 'I will not deceive you now, by saying I have discovered the truth. I will only confess the truth.'

'Then you can confess it to your own priest,' said Father Brown, and strode towards the garden gate, followed by his staring friend. Before he reached the gate, another figure had rushed athwart him like the wind; and Dunn the gardener was shouting at him some unintelligible derision at detectives who were running away from their job. Then the priest ducked just in time to dodge a blow from the horse-pistol, wielded like a club. But Dunn was just not in time to dodge a blow from the fist of Flambeau, which was like the club of Hercules. The two left Mr Dunn spread flat behind them on the path, and, passing out of the gate, went out and got into their car in silence. Flambeau only asked one brief question and Father Brown only answered: 'Casterbury.'

At last, after a long silence, the priest observed: 'I could almost believe the storm belonged only to that garden, and came out of a storm in the soul.'

'My friend,' said Flambeau, 'I have known you a long time, and when you show certain signs of certainty, I follow your lead. But I hope you are not going to tell me that you took me away from that fascinating job, because you did not like the atmosphere.'

'Well, it was certainly a terrible atmosphere,' replied

Father Brown, calmly. 'Dreadful and passionate and oppressive. And the most dreadful thing about it was this – that there was no hate in it at all.'

'Somebody,' suggested Flambeau, 'seems to have had a slight dislike of grandpapa.'

'Nobody had any dislike of anybody,' said Father Brown with a groan. 'That was the dreadful thing in that darkness. It was love.'

'Curious way of expressing love – to strangle somebody and stick him with a sword,' observed the other.

'It was love,' repeated the priest, 'and it filled the house with terror.'

'Don't tell me,' protested Flambeau, 'that that beautiful woman is in love with that spider in spectacles.'

'No,' said Father Brown and groaned again. 'She is in love with her husband. It is ghastly.'

'It is a state of things that I have often heard you recommend,' replied Flambeau. 'You cannot call that lawless love.'

'Not lawless in that sense,' answered Father Brown; then he turned sharply on his elbow and spoke with a new warmth: 'Do you think I don't know that the love of a man and a woman was the first command of God and is glorious for ever? Are you one of those idiots who think we don't admire love and marriage? Do I need to be told of the Garden of Eden or the wine of Cana? It is just because the strength in the thing was the strength of God, that it rages with that awful energy even when it breaks loose from God. When the Garden becomes a jungle, but still a glorious jungle; when the second fermentation turns the wine of Cana into the vinegar of Calvary. Do you think I don't know all that?'

'I'm sure you do,' said Flambeau, 'but I don't yet know much about my problem of the murder.'

'The murder cannot be solved,' said Father Brown.

'And why not?' demanded his friend.

'Because there is no murder to solve,' said Father Brown.

Flambeau was silent with sheer surprise; and it was his friend who resumed in a quiet tone: 'I'll tell you a curious thing. I talked with that woman when she was wild with grief; but she never said anything about the murder. She never mentioned murder, or even alluded to murder. What she did mention repeatedly was sacrilege.'

Then, with another jerk of verbal disconnection, he added: 'Have you ever heard of Tiger Tyrone?'

'Haven't I!' cried Flambeau. 'Why, that's the very man who's supposed to be after the reliquary, and whom I've been commissioned specially to circumvent. He's the most violent and daring gangster who ever visited this country; Irish, of course, but the sort that goes quite crazily anti-clerical. Perhaps he's dabbled in a little diabolism in these secret societies; anyhow, he has a macabre taste for playing all sorts of wild tricks that look wickeder than they are. Otherwise he's not the wickedest; he seldom kills, and never for cruelty; but he loves doing anything to shock people, especially his own people; robbing churches or digging up skeletons or what not.'

'Yes,' said Father Brown, 'it all fits in. I ought to have seen it all long before.'

'I don't see how we could have seen anything, after only an hour's investigation,' said the detective defensively.

'I ought to have seen it before there was anything to

investigate,' said the priest. 'I ought to have known it before you arrived this morning.'

'What on earth do you mean?'

'It only shows how wrong voices sound on the telephone,' said Father Brown reflectively. 'I heard all three stages of the thing this morning; and I thought they were trifles. First, a woman rang me up and asked me to go to that inn as soon as possible. What did that mean? Of course it meant that the old grandfather was dying. Then she rang up to say that I needn't go, after all. What did that mean? Of course it meant that the old grandfather was dead. He had died quite peaceably in his bed; probably heart failure from sheer old age. And then she rang up a third time and said I was to go, after all. What did that mean? Ah, that is rather more interesting!'

He went on after a moment's pause: 'Tiger Tyrone, whose wife worships him, took hold of one of his mad ideas, and yet it was a crafty idea, too. He had just heard that you were tracking him down, that you knew him and his methods and were coming to save the reliquary; he may have heard that I have sometimes been of some assistance. He wanted to stop us on the road; and his trick for doing it was to stage a murder. It was a pretty horrible thing to do; but it wasn't a murder. Probably he bullied his wife with an air of brutal common sense, saying he could only escape penal servitude by using a dead body that couldn't suffer anything from such use. Anyhow, his wife would do anything for him; but she felt all the unnatural hideousness of that hanging masquerade; and that's why she talked about sacrilege. She was thinking of the desecration of the relic; but also of the desecration of the death-bed. The brother's one of those shoddy "scientific" rebels who tinker with dud bombs; an idealist run to seed. But he's devoted to Tiger; and so is the gardener. Perhaps it's a point in his favour that so many people seem devoted to him.

'There was one little point that set me guessing very early. Among the old books the doctor was turning over was a bundle of seventeenth-century pamphlets; and I caught one title: *True Declaration of the Trial and Execution of My Lord Stafford.* Now Stafford was executed in the Popish Plot business, which began with one of history's detective stories; the death of Sir Edmund Berry Godfrey.. Godfrey was found dead in a ditch, and part of the mystery was that he had marks of strangulation, but was also transfixed with his own sword. I thought at once that somebody in the house might have got the idea from here. But he couldn't have wanted it as a way of committing a murder. He can only have wanted it as a way of creating a mystery. Then I saw that this applied to all the other outrageous details. They were devilish enough; but it wasn't mere devilry; there was a rag of excuse; because they had to make the mystery as contradictory and complicated as possible, to make sure that we should be a long time solving it – or rather seeing through it. So they dragged the poor old man off his death-bed and made the corpse hop and turn cartwheels and do everything that it *couldn't* have done. They had to give us an insoluble problem. They swept their own tracks off the path, leaving the broom. Fortunately we did see through it in time.'

'You saw through it in time,' said Flambeau. 'I might have lingered a little longer over the second trail they left, sprinkled with assorted pills.'

'Well, anyhow, we got away,' said Father Brown, comfortably.

'And that, I presume,' said Flambeau, 'is the reason I am driving at this rate along the road to Casterbury.'

That night in the monastery and church at Casterbury there were events calculated to stagger monastic seclusion. The reliquary of St Dorothy, in a casket gorgeous with gold and rubies, was temporarily placed in a side room near the chapel of the monastery, to be brought in with a procession for a special service at the end of Benediction. It was guarded for the moment by one monk, who watched it in a tense and vigilant manner; for he and his brethren knew all about the shadow of peril from the prowling of Tiger Tyrone. Thus it was that the monk was on his feet in a flash, when he saw one of the low-latticed windows beginning to open and a dark object crawling like a black serpent through the crack. Rushing across, he gripped it and found it was the arm and sleeve of a man, terminating with a handsome cuff and a smart dark-grey glove. Laying hold of it, he shouted for help, and even as he did so, a man darted into the room through the door behind his back and snatched the casket he had left behind him on the table. Almost at the same instant, the arm wedged in the window came away in his hand, and he stood holding the stuffed limb of a dummy.

Tiger Tyrone had played that trick before, but to the monk it was a novelty. Fortunately, there was at least one person to whom the Tiger's tricks were not a novelty; and that person appeared with militant moustaches, gigantically framed in the doorway, at the very moment when the Tiger turned to escape by it. Flambeau and Tiger Tyrone looked at each other with steady eyes and exchanged something that was almost like a military salute.

Meanwhile Father Brown had slipped into the chapel, to say a prayer for several persons involved in these unseemly events. But he was rather smiling than otherwise, and, to tell the truth, he was not by any means hopeless about Mr Tyrone and his deplorable family; but rather more hopeful than he was for many more respectable people. Then his thoughts widened with the grander perspectives of the place and the occasion. Against black and green marbles at the end of the rather rococo chapel, the dark-red vestments of the festival of a martyr were in their turn a background for a fierier red; a red like red-hot coals: the rubies of the reliquary; the roses of St Dorothy. And he had again a thought to throw back to the strange events of that day, and the woman who had shuddered at the sacrilege she had helped. After all, he thought, St Dorothy also had a pagan lover; but he had not dominated her or destroyed her faith. She had died free and for the truth; and then had sent him roses from Paradise . . .

He raised his eyes and saw through the veil of incense smoke and of twinkling lights that Benediction was drawing to its end while the procession waited. The sense of accumulated riches of time and tradition pressed past him like a crowd moving in rank after rank, through unending centuries; and high above them all, like a garland of unfading flames, like the sun of our mortal midnight, the great monstrance blazed against the darkness of the vaulted shadows, as it blazed against the black enigma of the universe. For some are convinced that this enigma also is an insoluble problem. And others have equal certitude that it has but one solution.

Afterword

It is a horribly ironic fate for the preposterously prolific Gilbert Keith Chesterton that he should be remembered almost solely his invention of a certain round Catholic priest called Brown. Indeed, even when Chesterton's classic detective stories are read it tends to be from the selection you have before you. No matter, though. In these tales alone can be found something from almost every part of the author's varied career.

Chesterton wrote novels, poetry, short stories, plays, political pieces, biographies, literary criticism, religious works, philosophical books and journalism by the ton. In his lifetime he produced an astonishing 100 books (though by his own admission a great number of these were really extended ruminations on his own theories of life, reason and the experience of faith). His nearest counterpart is Dr Johnson, another productive writer whose very flexibility tends to baffle the modern reader and who is remembered chiefly for just one great achievement. Chesterton, though, published a considerable amount of material that was rum or plain boring, especially in his later years.

The popularity of anti-Catholic, anti-Chesterton writers such as Orwell has not helped his cause either. It is certainly true that Chesterton is hardly a bastion of modernity in his thinking. However, especially in his fiction, he proves himself a thoroughly ingenious and regularly profound writer. Less inexhaustible minds might have striven for consistency and quality above quantity but Chesterton cared not a jot for such niceties. He shared Father Brown's humility when acknowledging his digression-heavy style. Besides, no less a critic than T. S. Eliot put it this way: 'To judge Chesterton on his "contributions to literature" would be to apply the wrong standard.' This book serves, therefore, not as a greatest hits of the writer but as a window into his kaleidoscopic mind.

The indivisible link between Chesterton and his diminutive priest might be explained by the fact that these stories are some of the most ingenious and original in the history of detective fiction. The earlier tales concentrate on extraordinary events which Father Brown solves using his ability to see within the criminal mind. This is explained by the time he has spent listening in the confession booth. As he puts it, 'Has it never struck you that a man who does next to nothing but hear men's real sins is not likely to be wholly unaware of human evil?'. In later stories, Chesterton uses Father Brown to a greater degree as a mouthpiece for his own musings upon society, and his empathetic role is either irrelevant or assumed. Chesterton, comfortably established as a crime writer, takes the opportunity to clamber up every philosophical monkey puzzle tree he encounters. Their variety in terms of tone and theme is one explanation for the stories' enduring success.

Another striking feature of the stories is that although there is usually the sense that something unnatural or not of this world has occurred, there is always a reasonable explanation. Father Brown never resorts to blaming the divine for interfering in the petty realm of human affairs and it is precisely his clear-sightedness that makes him so good at seeing past criminal deceptions. Throughout, the author's own poetic voice can be heard in the lengthy and wonderful pieces of description that fill the pages, and there are moments of very modern observational humour. One London bus ride is described as follows in 'The Blue Cross' from *The Innocence of Father Brown* (1911): 'It was one of those journeys on which a man perpetually feels that now at last he must have come to the end of the universe, and then finds he has only come to the beginning of Tufnell Park.' As in P. G. Wodehouse's stories, society is presented in a comically garish way and the author draws on its absurd rituals to supply extraordinary events.

The sheer ingenuity of his discoveries is always unanticipated. So, in 'The Secret Garden', even his friend the doctor accuses him of lunacy as he details the circumstances that led to a man simultaneously leaving and not leaving Valentin's garden. Such paradoxes often form the basis of these tales. It is Chesterton's attention to how things are ignored and therefore misconstrued by over-casual casual observers that inspires such tales as 'The Invisible Man' (where a postman can carry a body in a sack because he looks as if he is doing his job), 'The Queer Feet' (where the villain exploits the fact that waiters and gentlemen dining differ in appearance only in the way they carry themselves), 'The Mirror of the Magistrate' (where the murderer accidentally shoots his own reflection) and 'The Flying Stars' (where a policeman can be thoroughly beaten up in front of a noble audience because he seems to be part of a hilarious charade).

In creating Father Brown, Chesterton did not stick to the rigid framework of the detective story as practised by his most obvious forebears: Edgar Allan

Poe and Arthur Conan Doyle. He himself noted provocatively in 1927 that 'Sherlock Holmes is not really a real logician. He is an ideal logician imagined by an illogical person.' Father Brown is much less severe than Poe's detective Dupin, and shows none of the arrogance of the indestructible Holmes. For one thing, Brown has no fawning Dr Watson to be blinded by his genius, so he must convince us on his own merits. The following lines from 'The Strange Crime of John Boulnois' sum up perfectly Brown's distinctive qualities: he 'differed from most detectives in fact and fiction in a small point – he never pretended not to understand when he understood perfectly well.'

It is instructive and impressive that when reading Chesterton's introductions to his non-fiction books such as *The Victorian Age in Literature*, only the lack of references to Father Brown give away the fact that this is not a modern critic but the author himself. If his opinions are Edwardian then the candour and self-deprecating wit of his style are distinctly more contemporary. He was much more prescient as a writer than many give him credit for. His deceptively quiet priestly hero is the original for detectives as wide-ranging as Brother Cadfael and Columbo.

Unlike other crime writers, Chesterton offers symbolic rather than tediously realistic murders and he does not make unreasonable jumps of logic that the reader could not have guessed. For those reasons, the Father Brown stories are satisfying both as detective stories and as philosophical discussions. Crucially, they continue to provoke thought even after the details of the crime have been solved and the means explained. In 'The Perishing of the Pendragons' the ominous symbols of the tower, snakes, shipwrecks and a map that is not what it seems fascinate more even than the exceptionally clever manner in which the villain has been killing off his kin. Similarly, although the precise way in which the murder takes place in 'The Hammer of God' is a little far fetched, it makes for an excellent mystery and morality tale. Moreover, the description of the vertiginous view from the church tower is extremely memorable and displays his distinctive use of elegant poetic metaphor to enhance a scene.

So to the allegedly varying quality of the Father Brown stories often noted by critics. A reason regularly cited for this is that Chesterton admitted that he wrote the later books because of a lack of funds. We should perhaps not take our modest author on his word. It is apparent that he did not write the stories unwillingly. He must have been aware that the tales he was producing by then were less sensational and more philosophical. It may just be that his dismissive stance reflected a concern that he was no longer giving his audience quite what they expected. Really, as ever, he fits the medium to suit his purpose and alters the character of Brown somewhat to give his own opinions room to breathe. Chesterton, like Conan Doyle, was understandably frustrated that his other writing tended to be ignored by readers far keener on reading murder mysteries than religious tracts. Given Chesterton's astonishing success with a 'biography' of Robert Browning that by his own admission had little to do with that poet and was riddled with misquotations, perhaps he should have been less anxious.

If we are unkind we might say that occasionally he

ran out of inspired puzzles for his priest to solve. Yet even when the story is less inventive we are given plenty of intrigue combined with Chesterton's own delightful commentary to make up for it. Although in 'The Green Man', from the final collection (*The Scandal of Father Brown*, 1935), the crime is fairly mundane and Brown's guesswork rather dubious, there is the brilliant description of the priest's horror at realising the murderer was right beside him and had betrayed himself with a throwaway remark. Memorable also is the naval officer who incriminates himself by waving a sword around in a pirate-like manner behind the doomed admiral because he thinks no one is watching.

In 'The Blast of the Book', from the same collection, it is (rather ironically) the clerk that we remember most vividly. He has been ignored and thus misjudged so completely that he can get away with inventing five fictional men and having all of them disappear to the superstitious terror of his employer, all the time using the silly disguise of a false beard. The questions that keep surfacing are those Chesterton asks concerning Gabriel Syme in his excellent but very peculiar novel *The Man Who Was Thursday*: 'Was he wearing a mask? Was anyone wearing a mask? Was anyone anything?' Reading these various Father Brown stories we sense that the author himself is switching between masks, just as frequently and subtly as his characters. He is the poet with his paradoxes, the novelist with his devious plots, the psychologist tapping into the minds of his subjects, the journalist offering his notes on society and the religious commentator analysing the moral significance of it all.

In spite of all his fascinating insights, Father Brown himself would have made a terrible priest. He is never in his parish, it would seem. His appearances and disappearances, like objects in the crimes, are wondrous and a little improbable. That is beside the point, of course, just as it is irrelevant that the number of murders in Inspector Morse's Oxford seems implausibly high. The Father Brown world is an exaggerated one, in which everyone is of some significance if only to tell us something of what we are. There is also a noticeable quaintness about these stories when compared with modern murder mysteries. The detail in Father Brown stories is only very rarely in the horror of crime. Usually, the gruesome is set aside so that the concept that forms the heart of the tale can take centre stage. Chesterton would no doubt be baffled by Patricia Cornwell's blurring of the boundaries of crime fact and fiction. He would find the modern delight in Hannibal Lecter's repulsive career even more shocking because it demonstrates that we are no more than voyeurs when it comes to evil.

Chesterton dwells on showman thieves and petty murderers who in the majority of cases kill for greed. He would have disapproved of the tendency towards amorality and focus upon sadism in modern crime writing. By means of enjoyable parables he exposes true, universal wrongs peculiar to man rather than the unbelievable wrongs of a peculiar man. The fascinating moral questions posed by the detective priest resemble those of Oscar Wilde's short stories more than they do the clever logical triumphs of Conan Doyle's. This is also the key to how well they have lasted compared to Chesterton's once popular non-fiction. Where some authors have tended to make the detective story something of a snack in literary terms, Chesterton makes it altogether more filling. At the same time he rarely loses his light touch. From the observation that two heads are not always better than one (when a second beheading has taken place) to the description of a young man trying to pick up golf hastily by 'practising particular strokes with a kind of microscopic fury', these stories remain as entertaining as they are inspiring and are a fascinatingly introduction to a larger-than-life author.

Biography

Gilbert Keith Chesterton was born in Kensington in 1874. He was a late developer, only reaching adolescence in his late teens, leaving him with a somewhat skewed perspective on life. His childlike qualities of clarity and belief inspired his most famous creation, Father Brown. During his life Chesterton produced an considerable number of works in various styles including novels, plays, poems and non-fiction but he remains best known for his ingenious short stories about crime. He converted to Roman Catholicism in 1922 and wrote a number of books about his faith, most famously *Orthodoxy*. He died in 1936.